Dov Silverman, win  tory Merit Award for M n in Brooklyn, New Yor US marine in the Korean duc-tor and as an auctio *ude*, from Stonybrook Un

The family, including children Barbara (now married and the mother of Anav) and Jeff (who died of leukemia in 1979 at the age of 18), moved to Safed, Israel in 1972. Dov worked as a teacher of English as a Second Language, advisor to English teachers and high school principal.

In 1985, Dov Silverman became a full-time writer. His wife, Janet, has been his helpmate and editor through all his endeavours.

By the same author

Legends of Safed
The Fall of the Shogun
The Black Dragon
The Good Shepherds (in Japanese)

Elizabeth Henderson, Ph.D.

DOV SILVERMAN

The Shishi

GRAFTON BOOKS

A Division of the Collins Publishing Group

LONDON GLASGOW
TORONTO SYDNEY AUCKLAND

Grafton Books
A Division of the Collins Publishing Group
8 Grafton Street, London W1X 3LA

Published in paperback by Grafton Books 1990

First published in Great Britain by
Grafton Books 1989

Copyright © Dov Silverman 1989

ISBN 0-586-20351-6

Printed and bound in Great Britain by
Collins, Glasgow

Set in Garamond

For my daughter, Barbara, and son-in-law, Ike
With love

Acknowledgements

FOR SUPPORT AND ENCOURAGEMENT ALONG THE WAY

Edyth H. Geiger
Malka Rabinowitz
Sylvia and Mel Springer

To the Reader

This book tells of the men and women who shaped Japan's destiny in the nineteenth century. It follows the real-life exploits of Mangiro – known to the world as John Mung – the man who brought western knowledge to the country of his birth. It is the story of a proud nation, and of the people who led it out of feudal isolation to take its place in the modern world.

You can read further of Mung's gripping adventures in the bestselling *The Fall of the Shogun* and *The Black Dragon*, also published by Grafton Books.

We shall fall behind
   Our fellows in the world
If, when we should advance,
   We make no move at all.

Emperor Meiji

MANCHURIA

Vulcan
Gavan

Samarga

Olga • Sapporo
Vladivostok

*SEA
OF
JAPAN*

KURIL
ISLANDS

HOKKAIDŌ

HONSHŪ

Kyōto
Tōkyō

KYŪSHU *SHIKOKU*
Kagoshima

*RYUKU
ISLANDS*

*PACIFIC
OCEAN*

- - - - - *The flight of the Vulcan pirates*

Chapter 1

Spring 1871: The port of Kagoshima on Japan's southern island of Kyushu

'Who are they?' Mung asked, pointing to a band of samurai moving out of the woods.

'Our escort, with more behind,' Rhee answered.

The Minister of Japan's Maritime Services nodded, and patted the Colt .44 under his obi. Rhee grunted. Mung had never learned to use a sword, even when he had two hands.

'Why are they taking the Kagoshima road?' Mung asked. 'I must inspect the *Kanrin Maru*.'

'To mislead a possible ambush. After we pass the crossroad, they will double back and the rear guard will take the point.'

Mung nodded his approval. Rhee had saved his life more than once. The first time, assassins killed Rhee's brother. After the burial, Mung had offered the Okinawan chief a life pension. Rhee refused, and vowed to make Mung's enemies his.

'Sire,' Rhee said, 'I wish to select an additional twenty bodyguards for our trip to Tokyo.'

'That number seems exaggerated.'

'I have no idea how talented these tattooed men are at murder. The warning was specific. The Yakuza have been paid to kill you.'

'If you must, take twenty from the Black Dragon Society.'

They entered the shipyard. It was here Mung had lived and worked for two years after returning from America. Here he planned, designed and built the *Shinto Maru*, Japan's first whaler. Five years aboard American whalers

13

and two summers working with his adoptive American brother at the Fairhaven shipyard in Massachusetts, had provided him with the experience needed to accomplish the task.

Mung turned from the past and gazed at the pride of Japan's merchant fleet – the *Kanrin Maru*. She had been built in Amsterdam, an 180-foot transoceanic steam sailer. Her paddle wheels humped up amidship. She mounted ten-pound cannon fore and aft. Mung had navigated the ship when she carried the first Japanese ambassadorial mission to America. She was now being refitted for another journey across the ocean, this time to Prussia.

Mung summoned the master shipbuilder and questioned him until satisfied the work schedule was being maintained. He then wandered through the yard. Although few Orientals or Occidentals knew of it, the yard was the finest shipbuilding facility in the Far East.

Eighteen years before, upon his return from America, Mung had proved to himself and a few others that Japan had the ability to modernize. According to law, he should have been executed for having been out of Japan. Instead, after his background became known, Lord Nariakira of Satsuma ordered him to build a modern whaler. From every town, village and city in the fiefdom had come master shipbuilders, carpenters, smiths, sailmakers and seamen. Not one had ever seen a ship as large as they were commanded to build, and sail. None understood the concept of a fixed keel, or the western method of tacking against the wind. Yet, in the ensuing years, they constructed five whalers, the hulls for three steam tugs, and several cutters. Mung was quietly proud of having given birth to Japan's only two modern industries – shipbuilding and whaling. Soon he would be in Tokyo, attempting to persuade the lords of the realm to enter other areas of production and trade. He was dedicated to modernization as the only means of fending off western imperialism. He had to change Japan's rice crop economy to an industrial one. He fingered his bent nose, thinking that no matter how high he rose in the service of the Emperor, to Japanese nobility he would always remain the fisherboy from the village of Nakanohama. That attitude would hinder the reception of his plans when he presented them to the Great Council in Tokyo.

'Rhee,' he called, 'let us go to the school. I plan to spend the remainder of the day with my wife.'

Rhee whistled and the samurai moved out on either side of the road, hands on their swords.

Alerted by the guards, teachers and students bowed low as the tall Minister of Maritime Services entered the compound. Mung bowed to the teachers, then to the students. He passed his seventeen-year-old son, Yoshida, standing with the older boys, but neither showed any sign of recognition, or the affection they felt. It would have been bad manners.

Mung looked overhead at the kites held by the younger children in the schoolyard. The colourful kites hung motionless against the wind in a clear blue sky. The slips of bamboo fitted at their backs made them sound like a chorus of pump organs.

'I have not flown a kite in years,' he said to the children. 'Do you know that once I used special kite cord to escape British and French warships in this very harbour? Aaahh, but that is a story which will have to wait for another time.'

A teacher shuffled forward on wooden clogs, bowed and offered her kite line.

'Thank you.' Mung looked up. He tilted his head, listening to the wind-driven harmony in the sky. 'Let me see if I can play melody,' he said.

He tugged the cord left, then swung it right, sending the kite whistling into dips, dives and seesaw swings. It sang louder and flew higher than the others. As he worked the line, he remembered kite flying in Nakanohama. There were no elegant kites like these. He and his friends had shared one, each contributing scraps of cloth for the tail. At day's end, the scraps were untied and taken home. Mung's memories of the fishing village were always associated with a feeling of hunger. He had heard men speak glowingly of their childhood, of a desire to relive their youth. Not me, he thought. I look forward to tomorrow.

The kite dipped in a long swooping dive over the red tiled roof of the school. It shrilled as it bellied down, sang bravely and, defying gravity, soared up. Mung caught a flash of blue in the doorway. Ukiko, his wife, was standing there. The colour of her kimono matched the sky. It was decorated with pictures of yellow bamboo and bound at the waist by a light brown obi. Ukiko's jet black hair was pulled back but for two wisps that framed her oval face and sparkling dark eyes. She bowed to him.

Mung returned control of the kite to the teacher and went to his wife. She was the principal of this school her sister, Saiyo, had founded. After Saiyo, Mung's first wife, had been killed, Mung suffered the darkest days of his life, until Ukiko made him feel, and love again.

Ukiko bowed as he entered the school. She did not speak until after Mung tasted the scented tea and rice cakes she had prepared.

'I have arranged for Yoshida to remain here at the school until tonight,' Ukiko said. 'Your things are packed.'

Mung peered over his teacup and raised an eyebrow. 'Where am I going?'

'To the Emperor.'

'It was a secret. Only Jiroo, the senior Black Dragon, and Rhee knew. How could you?' he asked.

'From your message this morning that Yoshida and I would accompany you on a night outing.'

'From that you concluded I am travelling to Tokyo?'

'A picnic was one of the ways you said farewell to my

16

sister. Yoshida was a baby then and I took care of him while you and Saiyo went off together. We have been married fifteen years and you still have the same predictable habits. Very unJapanese.'

He smiled. 'Such as?'

'You take time to please an unworthy wife.'

Mung held up his hand and she understood the sign. It forbade her to speak of her inability to bear children.

Ukiko mourned her flawed body. She tried every potion and charm she heard of to become pregnant. Even now, powdered sea urchin was prepared for use before their next trip to the pillow. And if that did not work, there was her plan for the new western cure. For that she must persuade Mung to bring the bunn-iis from Tokyo.

'It is remarkable,' he said, 'how you always know of my journeys. I am supposed to be the master spy.'

Her eyelashes fluttered. 'You always do something special for us before leaving on an extended journey. It is unJapanese for a husband to be so concerned for his wife.' She smiled. 'But I enjoy it.'

'You have also become fond of other western innovations such as the indoor toilet, and our soaping each other in the tub.' Mung imitated her fluttering eyelashes.

Ukiko's eyes opened wide. She looked around to see if they could be overheard. 'Shhh,' she whispered. 'It is true I enjoy bad habits, but you taught them to me.' She leaned forward. 'If the neighbours ever learned . . . Aaiiiee.'

'What if they knew we have sex in the tub?' Mung grinned and popped another rice cake into his mouth. He leaned towards her. 'What would they say if they knew we touch tongues when making love? That would chill them.'

Ukiko turned red and she crumpled. For a moment Mung thought she would faint. The first time he had kissed her on the mouth, he had done it unconsciously in the heat of lovemaking – something learned from the girls in Honolulu. Ukiko had responded with her entire body, but

17

later wept for having done such a disgusting thing. Since then, their lips and tongues had met again, and she initiated the kiss as often as he.

'You are highly skilled at pleasuring,' Ukiko said 'And I have learned to be aggressive in bed.'

'Aggressive women please me.'

'The pleasure you give me is offset by the guilt I feel for enjoying our pillow time more than you.'

'Who says that is so?' Mung smiled and they gazed into each other's eyes. He reached out and touched her hand. 'Now tell me how you knew it is the Emperor I am going to see.'

Ukiko patted his hand. 'Few people in the empire can summon the Minister of Maritime Services. Fewer know you are the Black Dragon, the eyes and ears of the Emperor. If you are near Tokyo, you must report directly to him.'

'Yes, you are correct. He has summoned me.'

Ukiko reached out and brushed her fingertips over Mung's face. 'My touch will also see the descendant of Amaterasu, the Sun Goddess. When do you leave?'

'In three days. After I have questioned the Black Dragons returned from abroad. Based on their information, I will formulate my recommendations to the Emperor and the Rujo, the Great Council, on how to modernize Japan more quickly.'

'You will have Lord Koin to contend with,' Ukiko warned.

'At the age of sixty, he is soon to retire. It is Saga of Choshu who threatens to challenge the westerners.'

'I advise you to keep a sharp watch on Fujita Koin,' Ukiko said. 'He will not go to his grave until the three houses of Mito are in a position of power.'

'How could you know of him?' Mung asked.

'I by birth and you by adoption are of the Ishikawa family. In the imperial book of heraldry, ours is one of the oldest names recorded. As governor of Kagoshima, my father hosted Lord Koin and his sons on one of their winter vacations. I remember hearing Lord Koin say, "The Emperor has granted Mito honour without power. Before I greet my ancestors, that situation will be rectified."'

'That sounds like the vain boast of an old man.'

'He was not so old when I overheard him. It was the solemn vow of a samurai to his ancestors.'

'I met him in battle,' Mung said. 'I admit he was fearless, although a bad tactician. My Black Dragons report he will bequeath the leadership of the three houses of Mito to his youngest son. Is that possible?'

'Ho!' Ukiko tried to cover her surprise behind her fan. 'Count Iyeasu is a frog.'

'A what?'

'Lord Koin has three sons as different as the seasons. The oldest is a giant, the middle son a viper, and Count Iyeasu is a frog, although a nice frog. He, like you, breaks the harmony of height. You are long and thin. He is short and wide. You both have the same aura of power and serenity.'

'Would you prefer a husband with more flesh on his bones?'

Her eyes smiled and lids fluttered. 'I like the feel of your hard muscles against my softness. Will we have time for that before you leave?'

'You did say Yoshida would be busy until tonight's outing?'

'I arranged it so.'

'As the Great Buddha said, "He who procrastinates is lost."'

Mung took his wife's hand. They left the school compound, oblivious to the Black Dragon guards, or the sinister eyes that watched from the nearby forest. They walked as lovers, enjoying the view of the mountainside falling away to the orchards, and the orderly rice paddies sweeping down to the sea. They touched plum blossoms and picked wildflowers on the way to their house on the side of the hill.

Chapter 2

It was dark when Mung and Ukiko came out of their house. Armed guards and torchbearers preceded them to the school where Yoshida waited. Although his kimono, obi and short haircut were exact duplicates of his father's, Yoshida's thin body and delicate features resembled those of his dead mother. He bowed to his parents and they to him, the love for their only son blatantly evident.

'Can you tell me how fish are caught?' Mung asked Yoshida.

Believing his father was testing him on school work, the young man answered, 'By hook, net or damming a stream.'

'I know men who catch fish with birds. Did you ever hear of that?'

'No, sire.'

'What kind of fish do you suppose are caught by those birds?' Mung asked.

Fearing he was failing the test, Yoshida lowered his head. He did not see the twinkle in his father's eyes. 'I do not know,' he said sadly.

'Flying fish!' Mung laughed. 'You have heard of flying fish?'

Pleased to be able to give a positive answer, the young man straightened up. 'Yes. Only two days ago we saw a school of them at the mouth of the harbour.'

'Do not tease the boy,' Ukiko whispered.

Mung laughed again to cover his disappointment. At seventeen I was third mate on an American whaler, he thought, and my son does not even know when his leg is being pulled. Mung knew Yoshida was over-protected, but was never able to find time to rectify the situation.

'Ride up front with Rhee,' he ordered his son. 'We shall talk on our return.'

The Okinawan helped the young man into the saddle, and the two moved ahead of Mung and Ukiko's mounts. Twenty Black Dragons escorted the party. Others were stationed along the trail.

On the outskirts of town, Mung tossed a coin to an itinerant mountain priest carrying his portable altar. In one deft movement, the priest caught the coin and bowed his head to the ground. He remained in that position until the rear guard passed, but his scornful eyes followed the column until it was well onto the river road.

The man slipped the coin into his obi and took a lamp out of the altar. He turned up the flame and raised the lamp over his head. His loose sleeve slipped down his arm to reveal the grey-black head and beady eyes of a weasel tattooed on his skin.

Mung and Ukiko rode side by side under a star-filled sky. The pungent aroma of spring wafted up from the newly tilled rice paddies. Mung noticed Ukiko worrying the corner of her lip. It meant there was something she wanted to ask. Good. It could make his own request easier.

Ukiko glanced at Mung. Her large, innocent eyes were childlike, but he knew that behind the pixie face was a keen, although sometimes naïve, mind.

'Do you know what bunn-iis are?' she finally asked.

'No. What are they?'

'I am not certain. My cousin wrote from Tokyo that bunn-iis are the newest fad in the capital.'

'What are bunn-iis for? Who uses them?'

'I thought you could tell me. They come from America. Sales of five hundred American dollars for each bunn-ii are quite common. They have been sold for as much as a thousand dollars each. It is a wonderful investment.'

'You have the inheritance from your father, enough for several lifetimes. Why do you wish to speculate?'

'I thought to invest for Yoshida.'

'The money Lord Nariakira willed me is enough for Yoshida and his children's children.'

'You rarely use money.' Ukiko pouted. 'You do not know what wealth really is. A little more never hurt a young man's prospects for an advantageous marriage.'

Had Mung not been so intent on his own request, he would have paid more attention. 'I still do not know what bunn-iis are,' he said.

'They are not native to Japan. That is why the price is so high. They are large furry rodents with long ears and short tails. They hop with their little feet held in front like this.' Ukiko dropped the reins and curled her hands under her chin. 'My cousin says they sniff a great deal.' She twitched her nose. 'I hope I am doing it right.'

'Rabbits!' Mung laughed. 'You mean rabbits. Bunnies is an English word children use.'

'Well these rabbits, or bunn-iis, are good investments. I would like to speculate on a pair.'

'Start with a pair and you will soon have a hundred. They multiply rapidly.'

'How wonderful. My money will grow too.' She could have hugged herself with joy. Mung had confirmed Ginko's report that the furry little animals were fertile beyond belief. Although she had never tasted red meat, she was prepared to eat bunn-iis, fur and all, if it would help her conceive. 'When you are in Tokyo, would you purchase a pair of bunn-iis for me?'

'You need a place outside the house to keep them.'

'That will not be a problem. I may even have them sold before they arrive.' Ukiko was so excited, it was difficult for her to sit still in the saddle. In my next letter to Ginko, I will ask how the animals should be cooked to increase my fertility, she thought.

The procession arrived at the river where five long, narrow boats were tied. Mung helped Ukiko dismount.

23

With Rhee and Yoshida, they walked down to the dock. Their guards took positions several yards back along the road and paralleling the water.

The master fisherman bowed. 'Sire, everything is ready.'

'My son has never seen a bird catch a fish. Will you show him?'

'I would be honoured. Will your son be the kako in my boat?'

'What does a kako do?' Yoshida asked.

The fisherman handed the young man a heavy bamboo clapper. 'You must bang this against the side of the boat and call out, "Dive! Gulp! Catch!" That encourages the birds.'

'I see no birds.'

'Ichi,' the master fisherman called.

A parade of twelve large duck-like birds waddled into the torchlight. Their webbed feet tracked the sand behind Ichi, the grizzled old leader. He had a sharp hooked beak and was greying under the neck. Black and green feathers covered his plump body. He hopped up into his master's arms and allowed Yoshida to pet him.

'Why is there a ring around his neck?' Yoshida asked.

'That is to stop him from eating the fish he catches.'

'If he cannot swallow because of the ring, how does he eat his own food?'

'I have made the ring just large enough for little fish to pass through to his belly. In that way he feeds himself and supplies me with produce to sell.'

'Does he always return so quickly when you call him?'

'No. Cormorants are independent creatures, and Ichi is a leader. Sometimes I must wait for him. But now we will get to work. Ichi and the others wear harnesses with lines attached. When you tell me a bird has stopped diving, I will pull him in, empty his beak and send him out again. Are you ready to be my kako?'

'Yes.' Yoshida stepped into the boat and swung the heavy clapper against the side.

The cormorants were loaded into the master fisherman's boat. Rhee and Mung helped Ukiko into the next one. In the bow of each boat, a man tended three torches. The five fishing boats put out and were sculled up-river by helmsmen at the long sweep oars. The master fisherman's boat led them to a quiet pool not far from the river bank, where they formed a wide circle. The flickering torches illuminated the surface and drew fish up to the light. Mung and Ukiko saw Yoshida point out the rising fish and ready his clapper. The cormorants were lowered into the water.

In the shadows along the river bank, two Yakuza scouts tensed at the sound of the clapper and Yoshida's cries to the cormorants. In whispers, the tattooed men identified the Minister of Maritime Services, his foreign bodyguard at the sweep oar, and his son in the next boat. They slipped away along the edge of the river as the lead bird was pulled in to disgorge its catch.

Ukiko trailed her finger in the water. 'I would like you to tell me what is on your mind,' she said to Mung. 'You are looking at our son but thinking of something else. That usually means you are seeking a tactful way of saying a disturbing thing.'

'If I am so predictable, have I become boring?'

'Never.'

Rhee leaned on the sweep oar, holding the boat in position at the edge of the pool.

Ukiko watched Mung's face in the flickering torchlight. She could see it was a serious matter.

'Some time ago I sent three of my Black Dragons to China to replace Udo,' he said.

'He is the surviving son of the ashigara, one-sword samurai, who gave his life to save yours?'

'Yes, I told you how Udo's brother, Uraga, died saving me from the tong-men in Canton.'

'Does your relieving Udo of duty in China mean he has been delinquent?'

'The opposite,' Mung said. 'I doubt three men will be sufficient to replace him. But they are the only ones I have who speak Mandarin Chinese. I have called Udo back to command the Black Dragons accompanying the ambassadorial delegation to Prussia.'

'Does he speak German?'

'Fluently. As well as French and English. He also has close ties to the most powerful tong chief in southern China.'

'Skill in foreign languages is an asset. But of what use can a tong chief be?'

'Kang Shu has strong connections with Chinese communities in Europe, England and America. He passes accurate information from them to Udo, who forwards it to me. The information is about innovations in science and industry. Things that are described in journals and newspapers. Udo uses the overseas Chinese to obtain advance knowledge of each country's needs, surpluses and plans for investments at home and abroad. Knowledge that helps us predict markets, to be able to buy low and sell high.'

'I know merchants have been given higher status since the Emperor returned to power, but it still irks me to hear you speak like one,' Ukiko said.

'What about your investment in bunn-iis?'

'I am a woman. There is a difference.'

'In the new Japan there will be many differences. Change will take place as fast as rabbits multiply. One of them will be the elimination of rank.'

Ukiko grimaced. 'I prefer not to speak of this. When will Udo arrive?'

'Soon. That is the problem.'

'I will see he is looked after.'

'It is more complicated than that. Until only a few years ago the penalty for leaving Japan, even boarding a foreign vessel, was death. Lord Nariakira and I had to meet secretly at sea with Commodore Perry. It was Udo and his brother who rowed us out to the American flagship. To keep the meeting secret, Lord Nariakira ordered me to be certain the brothers never returned to Japan. He meant they should die. Instead, I sent them to China where Uraga was killed. The order still stands, but Udo is already on his way home.'

'Surely a verbal order from a dead man can be overlooked?'

'It was not just any man. It was Nariakira of Satsuma. He raised me to the rank of samurai. According to the code of Bushido, his order is more binding than another since the man who issued it cannot be petitioned to rescind it.'

'Your eyes tell me you have a plan.'

'There is a way to satisfy my conscience regarding the order from Lord Nariakira and the vow I made to Udo's father to guide his son in the service of the Emperor. I need your help to create a legal fiction, as your father did when he adopted me.'

'My father adopted you to raise you to a rank high enough to marry Saiyo and perpetuate the family name because he had no sons.'

'If we were to adopt Udo he could return to Japan as an Ishikawa, not Udo, son of Yaka, who was banned forever.'

Ukiko's back stiffened. 'As head of the family, you need not consult me.'

'I know,' Mung said gently, 'but as I was adopted by your father, and you were born to his honourable name, I thought we should discuss it.'

Her eyes flashed. 'There is a saying, "If you do not want to take the priest's advice, do not ask his opinion."'

'You are not a priest, but my wife whom I love and do not want to hurt.'

'So I would have two sons. Neither my own. Is he older than me?'

'Udo is thirty-one. Two years younger. It is a shame he will never see thirty-two.'

'Why is that?'

'I will have to order him killed before he comes ashore.'

'What of your vow to his father? It would violate Bushido. You cannot.'

'The adoption papers are in the governor's office.'

Ukiko sighed. 'You tricked me.'

'Will you sign them?'

'Your sense of democracy as you explain it and practise it, differ. You request permission you do not need, then tell me what it is you want done. My master commands and I obey.' Ukiko bowed.

The squawking cormorants, Yoshida's cries and the bamboo clapper made it difficult for Mung to be heard. He waited a few moments, then said, 'Your anger is not because of me or the adoption. For you and for our happiness, I pray you will conceive.'

Ukiko turned away to hide her tears and stifle the pain in her heart.

Half a mile up-river, a large group of men separated into two parties. Those armed with six-foot bows and steel-tipped war arrows glided silently through the trees along the river bank in the direction of the boats. The others stripped and waded into the river. The faint light of the sickle moon reflected their tattooed bodies in the slow moving water. Each man carried a three-foot-long metal hook and a steel dagger. They paddled downstream under the drooping willows.

Twenty yards from the circle of torchlight around the pool, the swimmers trod water. Their leader, a man with plucked eyebrows and the head of a golden lizard tattooed on his shaved skull, surfaced in their midst.

'Now remember! Three men attack each of the four boats,' he whispered. 'Kill everyone, then make your escape down-river! You three,' he pointed with an arm covered by tattooed golden scales, 'we will kill the Black Dragon!'

The Golden Lizard paused, then gave the order, 'Yakuza, follow me!' The wind whistled through his nose as he inhaled. Sixteen men disappeared beneath the water's surface.

On shore, tattooed men knelt and set the end of their long bows in the soft earth of the river bank. They notched their arrows and drew their bowstrings taut.

Chapter 3

Rhee leaned on the long oar to scull the boat back into position at the edge of the pool, and the motion saved their lives. A three-foot-long war arrow buried itself in the oar handle. Others whizzed by Mung and Ukiko. The feathered shafts whipped their clothing.

'Attack, attack!' Rhee shouted as he dived on top of Mung and Ukiko, knocking them to the bottom of the boat. A second flight of arrows whistled over their heads.

War cries erupted from shore. The Black Dragon guards charged into the undergrowth – slashing, chopping and hacking men, trees and shrubs with their long two-handed swords. The tattooed archers were cut down before they strung their third arrows.

Rhee grasped the side of the boat to raise himself up and a hook flashed out of the water. Its steel point pierced the back of his left hand, pinning it to the wood. He stifled a cry as a blue and red tattooed face, using the hook for leverage, pulled itself out of the water. Rhee cocked his right arm. He set his feet and threw a wedge punch, driving the Yakuza's nose bone up into his brain. The colourful face grimaced, the dark feverish eyes filled with blood, and he slipped back into the water.

Mung drew his pistol. 'Ukiko, stay down!' he warned.

Mung shivered as Rhee pulled the hook from his bloody hand. Then another hook flashed out of the water at the bow and buried itself in the torch-man's leg. He screamed and was dragged thrashing over the side.

A third hook dug into the bow. A tattooed Golden Lizard slithered onto the front of the boat. In the eerie torchlight the lizard stood erect. Golden, black-edged

30

scales covered its body. They rippled down the muscular torso and powerful legs. It looked up with the face of a man and Ukiko screamed. She jerked back, hitting Mung as he fired, and the shot went wild. The lizard-man jumped forward, a lethal hook in one hand, a dagger in the other.

'Yakuza!' Rhee shouted. He vaulted over Ukiko and Mung to challenge the lizard-man. Despite the rocking back and forth of the boat the Okinawan chief, expert in his native art of karate, maintained his balance. The Golden Lizard stalked forward with weapons poised. Rhee offered his wounded hand as a target and the hook slashed out, catching his sleeve. Rhee jerked back, pulling the Yakuza chief off balance. The lizard-man stabbed with the dagger but Rhee, using a sweeping arm block, deflected the knife. He turned sideways and kicked, his foot catching the Yakuza in the chest. The lizard-man spun, gasping for air. He tripped and fell over the side, face down, exposing the scaly tail tattooed on his buttocks and down his legs. He twisted his body.

Mung aimed down into the face not three feet away, but he was jerked backward. A hook tore a two foot gash in the back of his kimono. He spun and fired. The tattooed face coming over the side snapped back with a black hole in its forehead. In the flickering torchlight, Mung saw another painted body coming up towards the surface. He fired when the head broke water.

'Where is the lizard-man?' he shouted.

Rhee pointed at the gasping serpent in the water. 'There!'

Mung aimed his pistol.

'Yoshida!' Ukiko cried.

Just beyond the struggling lizard-man, Mung saw a Yakuza kick the lifeless body of the torch-man off the bow of the first boat. He advanced on the master fisherman who stood with Ichi cradled in his arms. Behind the fisherman, Yoshida sat like a statue, the bamboo clapper clutched in his hands. A slick green and red hand reached up from the water with a hook aimed for Yoshida's back. Mung snapped off a shot that splashed water near the Yakuza and kept him away. The master fisherman turned and launched the cormorant at Yoshida's attacker in the water. Ichi beat his wings in the man's face and slashed with his sharp beak. The Yakuza pushed away from the enraged bird. Mung aimed more carefully, fired, and the Yakuza died.

The tattooed man in the bow came up behind the master fisherman and drove a knife into his back. The fisherman cried out, and fell dead in the bottom of the boat. The Yakuza started for Yoshida. Ichi squawked and flew up to attack his master's killer. A vicious hook swished through the air, impaling the bird on its point. The Yakuza dropped the hooked bird on top of the dead fisherman. He stepped over the bodies, advancing towards Yoshida.

For a moment Mung froze. Then he fired, and missed. The gun hammer clicked, and clicked again on empty cylinders. He and Ukiko could only watch the Yakuza push Yoshida's head back, baring his throat and raising the knife.

Ukiko was on her knees in the bottom of the boat. 'Do something!' She tugged at Mung's kimono, screaming, 'Do something!'

Mung's lips worked but no sound came out. He watched the tattooed man bring the knife down to slash his son's throat. Suddenly Yoshida swung the bamboo clapper up into the Yakuza's groin. The tattooed body arched. He screamed and fell back.

'Musashiiiii!' Yoshida bellowed, exploding off his seat. He swung the heavy clapper in a wide underhanded arc into the Yakuza's jaw. Mung saw the tattooed face disintegrate. Yoshida swung again, striking the man's head and knocking him from the boat with the force of the blow.

Ukiko looked up at Mung. Neither could speak.

'Your son is a warrior,' Rhee said.

The two men looked at each other. 'Did you teach him karate?' Mung asked.

'No, sire, but look.'

Yoshida had removed the hook from Ichi's body, thrown the bird overboard, and stood ready for the next attack.

'Take me to him,' Ukiko cried. 'Take me to our son.'

Rhee jumped to the sculling oar and Mung to the bow. They moved their boat alongside Yoshida's. His back was towards them.

'Yoshida,' Mung cried, 'come in our boat.' He held out his hand.

The young man turned. His face was placid. He looked down at the hook and bloody bamboo clapper in his hands, then at his parents, as if questioning why he held the gory weapons. He dropped both and took Mung's hand.

'Be careful not to fall,' Ukiko said.

'Were you frightened?' Mung asked.

'I do not remember,' Yoshida answered.

'That is the way of a warrior in the heat of battle,' Rhee said. 'You invoked the name of Musashi, and the Sword Saint came to your aid.'

Yoshida turned to his father. 'Will you teach me how to swim? I feared I would fall into the water.'

The request seemed strange. It flustered Mung.

A command was shouted from shore and the Black Dragon guards released arrows at the attackers in the water. Mung followed their flight down-river and saw them fall harmlessly. He caught a flash of gold swimming away in the darkness.

'Father, I would like to learn to swim.'

Mung embraced his son. 'I must leave for Tokyo and will not have time to teach you in the near future, but there is someone who will. His name is Udo. I taught him to swim Hawaiian-style some years ago. He will arrive soon.'

'Sire.' Rhee pointed to shore where the Black Dragons were laying out tattooed bodies along the river's bank.

'The lizard-man escaped,' Mung said. 'In the future, our guards will be more alert. After my family is taken home safely, assemble those who failed to protect us.'

In the Kagoshima council house, twelve samurai warriors stood before the Black Dragon.

'Your duty was to guard my family and protect me. It is only luck that we were not killed. I have the power to strip each of you of your titles. To bring everlasting shame on your families and your ancestors.'

Mung watched the men's reactions. He had calculated his every word, and still marvelled at how easy it was to control with fear. He had condemned such a method when others employed it, but here in Japan it was effective, and expected.

'I have the right to order all twelve of you to commit seppuku now. If I give the order you will fall on your knees and slit your own bellies!'

The young men raised their heads and pulled back their shoulders. They were brave and proud. Mung would make use of their humiliation.

'I know you do not fear death. I shall not command it. Upon entering the Black Dragon Society, you swore an oath superseding all others. You vowed to serve the Emperor as his eyes and ears. Tonight you neither listened nor watched. You have failed in your duty.

'Yet, your honour is retrievable. This is your punishment and path to redemption. You will travel in threes, each group to a different destination. The first two go to the fiefdoms of Choshu and Mito. They are ruled by Lords Saga and Koin, who both openly oppose my plan for using foreigners in the modernization of Japan. It may be that they hired the Yakuza to assassinate me. Find out! The other two groups will travel to Kyoto and Tokyo. You are to arrange a meeting for me with the chief Yakuza in those cities.'

'Sire,' a short young man said, 'for two years I and others were assigned such a task, and were unsuccessful. The organization of tattooed men is more ancient than our Black Dragon Society. They have their own secret language.'

'Down on your faces!' Rhee shouted. 'Do not dare tell the Black Dragon what you cannot do!'

Mung spoke slowly and distinctly to the prostrate men. 'Until you arrange a meeting with a Yakuza of national prominence, you are all exiled from Satsuma. Forbidden contact with your families or friends. You will abstain from food and drink between sunrise and sunset. You will not sleep with a woman. Should you die before your mission is accomplished, your families will be sent penniless into exile and the graves of your ancestors obliterated.'

'So it is ordered, so it is done,' the twelve samurai chanted. They came up on their knees, touched their heads to the floor, and crawled out of the room.

'Rhee,' Mung said, 'should they fail or I die first, nothing is to be done to them or their families.'

'I think you should have ordered them to kill Lord Saga and Lord Koin, sire.'

'I met both men in battle at the Hakusar Valley when they sided with the shogun. Saga's archers were more accurate than the Yakuza.' He held up the stump of his arm. 'That is where I lost my hand. See to your own wound now.'

'Thank you, sire. But why will you not order Saga and Koin dead?'

'A battle with Choshu and the three houses of Mito could spark a civil war between those who want modernization and those opposed. Secondly, the young man was correct when he said the Yakuza are members of a more ancient organization than our Black Dragon Society. A clash between the two could result in a battle similar to the Chinese tong wars. Thousands were killed, and the Chinese imperial government has yet to recover. This country could explode. As a military observer in the American Civil War, I saw what can happen. I do not want such a disaster to befall Japan.'

'Yes, sire.' Khee pointed to a room off the large hall. 'I have arranged sleeping quarters in there. Tomorrow morning you meet the returning Black Dragons.'

'How many of them were lost?'

'None, sire. All twenty-four are camped outside the city.'

'Keep them isolated until I am through with them.'

It was the first day of the Plum Blossom Festival. The twenty-four men gathered in a grove outside Kagoshima had not come to view the delicate blossoms, nor listen to the nightingales and ponder life's mysteries. Five years before, they had been ordered to meet here on this day. Now, having completed their assignments, they waited, and wondered how time had dealt with the man who sent them from Japan.

In the council house, Mung addressed four senior Black Dragons. 'We are not monks, able to divorce ourselves from reality. It is our duty to see things as they are and will be. The superiority of foreign technology you will soon hear about from the returned Black Dragons should not overwhelm you. It does not indicate Japan's moral or intellectual inferiority. It does show we have much to learn from the West.'

'How can we absorb western ideas without disrupting our social system?' Jiroo asked.

'We cannot,' Mung answered. 'Japanese society must change. Our task is to harmonize western technology with our way of life. The Emperor took the first step to eliminate our feudalistic society by removing the shogun and replacing the military government with the Rujo.'

'Yes,' Jiroo said, 'but many of those in the Bakufu who were opposed to modernization, wield power in the Rujo.'

'Social change of any kind causes disruption. Even those who will benefit most from a more democratic government may fight us at first. But the Emperor now controls the rice-producing Kanto Plains and Japan's major seaports.'

'He has no army,' Jiroo said.

'He has the loyalty of the Fujiwara in Tokyo, and Satsuma in the south. These two powerful fiefdoms will aid us in establishing a parliamentary government with the Emperor at its head. Four of the men waiting for us have each studied one of the political systems in America, England, France and Prussia. What they have to tell us will influence which administrative structure Japan should adopt. The other twenty learned foreign methods of education, agriculture, mining, finance and military. We shall copy the best from the West so that thirty years from now Japan will leap into the twentieth century as an equal among the modern nations of the world.' Mung removed a scroll from his sleeve. 'The Emperor has summoned me to the capital. I leave in two days. In that time I must drain every bit of information possible from the returnees. You four will assist me. Until my departure, no one sleeps. Prepare stimulants.'

Mung stood up and bowed to the senior Black Dragons. 'I will meet you in the grove at noon.'

Outside the council house, Rhee sent his samurai to scout the trail to the cemetery. He accompanied Mung up the hill.

At Yaka's grave, Mung bowed. 'Your surviving son will visit here soon, old friend. I shall guide him in the service of the Emperor, as I promised you. He will have the opportunity to achieve his potential in the Black Dragon Society, and will be as a son to me. Rest easy.'

Mung moved to stand between the next two graves. On the left was his father-in-law's resting place. He addressed the grave. 'Father-in-law, as you adopted me I have adopted Udo, son of Yaka, into our family. I believe he will bring honour to the name of Ishikawa. He was a modest, unsophisticated boy who has lived up to the intellectual capabilities I saw in him years ago.'

Mung bowed, then turned and crouched down beside the grave of his departed wife. 'Saiyo, my first love, I hope it is well with you. I picked wildflowers for you from the path we used to walk behind our house.' He lay the bouquet of white, yellow and purple blossoms on the grave. 'Spring is here. You always looked forward to the warm weather and sweet smelling flowers.' He fingered his bent nose. 'I come to you now with a problem. It is our son, Yoshida. He acts strangely, although Ukiko says he is at the age for such behaviour. We will soon be sending him to school in Kyoto. Last night I feared he would join you. We were attacked and he was almost killed, but he saved himself in a way I could never have imagined. He is not athletic and does not study the martial arts. Yet he killed a man with a blow from a wooden instrument. There is another thing. He forgets. I have seen him walk into a room, stand and look around trying to remember why he is there.

'Your sister loves him as if he came from her body. Sometimes I think she is over-protective. She is still trying all the potions, salves and amulets the crackpot doctors, priests and shamans sell for pregnancy. You should have seen her face light up when I told her rabbits are fertile. I hope I do not have to contend with rabbits the next time we go to the pillow. Our sleeping place is already crowded with all the charms she uses.'

Mung looked up. 'The sun will soon reach its zenith. I go now to question the returned Black Dragons. Then I will travel to Tokyo for an audience with the Emperor.'

* * *

38

At five feet eight inches, Mung was taller than any of the young men in the grove. At forty-three, he was still lean and hard, and his skin glowed. He signalled everyone to be seated.

His voice filled the clearing, blending with the timber of the tall pines. 'I welcome you back to Japan and look forward to hearing about all you have seen and learned. Since your departure the name of Yedo has been changed to Tokyo, which means eastern capital. The Emperor moved there from the traditional capital of Kyoto after the armies of the Fujiwara and Satsuma were forced to sign unequal treaties with British, French and Russian gunboat commanders in Tokyo bay. The foreigners outmanoeuvred our infantry, smashed our outdated artillery, and burned our wind-driven ships. We were defeated not for lack of courage, but for lack of modern weapons and a powerful economic base from which to negotiate. Those of us who work to modernize Japan have waited for your return at the time of the blossoming plum trees. Your reports will affect the future of our country. The task of modernization will not be easy. We who support this policy are in the minority. Two of our greatest leaders are gone – Lord Nariakira of Satsuma and Lord Takai of the Fujiwara. Both committed seppuku after being forced to sign the unequal treaties with the West.'

The young men in the grove clenched their fists. Blood pounded in their heads as with each pump of their hearts they silently vowed to regain Japan's honour.

'The loss of Lords Nariakira and Takai created a power vacuum,' Mung continued. 'The Emperor's move from Kyoto to Tokyo was an attempt to fill that void. His majesty wants a centralized government and an industrialized economy. Difficult though it was, the Emperor has already influenced the Rujo to consider land reforms, reduction of taxes and law changes regarding class differences. Merchants are now considered equal in status to

39

farmers. They have the same rights of ownership and tax obligations.' It amused Mung to see the shocked expressions of the young samurai. They would soon learn to accept the new status of the despised businessmen. 'There are many in the empire who oppose these changes. It threatens their power. Lord Saga, of Choshu in the south, has vowed to expel all foreigners. Fujita Koin, of Mito in the centre of the country, and others, support his policy. The Emperor opposes it but cannot do so openly for fear of a civil war. The people of Japan believe that what the Emperor orders will be done. This, you know, is a myth. The Emperors have not held power for the past 250 years, since the first Tokugawa shogun. The Black Dragon Society is dedicated to restoration of the Emperor to power.

'We have enemies. Your return to Kagoshima is no secret. We are quite noticeable with our top knots shaved.' Mung touched the short dark bristles of his close-cropped hair. 'Our western style haircuts set us apart as an easy target. This is a risk we must take. Although today you appear before me in traditional dress, which is comfortable and less conspicuous, when you leave Kagoshima do so in European clothing. Our aim is to promote foreign learning, and you must become walking proclamations of modern ideas.'

The young men shifted uneasily, thinking of the stiff collars, crotched trousers and tight shoes.

'Like the entertainer who walks a thin rope, my policy of inviting westerners to help us close the technological gap can be dangerous. Foreign governments are interested in capitalizing on our industrial backwardness. They hope to put us in debt and use our people as a cheap source of labour. Some want to missionize. The balancing act we must perform is to invite their experts, glean that knowledge we deem important, and screen out that which is abhorrent. The empire is on the verge of economic collapse.

Our overworked feudal system has run its course. To prevent famine, and a possible civil war, we need those same western nations. Some of their leaders are honest and interested in helping us without conditions. They are in the minority.

'We can resist the negative aspects of the West. Unlike China, India and the Pacific island nations now being managed by western powers, Japan has a common culture, language and customs. We have the Emperor to lead us. You are his eyes and ears. Be alert, and teach Japan what you have learned.'

Mung, of all people, knew what these men would soon face. He had been ten years out of Japan after being shipwrecked and rescued by an American whaler. The knowledge he gained had been so advanced that upon his return it was almost impossible to convey to the most learned Japanese scholars. He had suffered and almost died because of it.

'When you leave Kagoshima,' Mung said, 'there will be time to spend with your families. After that you will travel to the capital as advisors to the Rujo. Tokyo, with its one million inhabitants, is Japan's largest city. Its people set the trends, fads and fashions in the empire. Go among them. Tell them of the West. Give lectures. Translate the books you have brought back. Start self-improvement societies to learn western ways. Offer business advice free. Your message is that to enable Japan to resist the foreigners, we must first learn from them.' Mung motioned to Jiroo, Takura and the other two senior Black Dragons. 'In a few moments we shall begin questioning you. In two days I must leave. You will remain here writing reports for at least a month. I anticipate the return of another member of our society. He has been successful for many years in supplying information from China, Korea and Manchuria. It would be most beneficial for you to meet with him. His name is Udo. I have adopted him as my son.'

Chapter 4

Canton, The House of a Thousand Delights
The room was bathed in purple light from paper lanterns strung across the ceiling. Three naked bodies were misty shadows on the soft down quilt in the centre of the floor.

The girl at his back gently raked his skin with her lacquered nails. She cupped his buttocks and brushed her breasts against his back. The girl in front caressed his chest.

'I have an appointment,' Udo said in Chinese.

'Allow us to pleasure you before you leave,' the girl in front said in English. Her lips brushed his. 'We must prove ourselves.'

Gently but firmly, he pushed her away. 'I need the potency you have aroused for someone else.'

The girl behind slid her arm over his thigh. Her hand encompassed his erection. She squeezed gently and he moaned, 'Do not do that.'

'Why can we not satisfy you?' she asked in German.

'You can,' he replied in the same guttural tone, and prised her fingers from his rigid penis. 'But like you, I too am a whore. I need my potency to perform.'

'I do not understand German,' the girl in front pouted.

Udo laughed. The pain in his scrotum assured him he would be able to satisfy the Frenchwoman. 'You are both accepted into The House of a Thousand Delights,' he said in Chinese.

Happiness blossomed in the girls' faces. They knelt and bowed repeatedly, until Udo held up his hand.

'Important as it is to pleasure our western patrons,' he said, 'you can earn more from talking to them. I want information. There is one woman who is already twenty-five but still working because of her ability to loosen tongues. Learn to drink western liquor, and improve your knowledge of their languages. Your German and English are still Biblical. Continue studying with the missionaries during the day, but at night talk, talk, talk to our guests.'

'Do you want us to convert?'

'Not unless the Christians threaten to throw you out. They give prospective converts more lessons and better teachers than those who have accepted their god. Now help me with my clothes. I have a chore to perform.'

Dressed in the silk embroidered robe and round hat of a wealthy Chinese merchant, Udo left The House of a Thousand Delights in his private rickshaw. His body servant cleared a path through Canton's crowded streets towards the fenced-in foreign compound.

The lane separating the Chinese houses from the fence was a hundred feet wide. Beyond the fence were cobbled streets, polo and cricket fields, and manicured lawns that rolled down to the giant warehouses on the water. Several western ships were unloading cotton, opium and manufactured iron products, while taking on tea, silk and spices.

The rickshaw stopped at a dignified Chinese house across from the French compound. Udo entered and walked directly to the drawing room. Furniture from Bombay stood on Persian carpets. The Austrian chandelier sparkled its light on European paintings decorating the walls. He waited until the servant left the room.

Udo touched the pouch of opium in his sleeve, hoping it would secure the information he needed. Time was short before his departure from China. He had controlled Denise Dubois through this drug for years, and endured a personal relationship to help her maintain her self-respect. He smoothed his robe and opened the double doors into the boudoir.

Denise Dubois lay propped by silk pillows on the canopied bed. At the age of forty, she was still a beautiful woman. Each curve of her sensuous body was highlighted by the sheen of the sheer Damascus silk nightgown. From neck to toe the thin material covered, yet revealed every contour. Her face was strong, her lips wide, but the colouring she used to hide the lines under her sunken eyes made them appear deeper, accentuating the ravages of opium. The once bright grey eyes that had caused men to tremble were now dull, flat balls of slag.

'I prefer you dressed in western clothes,' she said in a voice made husky by years of sucking an opium pipe. 'That way you almost look like one of us.'

Udo sat next to her on the bed. He placed the palms of his hands over her breasts and massaged the nipples.

'Did you bring a fresh supply?' she asked.

He used the tips of his fingers to trace a delicate line from her cleavage to her navel. Her soft belly rose to follow his touch. He leaned down and kissed it. She pressed his head into her.

'Do you have it?' she asked again.

'Yes,' he murmured into her stomach, feeling her breathe a sigh of relief.

'Pack a pipe for me. Please.'

He lifted his head and took her wrists, putting her palms on his lips. 'Do you have the information from your friend about the coolies?'

'Those women aren't my friends. They come to this house to drink, gossip, and for the privacy of using the free opium you provide. They think because I'm an outcast, I need them.'

'The amount of opium you request has increased considerably these last months.' Udo raised his eyebrows to emphasize his point.

'Isn't the information you receive worth it?'

Udo remained silent, staring at her.

'Those women need me,' she went on. 'Half of them are as addicted as I am. Some have been attending my special teas for years. Two are becoming bothersome.'

Udo took the pouch from his sleeve and placed it on the night table. Her eyes followed every move of his hands as he removed an ivory pipe from the drawer and packed it.

'I do not want you going to sleep on me,' he said. 'I need you.'

For just a moment he saw the flash in her eyes as he remembered it from years before. The first time he met her was soon after she departed from the British consul's party on Mung's arm. From that day, no member of the foreign community would speak with Denise Dubois in public. Her husband divorced her. Mung had bedded the French-woman that night, and later passed her on to Udo. It was Udo who introduced her to opium. He knew Mung would disapprove but it had given him control, and the information was so appreciated he was now summoned to return to Japan. He had succeeded, and that was his first priority.

Denise Dubois reached up and took the pipe from his hands. He lit it for her. She inhaled deeply and blew a cloud of smoke into his chest. The lines on her forehead smoothed as the narcotic took hold.

'How long can you stay?' she asked.

'Tell me which women have become bothersome.'

'Caroline from the German compound and Tala, the Russian. They pester me for more and more opium. It has almost come to begging.'

Denise undid her gown and pulled it back. Udo caressed her thigh. She inhaled, holding the smoke down in her lungs, letting it drift slowly from her nostrils. 'Tala makes me nervous. When we are alone she speaks badly of her husband. She cannot stand having sex with him, or even letting him touch her.'

'Has she mentioned a lover?'

'No.'

'Is she a lesbian?' He kissed her breasts.

'She touched me a few times, but I let her know I will have none of that.'

Udo harried the swollen nipples with his tongue and teeth. 'If Caroline has provided the information I need, give her as much as she wants. But not Tala. When do you expect her again?'

'Tomorrow.'

'Tell her you will introduce her to a person whose supply is unlimited.'

'When?'

'In two days.'

'She is already in great need.'

Udo reached behind the Frenchwoman's back and lifted her up. He pulled the nightgown off. 'She cannot buy it herself or ask her servants,' he said. 'She and her husband would be disgraced in the foreign compound. I want her so desperate for the pipe she will do what I ask of her.'

Denise reached under his robe. She looked up through half-closed eyes. 'You are hard, in more ways than one.'

'I will need privacy with the Russian,' he said.

'I should despise you. I took you in as my Oriental student lover.' She held up the pipe as in a toast. 'Now I work for you.'

'Tala will too.'

'It would give me pleasure to see that haughty Russian bitch in bed with a Chinaman, a Japanese, or whatever you are.' She gave Udo a mocking smile. 'Until she does, she won't know what she is missing.'

Udo did not expect to make love to Tala Derzhavin. Not if his spies proved his suspicion of who her lover was. He disrobed and lay alongside Denise Dubois. 'The information about the contract labourers?' he asked.

'Yes, Caroline told me what you need to know,' she teased. 'Her husband is involved in the transaction. But you will have to love the information from me.'

Udo took the pipe from her hand. He inhaled and blew the smoke into her mouth. 'Before I finish loving you, your lips will plead for me to stop, while your body continues like an inexhaustible steam engine. And even when you have told me everything, I will not stop.'

She ran her hands over his face and through his thick, cropped black hair.

'This will be our last lovemaking,' he said. 'I am leaving China.'

A look of desperation entered her eyes. She pulled his head into the hollow of her neck and her body tensed.

'Do not be frightened,' he whispered. 'You will be taken care of. There is a young man. He will supply all your needs.'

She kissed his ear, neck and shoulder. 'There is always a young man,' she sighed. 'You were young when you came to me. I taught you many things.'

'I am only thirty-one now.'

'In your body. Your mind has absorbed centuries of cunning from these Chinese. If this is our last time, come, show your teacher how much you have learned.'

The following evening, Udo was rowed across the harbour in his private fifteen-man fast-boat. Although he was an invited guest, his men approached Kang Shu's enormous ornate barge with caution. Long scrambling dragon-boats with eighty armed rowers in each patrolled the outer perimeter around the barge. It lay anchored in the only clear space among a quarter of a million boat-people in Canton harbour, and was lit by hundreds of gaily coloured lanterns.

Udo was thoroughly searched before being allowed to board. He passed between rows of guards and descended the polished teakwood stairs into the bowels of the giant craft. A mahogany door inlaid with silver and gold swung open before him.

Kang Shu, the most powerful man in southern China, sat cross-legged behind a low table covered with trays of food. 'Welcome. Welcome. Please be seated,' he said. The smile of his gapped yellow teeth and black marble eyes was the warmest he had given any man. He held a thin black cheroot underhand and puffed repeatedly. The smoke drifted from his pursed lower lip, up in front of his face, and curled around the brim of a proper black bowler hat that sat squarely on top of his head. 'I have ordered a special meal in honour of our last meeting.'

'Your hospitality has always been more than generous,' Udo said. 'I have never left your table without having had a unique experience. It will be difficult returning to Japan's gummy rice and bland tastes.'

Kang Shu clapped his hands and a servant entered. 'Prepare a supply of spices and delicacies selected by the chef to serve two people for a year. Have it delivered to Mr Udo at the Tillim Trading Company in the American compound.'

Udo bowed his gratitude as Kang Shu waved his cheroot over the food in front of them. 'Tonight I promise a culinary adventure you will long remember.'

Udo looked not at the food but at the ebony table top on which it sat. The grain of the wood ran horizontal to his seat. It meant he was afforded most honoured guest status. On the table were four dishes of fresh and dried fruits, sweets and cakes.

Kang pointed to a golden mass settled on a bed of dried seaweed. 'Will-Not-Stick-Three-Ways,' he said.

'I have never heard of it.'

'It is a sweet that will not stick to the ladle during preparation, to the chopsticks in the eating, or to the teeth when chewing.'

Udo smiled. He loosened his robe and congratulated himself for not having eaten since morning. 'What else have you planned?' he asked.

'Drunken Chicken, named in honour of a fun-loving empress. Sunflower Duck, Braised Prawns, Five Fragrant Kidney Slices, and Shark-fin Soup. And there is more.' Kang rubbed his hands together. 'All is prepared by a former chef from the imperial palace in Peking. I bought him for a very delicate price.'

Once again Udo bowed in appreciation of the honour bestowed upon him by the unofficial sovereign of southern China. Kang Shu owned Canton. He controlled two and a half million people. All the city administrators were obligated to the little man. No business deal on land or water, big or small, took place without Kang Shu receiving his share of the squeeze. Even the imperial Chinese army asked Kang Shu's permission to enter certain provinces.

'Will it disturb my gracious host and this carefully planned banquet if we discuss business while we eat?' Udo asked.

'The first time your Mr Mung visited, we ate and spoke business at the table. The British lord had paid me to poison Mr Mung.' Kang Shu smiled. 'But then I took into account that Mung and I are both Orientals. To hell with that pasty-faced Englisher, I thought. So I listened to Mung. Since that day my digestion and fortune have improved. He appears a quiet fellow but he has a sense of the dramatic. Things happen around him. In one glorious night of battle in Canton harbour, he made me the most powerful tong chief in Canton. Since then, my situation has improved.'

Udo remembered the battle well. His brother had died blowing up a ship full of explosives surrounded by five of Canton's strongest tong chiefs and four hundred men. Uraga gave his life to ensure Mung's escape.

Udo reached into his robe and gun barrels clattered through firing ports concealed in the walls, all aimed at him. He bowed slowly without removing his hand. 'Please excuse me,' he said. 'In the excitement of so many honours bestowed upon me, I forgot.' He had known very well what would happen, but wanted Kang Shu on the defensive to complete this final business deal.

The tong chief was not deceived. He smiled and waved his hand, and the gun barrels withdrew 'Pardon me for not informing my bodyguards a friend was dining. You may remove your hand.'

Udo pulled out five silk pouches and placed them on the table in front of the tong chief. 'Every three months, as Mung promised,' he said. 'After my departure, you will continue to receive this symbol of our friendship.'

'Five pouches of gold is more than symbolic,' Kang said. 'It is what helped put me in power. I shall continue to supply information to your people.'

He clapped his hands and a servant removed the gold. Others brought in the first hot dishes.

Udo concentrated on eating and praising the cuisine. He waited for Kang's inevitable question about the contract labourers. The information Caroline supplied to Denise was exactly what Udo needed for this meeting.

Finally, in a tone that belied the importance of the subject, Kang said, 'I have not heard from the Germans as to when they will take possession of my coolies in Macao.'

Udo tweezered a morsel from a serving dish and dipped it in a spicy brown sauce. 'Unfortunately,' he said, 'the Germans are no longer willing to do business with you.'

'Why so?' Kang asked, feigning innocence.

'They say twenty-five per cent of the last group of coolies you sold them died in transit to Hawaii. The remainder were dead before the sugar cane was harvested.'

The tong chief laid aside his eating sticks. 'I bought two thousand men for the German deal. They have been sitting idle, eating my food, and complaining about the conditions. It is costly. My good name is being tarnished.' Kang Shu gulped some rice wine. He looked over the cup and was surprised by Udo's smile. 'My friend, this is no joking matter.'

'Kang, you are rich enough to buy Germany. If only you would feed those poor bastards in your barracoon, there would be no problem.'

'I have known poverty those shit coolies never dreamed of. Maybe I will let them starve. It would be cheaper.'

'There is a two hundred dollar profit to be made on each coolie.'

'That is seventy-five dollars more than I would get if the Germans transported them to Hawaii. How?' Kang demanded.

'I sell their contracts to the railroad in California. Did you know the Russian spring convoy from Vladivostok is already moving south?'

'Your spy network is as efficient as mine.'

'Spring came early up north,' Udo said. 'Pigeons brought word from Korea that the Russian trade convoy has sailed. They plan to buy tea, silk and spices here in Canton, offload in San Francisco, and go on to the Russian fur traders in the Oregon Territory.'

Kang leaned forward. 'What can you offer the Russians to make up for the loss of income from tea and spices?'

'They will earn as much carrying coolies to San Francisco. And if they pick them up in Shanghai, the convoy will save a thousand miles. They will arrive in America two months early. With your tong connections in San Francisco and Los Angeles, you can arrange for them to earn money ferrying goods up and down the west coast until it is time for them to take their furs back home.'

'This is quite a scheme. How do you intend to transport my two thousand coolies to Shanghai in time to meet the convoy?'

'I do not.'

'So who has two thousand coolies there?'

'I do.'

51

Kang pushed his bowler hat to the back of his head. 'And how does that help me?'

'I will sell your coolies in Macao to the Germans here in Canton. You sell mine to the Russians in Shanghai. I hold the contracts but have no place to house the labourers, or agents to conclude the deal in Shanghai. You do.'

Incredulous, Kang Shu scratched his head. 'You intend to sell the Germans the same coolies they turned down from me?'

'Easily. I bribed one of the German officials. Just move those men from your barracoon in Macao to the one in Amoy. I will lend you six Tillim Trading junks to help transport them.'

Kang warmed to the idea. 'If you succeed in this and we trick the Germans, my name will be honoured throughout all the tongs of China. That is very pleasing to me. How do you intend to get the higher price?'

'Through my American trading company.' Udo smiled. 'Just be certain to feed those coolies fresh fruits and vegetables. Give them meat and milk two days before the Germans come to inspect.'

Kang Shu grunted his agreement, although he had no intention of wasting his money. I will invest in the fruits and vegetables, he thought, but to hell with the meat. A double dose of cod-liver oil before the inspection will make their skins shine.

'Do the round-eyes continue to believe you are merely the manager of Tillim Trading Company?' Kang asked.

'In all of China only you know I bought Jake Tillim out for Mr Mung. My position as comprador allows me to bargain like a Chinese at the prices of a European. Also, as an employee, I can live in the foreign compound, something no Oriental could do otherwise.'

'If you put this deal together, what is my profit?'

'All the money goes to you,' Udo said.

Kang pulled his hat down, shading his eyes. He shot Udo a dark look. 'Now I begin to worry.'

'We divide the profits evenly. You hold my half but it will be our secret, separate from any dealings with Mr Mung. If I need the money, you will receive a coded message through my replacements, although they know nothing of this arrangement.'

Kang Shu breathed easier. 'I am pleased to see you have at least one vice.'

Udo shrugged. 'I have become accustomed to living well in China. In Japan my family had little. There, title is everything. I was born a one-sword samurai, and so I shall die.'

'You are a financial genius. Why return to a country where merchants are considered lower than dog shit? Join me. Together we could run all of China.'

'I know you will find it hard to understand when I say that Bushido, the warrior code of the samurai, draws me back to Japan. No matter what I have become here, I am still a servant of the Emperor and the Lord of Satsuma.'

Kang speared a prawn and swished it around in a sizzling red sauce, then popped it into his mouth. 'My loyalties are to a good life and a few special friends like yourself. Tell Mr Mung I will shepherd his three new agents and continue to supply information.'

The tong chief tapped a small gong and a servant appeared with a sheaf of papers. He set them before Udo and placed a small lacquer box on top.

'The papers are for Mr Mung,' Kang said. 'I had my agents in Manchuria and Korea compile information about the Russians there.' He pushed his bowler hat up. 'Someday we Orientals will have to chase the Russians back to Siberia.' He shrugged. 'The information is a hodgepodge of material regarding imperial Chinese policies, and about the round-eyes in the Far East. It was gathered by people of varying talents and will require patience to unravel.'

'In the name of Mr Mung and for myself, I thank you,' Udo said.

'The lacquer box is your gift. Open it.'

Udo took out a large gold earring. To it was attached a teardrop of gold inlaid jade with an intricate geometrical pattern.

'If you ever need help and are near a Chinese community, even in foreign lands, clip this to your left ear,' Kang said. 'It will identify you as one favoured by Kang Shu, greatest of all tong chiefs in China.' The thin, sallow-complexioned man appeared to grow as he spoke. 'My tong controls Chinese labourers in Malaya, Hawaii, Panama, Peru and Cuba. There are concentrations of our people in Paris, Vienna, London, San Francisco, New Orleans and New York. With that earring you may draw on my power and wealth in all those places.'

The kowtow Udo performed was genuine. 'I am humbled before such generosity, and ashamed I came to our last meeting without a gift for you.'

'The five pouches of gold are a sign you have not forgotten your pledge. With all my wealth I, Kang Shu, am still a lonely man. It is dangerous for me to allow people close. You have placed your trust in me and I in you. The profits from the coolie transaction will be safe, that is if the Russians and Germans agree.'

'I have a meeting with a Russian lady tomorrow afternoon, and my weekly poker game with the German consul in the evening. After losing a hundred dollars or so, I will know if they agree.'

Chapter 5

'Madam Derzhavin,' Udo said in French, 'anything can be bought in Canton. However, as in Russia, there is always the price to consider.' He bowed.

'My house servants deal with peddlers,' the tall, angular blonde woman replied.

'This gentleman is more than a street hawker,' Denise Dubois said. 'He is one of the most influential merchants in Canton, and comprador of the Tillim Trading Company.'

Tala Derzhavin worried a lace handkerchief in her white-knuckled fists. Her square shoulders twitched with the need for opium, but she stiffened her back and said, 'Your references may be as handsome as your western style clothing, Mr Udo, but you are a tradesman nevertheless.'

Udo felt no anger towards the elegant Russian woman, but he made it appear so in his stance and voice. 'You mean an Oriental tradesman.'

'However you wish to interpret my words.'

The time had come for Udo to show his power. With a simple flick of his finger, he motioned Denise Dubois from the room. She left without question.

A moment later, a beautiful Eurasian woman entered and closed the boudoir doors behind her. Her clinging silk gown revealed a voluptuous body. Tala Derzhavin stared in a way that told Udo his information about her was correct. He stepped closer to Madam Derzhavin and she withdrew, backing into the canopied bed.

'Do not be afraid,' Udo said.

'You are impertinent. I am a white woman.'

'You are in need, Madam. It is why you are here speaking to me.' He waved the Eurasian woman forward.

Tala watched the exquisite creature glide across the carpeted floor and hold out a long-stemmed ivory pipe. The Russian woman could not move. She saw the Eurasian reach out, felt her soft touch behind the elbow. The fingers lingered and caressed. Then Tala's arm was raised, the pipe placed in her hand. Her glance locked with the other woman's eyes.

'Shall I light it for you?' the beautiful lips asked in Russian.

'Where did you learn the mother tongue?' Tala whispered.

Udo remained motionless, forgotten.

'My father was exiled from Moscow to Khabarovsk near the Manchurian border,' the Eurasian said. 'My mother was Mongolian.' She moved closer, took the pipe from Tala's hand and lit it. She blew the sweet smelling smoke against the taller woman's lips.

Tala Derzhavin inhaled. She leaned forward, her eyelids fluttering. She raised her hand to take the pipe and quivered as their fingers touched.

'Come here,' Udo commanded in Chinese.

The Eurasian woman drew back next to him.

Tala cried out like a wounded kitten, then glared at Udo with the ferocity of a lioness. 'What did you tell her? Where is she going?'

'Where I say. She is my property.' Udo's voice was harsh. 'I own her, this house, and the opium you need.' He stroked the Eurasian's long black hair.

Tala bridled; anger sparked from her eyes.

'Madam Dubois called me a merchant,' Udo said. 'You say I am a tradesman. I accept your definition. Let us trade.'

Tala Derzhavin squared her shoulders and raised her

chin. 'I can do without opium and slime like you!' She started forward to leave the room.

Udo reached under the black hair. His fingers probed the vertebrae of the Eurasian's spine, then pressed hard. Her eyes flew open, her body went rigid.

Tala, directly in front of her, cried out, 'What have you done?'

'I have paralysed her,' Udo said. 'She cannot move or speak, although she feels and hears everything.'

He reached over and undid the loops of the silk gown. It opened, revealing a statuesque figure so beautiful that Tala gasped. She tried to turn away but her eyes scoured the unblemished body. Udo pushed the gown from the Eurasian's shoulders. It dropped to the floor. Tala remained as frozen as the woman before her.

'Please take the pipe from her hand,' Udo said. 'It might fall and burn the carpet.'

Trance-like, Tala edged closer to the naked bronze figure. Her eyes roamed the exquisite breasts, narrow waist and strong thighs. She took the pipe from the clenched fingers and breathed in the aroma of the perfumed body. 'Please do not hurt her,' she begged.

'Why not?' Udo asked.

'I want her,' Tala whispered.

He nodded. 'She can be yours.'

'How?'

'We trade.'

Her head nodded up and down. 'What do you want?'

'This lovely Oriental lady will be yours,' Udo said softly. 'Madam Dubois will see she is housed here in a private room only for you. The room will be supplied with opium for your needs.'

Tala Derzhavin exerted supreme self-control. She stepped back, dropping her handkerchief, and rubbed the warm bowl of the ivory pipe. 'What do I pay?' Her eyes remained on the nude figure before her.

'I must meet with your husband under favourable conditions to conclude a business deal.'

She turned to face Udo. 'Is that all?'

'Your husband has never dealt directly with Orientals, but for this arrangement it is imperative we meet face to face.'

Tala flashed a haughty look. 'My husband will kiss an Oriental's arse if I tell him to. But certainly there is more, Mr Tradesman!'

'As long as you continue to supply information regarding Russian policy in the Far East, the arrangement in this house will continue.'

'Ha! You want me to spy on my husband.' She sucked deeply on the long-stemmed pipe and sent smoke spiralling to the ceiling. 'I'll need money. That crude son of a bitch of a husband never gives me enough to even dress properly. He thinks our marriage conferred the right to slobber over me twice a week without paying.'

'Money will be forthcoming based on the value of the information.'

The tall Russian woman looked longingly at the Eurasian beauty frozen in her naked splendour. 'How much would it cost to kill him?' Tala asked.

'Who?'

'My husband. I understand you Orientals can arrange things like that.'

'Damn it, no!' Udo shouted. 'Your husband has the information we need, not you.'

'What information would be worth your killing him?' she insisted.

'If he dies, everything we agreed upon is finished.' Damned women, he thought. Every time I think I am in control, they do something unexpected. 'My appointment with your husband must be soon,' he snapped.

'My house, eight tomorrow morning. He will be waiting.'

Udo removed his hand from the Eurasian's neck and she slumped forward. Tala dropped the pipe and caught the naked body in her arms. 'It will be all right,' she whispered. 'Everything will be all right.'

Udo retrieved the fallen pipe. He whisked up the ashes with Tala's handkerchief and put it on the night table with a new pouch of opium.

Of the four Black Dragons seated on the floor in the Canton office of the Tillim Trading Company, there was no doubt who the leader was. Udo's robe was of the finest crimson and gold Chinese silk. He held himself straight and tall and the other three listened to his every word.

'I would prefer another year to prepare you three,' he said in Japanese, 'but I leave for Kagoshima tonight. Your roles are as I outlined them. One – The House of a Thousand Delights and Madame Dubois. Two – the Chinese Trading Company. Three – the Tillim Trading Company. Your primary objective is to gather information and supply the Black Dragon with up-to-date reports. If you can make a profit while doing so, all the better. Remember to use the carrier pigeons for only the most urgent messages. And work at improving your knowledge of foreign languages.' Udo pointed at the first Black Dragon. 'I have arranged with two marine guards from the American consulate to continue your poker lessons.'

'Excuse me, sire, but last night I watched you put away three of a kind, allowing the German ambassador to win with two pair. According to Mr Hoyle's book, you should have been victorious.'

Udo sighed. 'My only hope for you is that I knew less when I arrived in China. Westerners consider winning or losing in poker a matter of honour. You must not. That weekly game was established thirty years ago by Jake Tillim, the founder of the Tillim Trading Company. His purpose was to transact business informally. The game allows Orientals like ourselves a personal contact with people who would not recognize us in public. You must never win large amounts, or make the round-eyes appear foolish.' He looked around at the attentive faces. 'If you should come up against any problem you cannot handle, go to Kang Shu. He is our best counsellor in China. Always pay him the greatest respect, and the five pouches of gold every three months.'

Udo pointed at the first young man again. 'You will sleep with Madame Dubois, but never approach Tala Derzhavin. She would eat you alive. And turn down all her requests to kill her husband. He was quite receptive to an idea I put to him yesterday morning. He mentioned the presence of Russian traders in the Chinese city of Hunchun. It could mean the czar's first move south since he founded Vladivostok. I spoke of it in the poker game last night and it disturbed the westerners. They worry that if the Russians establish a warm water port in Korea, they will be competitors in commerce and fishing in the Far East.' Udo spread a map before the three Black Dragons. 'For Japan, a Russian-dominated Korea is dangerous.' He put his finger on the southern peninsula of South Korea. 'It points like a dagger at the bowels of Japan, and is only one hundred miles away. Any foreign invasion of Japan must come from here. Pay close attention to all information from the north.'

'One of the girls in The House of a Thousand Delights reported a missionary killed and his family hacked to death up north,' the first Black Dragon said. 'The Christians kidnapped Chinese children and were drinking their blood and eating their flesh.'

'Nonsense,' Udo said. 'They only playact doing that with the body of their god. Christians are definitely not cannibals.'

'Sire, I have witnessed round-eyes eating beef so rare, blood oozed from it. I confirmed the missionary incident from three different sources. Fifty-four graves were dug up and the remains of children identified.'

'About them eating raw meat, you are correct,' Udo said. 'But they do not eat people. Often information like that can be clarified at the poker game, as I did last night. The children were sickly and close to death. They were purchased from poor families by the missionaries. Christians believe if they pour their holy water on the little ones, it will keep them out of Hell and allow direct passage to Heaven. The Chinese mob invented the story for an excuse to loot the mission.

'This brings me to the last point. Life in China can be very pleasant. It is far more luxurious than Japan. Enjoy its benefits, but always remain alert. It can also be extremely treacherous here. Mung, the Black Dragon, left Canton under attack. My brother was killed, as was Ariwara Motokata, by a jealous business rival. I killed Motokata's murderer, and others to stay alive.' Udo drew a short, two-barrelled pistol from one sleeve, and a long knife with a triangular blade from the other. 'These are both American weapons. The pistol is called a derringer and the knife an Arkansas toothpick. Americans favour the bowie knife, but it was really made for work.' He held the long shiny blade up to the lantern. 'This has only one function – to kill.' He pointed to three boxes in the corner of the room. 'In those cartons you will each find a set of these weapons. They are my parting gift to you. I will burn incense in the great temple of Kagoshima and put prayer notes for your success on the gate of the Shinto shrine.' He stood up and bowed. 'Now I leave for Japan, and my new parents.'

Chapter 6

From the huge wooden gateway of the Yasukune shrine to the Emperor's palace, three thousand imperial guards in blood-red uniforms lined both sides of the road. White ostrich plumes waved from their gleaming helmets. The glittering blades of their long swords formed a sharp-edged gauntlet between which ran a crier shouting, 'He comes! He comes!'

Mung could feel the excitement sweep the crowd. Balconies and second storey windows were thronged with onlookers. People craned their necks. A trumpet sounded and a band marched into view. Five hundred lancers followed. Fifty lords of the realm on horseback, each with scores of retainers, preceded the Emperor returning from his daily prayers. He rode in a coach with windows shut and shades drawn. Hundreds of archers circled with bows strung, ordered to kill any person who looked upon the imperial carriage.

The carriage approached and people prostrated themselves full length on the ground, eyes shut tight. Mung saw balconies empty and heard shutters bang closed. He and his guards lay down on the ground. It was forbidden to look on the descendant of the Sun Goddess, Amaterasu-o-mi-Kami, without imperial permission.

The carriage passed and Mung stood up in time to catch sight of the eight ornate wagons carrying the Emperor's personal effects. Each displayed the imperial crest – a blazing sun and sixteen expanding rays. A regiment of priests passed, garbed in white silk robes with the sacred lotus emblazoned on their garments in gold leaf. The horse artillery pranced forward with ammunition wagons, loaders, gunners and outriders.

A battalion of cavalry cantered ahead of the imperial infantry, for whom Mung felt humorous compassion. The rugged foot soldiers' swaggering attempts to maintain military decorum despite the warm horse droppings, made their each step into the steaming piles of manure more hilarious. It was a daily occurrence the people enjoyed. They giggled politely behind their fans. The long white plumes of the imperial guards quivered and their armour jingled as they tried to suppress their laughter at the infantry wading through the dung.

Mung had begged to have the infantry precede the horses, but Japan remained a rigid status society. Shortly he would be meeting with the Emperor to give his report and recommendations for reforming the traditional system of hereditary rank and privilege.

The master of protocol in the imperial court motioned Mung to enter. He lay face down, legs together, arms outstretched, and wriggled on his belly into the presence of the Son of Heaven.

'Rise and be seated,' the familiar voice commanded.

Mung rose to his knees. He touched his head to the floor, then sat back on his heels.

The Emperor of Japan sat on a raised wooden platform in a room devoid of furniture. A curved black hat, held by leather thongs tied under his chin, framed his smooth young face. His silk brocade robes hid the shape of his thin body.

'Black Dragon,' the Emperor said, 'how is it that common criminals threaten you, my personal representative?' The precise diction lent weight to the question.

'Sire,' Mung replied, 'even with advance warning, it is difficult to prevent assassination attempts when the killers are prepared to die. Few Yakuza escaped, none were captured alive. My men continue the search to discover who paid for the attack.'

'The Yakuza do not usually involve themselves in national politics,' the Emperor said. 'I have been informed they are a clandestine organization prone to smuggling and robbery. Why have they stepped out of character?'

'I suspect this may be a renegade group hired by opponents of my modernization plan.'

'When you find those responsible, their names and those of their ancestors will be obliterated from the minds of men.'

The Emperor's dark, intelligent eyes studied Mung, the only common-born subject to whom he had ever spoken. In previous meetings he had questioned the Black Dragon about his boyhood village life. More often it was about his stay in America, whaling in the Pacific, and gold-mining in California. Twice he had asked to hear how Mung's nose had been broken in the fight with a French sailor in Honolulu. Today he would have liked to hear a detailed description of the Yakuza attack on the river, but there was no time.

'My dedicated servant,' the Emperor said, 'you are about to enter another period of intense activity. There are factions here in the capital who oppose your methods of modernization. Some may try to outmanoeuvre you politically, while others look for more direct means. Be alert!' The Emperor paused, then said, 'I have had news of John Whittefield's resignation from the American Navy to take up the post of Chief of the Japanese Section in the Foreign Bureau.'

'That is good for Japan,' Mung said. 'It indicates my brother, John, could one day become America's ambassador to your court.'

'An appointment I shall encourage. Your adoptive family across the ocean has helped Japan, and they continue to fight against the unfair international treaties. John predicts

64

that France and Prussia are on the verge of war. The British prime minister, Gladstone, sends a similar message. I was under the impression that France and Prussia were allies.'

'The returning Black Dragons confirm the war talk. They say von Bismarck is purposely pressuring Napoleon III to fight by violating a secret agreement and informing the European press of France's intention to annex parts of Belgium and Italy.'

'Will there be war?'

'Yes, sire.'

'Who will triumph?'

'My agents from France say the French, but those from Vienna say Prussia.'

'And you?'

'I think it will be the Iron Chancellor. Von Bismarck is the stronger personality, and an army is a reflection of its leader.'

The Emperor lifted his hand and rang a tiny silver bell. Before the musical chimes faded, a door slid open. Lord Hotta, first advisor to the Emperor, wriggled forward on his stomach and was seated next to Mung.

The Fujiwara lord, one of the most powerful men in Japan, was Mung's trusted ally, although they had once been enemies. The old warrior, a veteran of thirty years of field battles, court intrigues and political manoeuvring, had been at Mung's side in the defeat by foreigners at the battle of Tokyo bay. Afterwards they had sworn a pact to establish Japan as a world power.

The Emperor nodded to Lord Hotta, who addressed Mung. 'Your wife has arrived aboard the *Kanrin Maru*.'

Mung's surprise was so apparent that the Fujiwara lord answered his questions before they were asked. 'I ordered it. The Emperor requires the services of the Black Dragon here in Tokyo. Pressures are rapidly building up from within and outside the country. Coming events may require a more immediate response. Therefore, you must remain near the decision makers. Do not be concerned. Your son is well protected at his studies in Kyoto.'

'I am honoured,' Mung said. 'This will allow me to centralize and increase my control of the Black Dragon Society. But will it not appear strange that the Minister of Maritime Services remains so far from Japan's largest shipyard in Kagoshima?' he asked.

'The Emperor has recently accepted the British Lord Alcock's offer to provide advisors and loans to build an even larger shipyard in the nearby village of Yokohama. Count Iyeasu of Mito arranged this before his return from Britain.'

'You will work with the count,' the Emperor said. 'He will oversee the building of the shipyard.'

'Sire,' Mung said, 'the count is the youngest son of Fujita Koin who is most antagonistic to my plans.'

'Iyeasu Koin is brilliant,' Lord Hotta said. 'He is also energetic, with one predictable trait. Whatever task he undertakes, it absorbs all his time and energy until completed. By appointing Iyeasu to this position, we gain a most competent manager for our project. And we deprive Mito of their most valuable asset for opposing our plans. The Emperor invited both father and sons, along with Lord Saga, to hear your report on the returning Black Dragons, whom you are to refer to as your students.'

'Once again I must question the wisdom of sitting with those so opposed to our policies,' Mung said.

'First of all, you should differentiate between Lords Koin and Saga,' Hotta said. 'Fujita Koin is not opposed to modernization. He prefers western-trained Japanese to reorganize the country rather than your method of using foreigners. Saga opposes all change, and only itches to expel the barbarians.'

The Emperor raised a finger and the two advisors fell silent. 'Mung,' he said, 'never forget that I may command religious respect, but for the most part I am only obeyed by those lords who agree with my policies. Saga of Choshu and Fujita Koin of Mito hold sway over a majority of lords in the Rujo. They can field more armed men than I can, even with my support from Satsuma and Lord Hotta's Fujiwara. We cannot implement our policies and antagonize Choshu and Mito at this time. You have been summoned to Tokyo to prevent a civil war. The foreigners would like nothing better than to watch us fight each other. Then they could demand more concessions from a weakened winner.'

'Sire,' Mung said, 'I believe if you were to demand that the lords of the realm follow you, they would. Respect for the Emperor is so deeply engrained in your people, it would be unthinkable for them not to obey.'

'I trust I will never have to test your theory. Even now, Lord Saga may be the first to openly oppose me. He has not answered my summons.'

'According to my agents, he has not left Choshu,' Mung said.

Lord Hotta flashed the Emperor a knowing glance. 'It could signify open rebellion.'

'Let us not jump to conclusions,' the Emperor said. 'What cannot be changed will not be discussed. Let us meet with Fujita Koin and his sons.'

'Sire,' Mung asked, 'may I know more about Iyeasu Koin before we meet?'

The Emperor nodded and Lord Hotta explained, 'Three months ago he returned from England where he had been studying for seven years. He speaks English and French fluently. In our society where it is said the protruding nail is pounded down to the level of all others, the young count is an exception. He is his father's experiment. The old man educated him from childhood in western sciences, then sent him abroad to learn more. This has earned Iyeasu the hatred of his middle brother, Hideyoshi, who is overly ambitious. He fears Iyeasu, and makes jokes at his expense.

The latest is that Count Iyeasu is suing Tokyo municipality for building the streets too close to his arse.'

The Emperor's robes jiggled. His lips compressed and Mung saw a tear of laughter slip down his smooth cheek.

Lord Hotta hid his giggle behind a fan. 'Count Iyeasu is rather short and eh . . . eh . . . fluffy. Yes, I would say he is very fluffy.'

The young Emperor bit his lip to maintain his composure, but his shoulders shook with mirth and he rocked back and forth. A second tear followed the first down the reddening cheeks.

For Mung the Emperor suddenly became a man before his eyes, no longer the god he had believed in, and Mung felt himself vulnerable. He knew the Emperor was correct. There were those who would defy imperial authority. 'Why does Hideyoshi undermine his younger brother?' Mung asked. 'Would not the older Danjuro be more of a threat in the order of inheritance?'

Lord Hotta smoothed his robes. 'Danjuro is a courageous man. Tell him to storm a fortress and he will charge. But the Mito giant is no leader. Whereas Hideyoshi is sly like a fox, and his father knows it. So Hideyoshi, the middle brother, fears their father will pass leadership of the fiefdom to Iyeasu. However, whatever differences separate the three brothers, they all agree with their father on one thing.' He pointed at Mung. 'Your plan for modernization is a threat to their way of life, and they believe a threat to the survival of Japan. Hideyoshi especially fears a society based on advancement by merit, not birth.'

'It is time,' the Emperor said.

'Admit Fujita Koin and his two sons,' Lord Hotta ordered.

The shoji screen door slid open. The old man, leader of the three houses of Mito, went down on his belly and wriggled forward. He knelt before the Emperor.

Mung, watching Lord Koin from the corner of his eye,

glimpsed something else that raised the hair on the back of his neck. A large mound of silk moved across the polished teakwood floor. A close-cropped, melon-shaped head and five pudgy fingers on either side, protruded from the moving pile of silk. Two white tabi socks poked out from behind the silken hump. Mung glanced sideways, watching the youngest count of Mito push himself up on to his knees before the Emperor and roll forward to touch his head to the floor. Then, for the first time, Mung saw the smooth childlike face of Iyeasu Koin. He had wide shoulders and an enormous chest. Mung's lips curled in a smile. The youngest count of Mito fitted Ukiko's description of a friendly frog.

The doorway of the room was filled by the oldest brother. Even on his knees, Danjuro Koin, the Mito giant, was almost as tall as the master of protocol. He crept forward and took his place near his father.

'The Emperor welcomes the leader of the three houses of Mito,' Lord Hotta said. 'Your son, Iyeasu, has spoken with great skill in the Rujo. This being his first time in personal audience with the Emperor, he is not to feel inhibited.'

Iyeasu's wide innocent eyes closed as he again pressed his head to the floor, acknowledging the honour.

'I have instructed my son to answer without hesitation,' Fujita Koin said.

'The Minister of Maritime Services will now present a condensed account of his students' observations while abroad,' Lord Hotta said.

Iyeasu listened carefully to Mung's report, hearing the Minister of Maritime Services quote names, dates, places – Japanese and foreign – shipping, tonnage and import-export figures, all without consulting notes or pausing to rethink a fact. Iyeasu had heard of Mung's exceptional memory, and wondered if he too could learn to remember everything he saw and heard.

'Since Commodore Perry entered Tokyo bay seventeen years ago,' Mung said, 'Japan has begun to emerge from 250 years of self-enforced isolation. The shogunate's policy of withdrawal from international commerce and politics served the empire well in its time. But that era is over. The shogun's defeat, and return of power to the Emperor, were the first steps in a new policy of political, economic and social intercourse with the outside world.'

'Some in Japan think the intercourse you speak of has turned into rape,' Fujita Koin said. 'First the foreigners forced coal and supply stations on us for their transoceanic steamers and whaling fleets. Then we were made to sign unequal trade agreements under the shadows of their guns. Now Christian missionaries are free to roam in whichever port their countries have trading rights.'

'The progress made among our people by missionaries is insignificant,' Mung said. 'It is offset by the general educational benefits our people receive from the missionaries. Rescue and supply stations are a humanitarian responsibility undertaken by all civilized nations. The treaties may be unequal, but they established a basis for trade with the West. At a later date, they shall be revised.'

The low, deep voice of Danjuro filled the room. 'Our economy has done well for centuries without the round-eyes,' he rumbled.

'That is a commonly accepted fallacy,' Lord Hotta said. 'The 250 years of peace during the reign of the shoguns was based on a thriving economy centuries old. Our ancestors were once energetic seafaring businessmen. Japanese merchants travelled to China and Hawaii. They traded in India and Arabia. Some even reached the west coast of North America before the policy of isolation. But the years of peace have resulted in a population boom without improved methods of farming, taxation or distribution of wealth. We are a one-crop nation unable to produce enough rice to feed our people. For the first time in our history, there have been food riots. With international commerce, we would be able to borrow in time of need and sell in time of plenty.'

'And if the Christians lend us money, they will demand our souls in payment,' the old man of Mito said. 'More and more of their priests go among our people. Lord Hotta deleted one point in his history lesson. The shogun rose to power because the Franciscans had converted a quarter-million of our people, and the Emperor had done nothing to stop it. The shogun searched out Christian priests and converts and killed them. Because of his actions, Japan has lived in peace longer than any European nation. It is true Japan must modernize. But Saga of Choshu is correct. We must drive the western consuls and Christian clergy from our land. I would not mind sending some Shinto priests and Buddhist monks along with them.'

'The consuls serve a beneficial purpose,' Mung said. 'They represent foreign business interests, and reduce friction between our people and theirs.'

'These same consuls also set Japan's gold standards,' Count Iyeasu said. 'They keep the price of gold artificially low when buying from us, and sell at a large profit in Europe.'

'I admit some foreign consuls have taken advantage of their power over the precious metals,' Mung said.

'Mr Minister,' Iyeasu said, 'what would you do if the westerners applied their controls on gold to everything we produce?'

'They would have no basis for such a policy.'

The round little man cocked his head and aimed his eyes at Mung. 'They might approach the pope in Rome. With his new concept of infallibility, they could ask him to condone any price on any product.'

For a moment Mung felt trapped. He had not yet reported to the Emperor the information being drawn out of him. 'My students who were abroad do not foresee papal infallibility influencing Japan,' he said.

'Obviously Count Iyeasu does,' Lord Hotta said, shooting a hard look at Mung. Hotta did not like surprises. 'Explain this papal infallibility,' he ordered Iyeasu.

Mung watched and was fascinated by the young count who, despite this being his first audience with the Emperor, spoke without a hint of uneasiness.

'In the latter part of 1869,' Iyeasu said, 'Pope Pius IX decreed that he, and all successors to the throne of Saint Peter, are endowed with the Holy Spirit when speaking on matters of faith and morals. They cannot err. Of course Catholic businessmen, bankers and merchants know the pope's favours can be bought, and his faith and morals applied to financial endeavours.'

'I have also found it expedient to be infallible,' the Emperor said, 'but that does not mean I am always correct, or that people will do as I say.'

Five startled men stared at the young monarch. 'Does this pope have advisors?' he asked.

'Yes, sire,' Iyeasu replied.

'Then he and I are equally infallible.'

'But you are the direct descendant of the Sun Goddess, Amaterasu,' Danjuro blurted out.

'Eh ... Ahh ... Yes. Then ... there you have it,' the Emperor said.

Mung diverted attention away from the ruler by addressing Iyeasu. 'The Roman Catholic pope represents only one faction of Christianity. Protestants reject him. My students tell me that Napoleon III, who was the pope's strong right arm, has withdrawn his army from Italy to prepare for war with Prussia. The Italian government itself has not taken kindly to this new concept of papal infallibility. They have confined the pope to a small area of Rome called the Vatican. In effect, the pope is not a threat to Italy or Japan.'

It was Mung's turn to watch the young Mito count shift

in discomfort. Iyeasu lowered his innocent-looking eyes in respect as Mung continued speaking. 'The danger to our people is not so much religious or moral, but in the way we look at ourselves. We believe ourselves superior to all peoples, yet our every contact with the West proves our scientific and military inferiority. There are those like Lord Saga who, faced with this situation, want to return to the policy of isolation. But we can no longer hide from the outside world. We need foreign teachers in order to equal their accomplishments.'

'My time abroad convinced me that Japan must modernize,' Iyeasu Koin said. 'My father accepted that fact when he sent me to England some years ago. The Minister of Maritime Services and I differ on methods. One thing he should know. Westerners will never accept us as equals. The Christian world is divided into two groups, those who explain the universe by creation and those who do so by science. They may disagree on papal infallibility, but both sides accept the colour of a man's skin as an indicator of his moral or biological development. The religious Christian sees darker-skinned people as the sons of Ham – meant to be hewers of wood and drawers of water. In effect, slaves to the white man. The white secularist quotes Darwin's theory of natural selection to prove racial superiority.' Iyeasu addressed the Emperor. 'Your imperial highness, due to their racial beliefs the white nations will allow Japan, at best, the status of vassal state.'

'Knowledge will earn Japan equality and respect from all white nations,' Mung said.

'Equals! Ha!' The old Lord of Mito grunted, and his soft lips fluttered. 'Yes, I agree we must learn from the barbarians. I agree we have buried our heads in the sand for too long. I will send hundreds of students abroad to learn from them. But I will not allow the round-eyes in my country. I will fight to keep them out.'

'War serves no purpose,' Mung said.

'That is the difference between us, Fisherman,' the old man thundered. 'War is the sole purpose for my existence. The samurai is born and bred to fight.'

Mung burned at the insult. It was common knowledge his father had been a deposed samurai. He swallowed his pride and said, 'Lord Koin, if you send hundreds of students abroad to study, what will you do when they return with the concept of the equality of man? Your own son must have been exposed to the idea that all men are created equal and should be treated as such before the law. The whites may be prejudiced, but their ideas have no colour.' Mung challenged Iyeasu with his eyes. He received a complacent smile, as if to say, You must win your own argument. I will not do it for you.

'We shall send abroad only those of samurai rank,' the old man said. 'They will return to protect their interests.'

'In doing so they would be serving themselves and not the people of Japan,' Mung said.

'Of course,' Fujita Koin exclaimed. 'It has always been so. Each person is born into a certain class with defined responsibilities to society, and all serve the Emperor.'

'For Japan to meet the challenge of the West, our laws must be changed to benefit all the people,' Mung said. 'My students will recommend to the Rujo that we begin to invite judicial experts from France and agronomists from America. England will become our maritime model and von Bismarck's army our military example.'

'It is a long way between your students' recommendations and acceptance by the Rujo,' the giant Danjuro said.

With a motion of his fan, the Emperor signalled for silence. 'Lord Koin,' he said, 'the strength of this nation will be determined by the level of education of its entire population. The hundreds of students you send abroad will return to educate all our people.'

The three men from Mito lowered their heads as the

74

Emperor spoke. He was showing himself a diplomat by complimenting the Lord of Mito, yet telling him what to do. However, even Mung was startled when the Emperor added, 'Women will participate too. If it is a fight for the survival of the Japanese people, we cannot disregard fifty per cent of the population. Women will receive a basic education.'

The Lord of Mito, trapped by his loyalty to the Emperor and strict adherence to the code of Bushido, gummed his soft wet lips until they were sucked into his toothless mouth. He touched his head to the floor. 'Your imperial highness, protocol dictates this matter be brought before the Rujo. If Mung's students present his view of using foreign advisors, I request Count Iyeasu be allowed to set forth mine, which is to educate an élite group abroad who will return to teach our people.'

'Granted,' the Emperor said. 'Your son, Iyeasu, has impressed me. I am considering that he become one of my advisors. For now, I place him in charge of constructing the new Yokohama shipyard he was so instrumental in persuading the British to help us build.'

Count Iyeasu bowed. Once again the house of Mito is being given honour, but no power, he thought. In one stroke the young Emperor has reduced my ability to influence the future of Japan. He wants me kept busy and away from Tokyo. Father and son's eyes met, both knowing that the fight for Japan's nobility to retain its rights had begun.

'Your imperial majesty,' Iyeasu said, 'it is my honour to serve the Emperor and Japan. Yokohama will have the best shipyard that can be constructed there.' He raised his round head. 'I request, from the son of a samurai, some of his precious time to advise me. If the Minister of Maritime Services will be so kind?'

Mung bowed his appreciation to the round little man for mentioning Mung's father's former rank. Iyeasu had, in effect, corrected his own father. 'I am at your service,' Mung said.

The master of protocol entered the room with a message for Lord Hotta. Hotta read the communication and looked up. 'Mung, your son urgently requests to speak with you.'

'But my son is studying in Kyoto.'

'It is your adopted son, Udo Ishikawa.'

Chapter 7

Mung received Udo in a private room of the Emperor's palace. The unsophisticated boy he sent into exile had grown to vigorous self-possessed manhood. Even on his knees, Udo seemed tall. He wore a royal blue kimono of fine Chinese silk. An ivory fan with matching pipe showed from one side of his deep purple obi, and a merchant's inkstand, abacus and sword from the other. His nails were manicured, and Mung caught the scent of perfume. He found himself irritated by the poise and composure of this young man on his first visit to the imperial palace.

'Explain why you have interrupted the Emperor,' Mung ordered.

Udo touched his head to the floor. 'Sire, there is trouble in the south. Lord Saga of Choshu closed the Shimonoseki straits to all shipping. There was a battle with European warships.'

Mung stiffened. He ground his teeth and his jaw muscles danced. The one thing he dreaded was a confrontation with the foreigners.

His worst fears were realized when Udo said, 'The British Lord Crest is leading an international fleet to Tokyo.'

'How did you come by this news?'

'The trading junk I boarded in Canton was stopped in the Shimonoseki straits by a Dutch war sloop. Her captain told me what happened. The Choshu blockade of merchant ships lasted one month before Lord Crest arrived with seven ships diverted from the international armada in Tientsin. Within an hour after they entered the straits, the

Choshu forts were demolished. Landing parties, with support from the gun-ships, routed the Choshu army and captured Lord Saga. Lord Crest is bringing him here.'

A groan escaped Mung's lips. 'Tokyo is seething with anti foreign sentiment. Bringing Saga to the capital is like placing a mad torchbearer in a fireworks factory. It could begin a war. Your interruption of the Emperor's meeting was warranted. I am not pleased, but the messenger brings joy to my heart. I must return immediately to the Emperor with this news. Accompany me to the anteroom in the event his majesty would question you. The master of protocol will instruct you how to act in the Emperor's presence if you are summoned.'

A short time later, Udo wriggled across the floor and then knelt between Mung and Lord Hotta. He bowed to the Emperor, and gave his report.

'When can the foreigners be expected?' Lord Hotta asked.

'Any time after forty-eight hours.'

'What kind of time segment is he talking of?' Fujita Koin demanded.

'Western time,' Udo said.

'You are in Japan now.'

'The foreigners could arrive in two days. Not sooner.'

'What demands will they make?' Hotta asked.

'Of this I have no direct knowledge. If the treaty of Tientsin is used as a model, it would be money, trading ports, lower tariffs, land concessions and extraterritoriality.'

'I do not believe anyone in this room understands the meaning of that last word,' Fujita Koin said. 'Neither have we heard of the treaty of Tientsin. Explain.'

Mung felt an uncomfortable degree of satisfaction that the self-assured young man, so calm on his first audience with the Emperor, had been rebuffed, even if it was by the

Lord of Mito. Where is the humility of our youth, Mung wondered.

'Before I left China,' Udo said, 'there was a riot in Tientsin. People were incited to believe Christian missionaries were kidnapping children, drinking their blood and eating their eyeballs.'

'Ha,' the old Lord of Mito exploded, 'so they eat eyeballs too! They are rumoured to be drinking blood and eating human flesh in the foreign compound not far from here.'

'They use wine symbolically as blood in their rituals,' Mung explained. 'And a wafer is the substitute for the flesh of their chief prophet. They are against cannibalism.'

'It sounds as if they are practising for it,' Danjuro said.

'They eat red meat every day,' Fujita Koin said. 'That is a form of cannibalism.'

Mung saw the Emperor turn pale.

'Were the missionaries really eating the children's eyeballs?' Fujita Koin asked.

'No, sire,' Udo said. 'They did purchase orphans, unwanted girl babies and sickly infants. It was to restore their health, if possible, and save their souls from Hell if the children died.'

'So,' Count Iyeasu said, 'in this instance the Christians were performing good deeds and charitable acts.'

'Yes. Local bandits incited the people intentionally. They used the riot to steal from the foreigners, and then fled. The crowd went wild. They murdered ten nuns and eleven other whites, including the French consul. The imperial Chinese army stopped the riot and hung the bandits. But the army was attacked by the western expeditionary force. Lord Crest used the incident as an excuse to send troops and ships against the capital, Peiping. The westerners defeated the imperial army. They forced the Chinese government to lease vast areas of land, open more trading ports, and cede extraterritoriality.' He glanced at Lord Koin, then said, 'This allows foreigners legal jurisdiction over their nationals and converted Chinese Christians in China. The foreigners also received the right to set taxes, import-export duties, and assume responsibility for municipal government in those cities designated as international trading ports.'

Hotta drew in his breath. 'It means China has given away part of her country,' he said.

'Given is not a strong enough word to describe it, sire,' Udo said. 'The Chinese were then forced to pay for the loss of foreign lives, properties and the entire expense of the western military expedition.'

'They eat pig meat and they act like pigs,' Fujita Koin said. 'If they come here making those demands, I will fight them!'

'It may not be necessary to fight them, sire,' Udo said. 'Certainly it is not advisable. Western military power is far superior to ours. They do not want war. Their aim is to promote trade and encourage Christianity.'

Mung was pleased by Udo's answer.

For the first time since Udo had entered, the Emperor spoke. 'Is their leader a strong personality?'

'Your imperial highness, Lord Crest is new to the Far East,' Udo answered.

'I am familiar with the Englishman,' Iyeasu Koin said. 'He was my lecturer at Oxford, and I was a guest at his Bournemouth estate. He is a direct individual. A most determined man. He wastes no time, nor brooks interference in his personal or public life. He has openly stated, in recruiting his fighting men, that with his brains and their guts he will win honours enough to become prime minister of England. They love him for it.'

'He sounds like a formidable person,' the Emperor said.

Lord Edward Crest addressed six international naval captains in his stateroom aboard Her Royal Majesty's cruiser,

Nemesis. 'Gentlemen. As you know, the heralds of civilization are commerce and Christianity. The two go hand in hand. It has fallen on the nations of the West to bring about emancipation from the thralldom of the eastern religions. We are here to accelerate trade in the kingdom of Japan and bring the word of our Lord, Jesus Christ, to these backward peoples. Our entrance into Tokyo bay must be accomplished in such a manner as to impress the little people and protect ourselves. I give you the battle order. The Spanish and Dutch sloops shall patrol the mouth of the harbour. No vessel is to enter or leave until negotiations are concluded. The Swedish and German frigates will sail on my port side, slightly astern. The French and Russian frigates on my starboard side. No one is to fire unless I give the signal. Our destination is a point five hundred yards off the Yedo docks. There we shall form a battle line facing the city. I will submit our demands through the British consul. If negotiations do not begin immediately, I will shoot the tops off their largest buildings, one every hour until the Japanese send a delegation empowered to receive our demands. As for the buck-toothed little bandit in my brig, I would like to hang Lord Saga but he too will become part of the negotiations. There is no sense losing a sum of gold for some greasy, obnoxious goose.'

'Hear! Hear!' The captains applauded.

'Gentlemen. I do forbid liquor aboard my ships, but let it not be said that Edward Crest went to battle without toasting his comrades in arms. I propose we do it with a prayer.' He bowed his head and said, 'May this endeavour be blessed. In the name of Jesus Christ do we venture forth for God and country. May our Holy Father guide the aim of our gunners.'

In the Hall of a Hundred Mats, the lords of the realm sat back on their heels and waited for the master of protocol to complete the ceremony of announcing new appointments in the imperial book of heraldry. Mung was seated alone on the dais before the leaders of Japan, and felt vulnerable. Fujita Koin had outmanoeuvred him. The young Emperor was tricked into appointing Mung the task of explaining the expected invasion by the foreign fleet to the Great Council. And that without imperial support. Fujita Koin had argued that if there was imperial sanction at this point and the vote went against Mung, it could mean civil war. Rumours were rife in the city; anti-foreign feelings ran high in the regiments.

When Udo's name was read with those newly raised to the rank of two-sworded samurai, Mung looked over at his son. He was asleep sitting up. Rhee and Jiroo elbowed him awake. Mung's own head had been nodding and he stiffened his backbone. For the previous thirty-six hours, Udo had been reporting to him on China and Kang Shu's mass of information. Another six hours had been spent summarizing the most important points for the Emperor and Lord Hotta, then preparing for this assembly.

'All lords are present or represented,' the master of protocol announced. 'Only Saga of Choshu is absent.'

Eyes turned to the empty place traditionally occupied by Choshu for more than six centuries. Slowly everyone in the hall turned to focus on Mung seated before them on the dais.

He breathed deeply, tightened his stomach muscles, and began to speak. 'These are the facts as I know them. Lord Saga of Choshu violated the agreement passed by this council declaring the Straits of Shimonoseki an international waterway. The members of this council guaranteed free and peaceful passage to ships of all nations. Lord Saga disregarded the council's ruling. He blockaded the straits to merchant ships. A foreign fleet took action to open the waterway. The Choshu forts were smashed from the sea, their army defeated on land, and Saga captured alive.'

Mung waited until the murmurs had died down. 'The western fleet that reopened the straits is on its way here.' Once again he waited for quiet. 'I do not believe the foreigners seek war. Two hundred of their fighting ships remain in China. To me this indicates they consider Lord Saga's action to be independent of imperial influence.' Mung hoped this was so, purposely injecting the Emperor's title. Mung did not have his public backing, but there was no harm in implying it. 'The Emperor assumes that the international status of the Shimonoseki straits remains unchanged. Are there objections?'

All eyes turned to the Lord of Mito. He remained rigidly silent. Hotta had gained this concession from the old man before agreeing that Mung would conduct the negotiations.

'As there is no debate on the issue,' Mung said, 'it is my recommendation to negotiate without a show of force. I would be honoured by a unanimous vote to that effect.'

This too Fujita Koin had conceded, but his middle son had not. Hideyoshi Koin snapped his fan open for recognition, and spoke without waiting for the master of protocol's formal consent. 'You certainly would be honoured by a unanimous vote.' The pockmarked face sneered at Mung. Of all those privileged to speak in the Hall of a Hundred Mats, only Mung was not highborn. 'You sent the *Kanrin Maru* and other fighting ships from the harbour,' Hideyoshi declared. 'Now it is impossible to challenge the foreigners at sea.'

'We made the mistake of underestimating western firepower in the battle of Tokyo bay,' Mung said. 'Our entire whaling fleet was sunk in five minutes.'

'If you were so unsuccessful then, why do you lead the negotiations now?' Hideyoshi demanded.

Mung was inwardly elated. He had skilfully set up the second son of Mito for that question, and he replied, 'It was your father who persuaded the Emperor that I should be appointed to this position. I recommended your brother,

Iyeasu, since he is acquainted with the British lord who leads the expedition against us. Count Iyeasu has spent time as a guest in Lord Crest's home in England.'

Murmurs swept the great hall. Mung looked to Iyeasu, who raised an eyebrow as if to say, one for you, old chap.

Hideyoshi was livid. His voice cracked when he said, 'Only seven barbarian boats, and the might of imperial Japan quails before them!'

'The ships you speak of are the most modern from a fleet of over two hundred warships and transports that recently invaded northern China and routed the imperial Chinese army at Tientsin. They went on to besiege Peiping and forced the Chinese Emperor to cede every point of their demands. That armada of foreign ships and army of troops is only three weeks sailing time from this very place. They are battle tested and looking for new countries to conquer.'

Silence blanketed the long hall.

A fan was raised by a politically uncommitted lord. 'We must not concede every demand to avoid battle,' he said. 'Honour requires us to fight.'

'Some concessions must be made,' Mung said. 'Others we will fight to prevent. I have sent a message requesting that the western consuls be prepared to greet Lord Crest.'

'What will they tell the Englishman?' Hideyoshi demanded.

'Nothing,' Mung said. 'I have asked them to ascertain why these warships come to Tokyo uninvited.'

'We know why,' Hideyoshi said. 'They want to suck our life's blood from us!'

Mung leaned forward. He lowered his voice as if speaking to an obstinate child. 'We may know why Lord Crest is on his way, but it is not always necessary to tell all one knows.' He straightened and raised his voice to carry to the far corners of the great hall. 'I will not recommend a fight we cannot win, nor agree to terms we cannot honourably afford. However Lord Saga, a member of this council, has violated international law. He is responsible for his actions to the Rujo, and we to the foreigners he blockaded.'

'Then you are preparing to accommodate the round-eyes?'

'I doubt some form of compensation can be avoided.'

'So you will bargain like a merchant to reduce the price?'

Mung's face reddened at the insult. 'I will do what is needed to prevent Japan from being dominated and manipulated like China.'

Now Fujita Koin opened his fan. When he was recognized, he pointed at Mung. 'Should Lord Saga die at the hands of the foreigners, I will fight you! I will fight everyone in this hall, and all of Europe! The army of Mito will march against any barbarian who tries to discipline a lord of the realm.'

Like a volley of shots, fans snapped open throughout the great hall to signal agreement. Mung looked over the steely-eyed warriors before him. Not a fan was closed. I must save Lord Saga from any form of punishment, he thought, and that requires a secret meeting with the American consul. He bowed and said, 'I accept Lord Koin's declaration and the agreement of the lords of the realm to fight if Lord Saga is harmed, and to negotiate without a show of force if he is safe.'

Udo looked around the hall, then whispered to Rhee and Jiroo, 'The Black Dragon has just avoided a blood bath.'

'For the present,' Jiroo said.

In his private apartment in the imperial palace, Mung spoke to Jiroo. 'Arrange for Black Dragons to guard my route to the American consul's residence at 7 p.m. If it is discovered I am meeting with him, it could set off riots in the city. I need Townsend Harris' help to guarantee Lord Saga's safe release.'

'Even if you succeed in maintaining the peace,' Udo said,

'you must make concessions, and that will be held against you later.'

'At this point my personal well-being is not important. The future of Japan is.'

'Sire,' Jiroo said, 'your fate and the empire's are bound together.'

Chapter 8

Dressed as a one-sword samurai, with Udo as his body servant, Mung stepped into the rickshaw drawn by Rhee.

'The foreign compound,' Mung ordered.

Rhee lifted the pulling tongs and started forward. Udo trotted alongside.

Mung leaned back against the seat and relaxed. 'How does Tokyo compare with Canton?' he asked Udo.

'This is a much sterner city. The streets are wider and cleaner. There is more order, fewer people and shops.'

'But this is the Ginza we are passing through,' Mung said. 'It is Japan's largest commercial district.'

'It has been sixteen years since you were last in Canton. Almost the entire city has become a commercial district, and the population is now twice Tokyo's one million.'

Mung saw Udo tense, then reach into his sleeve for a weapon as he ran. 'What is it?' Mung asked.

'Those two dressed as merchants on the right are watching us. They wear swords under their robes.'

'Iewetsu and Ywata are Black Dragons guarding my route. I compliment you on your powers of observation, and on your conditioning. I expected you would be too winded to talk by now.'

Udo smiled. 'Canton's life style is overly relaxed. I studied with a master of tai chi to keep myself fit.'

'Is that more effective than Rhee's karate?'

'No. Like many Chinese practices, it has become stylized. It is now comparable to European ballet, and used mostly to achieve mental and physical harmony.'

Mung marvelled at Udo's polished manners and bearing, even while jogging alongside the rickshaw. 'I would like to spread some harmony among the lords of the realm,' Mung said. 'Several, including Mito, are preparing their armies to march against the foreigners.'

'Unless they can walk on water like the Christian god, they will not get close to a western warship.'

Mung did not appreciate the reference to Jesus, but made no comment. Only Ukiko knew of his past conversion to Christianity. He had reverted to the Shinto-Buddhist faith of his parents upon his return to Japan. Then, after American privateers murdered Saiyo, he privately renounced Christianity.

'Will I be allowed to meet the American consul?' Udo asked.

'Yes. You are to listen carefully but act as if you do not understand English. I will ask for your impressions later.'

'You do not trust the American?'

'Townsend Harris is a friend to Japan. I have a gift of memory but sometimes tend to colour it in the light of my own concepts. A second opinion is often helpful.' Mung also wished to judge Udo's ability to observe and evaluate in order to better assess the information he had brought from China, and before he was sent to Prussia.

'That must be the foreign compound.' Udo pointed to a group of houses whose front yards were lit by ships' lanterns. All had flagpoles, and some had uniformed guards at the low picket fenced gates.

'The American consulate is the first building on the right,' Mung said.

'In Canton, the entire foreign compound is fenced in and heavily guarded.'

'I would feel better if it were so here. They might be safer.'

Rhee stopped in front of a western-style house. A marine guard came forward to challenge them.

Mung stepped from the rickshaw. 'I have an appointment with the American consul.'

The marine gaped at the one-handed samurai who spoke perfect English. 'You speak American better than me granny.'

'I probably lived in America longer than the dear old lady,' Mung replied. 'I am Moryiama Ishikawa. The consul is expecting us.'

'Oh yes, yes, sir. That name sounds about right.' The marine opened the front door. 'Go inside, please.'

Townsend Harris came out from behind his desk. He bowed and smiled. 'Once again it is an honour to greet you, Mr Minister.'

Mung bowed. Then he held out his hand and the two men greeted each other American-style. 'Mr Consul, this is my newly adopted son, Udo Ishikawa.'

Udo felt Townsend Harris examining him closely. He took the consul's proffered hand. 'My pleasure,' the American said, and turned back to Mung. 'Come. Please be seated. What brings the Minister of Maritime Services to my door at such a late hour, and in disguise?'

'Have you heard about the treaty of Tientsin, or the trouble in the Shimonoseki straits?'

'No.'

Mung related the events, and added, 'I have sent messengers to the other foreign consuls involved, informing them that seven European warships are approaching Tokyo. I asked them to ascertain the reason.'

'But the reason is clear,' Harris said.

Mung ignored the comment. 'The Englishman must set Lord Saga free,' he said. 'Any attempt on his part to discipline a lord of the realm will be cause for all the feudal armies to march.'

'They would lose,' Harris said.

'They know it. I want Lord Crest to know that if Saga is harmed, I can do nothing to prevent the blood bath. It is Bushido.'

'I assume you speak for the Emperor?'

'Yes.'

'If Saga has not been harmed by the time he reaches here,' Townsend Harris said, 'his safety is negotiable. But the price will be high. Edward Crest will make the same demands he did in Peiping.'

'I would like you to remind Lord Crest that we are not China. She has great land mass and population. She can afford to allow western countries to attach themselves like parasites to the outer skin of an animal's body. Japan is an island nation, cut off from international trade for too long, and lacking in natural resources.'

'Do you consider America to be one of the offending ticks, Mr Minister?'

'I have approached you because the United States does not and has never demanded monetary or territorial concessions from China, Korea or Japan. Furthermore, my brother, John Whittefield, and my adoptive father before him who held the same position of Director of the Japanese Section in the American State Department, have always advocated fair policies in the Far East.'

Townsend Harris stiffened. 'Mr Minister, I hope your reference to family connections in Washington is not an implied threat. Family ties will not dictate American policy. Washington is a long way from Tokyo.' He stared hard at Mung.

The Black Dragon's gaze never wavered. 'I try not to threaten, Mr Consul. The mention of my brother's new position was to remind you of your country's policy of helping backward nations achieve a democratic form of government. If there is war now, your children and mine will never see peace in Japan. Will you help, Mr Consul?'

'I will, Mr Minister, but in the future please do not remind me of my nation's policies.'

Mung acknowledged the rebuff with a bow. 'Will you speak with Lord Crest when he arrives?'

'I will.'

'A word of caution,' Mung said. 'I came here in disguise because anti-foreign feelings are high. It would be advisable for the foreign compound to increase its guards, and for westerners to refrain from entering Tokyo. If church services are held, it would be best that Japanese converts did not attend until tempers cool.'

'Thank you for the advice, and the opportunity to assist the imperial government of Japan.'

'I shall inform the Emperor of your cooperation,' Mung replied.

Townsend Harris turned to Udo. 'And I should like to inform your recently adopted son that his young replacements in Canton are moderately successful in their new positions.'

Caught off guard, Udo bowed but remained silent.

It was close to midnight when Rhee pulled the rickshaw into the wide avenue of the deserted Ginza.

'Now tell me what mistakes I may have made in my meeting with Townsend Harris,' Mung said to Udo. 'And do not spare my feelings. I need a critique of my actions.'

'I think you should not have said that Saga must be released. It meant you will pay their price.'

'Go on,' Mung encouraged.

'You accept the American consul as a friend, but he was lying to you.'

'Some say prevarication is the art of diplomacy. What do you think?'

'Harris must have been aware of the Tientsin Treaty and the defeat of Lord Saga if he knew about my departure from Canton.'

'Why do you think the American revealed that?' Mung asked.

'A boastful mistake to show that his spy network in China is efficient.'

'Kang Shu has trained you to distrust everyone.'

Udo remained silent as they moved down the centre of the Ginza. The shops were closed, their gay coloured lanterns extinguished. The moon bathed the wide tree-lined street in silvery light.

'Townsend Harris is the longest serving consul in Japan,' Mung said. 'I respect and trust him as a friend of the Japanese people.'

'He turned coldly formal after a warm greeting.'

'I did not say Harris approves of Japan's present form of government. For that matter, neither do I. When he spoke to you about Canton, he was telling me that the other consuls have received the news of Tientsin, Shimonoseki and Lord Crest's intentions. I expect the Englishman will arrive very soon.'

'Why didn't the American just come out and say he knew?' Udo asked.

'Probably restricted by some gentleman's code. Remember, the West has its own form of Bushido. Neither did I err in mentioning Saga's release. If you recall, it was then that Harris turned formal. If Saga is harmed by Lord Crest, Townsend Harris and I may next see each other over gun barrels, and we both know that.'

In the shadow of the same shop doorway, Udo recognized the figures of the two Black Dragons dressed as merchants, but he sensed something different in their stances.

'You are trained in the middle echelon of business and the lower level of politics,' Mung said. 'You leave for Berlin shortly to serve as one of our military observers. In Prussia you will have to deal with the highest, the most refined and more dangerous statesmen. That is one reason I wanted you with me tonight.'

'Rhee,' Udo called, 'something seems odd with those two Black Dragons in the doorway.' He dropped back to protect the rear of the rickshaw.

Rhee hoisted the pulling tongs and moved faster. As they

passed the doorway, Mung saw the two Black Dragons crumple. Two armed men came leaping over their bodies.

'An attack!' Udo warned, and Rhee sprang ahead.

From the street corner fifty yards away, ten men charged forward. 'Kill the traitor!' they shouted.

Mung cleared the Colt .44 from his obi. Three attackers fired muskets and the lead balls whistled by his head. They dropped the firearms and charged with the others, all brandishing swords. Rhee let go of the rickshaw's tongs. They dug into the cobbled street and Mung was thrown forward onto the ground. Another bullet whizzed by his head. He snapped off a shot and killed an attacker coming from behind.

Rhee whipped out two sticks attached by a metal chain. With a bone chilling cry, he charged the assailants. They stood still, raising their weapons to strike at him. At the last possible moment, Rhee leapt sideways. Sword points flicked his canvas jacket and trousers, but he was untouched.

The ten were perfect standing targets for Mung. He aimed and fired, aimed and fired, until his pistol was empty. Three men died, one was wounded. Rhee roared a terrible war cry and smashed another's skull with his flailing sticks. The remaining attackers broke and ran.

Behind Mung, two shots rang out. He turned to see Udo, holding a smoking derringer in his right hand, avoid the slashing long sword of a wounded attacker. Udo's left hand drove the long, thin blade of an Arkansas toothpick to its hilt into his assailant's body. Visibly shaken, he let the body slip off his blade to the ground.

'That peashooter of a derringer may stop a Chinese, but not a determined samurai,' Mung said.

'These are not samurai,' Rhee called. 'They are ronin, unemployed warriors.'

'Do they have tattoos?' Mung asked.

'No, sire.'

'Check the one Udo killed,' Mung ordered. He saw Udo holding onto the rickshaw for support. 'Are you wounded?'

'No,' Udo gasped. He held out his trembling hand. 'I killed in China but thought that was finished when I came home. Look how I shake.'

'This may be just the beginning.' Mung reached down to pull the clothes off the dead body at the rear of the rickshaw. 'I almost wish they did have tattoos.' He shook his head. 'These attackers were not professional killers. Their planning was bad and their timing off. Nothing like the assassins on the river. I expect these men were persuaded that eliminating me would protect the Emperor and Japan. This could be the first battle of a civil war, although I hope not. I was a military observer in the American Civil War. The loss of life and devastation of property was terrible. It will take America a hundred years for the people to reconcile their differences. We must see that does not happen here in Japan.'

Jiroo led a band of armed Black Dragons, followed by a host of Tokyo policemen, into the Ginza at a dead run. They surrounded Mung and whisked him away.

'When Lord Crest arrives, observe and report to me at Ukiko's house,' he called back to Udo and Rhee.

Chapter 9

Mung gazed across Tamieka Pond at the Shoin-style villa bathed in moonlight. It nestled amidst ancient pines and wind-sculpted evergreens. Velvet moss covered the stone steps from the porch to the water's edge. He was reminded of the hut he had grown up in, in Nakanohama. There his wooden pallet, in a hut of mud and thatch, was only a short distance from the ocean waves. This villa's roof was peaked and expertly shingled, the porch in perfect balance to the length and width of the house. It had been constructed by an artist centuries before.

'Sire,' Jiroo interrupted his thoughts, 'I have positioned ten Black Dragons around the villa.'

'Has there been contact yet with a senior Yakuza in Tokyo?'

'None, sire.'

'How many casualties did we suffer tonight?'

'Two. But we captured one of the attackers and drew the story from him. Ronin from small clans in the south were drinking in the Yoshiwara pleasure district. They heard you were meeting with the American consul. The saké put it into their heads to attack you.'

Mung stiffened. 'My visit to the American was intentionally revealed. I want to know by whom. Direct our men in Tokyo to press harder for contact with the Yakuza. Have them listen for news of possible attacks against the foreign compound. Whoever revealed my whereabouts may plot to kill some westerners to cause an incident. I want Udo and Rhee here tomorrow morning.'

'Yes, sire.' Jiroo bowed, then pointed to the villa. 'Your wife.'

Mung looked up and saw Ukiko's shadow slide open the shoji screen door. She stepped out on the porch and slowly walked down the stone steps to the water's edge. The moonlight played on the ebony hair cascading over her shoulders and down the back of her silk gown. She gazed into the water and her moon shadow drew the golden carp to her feet.

Mung moved silently around the water's edge and down the moss-covered steps. He went up behind Ukiko and whispered, 'You look beautiful in the moonlight.'

'Oh!' She turned and clapped her hands in happiness. She reached out to touch him, then remembered to bow. 'I am so pleased to see you safe. And Udo and Rhee? Were they injured?'

'They are well. But how could you know of the attack so quickly?'

'My cousin, Gin-ko, sent word of the battle on the Ginza.'

'How is it I have never met this cousin who is so well-informed?'

'Gin-ko has ways of learning things. Sometimes even before they happen.'

Mung smiled. 'I should enlist her as a Black Dragon. Perhaps she could help me locate a senior Yakuza.'

'Are there women in the society now?'

'Not yet. It is a man's organization by tradition.'

'But are you not trying to modernize our country? Did not the Emperor break tradition when he appointed you Black Dragon? It was always a Buddhist fighting priest who held the rank.'

Mung took his wife's arm, leading her up the steps to the porch as he spoke. 'Before his death, Gompachi recommended to the Emperor that I replace him as Black Dragon. His reasoning was simple. The Buddhist and Shinto priests had become too powerful an economic force in the empire. Property tax exemptions allowed them to accumulate vast areas of prime rice-producing land. With financial power they wielded influence on too many lords, and affected votes in the Great Council. Because I had returned from the West with no religious or political allegiances, no power base, and I posed no threat to anyone, I was appointed.'

'You forgot to mention your genius at shipbuilding, whaling and war.' Ukiko smiled. 'It could be said you were honoured with the position of Black Dragon for returning the Emperor to power and maintaining peace between the feudal lords.'

'Peace may fall by the wayside when Lord Crest comes sailing into Tokyo bay.'

'I do not think you will allow that to happen.'

'How can I prevent it?' Mung said.

'But you are lucky, and my father told me luck is often more important than ability.'

'You, a schoolteacher, are agreeing that the future is dependent more on fortune than education?'

'Not exactly. My father meant that a lucky intellectual is more successful than an unlucky one.'

'I certainly am lucky to have you as a wife.'

Ukiko blushed. She reached out and touched his arm. 'Let us take off all our clothes, go to the pillow and see what happens.'

Mung nodded and followed her. 'What do you think will happen?'

She squeezed his hand and smiled.

Before breakfast, Mung had consulted with Jiroo and three other Black Dragons, heard a report on Lord Iyeasu Koin's arrival at the new shipyard site in Yokohama, and received two messages from Lord Hotta. Now he knelt at the low table with Ukiko.

'Come, little brother,' Mung called, 'join us.' The three had agreed that Udo's family relationship would be that of younger brother rather than adopted son.

Udo left Rhee guarding the porch and knelt at the table. He waited until they had filled their bowls with rice, pickled vegetables and fish before helping himself.

'For a tall man, you eat little,' Ukiko said.

'I have already eaten,' Udo lied. The truth was he found the return to Japanese food bland and boring. It was always the same – morning, noon and night.

'How is your Chinese chef?' Ukiko asked.

Udo explained to Mung. 'The chef was a surprise gift from Kang Shu.'

'That wily Chinese tong chief may have sent the cook as insurance,' Mung said. 'If you displease Kang, he can order you poisoned. Chinese chefs are good at that.'

Ukiko almost blurted out what was foremost on her mind. Instead she asked, 'Would your cook know how to make Chinese dishes pleasing to the Japanese palate?'

'Food is food,' Mung said, taking more of the gummy rice.

'This man was chef to the Chinese Emperor,' Udo said. 'Each meal he prepares is an adventure. I am certain he could fix something you would both like.'

'Not for me.' Mung flicked gobs of rice from his bowl into his mouth with his eating sticks. 'I must be getting old. I can remember looking forward to a good beefsteak when I was in California, but now I think of food as fuel. Why don't you two arrange for this wonder-cook to prepare a Chinese meal sometime soon.'

As Ukiko cleared the table, she stole quick glances at Udo, wondering if she could trust him with her secret. To Mung she said, 'I would like to visit my cousin and see about the bunn-iis.'

'Do it. Take Udo with you. He has some experience with rabbits from China.' Mung winked at Udo.

'Yes, I would like very much to go,' Udo said.

'I will change my clothes,' Ukiko said, and hurried from the room.

'I know nothing about rabbits,' Udo whispered to Mung. 'Have you ever seen one?'

'Yes.'

'Then you are the expert. What is there to know? If you have seen one rabbit, you will recognize another. Three guards will accompany you, but I really want you to look out for Ukiko. I also want to find out about this cousin, Gin-ko. She knew of last night's attack in time to inform Ukiko before I returned home.'

'I will also report on the bunn-iis.' Udo smiled.

'A waste of money,' Mung said, 'but if it makes her happy it is good. Where are you quartered?'

'I have taken private rooms on the edge of the Yoshiwara.'

'The ladies of the Willow World will be honoured to have the former proprietor of Canton's House of a Thousand Delights as a patron.'

'I have always found professional pleasuring far superior to friendly lovemaking.'

Udo's attitude was so matter-of-fact, Mung wondered if the younger man would ever be interested in a true relationship with a woman. 'To ensure that you live to make the ladies happy,' Mung said, 'take this.' He placed a Colt .44 on the table with a pouch of bullets. 'One shot from this would have stopped that samurai last night.'

Udo picked up the pistol and hefted it in his hand. 'Thank you.'

'Practise shooting and reloading. It is a heavy weapon to aim, but it fires true.'

Ukiko appeared in the doorway wearing a fresh kimono and carrying a parasol. Udo tucked the gun into his obi at the back and stood up.

'Dear husband,' Ukiko said, 'I wanted to tell you I am pleased our son, Yoshida, will soon be with us. What made you decide against the school in Kyoto?'

Mung looked up at her. 'I did not order his return.'

'But . . . but I assumed it was you when the message reached me in Kagoshima.' There was concern in her voice and a question in her eyes. 'I sent an immediate reply by pigeon that he was to meet us here in Tokyo.'

'The exact thing to do,' Mung answered with a confidence he did not feel. 'I am certain there is an explanation, and that he is safe. My Black Dragons guard him. Now go with Udo and enjoy buying bunn-iis. I have reports to examine, messages to answer and documents to prepare for the Emperor.' He waved them to the door. 'Send in Rhee, please,' he told Udo. Ukiko turned back to look at Mung and he waved her on. 'Go. Enjoy yourself. Do not be concerned.'

Rhee came into the room. 'Find Jiroo!' Mung said. 'Tell him my son may be in danger. Yoshida should be coming down the Tokaido road. You, Jiroo, and as many men as can be spared are to ride the length of the road, all the way to Kyoto if necessary. Find Yoshida!'

Udo and Ukiko walked along in silence. On the other side of the pond, he said to her, 'Have you ever ridden in the new English invention the westerners call the jinrikisha?'

'No.' She cast a worried glance back towards the villa.

'Then I shall hail one. They say whoever rides in a rickshaw will never again agree to be carried in a kago.'

Within seconds of her first ride, Ukiko forgot her concern about Yoshida. She giggled at Udo's stories of strange Chinese customs, and their risqué jokes about Europeans.

'Oh look,' Ukiko cried, 'see how many more shops there are in the Ginza since I was last here. Not like in Kagoshima. Here they have a separate store for everything. And there is the artist section. Do you think any of those people are famous artists?'

'I would imagine so,' Udo said.

'See, there is the renowned Tokyo No theatre.'

Udo looked for signs of the previous night's battle. It was close to the theatre's entrance where the two Black Dragons were killed. He was glad to see the blood had been washed away.

'How will we find our cousin in this crowd?' he asked.

'Our cousin?' Ukiko puzzled.

'Am I not your little brother?' He smiled.

She giggled. 'Gin-ko is not a real cousin. She is a dear friend I came to know on my last visit here. We have corresponded ever since. If you will tell the rickshaw man to stop at the bonsai shop on the left, we are to meet her there.'

Udo gave the order but they were delayed by a large group of pilgrims straggling past on their way to Mount Fuji.

'Sometimes an older sister may share a secret with a younger brother, which the younger brother would not tell an older brother,' Ukiko said. 'Do you agree?'

'This younger brother would never dream of betraying his older sister's confidence.'

Ukiko leaned closer and said, 'There are people in Japan who eat red meat.'

'That is true,' he answered.

'They are not many, and fewer know how to prepare it.'

'Very few,' Udo said.

'This subject must be repulsive to you.'

'I am not yet certain of the subject.'

'Why, cooking and eating red meat.'

'That is not repulsive to me. In China, I acquired a taste for beef and pork. I understand venison is also available in Tokyo.'

Ukiko's eyes widened and Udo understood it to mean she was interested in hearing more. He leaned closer and said, 'Since red meat is against religious law in Japan, there is a little ditty that tells how to find it in Tokyo.' He recited,

> 'If you want red meat to eat
> And it has a tail.
> Look for the man proclaiming,
> Mountain whale for sale.

Little sister, if you wish, I will order mountain whale for you.'

Ukiko tried to speak but could not. She shook her head from side to side.

'No? You do not want me to order the meat?'

Through tight lips Ukiko forced herself to ask, 'Does your Chinese chef know how to cook bunn-iis?'

'You mean rabbits?'

'Yes.'

'Chinese can cook anything. I remember the first time I saw one of them slap a blood-filled liver on the cutting board.'

Ukiko swooned. 'Please,' she choked, 'do not tell me about it.'

'I apologize,' Udo said. 'I misunderstood you.'

'It is not you who are at fault. I am to blame. Will your chef cook bunn-iis for me?'

'Yes, but why, if it upsets you so?'

'It will help me become pregnant.'

'Eating bunn-iis will do it? Just cooked bunn-iis?' Udo choked back a laugh.

'Oh, I am not so naïve.' Ukiko sat up. 'My husband must make me pregnant, but Gin-ko says the bunn-iis are so fertile that eating their meat will help me conceive.'

'It is late in life for you to have a child.'

'I wish only to give Mung a son. I love Yoshida with all my heart, but my flesh and blood son will honour my grave. Will you help me?'

'Of course. And I promise that my cook will mask the look and taste of the rabbit so you will think you are eating fish.'

Ukiko's face brightened. 'Thank you.' She looked around. 'Oh, there she is. Gin-ko!'

They stepped on to the street from the rickshaw. Udo saw a group of people clustered around a woman whose back was to him. They stepped away when she turned to greet her friend. She approached and Udo saw her as through a fishbowl – each feature elongated, yet in sublime proportion. Her dark, dancing eyes smiled. Her arched brows, her coiffure with tortoise-shell combs were perfect. She glided forward on wooden clogs and his left eyelid began to flutter. Her greeting to Ukiko tinkled like the temple wind chimes.

Ukiko turned to him. 'Udo, I am pleased to introduce Gin-ko.'

His heart pounded and he gulped for air. He bowed as if to a two-sword samurai. Her bow was modest. He realized what was happening to him, and he was afraid. It had come, not as the Chinese poets said – under starry skies and silvery moon – but in broad daylight. The love lion had ambushed his heart and was clawing at the depths of his emotions. To regain his composure, he looked away and concentrated on a dishevelled ronin near the bonsai shop. The man lowered his eyes and moved on.

Udo cleared his throat. 'Have you ladies made plans?' he asked, trying not to stare at the beautiful woman before him.

'Yes,' Ukiko said, 'we are going to buy a pair of bunn-iis.'

'Ahh, but they are no longer for sale in the Ginza,' Ginko said. 'The price has fallen drastically because they multiply so quickly. We shall find them in the Shimbashi.'

'Is that far from here?' Udo asked.

'The Shimbashi neighbourhood begins just behind the No theatre and stretches back. The street of the bunn-iis is not far.'

Udo's knees weakened. The sound of Gin-ko's voice was

beautiful. 'I must inform the guards,' he said, wanting to distance himself from her before he spoke foolishly.

'I did not see any guards,' Ukiko said.

'Is it because of last night's attack?' Gin-ko asked.

'Yes,' Udo replied, and remembered his orders from Mung. 'It was good of you to inform the minister's wife of his safety. And so quickly. He was surprised his wife knew there had been an incident, before he arrived home.'

'I live in the Yoshiwara, not far from you.' Gin-ko smiled and Udo's stomach went weak. 'A messenger on his way to me passed the Ginza and heard about the attack just after it happened. I sent him directly to Ukiko to reassure her of Mung's safety.'

Udo realized he had been too blunt. The beautiful woman had rebuffed him by using Mung's personal name rather than his title. Udo bowed to her again and turned away to speak to the guards.

A solid square mile of winding streets, narrow alleys and foot paths snaking between crowded houses and shops made up the area known as the Shimbashi. The commoners' marketing quarter was crammed with food stalls, noodle shops, artists, sweet vendors, strolling players, students, tea houses, shoppers. Acupuncturists, genealogists and astrologers took up entire streets. In the lane of silk merchants, sellers used bird calls to attract customers.

A burly head-porter moved through the crowd singing, 'What fools drink makes of men.'

The line of porters behind him chorused, 'It is true, true indeed.'

They stopped and rested their loads. They drank saké and laughed with the people around them.

On the street of booksellers, Ukiko pointed to an advertisement for the latest edition of HOW TO BEHAVE POLITELY WITH FOREIGNERS. It included a special section on eating spaghetti with knife and fork.

'Is it true,' she asked Udo, 'that westerners blow their nose slabber into a cloth, wrap it up and save it?'

'They put it in their pockets and later wash the cloth.'

'Do they really use the cloth again?' Gin-ko asked, her eyes wide in amazement.

'Yes, a very disgusting habit.' He pushed his handkerchief deeper into his sleeve, promising himself to discard it at the first opportunity.

'Here is the bunn-iis shop,' Gin-ko said, leading Ukiko inside.

Udo, thinking of how to meet Gin-ko again, did not notice Ukiko's shock upon coming face to face with her first pair of rabbits.

'These are the finest bunn-iis in Tokyo,' the shopkeeper said. He bowed deeply to the three. 'The correct scientific name in Latin is rabbits.'

Gin-ko, seeing Ukiko's distress, moved between her and the animals. 'Are they fertile?' she asked.

'Unfortunately, yes. These creatures are so prolific, the price has dropped a hundredfold. This pair in particular are great fornicators.'

'Send them to my home,' Udo said. 'That is, if they please the lady?' He turned to Ukiko.

'I cannot,' she whispered, hiding her face behind her fan. 'I cannot eat those darling little creatures. If I remain barren the rest of my life, I cannot do it.' Tears welled up in her eyes.

Gin-ko took Ukiko's arm and led her from the shop. Udo politely looked away and his eyes fastened on the same short, muscular ronin he had seen in the Ginza. He started towards him and the man bolted, directly into the arms of a guard. The guard drove his sword hilt into the ronin's stomach. The ronin doubled over and the guard clasped his hand in a jujitsu grip that paralysed his arm. Without drawing attention, the guard walked the ronin into the rabbit shop.

Udo signalled the other two guards to watch the women. To the proprietor he said, 'Allow no one to enter.' He pushed the ronin to the rear of the shop.

Udo pulled out his Arkansas toothpick and passed the gleaming blade before the man's eyes. 'The gods gave man four balls,' he said. 'Two in a sack between his legs and two in his head.' He placed the knife's needle point in the man's crotch. 'I will pierce each one of your balls if you do not answer me quickly and truthfully. Why do you watch us?'

'Mother of autumn,' the man said.

Udo was stunned to hear the Black Dragon code words.

'You are Udo, recently adopted son of Moryiama Ishi-kawa, known as Mung?' the ronin asked.

'Yes.'

'Then please give me the countersign and tell this fellow Black Dragon not to break my arm.'

Udo motioned for the guard to release his grip, and said, 'Father of spring.'

The ronin massaged his arm, then opened and closed his fingers. 'I heard about you,' he said. 'A fancy dresser even taller and broader than the Black Dragon. They were right. You could almost pass for a round-eye.'

'What is your name and why are you following me?'

'I am Sandanj, one of the twelve who failed to protect the Black Dragon on the river. My punishment obliges me to establish contact with a senior Yakuza.'

'And you think I will lead you to the tattooed men?'

'Not you. The lady, Gin-ko. She has an admirer who is a Yakuza. I do not know what rank he holds.'

'Did you expect him to meet with her on an outing such as this?'

'I made one mistake and am punished because of it.' Sandanj hunched his broad, muscular shoulders and gritted his teeth. 'I will not make another.'

'You almost became a eunuch,' Udo said, replacing the weapon in his sleeve.

A guard whispered into the shop, 'The ladies wish to be off.'

'Sandanj,' Udo said, 'follow us if you will, but be sure to come to my quarters later. We have matters to discuss.' He went out to join the women.

'Ukiko is feeling better,' Gin-ko said. 'We would like to go to the Kabuki theatre. It is just around the corner.'

'Aristocrats cannot enter such a low class place in broad daylight,' Udo said.

Gin-ko cocked her head and flashed an indulgent smile. It pleasured his heart and hurt his pride, causing him to blurt out, 'The last time I was in Kagoshima, the Kabuki actors were listed with the livestock in the census.'

'You have been away many years,' Gin-ko said. 'Now the Kabuki actors are on a par with farmers.'

'And it is acceptable for women of samurai family to be seen there?'

'Many changes have taken place since your departure,' Ukiko said.

'But in my case,' Gin-ko said, 'any rank accorded me is honorary. A senior courtesan of the Yoshiwara was never restricted from entering a Kabuki theatre.'

Udo was struck dumb, and this time the woman clearly saw it. Gin-ko's face smiled but her eyes hardened. She sighed, and his heart broke. 'Ahh,' she said, 'you are one of those conservatives who do not approve of pleasure-women being any place other than the bedroom.'

Udo wanted to tell her he was a pleasure-man, but there was no word to explain in Japanese. He remained speechless.

'But you must not feel that way,' Ukiko said. 'Please, Udo,' she pleaded, 'Gin-ko is one of the most famous courtesans in the empire. The people crowded around her when we arrived were asking for her autograph. She is greatly respected.'

Gin-ko shrugged. 'Udo is a product of his upbringing. His moral concepts cannot be changed by request.' She turned her back on the man who had fallen in love with her.

Udo trailed behind the two women into the darkened theatre. They were seated on a mat near the stage and were informed the show had already run three hours, with two more to come. Ukiko and Gin-ko ordered lunch while they watched the acts, but Udo declined.

On stage there was a stylish mixture of dance, music and mime. The actors were dressed in garish costumes, colourful masks and heavy makeup. They presented comic and tragic skits portraying the conflict between man and man, man and nature, and ending each one with a moral lesson for the audience to ponder.

Udo's thoughts were on the woman in front of him. He sniffed the fragrance of Gin-ko's perfume and gazed at the nape of her elegantly curved neck. In his mind he formulated a detailed apology and explanation. He became angry at himself, then at her. He had called himself whore but could not apply the term to her. In the darkness of the theatre he reached out and touched her kimono with his fingertips, then pulled back, furious at his lack of self-control.

I was the master of the House of a Thousand Delights, he thought. I manipulated women. His mind raged through fantasized alternatives of controlling her. He had but to reach out, touch that beautiful neck and she would be paralysed, powerless to resist him. His hand remained frozen in his lap.

Of all Udo's imaginary speculations, none were about sex. He wondered why, because it was in lovemaking that he excelled. I will buy her contract. I will own her, he thought. Then a sense of caution crept into his planning.

As a Black Dragon he would need permission to enter into such an arrangement. An idea struck him. Suppose he established a house in Tokyo for gathering information? Silently he composed a message to Kang Shu for the necessary funds. He was certain he could justify the house to Mung.

Udo sat straighter now that he had resolved a plan. Yet there remained a seed of fear deep inside him. Love was something he had never considered. So he attempted to disregard the gnawing in his gut. The silence from the noisy audience took his attention to the final performance on stage. Actors in outlandish costumes were portraying Japanese tourists on holiday in San Francisco. They had entered a restaurant where, after a meal of strange foods, they were surrounded by bright red Indians. To save themselves, the tourists convinced the Indians they were their long-lost tribesmen. The Japanese were invited to the Indians' opera tent. There, the Kabuki version of an Italian prima donna bellowed, screeched and wailed, mimicking hands to bosom, hands to audience, hands to ears. The audience tittered, they giggled, they convulsed with gales of laughter. They laughed and held their sides, and begged the actors for mercy, but the talented mimes gave no quarter. People gasped, and stuffed their sleeves in their mouths to control themselves.

When the prima donna took her final bow, everyone but Udo was exhausted from the experience. They remained in their seats. In the lantern light brought in to illuminate the theatre, Gin-ko was recognized and asked to autograph fans. Udo watched her oblige with courtly grace.

An older man stepped up to Gin-ko and her other admirers fell back. He wore no sign of rank but held himself with authoritative dignity. As he spoke with the Yoshiwara beauty, Udo saw the other people put away their fans and leave. He caught sight of Sandanj watching from a short distance away and turned back towards Gin-ko. The distinguished man reached out to retrieve his autographed fan from her and the edge of a tattoo peeked out from under the sleeve. Udo looked to Sandanj, who nodded.

If she is involved with the tattooed men, Udo thought, I will punish her. He beckoned to one of his guards. 'I want to know who that man is talking to Mistress Gin-ko. And tell Sandanj to wait for me at my home.' He stepped forward and touched Ukiko's arm. 'Older sister, I have been wondering whether our cousin, the courtesan, would know how to contact a senior Yakuza. Since the attack on the river, Mung has been trying to do that with little success.'

'I never thought to ask her,' Ukiko said. 'She is wise in the ways of Tokyo.'

'As I keep your secret about the bunn-iis from older brother,' Udo said to Ukiko, 'could this request of mine remain between us?'

Ukiko blushed and nodded. Udo watched the older man with the tattooed arm leave the theatre. A Black Dragon followed him.

Chapter 10

The Emperor glared at Mung and Hotta. 'Two attacks on the Black Dragon, and now I hear his son, Yoshida, is threatened. Hotta, this must cease. You are the most powerful feudal lord in Tokyo. The former Black Dragon was killed here in the capital and now these attacks. Mung, you are not blameless. It is a . . .' The Emperor paused to avoid the word disgrace. Its use would oblige both Mung and Hotta to commit seppuku. 'It is a sign of disorganization that neither of you has been able to prevent these attacks.'

Mung and Hotta both knew that imperial decrees would not stop the assassination attempts. Already fifty samurai and ronin were locked in the municipal jail, charged with incitement. The slogan sweeping the ranks of warriors was, 'Sonno-joi! Revere the Emperor and expel the barbarians!'

'I do hope your son arrives safely,' the Emperor said.

Before Mung could express his gratitude he was startled to hear the young Emperor add, 'My sister, Princess Atsu, would like to publish a book.'

Mung kept his eyes lowered, wondering what connection this could have with him.

'Her book will inspire people to do good works,' the Emperor said. 'It will list those whose deeds benefit others but go unnoticed by superiors and government officials. I want your Black Dragons to be alert for people who deserve recognition. The names are to be forwarded to the princess. Mung, your wife, born to the Ishikawa family, is ranked high enough to act as liaison for the princess in this matter.'

'Thank you, your imperial highness.' Mung touched his

111

head to the floor. The young man who ruled an empire had extended his protective mantle over Mung's family. Yet the Black Dragon knew that if the Emperor accepted his recommendations for reform, the honour given would be a thin shield against the anger aroused. He slipped a scroll from his sleeve and passed it to Hotta. 'This is the proposed list of changes.'

'The Emperor will peruse this at his leisure,' Hotta said. 'You have something more to report?'

'Yes, my lord. The foreign fleet will arrive this evening.'

'How can you know this? My scout boats and the Fishermen's Guild have not reported a sighting.'

'When I ordered the *Kanrin Maru* to sea, it was to spy on the foreigners. Our balloonists sighted the fleet and sent pigeons back.'

'I witnessed your balloon demonstrations with the imperial artillery,' the Emperor said. 'But can you really send men aloft from the deck of a ship?'

'Yes, sire. My first ascent was from an American cruiser in the battle of Mobile Bay.' Mung saw the Emperor cock his head in question, and remembered the Emperor was only ten years old then. 'I was Japan's naval observer during the American Civil War, my lord.'

'What plans have you made to receive the foreigners coming to Tokyo?' Hotta asked.

'As the United States was not involved at Shimonoseki or Tientsin, the American consul will be first to greet Lord Crest. Townsend Harris will attempt to reduce European claims against us.'

Hotta nodded his approval. 'I would suggest including other consuls whose nations were not involved. Then play one off against the other.'

'My informants in China say the westerners have become accustomed to this manoeuvre. They have instructions to insert an equal status clause into every agreement, which gains them all rights and benefits achieved by other nations.

I chose the Americans because they suffer from anglophobia, a fear of the English. Little more than fifty years ago the English burned the American capital city of Washington. It is less than five years since the English supported the Confederacy against the Union during the Civil War. The Americans will attempt to stop England from dominating Japan, as she does China and India, because of fear, and because of the democratic principles the United States is founded on.'

'Count Iyeasu Koin will assist you in the negotiations,' the Emperor said.

Mung looked from the Emperor to Hotta. 'I thought Count Iyeasu was to be kept busy with the Yokohama shipyard.'

'His father, Lord Fujita Koin, is a crafty old man,' Hotta said. 'He made us believe he accepted his son's appointment. Then he campaigned against it among members of the Rujo. They accepted his argument that Iyeasu, who is familiar with Lord Crest and the British Consul Lord Alcock, should be included in the negotiations. The majority of our lords feel the contrasting objectives of the two English lords can be utilized to reduce foreign demands. Lord Alcock is supporting Japan in developing the Yokohama shipyard, while Lord Crest is coming to make demands on us. The Emperor received a petition that must be honoured.'

Mung felt himself boxed in by Fujita Koin and his supporters. It must have shown in his face for Lord Hotta said, 'In your favour is Lord Maeda's public statement that Lord Saga was a fool to blockade the Shimonoseki straits. Maeda has put his army at my disposal.'

'I request that you use his troops and your Fujiwara to sweep the harbour area of all armed men,' Mung said. 'And take up blocking positions to stop any troops from advancing to the port.'

'Do you have information of an uprising?' Hotta asked.

'No, but then I had no information of the two attacks that did take place. I do not want any more surprises. No drunken samurai or foreign sailors causing an incident. Nothing must disrupt the negotiations.'

'I will order the troops into position.'

'Please keep all boats docked, including those of the foreign consuls, until I have met with Townsend Harris and with Lord Crest.'

'We expected the round-eyes sooner,' Hotta said. 'Where have they been?'

'The British flagship was observed being towed out to sea. It lay dead in the water for two days. That usually means engine trouble.'

In fact, the *Nemesis* had burnt a main bearing. Now, with her furnaces glowing, her steam safety valves tied down, and smoke trailing from her twin stacks, she led the fleet heading for Tokyo bay.

'I will kill Mung, but not his son.'

'You were prepared to kill his son on the river,' Hideyoshi Koin said. 'Why not now?'

'I do not kill sick children.'

The second son of the house of Mito could not take his eyes from the muscular arms and glistening chest of the Golden Lizard. The effect of the tattooed scales rubbed with sweet oil fascinated him.

'Mung's son is seventeen,' Hideyoshi said. 'He is man enough to seek revenge, and man enough to die.'

'He is two young men, and I refuse to kill either. It is bad luck. You have already paid for Mung's death, so he shall die.'

'His guard has been increased since the last attempt.'

'That is my problem,' the lizard-man said.

'What is your purpose?' Hideyoshi asked. 'What else do you want?'

The lizard-head lowered and the tattooed scales on the

skull shone in the lamplight. The eyes peered out from hooded lids and fastened on the Count of Mito. 'You desire to control the Emperor and rule Japan. The Golden Lizard wishes to rule the underworld as chief Yakuza.' He flexed his muscles and the scales undulated. 'Nothing less will satisfy the Golden Lizard.' The reptile eyes widened into a maddened glare.

Hideyoshi feared he would be attacked. He was transfixed by those vicious eyes and could not move. Then suddenly the spell seemed to pass. Hideyoshi let out his breath. He had no choice but to deal with this madman. 'I will pay for the death of Lord Maeda,' he said.

'What has he done to offend you?'

'He has given public support to Mung's policies, and damned Saga of Choshu.'

'If it rains tomorrow as predicted,' the lizard-man said, 'Maeda will die the moment he leaves the imperial palace.'

'What kind of person is Udo?' Gin-ko asked.

'Bright and thoughtful,' Ukiko said. She held up a vial. 'He sent this powdered rhinoceros horn to me. The Chinese use it to increase fertility and virility. There is enough for me and for Mung.'

'I do hope it is successful. What has Udo done with the bunn-iis?'

'The note said he found a pleasant home for them.'

'What position did he hold in Canton?'

'Something for Japan's maritime service involving import and export.' Much as Ukiko loved Gin-ko, she would not reveal Udo's role in the Black Dragon Society.

'Is he a merchant?'

'Does he interest you?'

The beautiful courtesan blushed. 'I ask because of his request about the Yakuza.'

'In that, Udo is working for my husband. It has to do with the attack on us while cormorant fishing.'

'The little I know of the tattooed men is that they use pressure in their illegal works, rarely violence.'

Ukiko shuddered. 'That night on the river was certainly violent. Mung believes the attack was not sanctioned by Japan's senior Yakuza. If my husband can establish contact with them, the situation might be clarified.'

'Why was Udo chosen for the task?'

'A government minister cannot openly seek a meeting with the Yakuza. He would lose face. Mung thought highly enough of Udo to adopt him, and has assigned him this mission.'

'I will try to help your new son,' Gin-ko said. Both women giggled.

'He has invited us for a Chinese lunch tomorrow. Will you come?' Ukiko asked.

'If he serves anything that looks like rabbit, I am leaving on the first rickshaw.'

The two giggled again.

'I am certain Udo is a kind man and the bunn-iis are well cared for,' Ukiko said.

'Have another piece of rabbit,' Udo said.

Freshly bathed and robed, Sandanj tweezered a crispy morsel from among the sculpted radishes. 'I cannot tell the difference between this and chicken. It is delicious. I am very interested in foods of different lands. In my home I have many foreign cookbooks, but alas I cannot return there until my punishment is over.'

'How do you read the western cookbooks?'

'I am proficient in French. It is said the best cooking in the world comes from there.'

'Do not believe it.'

'You are familiar with French cooking?'

'Yes, and other European styles too. Finish this meal and tell me if our Chinese cousins do not surpass the Europeans in the art of gastronomy.'

'You and I shall be good friends,' Sandanj said as he stuffed his mouth. 'And when I am wealthy, we will taste all the best foods from different lands. I save every penny and pay to have my cookbooks translated. It helps me to learn the languages and the customs of the foreigners. One day I will publish the translations in Japanese to regain my investment.' He helped himself to more rabbit, then pointed at Udo with his eating sticks. 'Japanese are becoming more interested in western things. I could have a big seller in translated cookbooks.'

Udo marked his new friend as one who would help him secure a power base in Tokyo. 'I offer you my chef and my house whenever you wish,' he said. 'Use them as your own.'

'I am truly grateful.' Sandanj bowed low. 'My brothers in the Black Dragon Society do not recognize me since my punishment.'

'What about the two others assigned with you to this city?'

'They have each other. They are lovers.'

'I thought sex was forbidden as part of your punishment.'

'The Black Dragon ordered us not to have relations with women.'

'So they have become homosexual?'

'Yes. And I have heard that many of those returning from Europe are sexually inverted. When your new father sent them abroad, he ordered them to devote themselves totally to absorbing the languages, cultures and professions assigned to them. He can be very impressive, that father of yours. His height, that bent nose, and his sincerity, have quite an effect.' Sandanj studied Udo. 'You could be taken for his real son. You are even taller.'

'I would have to flatten my nose and give it a little twist.' They both laughed.

'They were a young, dedicated group who were sent out

117

to learn about the West,' Sandanj said. 'Rather than waste time and money seeking women to sleep with, they studied more and slept with each other.'

'Are you that way?'

'Oh no. I screw every female I can. Once I was shepherding at the French compound and met a most charming lady sheep.'

'No, no,' Udo laughed, 'no animal stories. I have had enough with rabbits today. But tell me how you recognized that Yakuza.'

'My two partners sniffed him out. He is also a homosexual.'

Udo breathed a deep sigh of relief. Part of his afternoon had been spent in the agony of imagining the older man with Gin-ko. 'Do you know if he is a powerful Yakuza?'

'From the way he acts and the respect accorded him, I would say if he is not, he could lead us to someone higher.' Sandanj pointed two fingers at his eyes, then at his crotch. 'We must try the four ball story on him with that big knife of yours.' He smiled. 'I can tell you from experience it is quite persuasive.'

'You and your companions continue to watch this Yakuza. Tomorrow I lunch with someone who may be able to clarify his status among the tattooed people.'

'I toast your success.' Sandanj raised his cup. 'No eating during daylight and no screwing at all is bad for one's health. Even my partners are starting to look good. If you had not given me this meal, I would have caught a dog and eaten him with the hair on.'

The two men laughed, one pleased to have found a friend, the other because he wanted to believe his infatuation with the beautiful courtesan was over. It had been some time since he thought of her. He looked at his pocket watch. Almost a half hour.

Chapter 11

Tokyo's huge brass war gong boomed and people ran into the streets. In the port area only the rickshaw carrying Townsend Harris moved along the deserted avenue to the silent harbour. The Fujiwara army and Lord Maeda's troops enforced a strict curfew with naked blades and taut bows.

From the imperial palace, Mung watched the American consul being rowed towards the five foreign warships manoeuvring into a battle line opposite Tokyo's municipal pier. Two more warships patrolled the harbour's entrance, sealing it. With their daily supply of food from the sea cut off, the people of Tokyo would soon begin to suffer.

Udo and Sandanj were first to reach Mung. 'How may we help?' Udo asked.

Mung glared at Sandanj. 'Your companion is one of those guards I sentenced in Kagoshima,' he said to Udo. 'Why is he here?'

'He seeks to complete his mission,' Udo said. 'He may well have a connection to a senior Yakuza,' Udo said.

'For his sake, I hope it is so.'

Black Dragon couriers began arriving. 'Sire,' the first runner reported, 'Lord Hotta has the port area under control. The American consul is aboard the British flagship.'

A second messenger said, 'Samurai are gathering at the Hikawa shrine. Count Hideyoshi of Mito is whipping up anti-foreign sentiment there. They chant the Choshu war cry, "Sonno joi. Revere the Emperor and expel the barbarian!" They vow to attack all foreigners if Lord Saga has been injured or dishonoured.'

'Sire,' another runner gasped, 'the foreign consuls are demanding to visit their ships in the harbour. Some want to evacuate their families. The people of Tokyo are lining up at the shops to buy whatever food they can. I saw many samurai entering the Yasukune shrine. They vow to fight the barbarians.'

Mung pointed at the first runner. 'Tell Lords Hotta and Maeda to contain the hotheads at the two shrines. No one is allowed near a foreigner on land or at sea.' He pointed at the second runner. 'The foreign consuls are not yet permitted to enter the harbour area. They are to remain in the foreign compounds for the present.' He breathed deeply and ordered the third runner, 'Convey my request to Count Iyeasu of Mito to hold himself ready for an audience with the Emperor.'

Mung turned from the many couriers lined up to report. 'Udo, keep Sandanj with you. Await the American consul's return from the British flagship, and escort him directly to me.'

Shortly after nine p.m., in a room in the imperial palace especially designed for receiving foreigners, Townsend Harris sat crosslegged ten feet behind Lord Hotta, who was flanked by Mung and Iyeasu.

Lord Hotta sat before a raised platform on which stood a three-sided screen, its opening at a right angle to the four men. Within sat the Emperor. No foreigner had ever set eyes upon a descendant of the Sun Goddess. From his position forward of the other three, Hotta could see the Emperor's hands.

The Fujiwara lord addressed Townsend Harris without turning his head. 'If the American consul will apprise us of the results of his meeting with the foreign captains, I would be most grateful.'

'Gentlemen,' Harris said, 'I spoke with Lord Edward Crest, leader of the multi-national expedition. I made clear

120

to him as I do now to you, that I have offered my services to both sides in the hope of avoiding a military confrontation. In my capacity as arbitrator, I make no judgement. I act as a neutral party. However, I am the American representative to the imperial court of Japan. On behalf of my country, I also protest against Lord Saga's closing of the Shimonoseki straits.'

'We appreciate your position,' Lord Hotta said. 'Has Lord Saga been harmed?'

'No. Neither has he been judged. Lord Crest maintains the Rujo must do that.'

'Good,' Hotta said. 'Now what does the Englishman want?'

'Three million pounds sterling,' Townsend Harris replied.

Lord Hotta's head swivelled around so quickly, Mung feared the Fujiwara lord had harmed himself. The pained expression on the lord's face indicated his great discomfort.

'Would you repeat that, please,' Mung said.

'Lord Crest demands three million sterling as indemnity for the illegal closure of the Straits of Shimonoseki. Lord Saga has already agreed to pay.'

Count Iyeasu was first to recover. 'How could the Choshu lord consent to a sum of money the Japanese government cannot afford?'

'I met with Lord Saga,' Townsend Harris said. 'This whole affair does not appear to disturb him. He claims the Rujo will pay. In the meantime he finds his cell comfortable, the food interesting, and he has developed a taste for Lord Crest's cigars. The Englishman will be happily rid of him.'

'Mr Consul,' Mung said, 'Lord Crest must know Japan does not have the funds.'

'I informed him these islands are people-rich and land-poor. Without natural resources, precious stones or metals.

And that having been isolated for two and a half centuries, your national treasury is non-existent.'

'What was his reaction?' Iyeasu asked.

'He demands that a Japanese delegation empowered to negotiate meet with him by ten tomorrow morning, or he will shoot the tops off the tallest buildings in Tokyo. He promises to demolish one building every hour until discussions begin, or the city is levelled.'

Count Iyeasu rolled forward on his massive stomach and touched his head to the floor. He addressed the Emperor behind the screen. 'Your Imperial Majesty, I have made a study of fires in Tokyo. Such a bombardment striking throughout the city would be catastrophic. Even the rain which has begun to fall will not stop the oil-soaked paper and wood-framed houses from igniting. The explosive shells will scatter burning embers in all directions.'

'Sire,' Mung added, 'I recommend that Count Iyeasu and I leave immediately for a secret meeting with Lord Crest. Perhaps we can persuade him to modify his demands. It would be impossible to evacuate the one million inhabitants of Tokyo before tomorrow.'

Hotta looked towards the screen and saw the Emperor's hand move. 'Permission granted,' Hotta announced.

Mung turned to Townsend Harris. 'I respectfully request that you accompany us to verify our credentials.'

'Certainly. I consider it my Christian duty.'

Mung winced. He ignored the word 'Christian' in his translation. How can I use these events to manipulate the foreigners into helping speed up the modernization of Japan, he wondered. During the formalities of being excused from the Emperor's presence, and the journey to the meeting, his mind raced over possibilities.

Mung, Iyeasu and Harris were driven in a closed carriage to the municipal pier, then rowed out to the HMS *Nemesis*. It was midnight when they were piped aboard and taken directly to Lord Crest's stateroom.

The British lord wore a cocked hat with plumes that brushed the ceiling. He carried so much gold braid on his shoulders, Mung thought the man should sag under the weight.

'Gentlemen,' Lord Crest said, 'I apologize for the lack of an official interpreter.'

'Your lordship,' Townsend Harris said, 'both Count Iyeasu and the Minister of Maritime Services speak English fluently.'

'Fine. The hour is late so let us get on with it, shall we? You gentlemen are empowered to negotiate for the government of Japan?'

'I vouch for their authority to conduct preparatory discussions,' Townsend Harris said.

'At the risk of appearing impolite, I must inform the honourable Japanese gentlemen that I will not suffer the long-drawn-out bargaining procedures expected by Orientals. The American Commodore Matthew Perry signed the first western treaty seventy-two hours after his arrival. I intend using that time schedule as my guide.'

'But Commodore Perry gave a year's notice of his intentions,' Mung protested.

'Then I shall have bettered the commodore when the history of this event is written, shan't I?' Edward Crest pointed to a calendar. 'It is now June 18, 1871. If agreement is not signed by midnight of the 21st, I will burn Tokyo. It is that simple. Official negotiations will start tomorrow morning at ten, or the shelling begins.'

Mung felt his testicles shrivel. He saw Iyeasu blanch.

'You will earn the undying hatred of the Japanese people by an act of such destruction,' Townsend Harris said.

'I disagree,' Lord Crest replied. 'The Oriental respects power. If we have to show it, we will. Tokyo's punishment will forever guarantee Japan's adherence to international laws and treaties.'

'You know our government does not have three million sterling to pay the indemnity,' Mung said.

'So the American consul has informed me.'

'How did you arrive at such a sum?' Iyeasu Koin asked.

'The cost was determined by the expense necessary to reopen the Straits of Shimonoseki, plus damages incurred in the battle, and losses to the merchant fleets of seven countries caused by the delay.'

'The price appears steep for a seven-ship expeditionary force that took only hours to accomplish its mission.'

Mung was shocked, although respectful of Iyeasu Koin. The Count of Mito was going against everything in his aristocratic breeding and actually bargaining with Lord Crest.

The British lord stiffened. His face reddened. 'The accounting is mine.'

'You have figures to support this claim?' Iyeasu asked.

Edward Crest leaned forward and peered down into the round, placid face of the Japanese nobleman. 'I do not intend justifying anything. Overcharges may be accredited to the column called punishment. Japan will be taught a lesson in international law.' He straightened up. His brow creased as he studied Iyeasu Koin. 'You are familiar to me.'

'I had the honour of attending your lectures and being your house-guest in Bournemouth.'

'Yes, yes,' Edward Crest said with genuine enthusiasm. 'You are that bright little fat fellow whose shirt-front was always popping out. I did not recognize you in traditional dress.'

'I apologize for not having informed the American consul of our past acquaintanceship,' Iyeasu said.

'One never knows who one will meet out here in the Far East. But this pleasure cannot be allowed to interrupt the business at hand. Perhaps we can share memories another time.'

'Will that be possible?' Iyeasu asked.

'It depends on your response to our demands.' The Englishman smiled.

'Lord Crest,' Townsend Harris said, 'the closure of the straits was the act of a single lord who violated Japanese law in doing so. Saga had no legal endorsement for his aggression, nor the right to commit Japan to your terms of compensation.'

'And the Rujo has no alternative but to pay. My guns are large enough to tear Tokyo apart. Lord Saga, as a member of the Great Council, speaks and acts with governmental authority. I am prepared to let the Rujo discipline him.' Edward Crest removed his cocked hat. 'Gentlemen, when my crew see this hat, they know the admiral is aboard. When you look upon it, know that I am a warrior. Albeit, a warrior who does not wish to fight. I have persuaded my six allies to forgo the bombardment of Japan's coastal cities for the more interesting prospect of trade, and promotion of Christianity.'

Mung and Iyeasu both chose to ignore mention of an additional threat to Japan's major coastal cities.

'We do not want war,' Mung said. 'Neither do we have the funds to avoid it.'

'Three million sterling may appear a large sum for a backward country such as Japan,' Edward Crest said, 'but modern nations would consider it fair settlement, and pay without quibbling.'

Iyeasu had warned Mung of the Englishman's overbearing attitude towards non-whites, but both men smarted from his insults. Mung silently thanked the Emperor for having ordered Iyeasu to participate in the negotiations. Hotta, or any other Japanese of rank, would have attacked the Englishman or walked out on him.

'Lord Crest,' Iyeasu said, 'to use a Latin expression, you cannot squeeze blood from a stone.'

To Mung's surprise, the Englishman smiled. 'I remember

you were always rummaging for an idiom when a straight-forward explanation would have served. Once again you have misstated. I instructed you to study the Bible to understand idiomatic English. The misquote you used was taken from Moses, who in fact did strike a rock and cause water to gush forth. I would prefer not to bash Tokyo about with my cannon. Rather let us Europeans show Japan how to pump vitality into its economy so the indemnity will be paid without unnecessary hardship.'

'What do you propose?' Mung asked.

'In lieu of an immediate cash settlement, Japan will open seven new trading ports to be administered by each of the seven nations gathered here. Customs and taxes will be set and collected by representatives of these nations. The first act will be to reduce Japan's import tax from twenty to five per cent.'

'How do you intend to pump new life into our economy,' Iyeasu asked, 'if you reduce our income on imports?'

'The fifteen per cent reduction will be accredited to the three million indemnity minus service charges. Furthermore, a code of official etiquette and procedures will be implemented to ensure proper treatment of foreign nationals in Japan. The effective administration of European justice will be established in the treaty ports.'

'You are speaking of extraterritoriality as defined in the recent treaty of Tientsin,' Mung said. 'That included unrestricted movement of Christian missionaries.'

Edward Crest bowed slightly to Mung. 'You are well informed, Mr Minister.'

'These terms are unacceptable,' Mung said. 'Unlimited freedom for priests would result in many deaths. We could not protect them once they left the larger coastal cities. As regards the remainder of your demands, including extraterritoriality, they amount to legal annexation of seven of Japan's cities.'

'Yes,' Edward Crest said, 'Japan must learn a lesson and never again violate a treaty with Christians.'

'Your lordship,' Iyeasu said, 'you are violating your own premise put forth in the lecture hall, that in any negotiation no side should be so humbled and humiliated it would seek to avenge the insult at all costs.'

'Count Iyeasu is correct,' Townsend Harris said. 'These demands are outrageous.'

'If America is so opposed to the terms,' Lord Crest said, 'let her lend Japan three million sterling and we shall be gone from here.'

'I haven't the authority,' Townsend Harris said.

'Neither do these two Japanese gentlemen have the authority to reject my terms. Let the Rujo decide. And by ten a.m. tomorrow, or my gunners will begin their target practice!'

'Allow us until noon,' Mung said. 'No decision could be reached before then.'

'In return for the extension, I want all foreign consuls, their families and employees given free access to our ships.'

'It will be arranged,' Mung said. 'Will you release Lord Saga?'

'You may have the little bandit now.'

'Not now,' Iyeasu said.

Mung looked questioningly at Iyeasu, who continued speaking. 'The Choshu lord is a most volatile person. I prefer him not to enter Tokyo until we have prepared for him. We shall send a contingent from the palace guard to escort him back.'

Again Mung was grateful to Iyeasu Koin. Only a Japanese noble could have made such a request.

'Very well,' Lord Crest said, 'but I do wish to be rid of that awkward fellow. You have until noon tomorrow.'

Chapter 12

Mung and Iyeasu watched Townsend Harris leave the municipal dock with his escort. Then the Count of Mito turned away from the Fujiwara guards and shuffled towards the end of the wooden pier. He cast a glance over his shoulder and motioned Mung to join him. The two men, one tall and lithe, the other short and square, gazed over the water at the foreign warships in the harbour.

'Pompous baboon,' Iyeasu declared. 'Calling us Japanese gentlemen! Referring to us as backward people!'

'I doubt there is another nobleman in the empire who could have held his temper and served his country better than you have tonight,' Mung said.

'My contempt for those white-faces is only intensified by their actions,' Iyeasu said. 'They see us as inferior.'

'How do you see them?'

'They are a privileged race in the history of today, but the situation will change.' Iyeasu's calm tone of voice had more impact than if he had shouted his conviction. 'Mung,' he said, 'if we remain a technically backward people for much longer, Japan will fall so far behind it will never catch up.'

'That is why I see using foreign expertise to train the next generation of Japanese as twentieth-century men.'

Iyeasu grunted. Mung saw his eyes fix on a distant place. The two stood together, but alone with their thoughts.

Then Iyeasu asked, 'How long before you allow the foreign nationals passage to their ships?'

'Not quite yet. They make good hostages. And, speaking of hostages, I want to thank you for keeping Saga out of Tokyo.'

Iyeasu nodded, and pointed to the line of gunboats. 'One day we shall fight them.'

'We will lose,' Mung said.

'We must make Japan strong enough not to lose. For if the round-eyes win, we will become their slaves. You were shocked that I, an aristocrat by birth, could eat their arrogance.' Iyeasu smiled. 'All whites have a weakness regarding Orientals. They think of us as cowardly, lazy and stupid. When we finally do meet in battle, that will work against them.'

'Modernization has been my goal since returning to Japan. The battles I foresee are economic and cultural. Even Lord Crest says he wants trade, not war.'

'That is because he has the guns and warships to dictate his terms of trade.' Iyeasu looked directly at Mung and said, 'Your first title of Scholar of Satsuma was fitted to you – an intellectual more than a military tactician. Let us suppose you persuade the Rujo to invite western advisors into our country.'

'Not likely with your father's opposition.'

Iyeasu motioned at the warships. 'What if your predictions become reality and Japan jumps into competition for international markets with them?'

'Economic Darwinism,' Mung said. 'The survival of the fittest.'

'If one of those nations was to suffer a major economic defeat because of us, they would use a military solution to rectify it. All the wars of Europe, including the Crusades, were for economic reasons.'

'War with us cannot be profitable for them,' Mung said.

'Those captains out there did well for themselves in Tientsin. They intend to sail away from here with a pocketful of concessions. They believe they were meant to dominate the non-whites of the world.'

'Impossible,' Mung said. 'Including India, China and

Africa, the so-called coloured peoples represent seventy per cent of the world's population.'

'Mung, you are brilliant in some things, a patriot in every way, but often naïve.'

'Is it naïve to say that Japan, by virtue of her geographic position, her racial and religious similarities, is ideally situated to contest the Europeans for all the commerce and trade this side of the Himalayas?'

'Well said.' Iyeasu clapped his hands. 'You are brilliantly aggressive. But look out there.' He pointed again. 'Those captains and the financial wizards controlling them will allow Japan only as much international business as will serve their own purposes. They will fatten us like cows to be milked for their benefits. They already justify the rape of China with Christian morals and western science.'

'Iyeasu, I grew up in America. They have their prejudices, but the Americans do not take part in the unfair treaties throughout the Pacific.'

'Humph! A fledgling nation unique in history. Their constitution has not yet stood the test of time.'

'Time is moving faster than ever before. Japan must not be left behind. This is why I oppose your father. Time is of the essence.'

'Time is of the essence. Time is of the essence.' Iyeasu repeated Mung's phrase over and over in a dull monotone.

To Mung's amazement, Iyeasu began to strip off his clothing. Twice Mung started to speak but was stopped by a motion of Iyeasu's hand. Mung felt he had neither the authority to question nor could he leave the nobleman standing in his hakka shorts on the end of the pier.

'Do you carry a timepiece?' Iyeasu asked.

'Yes.'

'Rouse me in thirty minutes. I must explore the implications of a decision which, if made, will change my life. Your concept of time moving faster troubles and stimulates me.' Iyeasu sat down at the edge of the pier in the lotus position, his legs hidden by his giant stomach. He gazed out to sea.

Mung heard a low hissing sound. It seemed to be the waves swishing through the wooden pilings beneath his feet. Then he realized the sound came from Iyeasu. He was sucking air through pursed lips. Mung watched the count's massive chest swell, his back expand. The great muscles in Iyeasu's shoulders bulged. Mung had not seen a resemblance between the brothers of Mito until that moment. Iyeasu resembled a smaller version of Danjuro. He exhaled and Mung saw his eyes roll up into his head. The man was in a trance.

It had been years since Mung practised the meditation techniques taught him by his father, and he felt no desire to use them now. Instead he paced the end of the pier behind the seated figure, concentrating on the details of his plan for using Lord Crest to force Iyeasu's father and the Rujo into accepting an immediate policy of modernization.

It was three a.m. when Mung and Iyeasu crawled into the Emperor's presence. As a ranking nobleman, Iyeasu gave the report. He answered Lord Hotta's questions and clarified certain points for the Emperor.

'In conclusion,' Iyeasu said, 'the Minister of Maritime Services and I believe some of Lord Crest's demands can be reduced by negotiation.'

'Your highness,' Mung said, 'according to my informants in Canton, prior to the negotiations with the Chinese in Tientsin the concept of perpetual leasing was seen by the western leaders as a secondary position. In our case, it might be written as leasing of the seven ports until the indemnity is paid, plus twenty years.' The Emperor nodded, and Mung went on. 'Their demand for extraterritoriality is meant to protect foreign nationals from what they consider our archaic form of justice. This requirement could also be modified.'

'How do westerners judge an accused?' Hotta asked.

'Evidence is presented to a court by a legal representative. It influences the determination of guilt or innocence by the judge. Most European countries have abandoned the use of torture to obtain confessions. In many courts the accused even retains the right not to testify against himself.'

'You mean they actually convict people without an admission of guilt?' Hotta said.

'Yes, sire.'

'And you wish to implement that system in Japan?'

'As happened in Europe, the use of torture in Japan is sometimes abused. The strong criminal goes free while the weak innocent confesses to whatever is suggested to him.'

'The fault lies with the judges, not the system,' Hotta said. 'To convict a person without a confession reeks of judicial hypocrisy. What counteroffer will you make?'

'I propose the foreigners should judge their people in the port cities and we should judge ours, with their help. It would be the first step to establishing a modern legal system in Japan.'

'I can see why the Englishman would accept this offer, but why should he relinquish his demand for perpetual leasing?' Hotta asked. 'He has the military power to force our acceptance.'

'While in England,' Iyeasu answered, 'I learned that Lord Crest has enemies there. The opposition political party fears he will return to contest the premiership in the coming election. There are those in his own party who desire the nomination for themselves, and prefer him to remain in the Far East. Lord Crest is an ambitious man with a definite view of himself in history. He is determined to return home with the victories of Tientsin and Tokyo to his credit. Neither he nor his allies want to squander the profits acquired in China on a war with Japan.'

'I agree with Count Iyeasu,' Mung said. 'Lord Crest will

accept a reasonable alternative to war. The seventy-two-hour time limit can be used against him. He knows if he were to begin shooting, it would delay reaching a settlement with us. And he must return to England soon. I propose we offer the concessions he demands, in return for the help of the seven nations in industrializing Japan. That would be an agreement between sovereign nations, not a dictated treaty.'

'The opposition of Count Iyeasu's father, Fujita Koin, would doom passage in the Rujo,' Lord Hotta said.

'Sire,' Iyeasu said, 'prior to this meeting I meditated on just that problem. I reminded myself that the moral priority of every Japanese is first to his Emperor, then to the empire, and afterwards to his family. My father's idea of sending our people abroad to study western technology is sound, but not immediately effective. I have come to believe Mung's plan is the only way to prevent Japan from becoming a vassal state of the West. His idea of using foreign capital and advisors satisfies two important points towards progress. It would place foreign funds and foreign nationals in our hands. The more Caucasians and Caucasian capital we hold, the stronger our bargaining position. Money and men would become hostage if the West threatened us. Just as Lord Saga's release was effected in exchange for foreign nationals being allowed to board their ships. I will openly support Mung's position.'

Mung turned towards Iyeasu, overwhelmed that the youngest count of Mito had found the inner strength to defy his father and the tradition of generations.

'Have you contemplated the consequences of opposing your father?' Hotta asked.

'Yes. It will weaken his position in the Rujo and he will disown me. I have one request. That in the modernization of the empire, as much attention be given to the military as to industry and commerce. In this I agree with my father, not Mung. Eventually we will have to fight the round-eyes. We must be prepared.'

'Your highness,' Mung said, 'I believe it is time to reveal my true role to Count Iyeasu. His heroic sacrifice in opposing his father for the glory of the Emperor and Japan has earned him that.'

The Emperor nodded at his chief counsellor. 'Inform Count Iyeasu of Mung's secret role.'

'Mung leads the Emperor's personal intelligence organization,' Hotta said. 'He is the Black Dragon.'

'I was aware the position existed,' Iyeasu said. 'I am pleased such a talented person holds it.'

The Emperor addressed Iyeasu and Mung. 'Go to the Rujo with the Englishman's demands. I expect the lords will reject them. Return to negotiate the new terms with Lord Crest as you have outlined them to me. Reconvene the Rujo and present the revised offer. It will allow our nobles to accept and save face. May the gods smile on your endeavours.'

Chapter 13

At his quarters in the imperial palace, Lord Maeda was among the first to receive the summons for the Rujo's assembly in the Hall of a Hundred Mats. His kago was carried towards the meeting in a downpour, surrounded by sixty samurai wearing raincapes over their armour. Sealskin bags protected the hilts of their swords.

The guards paid little attention to the loiterers near the Hinzemon palace gate, or to a group huddled around an open fire ahead of them. It was common practice for people seeking favours to gather at the gate, although usually not in such bad weather.

The Golden Lizard waited for the palace gates to slam shut behind Lord Maeda, then signalled the men standing nearby to attack the rear guard. Although Lord Maeda's men were more numerous, the rain gear delayed them from clearing their weapons. Samurai on both sides of the kago dashed to their comrades' aid, leaving Lord Maeda unattended. The Golden Lizard whistled, and the group around the fire attacked the front of the column. In unison, the lord's samurai pressed forward, forcing the Yakuza back. Further and further, they drove the tattooed men away from the unprotected kago.

The Golden Lizard threw off his raincape and hat. His tattooed body was naked to the waist. He and two other Yakuza dashed to the kago. The first man threw open the door and was blasted back by a quick shot. He fell dead with a lead ball in his chest.

From inside the kago, the empty smooth-bore pistol still smoking in his hand, Lord Maeda stared up at the lizard-man. The last words Lord Maeda heard were hissed by the

Golden Lizard. 'You are dead!' He thrust a spear through the nobleman's heart, then turned and shouted to his men, 'Retreat! Retreat!'

Danjuro, the Mito giant, was never able to find comfort in the cramped quarters of a kago. On foot, he led the Mito samurai escorting his father to the appointment with the Emperor. Approaching the Hinzemon Gate, Danjuro heard shouts. 'Assassins! Assassins! Stop them!' Then he saw a band of armed rabble running towards him, pursued by imperial guards.

'Form up and protect your lord,' Danjuro bellowed. 'Prepare to defend.' He flung his samurai into formation around his father's kago, and turned towards the fleeing men. Unable to clear his sword from its sealskin bag, he ripped off his raincape with his right hand. He whipped out his iron fan with his left hand, and struck the head of the nearest Yakuza running by. The Mito giant parried a sword cut from another Yakuza with his fan. He reached out, caught the man by the throat and strangled him.

'Good work,' the captain of the imperial guard shouted as he passed, urging his troops after the tattooed men.

Danjuro dropped the limp body. 'Into the palace quickly,' he ordered his men.

Lord Hotta sat at the Emperor's side. All others in the room knelt in a line facing the raised platform.

'The attack was not on me, your highness,' Fujita Koin answered the Emperor. 'They were most likely anti-foreign extremists displeased with Lord Maeda's politics.'

'Not so,' Lord Hotta said. 'They were hired assassins.'

Fujita Koin shrugged. 'It is possible they were hired to incite those samurai gathering in the temples and shrines. The warriors in the city want to hear from Lord Saga.' He glared at Mung.

'Saga will be heard when he addresses the Rujo,' Hotta

said. 'Not before. Your second son, Hideyoshi, has been visiting those anti-foreign gatherings and stirring them up.'

The Emperor slapped his fan into the palm of his hand and Mung saw the Lord of Mito wince. Then the old man bowed and said, 'I shall speak to my son about his actions.'

'It is also the Emperor's wish that you heed your youngest son,' Hotta said.

Iyeasu bowed his head to the floor. 'Father, I am bound by Bushido to serve the Emperor. I have come to the decision to support Mung's plan of modernization as opposed to yours.'

Everyone in the room remained deathly still. They heard the breath whistle through Danjuro's teeth. His body swelled with anger until Mung thought his armour would burst. As Danjuro expanded, his father appeared to wilt. Mung sensed the old man had been aware of this possibility.

'Father,' Iyeasu said, 'there is no time to wait before expanding Japan's horizons into the modern world. We must begin immediately to eliminate the petty feudal thrones and unite behind the Emperor.' His sad eyes lit up with the rightness of his cause. The round body shook with emotion. He was acting against all he had been taught of filial piety. 'Father, we must invite advisors, instructors and teachers from the West, and sit our youth at their feet to learn. Then, armed with their knowledge, we shall focus our strength like the rays of the rising sun into a single burning point capable of cutting down any foreign force. In a relatively short period we will be capable of challenging the West economically, and later defending ourselves militarily.'

Perspiration poured down Iyeasu's face as he waited for his father's reply. Mung steeled himself for a burst of rage from the Lord of Mito, but the voice he heard was as soft as Iyeasu's had been at the end of the pier. Even the Emperor leaned forward to hear.

'We Japanese have an engrained tendency towards imitation,' the old man said. 'Our ancestors flung themselves onto Chinese culture like monkeys jumping for bananas. There is not a scholar in the empire who recalls our original culture. We say the old religion is Shintoism, but there was another before that, which is lost. We preach Confucian ethics, our children are born with the blessings of a Shinto priest, and are buried with Buddhist rituals. I fear we Japanese will never again know who we really are because we copy everything.

'In 1542 the Spanish Jesuit, Francis Xavier, came to Japan to proselytize. Fifty years later he and those followers had converted three hundred thousand of our people. In Kyoto, his disciples paraded the streets in Portuguese balloon trousers, striped socks, high-topped shoes and feathered hats.

'In the seventeenth century a few powerful Japanese noblemen took steps to save our culture, and set out to establish a unique Japanese society. They elected the leader of the Tokugawa as shogun, and he killed off the Christian converts. Then he chased the round-eyes away and sealed Japan off from the outside world. In the 250 years of isolation we developed our own unique social order. There was peace in the land. Now the Christians return, and we are fighting each other.'

'My lord,' Mung said, 'the long period of peace you speak of was maintained by heartless control of the population. Our people were pressured into rigid class structures. They were forbidden to use their initiative and natural talents. Their most creative instincts were smothered. I too know something of our history. Before the Tokugawa shogun's reign, we were a vigorous, hardy nation of master mariners. Then we became a recluse nation. Now, like a hermit crab poking its head into the light, we are frightened by what we see.'

'Few things in life frighten me,' Fujita Koin said, 'but I

am appalled at the first sign of breakdown in Japan's social order. It begins with a son who does not honour his father.' The old man looked at Iyeasu.

'The lord of Mito is mistaken,' Hotta said. 'Rather than oppose you, Iyeasu was prepared to commit seppuku. Only the Emperor's order stayed his hand. In serving the Emperor, your son honours his father.'

'It would have been better had he slit his belly than betray his ancestors. He is my son no longer.'

'Father!' Iyeasu gasped.

'Rescind that vow,' Lord Hotta demanded.

'I will not!' The old man glared at Hotta and clasped his short sword. 'Nor will I allow my son to speak against his father in the Rujo. All properties, income and titles heretofore his right by birth are now and forever withdrawn. Without his rank he cannot speak in the Great Council. If I am ordered to revoke this oath I will commit seppuku here and now.' He drew his blade halfway from its scabbard before his hand was stayed by the Emperor's voice.

'Neither you nor your son will commit seppuku. This is my command and it will be done. Do you both understand?'

'Yes, your highness,' father and son answered, touching their heads to the floor.

'And your son shall speak in the Rujo, for I command it,' the Emperor said. 'Although I cannot confer hereditary title, I can appoint Iyeasu minister of the newly formed Department of Education. He and the Minister of Maritime Services will present Lord Crest's terms to the Great Council!'

'Your highness has put me in an awkward position,' Fujita Koin said. 'To oppose you in the Rujo in the face of this appointment might be construed as open defiance.'

'You would not be alone,' Hotta said. 'Those who killed

139

Lord Maeda challenged the Emperor's authority. Will you join that rabble?'

'If I did, it would be with the support of the fiefdom of Satsuma,' Fujita Koin said.

'How can that be?' Mung blurted out. 'Nariakira of Satsuma was the foremost leader in favour of modernizing our country.'

'That was some time ago,' Fujita Koin said. 'Since Nariakira's death and the retirement of his generals, my people and Saga's have influenced the Satsuma samurai to a more traditional view. You, Mr Mung, have been too long building big boats while we loyal Japanese have strengthened our military position.'

Mung, so certain of Satsuma's loyalty, had not assigned his overworked Black Dragons to that fiefdom. For several years he had relied on reports through normal military channels. If the old man spoke the truth, his anti-foreign faction had an overwhelming superiority of men, weapons and votes in the Rujo.

'Will the houses of Mito oppose the Emperor?' Hotta demanded.

Iyeasu interrupted, thinking to save his father from saying in anger what might cost him his life. 'To do so would make you guilty of the same crime of which you accuse me – filial impiety,' he said to his father. 'If you impede Mung's plans to move Japan forward it will be done from anger, not Bushido. You have agreed that Japan must modernize to defend herself from the West. The dispute is whether it will be now or later.'

'I shall give my answer in the Rujo,' the old man said. 'That is where the Emperor's loyal followers sit.'

Chapter 14

Udo received two messages at the same time. The first, from Ukiko, postponed their dinner date with Gin-ko because of a summons from Princess Atsu to begin work on the *Book of Good Deeds*. The second message was from Mung, telling of the death of Lord Maeda, and instructing Udo to contact the Yakuza immediately.

'Sandanj,' Udo shouted, 'get dressed. No Chinese food this evening. We have been ordered to meet your tattooed man.'

Udo's face was flushed, eyes bright, step quick as he left the house. He was on his way to see Gin-ko on official business, and needed no invitation.

Sandanj caught up with Udo in the street. 'Where are we going?'

'To the Yoshiwara,' Udo said, practising his greeting to Gin-ko as he hurried through the last part of a thundershower.

The pleasure district consisted of 150 brothels, 400 teahouses, and numerous restaurants and places of entertainment. Laughter and music floated out of buildings lining both sides of the fresh rain-washed streets. A heady fragrance of wet pine and sweet smelling flowers scented the silky clean air. Artists, writers and poets in the streets flicked their long brushes over delicate scrolls of rice paper.

Udo and Sandanj stepped aside for a beautiful woman leading a parade of girls aged eight to fifteen. Each of the girls held a hand-painted fan advertising the woman who led them – her skills at lovemaking and the house she came from.

'Are those young ones also prostitutes?' Udo asked a street artist.

'You are new to the Yoshiwara. Many tourists make the same mistake. The young ones are apprenticed to the courtesan leading them. They learn elegance, manners and proper speech for three years before being allowed to observe their mistress' techniques of romantic refinement. The one who shows the most promise, may some day replace her. The others will be taken on by reputable houses in the Yoshiwara. Or sold off to ply their skills in another city. They are greatly sought after.'

'I know some girls from the House of a Thousand Delights who could teach these Yoshiwara courtesans a few innovative romantic refinements,' Udo said.

'The House of a Thousand Delights was burned down several years ago,' the artist said. 'It was owned by a romantic Buddhist priest named Gompachi. He is missed.'

'How do we find the house of Gin-ko?' Sandanj asked.

'For out-of-towners you have good taste. It is that modest building set back from the street with the bonsai garden in front.'

'Thank you.' Udo turned to leave.

'Do not allow your passion to rule your mind,' the artist said. 'Mistress Gin-ko is someone special. You two cannot barge in there like farmers looking for a mare.'

'Mr Udo Ishikawa is also someone special,' Sandanj said.

'I advise you in the strongest possible terms to visit that teahouse across the street.' The artist pointed. 'Ask for a menu and read the instructions.'

'Thank you anyway,' Udo laughed, 'but we are not hungry.'

The two young men strode across the street and up the cobblestoned path between the dwarf pines and maples. Sandanj knocked on the door-frame.

A young girl came to the entrance and bowed. 'How may I help you?'

'My master wishes to see Mistress Gin-ko.'

The girl bowed again. 'I am so pleased my mistress finds favour in your master's eyes, but this is not the accepted way of introduction.'

'Tell her Udo Ishikawa is here,' Udo said. 'She knows who I am.'

The girl looked the handsome samurai up and down. 'I am first apprentice to Mistress Gin-ko and do not remember you. I have not been told of your arrival, nor heard your name mentioned. Please leave. Following the proper procedure for introduction is the only way.'

'There are other ways.' Sandanj started forward.

Udo held Sandanj's arm and looked down at the young girl. 'I tell females what to do, and they obey.' He put his hands under her elbows and lifted her up. Walking with her into the house, he then set her down. 'There we are.'

Udo looked around him. The rooms were built in a hollow square surrounding a beautiful open garden. There was Gin-ko, wearing a fawn-coloured robe. Her obi was of crimson and gold. She reclined on a carved stone bench, having her portrait painted by an elderly artist. Several delicate butterfly pins floated in her upswept hair, giving her the appearance of a fairy queen. His heart caught in his throat. The contrast of her softness and the hard granite bench was startling. He took a step towards the garden, but was stopped by a thin hag of a woman who limped into the room wearing a stark, black kimono. Slung over her right shoulder was a coiled snakeskin whip. 'Leave at once!' she croaked.

'I am Udo Ishikawa, senior samurai and son of the Minister of Maritime Services.' He looked past the old woman at Gin-ko.

The old woman cackled, her laugh sounding as if it came from a rusted throat. Four barrel-chested men moved to block Udo's way. 'So you are a senior samurai,' she said. 'Here in the Yoshiwara, money is rank. In this house I confer privilege. Now leave here while you can walk on your own.' Her right eye opened wide and glared at him. The corner of her thin mouth twisted up.

Sandanj moved to Udo's side.

'Out of my way,' Udo ordered the four men. The old woman was bluffing. Commoners would never touch a samurai. His eyes returned to Gin-ko. He went to push by the men and his outstretched arm was pulled forward. A hand gripped his collar from behind. Someone reached under his kimono and grabbed his golden spheres. Udo danced on tiptoe as he was turned around and hurried back past the apprentice girl. She bowed as he was tossed out the front door onto the cobblestoned path.

'Ooofff!' Sandanj landed on top of him, both sprawled on their faces.

Udo's anger raged as he struggled out from under the moaning Sandanj. He reached for his Colt revolver. The men at the entrance stepped aside and Udo caught sight of Gin-ko through an aura-like haze. He forgot the pain between his legs. He released his grip on the pistol and gaped up at her.

The old hag limped to Gin-ko's side. 'Do you know these two?' she rasped.

'That is Udo Ishikawa, son of the Minister of Maritime Services,' the beautiful courtesan said.

'His father has never been to this house,' the old woman said. 'Title makes no difference here. I have sent some of the highest lords of the land packing. Without proper introduction, formal gift giving and my approval, no one receives the favours of Gin-ko.'

'But this is the brother of my dear friend, Ukiko. He has come to speak with me.'

Udo saw a transformation come over the old woman. She gazed with adoration at Gin-ko. In a softer voice the hag said, 'Look at him. Like another lovesick puppy, kneeling there.'

Gin-ko hastened to hide a smile behind her fan.

Infuriated, Udo leapt to his feet, and doubled up from the pain in his groin. The humiliation, hurt and love he felt for the courtesan turned his shame into white hot fury. He forced himself to stand upright. Pointing down at Sandanj who sat in the path with outstretched legs and hands on his crotch, Udo ordered, 'Wait here!'

He walked straight up the steps. The old woman moved towards him. He saw Gin-ko's eyes widen with fear. 'I will talk with your mistress,' he said.

The old woman shrugged her right shoulder and the snakeskin whip slipped down into her gnarled hand. Gin-ko placed her fingertips on the woman's arm. 'Please, Little Mother, allow me to speak with this man.'

Udo suddenly realized Gin-ko feared the old woman would hurt him. He laughed. The hag's right eye glared at him while the other coolly measured the distance between them. The whip hand clenched and unclenched on the whip butt. Udo felt threatened but could not bring himself to believe it was by the old woman. He watched her step aside.

Gin-ko walked to the garden, and beckoned Udo to follow. Her tiny, soft-footed steps and the suggestive sway of her hips drove any thoughts of the hag from his mind. He followed and sat opposite her. Gin-ko arranged her robe carefully, then plucked a blossom and rubbed the petals against her delicate cheek as she looked at him.

'Ukiko asks to be forgiven,' Udo said. 'She cannot keep our dinner date. My sister has been summoned to the palace by Princess Atsu. I must also beg forgiveness. I have been ordered to establish contact with a senior Yakuza.' He breathed a sigh of relief. The first part of his prepared speech had gone well. It was the only thing going according to plan since Sandanj had knocked on the door.

'Is that the only reason you are here?' Gin-ko asked. 'To

contact the Yakuza?' She lowered her head. Her eyes peeked at him from under long curved lashes.

Udo's heart pounded in his chest.

'Is there nothing else you wish to say?' She cocked her head like an inquisitive kitten and looked into his eyes.

'Yes. Oh yes. Lord Maeda was assassinated by the tattooed men.'

'You mean the Golden Lizard.'

'You already know?'

'It has been arranged for you to meet with the chief Yakuza of Tokyo.'

'How could you do in one day what we have not accomplished in months?'

'It is the Yakuza who seek you. In the attack on Lord Maeda, the lizard-man deliberately identified himself. That was a direct challenge to the honour and position of the chief Yakuza. The Golden Lizard made a grave error when he entered this city without permission. Your meeting with the chief Yakuza has been arranged for nine tonight. You are to stand in the entrance of the bonsai shop in the Ginza where we first met. Someone will contact you.'

'When may I see you again?' Udo asked.

Gin-ko blushed, and covered her face with her fan. 'Do you wish to sit under the umbrella with me?'

Udo looked up at the clear blue sky. 'It has stopped raining.'

She smiled. 'To sit under the umbrella means the same as going to the pillow. You do understand that idiom?'

Now Udo blushed. 'Yes. Yes. I mean no. No, I do not wish to go to the pillow with you.'

'You do not?' Her eyes flew open in feigned surprise.

'Well yesss . . . I mean . . . It is not like that. Not here. I mean not in this place.' He waved his hand. 'It is not very nice here.' He clamped his mouth shut when she stiffened and raised her chin in defiance.

'I think this is a nice place,' Gin-ko said. 'I designed it.'

Udo's heart sank. He knew she was toying with him. He had seen his girls in Canton do it a thousand times, and had laughed at the fools who suffered the treatment. Still he could not stop. 'The building is quite nice, and,' he hastened to add, 'the garden is exceptional.'

'I am pleased you like this little park. I planted every tree. My father, who was a gardener, taught me. That is my room on the left. I can open the doors and look out on the garden. In the late evenings I sometimes watch fireflies, or the stars, or the moon casting shadows.'

'When may I see you again?'

'If you follow the rules, it must be arranged through Little Mother.' Gin-ko bowed.

The four burly guards entered the garden with the old woman. She pointed with her coiled whip to the front door. Udo bowed to Gin-ko, happy because she had said, 'If you follow the rules . . .' He did not intend to.

Outside the house Udo and Sandanj hobbled down the path, both walking slightly bowlegged to ease the pain in their groins.

'Wait,' the street artist called to them. 'Stand there just as you are. Do not move. I have been hoping for the opportunity to paint a portrait like this.' His brush attacked the canvas with vigorous slashes and strokes. 'Do not move,' he pleaded. 'Not an inch. I will have it in a minute.'

'You will have what?' Sandanj demanded.

'My room and board for the next two weeks. There. Take a look.' The artist turned the painting so they could see. It was a good caricature.

'That is me on the left,' Sandanj said.

Udo looked down at himself to see if he was actually standing as bowlegged as the painting showed. He was. 'What are you going to do with the painting?'

The artist dipped his brush in black ink and labelled it. Sandanj read aloud, 'Victims of the Grabbers of Golden Spheres. Yoshiwara, June 1871. By Kiyochika.'

'Who would buy something like that?' Udo demanded.

'I have a standing commission from a bordello down the street. The madam wishes to hang it in the hall by the front door. Tell me your names and I will pen them in. You will be famous.'

'You are mad.' Udo advanced on the man. 'We would be the laughing stock of Tokyo.'

The artist held the painting behind him. 'You cannot destroy my work. It is the way I earn my living. Come, you both shall be my guests at the teahouse and I will tell you how to meet Mistress Gin-ko.'

'You are also going to sell me that painting,' Udo said.

'Oh, that will be expensive.' The artist smiled.

While they waited for tea and the menu, Udo and the artist came to an agreement on price.

'I am forbidden to drink and you ordered tea,' Sandanj lamented. 'I am not allowed food and this blackmailing artist asked for a menu.'

'Friend,' Kiyochika said, 'you would have to be a cloistered ascetic not to order from this bill of fare.' He opened the menu and ran his finger down a list of prominent bordellos. There was a description of the courtesans and their special talents for pleasuring.

'You want Mistress Gin-ko,' the artist said. 'Here she is, alone at the top.'

'There is no background description,' Sandanj said.

'Not necessary,' Kiyochika replied. 'The lady is the most famous practitioner of her trade in the district. You have met the most sought-after courtesan in Japan. The instructions for courting her favours are written at the bottom of the menu. She is advertised in every teahouse in the Yoshiwara. I will select a bright girl from those serving us. You send her with a present for Little Mother and request permission to show your appreciation for the beauty of Mistress Gin-ko by offering an appropriate gift. The whole procedure may take two months before you even meet her for polite conversation.'

'Little Mother will get a swift kick,' Udo said. 'I never had to overcome such obstacles to meet a woman.'

'And I do not want to read another word about these raving beauties and what they can do or how they can do it.' Sandanj slammed the menu down.

'Are you forbidden sex also?' the artist asked.

'Only with women, so do not bend over,' Sandanj growled.

Udo picked up his painting and stood. 'I will meet with Mistress Gin-ko in less than two months, and without Little Mother's permission.'

'Beware of that old lady,' the artist called. 'She can be extremely dangerous.'

Chapter 15

In the Hall of a Hundred Mats Mung and Iyeasu sat side by side on the dais, facing the representatives of every fiefdom in the empire. The last name on the roll was called. 'Saga of Choshu.'

'Sonno joi!' he responded. 'Revere the Emperor and expel the barbarians!'

Many lords applauded the breach of custom by tapping their fans. Throughout the long, low-ceilinged room, eyes flashed, muscles twitched, and men caressed their swords.

Then the master of protocol declared, 'Kandocho ni tsukete!'

There was a hush in the Great Council hall. 'Kandocho ni tsukete!' he repeated. 'A public renunciation!'

Mung glanced at Iyeasu, then at Fujita Koin in the first row. Neither father nor son moved. Both appeared tired, sad and irreversibly committed.

'For disrupting community harmony,' the master of protocol said. 'For violating social convention and ignoring family authority. Lord Fujita Koin, who succeeds through the benign influence of his honourable ancestors in leading the three houses of Mito, does hereby disown his youngest son, Iyeasu, from this time and forever.'

The intake of breath whistling through the teeth of the assembled lords indicated Fujita Koin had not informed his allies of his intention.

'From this time onward,' the master of protocol said, 'the aforementioned Iyeasu is stripped of all rank, inherited wealth and benefits that were his right by birth. Ye who hear this, ye who see this,' he opened a scroll and held it up to the assembled lords, 'are witness to this renunciation.'

Mung watched Saga carefully. Would he try to use the uncertainty that spread through the hall? But the buck-toothed lord adjusted his wire-framed glasses and appeared content to await the main subject of debate.

'Having observed the solemnity of established procedure in this ancient meeting place,' the master of protocol said, 'let it be resolved to maintain the fundamentals of decorum and inherited virtues to continue intact the glorious tradition set by our ancestors. Hear ye and know ye, lords of the empire, that Iyeasu Koin, formerly Count of Mito, has been appointed to the newly created rank of baron.'

Without being recognized, Hideyoshi Koin shouted out, 'By whose authority?' His harsh voice was a challenge that echoed through the hall.

'By my authority,' Hotta snapped. 'I, Hotta, leader of the Fujiwara, senior advisor to the Emperor, have made this appointment.' He placed his hand on his sword.

Every hand in the hall went to a weapon. Eyes shifted to judge those sitting nearest as friend or foe. Outside, surrounding the great hall, thousands of samurai from the many fiefdoms stood to arms in ranks twenty deep – each commander with specific instructions whom to attack and whom to support in the event fighting did erupt.

Hideyoshi clutched his sword, but at their father's signal Danjuro gripped his brother's arm, immobilizing it.

'By imperial appointment,' the master of protocol's voice rose, aiming to force the lords to bow their acceptance of the Emperor's decree, 'Baron Iyeasu, now of the Fujiwara, has been designated Minister of Education.'

If the lords did not accept the appointment, the revolution had begun. Many bowed, but most watched for Lords Koin and Saga's signals.

Ever so slowly, Mung saw the old man of Mito bend his back and touch his head to the floor. Saga followed his lead, and then the others, all remaining in the obeisant position.

The master of protocol repressed a sigh of relief, and continued, 'The newly installed minister is instructed to modernize his department to keep pace with advancing civilization, while at the same time promoting national harmony and friendship with all nations. The Emperor wills this.'

'And so it shall be done,' the lords echoed, sitting back on their heels.

Few in Japan had heard of the title of baron. Mung had suggested the use of the European rank to the Emperor. The instruction to modernize was one more step in gaining acceptance from the Rujo for other changes. It set a precedent, although the crisis was far from over. Mung knew the majority vote was not in keeping with the feelings of most of the lords. And there were still Lord Crest's demands to deal with. He wished the members of the Great Council to be as bored and tired as possible before he and Iyeasu presented those demands. Mung and Iyeasu expected the Rujo would order them to renegotiate. Then they would be able to present their counterproposals to Lord Crest. The British lord's and the Rujo's acceptance of new terms would save face for east and west.

The master of protocol read out the third imperial edict, 'Baron Iyeasu and Minister of Maritime Services, Moryiama Ishikawa, represent Japan in negotiations with the foreign nations who seek compensation for the actions taken by the Lord of Choshu at Shimonoseki. At the Emperor's command, the two ministers met with the foreigners. They will now present their report to the Rujo. The Emperor wishes each lord's resolve to endeavour to promote the honour of Japan and her sovereignty. To be committed to the advancement of the welfare of the people, and to the prosperity of the empire.' He droned on in a sleep-inducing monotone, as Mung had instructed.

Finally the master of protocol recognized Baron Iyeasu. The former Count of Mito's presentation of the western demands was greeted with stony silence. Then lord after lord, from both political spectrums, voiced objection.

The debate was following Mung's predicted pattern, although Lords Koin and Saga had not yet spoken. It was midnight when they opened their fans to be recognized.

Several times Sandanj returned with the same report. 'The Great Council is still in session. They are united in rejecting the foreigners' demands.'

Udo lay on his sleeping pallet staring at the ceiling. 'If they are of one mind, why do they not vote and adjourn?'

'The Rujo is waiting for the Lords of Mito and Choshu to be heard, and they will speak last,' Sandanj said.

'How much time before we meet with the chief Yakuza?'

'An hour.'

Udo closed his eyes and contemplated his strategy for another meeting with Gin-ko. He knew in which room she slept, the number of guards, and he had her invitation. For those who follow the rules, she had said, a meeting could be arranged through Little Mother.

'Ha! Little Mother indeed. The chambermaid in the House of a Thousand Delights looked better than that old hag.'

'What did you say?' Sandanj asked.

'Nothing. Let me be.' He envisioned Gin-ko's house and planned the best way to enter without being detected. He thought of the garden and pictured her reclining on the stone bench. He forgot his scheme and kept her image fixed in his mind.

'Wake up.' Sandanj shook him. 'An urgent message from Ukiko. She requests we come immediately. There is a problem with Yoshida.'

Udo jumped up and shook himself. He handed Sandanj his derringer. 'Take this. There will not be time to return here before our meeting with the Yakuza. Hurry.'

* * *

Pale stars flecked the night sky above Tamieka Pond. Udo and Sandanj were challenged twice by Black Dragon guards before they reached the villa. Inside, a bedraggled Rhee was shovelling rice into his mouth from an upraised bowl. Ukiko handed him two cups of tea and he gulped them both down.

'What has happened to Yoshida?' Udo asked.

'He is ill,' Ukiko said.

'How serious?'

Tears filled Ukiko's eyes. 'Rhee does not know. It must be bad if they are sending him home at such a slow pace, accompanied by Kyoto's finest physician.'

'Rhee,' Udo asked, 'what did the doctor say to you?'

The Okinawan put down the empty rice bowl. 'He would not speak about the boy with me or anyone else. Yoshida is kept isolated. I saw him once. He is thin and nervous, but otherwise looks well.'

'Why the isolation?'

'I have no idea. We found them at an inn on the trunk road. Jiroo is accompanying them back. They will arrive in two or three days.'

'You must notify Mung,' Ukiko said. 'He will know what to do.'

'Of course.' Udo patted her shoulder. 'I will do that,' he said, knowing he would not interrupt Mung in the Great Council. 'Do not worry.' He led the Okinawan onto the porch and down the moss-covered steps to the edge of the pond. 'Tell me all you know.'

Rhee looked around to be certain he would not be overheard. He spoke softly. 'Yoshida is two people. At times himself, at other times a great warrior.'

'What name did the doctor call this illness?'

'He would not speak with me. My information comes from a Black Dragon who accompanied them from Kyoto as a bearer. He saw Yoshida sit rigid as a board in the kago for six hours without moving. He helped carry the boy to bed in the same position. He told me of another time when Yoshida became violent and had to be restrained.'

'Do you think anything can be done immediately to help?'

'Nothing except to inform Mung.'

Udo nodded. 'You rest here tonight. When you wake, come to my house. Say nothing of Yoshida's illness to anyone. Caution Ukiko. It is for the boy's safety. I leave now for a meeting in the Ginza.'

In the deserted commercial area, Udo and Sandanj stood in the shadowy doorway of the bonsai shop listening to the faint call of a town crier. 'Saru. Saru. Nine p.m. It is the hour of the ape.' They waited to be taken to a rendezvous with the Yakuza.

'Do not turn around!' The voice came from behind Udo. Out of the corner of his eye, he saw the shop door open. A hand reached out and rested on his shoulder. 'The one called Sandanj remains where he is until you return,' the voice said.

'When will that be?' Udo asked.

'No questions. Now back up.'

As Udo retreated into the darkness of the bonsai shop, he was passed by a man of similar height, build and dress. The man took his place next to Sandanj, and pressed the point of a short sword into Sandanj's back.

An aroma of evergreen and damp moss permeated the shop. 'If you have weapons, give them to me,' the voice from behind said.

Udo handed over his Colt and the Arkansas toothpick.

'Remove your clothing.'

He stripped to his hakka shorts.

'Everything.'

Naked, Udo was led in total darkness up a flight of steps. A lantern was uncovered in front of his face and he jerked back, but was pushed from behind through a doorway, still

155

blinded by the light. The lantern was removed and he was directed to a chair.

Slowly Udo's eyes adapted to a dimly lit attic room. He was seated at the end of a long table. On each side were five elderly men, all naked except for the tattoos covering their bodies. With painted arms crossed over multi-coloured chests, they stared at him with unmoving black eyes.

Seated on a raised platform at the opposite end of the long table was a man whose intricately tattooed body was visible, but his face remained perfectly shadowed by the single lantern hanging from the low, peaked ceiling. Udo remembered Kang Shu's words. 'The lengths to which people go to impress you are an indication of your worth to them.' His confidence was bolstered by the meticulous orchestration.

The voice behind him asked, 'Udo Ishikawa, do you represent the Black Dragon Society?'

'Yes.'

'Your father, whom you call Mung, named Moriyama Ishikawa, is he the Black Dragon?'

Udo remained silent.

The voice from behind spoke in a strange language. Then it said, 'We Yakuza also have oaths of honour. We shall respect yours.' A finger above Udo's shoulder pointed to the far end of the table. 'Gaze upon Wada Zenshichi, our honourable leader. He is descended from Wada Zenshichi of samurai rank, who was cast out from society by Shogun Tokugawa Hidetada in the year 1616. The Zenshichi family has led Japan's Yakuza for 255 years.'

Udo bowed to the leader of the tattooed men. 'Although I sit naked before you with no colour to cover my body, I wear the mantle of a Black Dragon. Our society is not as ancient as the Yakuza, but we have the honour of serving the Emperor. His imperial majesty is displeased with the violent actions of the tattooed men. They have attacked his representatives on two occasions. If imperial displeasure does not concern the Yakuza, there is no reason to continue this meeting.'

'If we did not honour the Emperor, you would not be here,' Wada Zenshichi said, his voice steeped in authority. 'Neither would Mung be alive. The warning of the assassination attempt on the river in Kagoshima came from me.'

'Are you saying the Golden Lizard is not Yakuza?'

'Look around you. Seated at this table are the most powerful Yakuza in the empire. We have voted to cast the lizard-man out. He has violated the rules of our organization. His attacks on Mung and Lord Maeda in Tokyo are a direct challenge to my authority.'

'The Black Dragon wants the Golden Lizard dead,' Udo said. 'Do you know of Kang Shu in Canton?'

Wada Zenshichi spoke to his tattooed men in their secret language, then said, 'I am told Kang Shu is the most powerful tong chief in southern China.'

'Kang Shu is indebted to the Black Dragon,' Udo said. 'The obligation can be beneficial to you in return for your cooperation in eliminating the Golden Lizard.'

'How can a Chinese tong chief help a Japanese Yakuza?'

'By selling your illegal gold to the newly created Shansi banks in northwest China at four times the artificially low rate maintained by the foreigners in Japan.'

'It is a long way from Tokyo to Canton, and further yet to northern China. A great distance to trust one's gold on the word of a Chinese.'

'In my clothing, there are three pouches of gold.'

Wada Zenshichi nodded. The gold was brought and placed on the table before Udo. He opened the pouches and tipped them over, one after the other, as he had done before Kang Shu. In the dim lantern-light, the pools of golden flakes shimmered.

'You have three choices,' Udo said. 'You can take this gold and kill me, which would mean war between our societies. You can take the gold, promise cooperation, and do nothing. In that case there would be distrust. Or you can send this gold to Kang Shu, establish the first trading link with China, and cooperate with the Black Dragon Society.'

'There is a fourth choice,' Wada Zenshichi said. 'I can take the gold and make no promises. That way my word would not be involved.'

'Then I would have to hunt you down and kill you,' Udo said. 'The future of Japan depends on the reforms being contemplated by the Emperor.'

The chief Yakuza leaned forward so his face was visible in the lamplight. Udo recognized the man who had spoken with Gin-ko at the Kabuki theatre. He understood that, having seen the Yakuza's face, the choice now would be his death or cooperation.

'The Black Dragon would aid my Yakuza in illegal enterprises?' Wada Zenshichi asked.

'He would not interfere if your people are nonviolent, do not oppose the Emperor, and pass along relevant information to support the new policy of modernization.'

'The Yakuza have never advocated violence. Our loyalty has always been to the Emperor. But what benefit can modernization have for us?'

'The Minister of Maritime Services issues sailing and trading permits. You can be first in the China trade. The elimination of the Golden Lizard will signal your cooperation.'

Chapter 16

The leaders of Japan tensed to hear the only two noblemen who had not spoken in the Hall of a Hundred Mats – Lords Koin and Saga.

'I have over-planned,' Mung whispered to Iyeasu. 'War appears inevitable. I have antagonized the entire Rujo, so much they will be against anything we propose now or later.'

'The lord of the three houses of Mito will address the assembly,' announced the master of protocol.

Fujita Koin, eldest member of the council, bowed. He allowed time for the hushed silence to heighten the tension in the already volatile atmosphere. Throughout the low-ceilinged hall anxiety and body heat added to the highly charged environment. The heavy breathing of Japan's warrior chiefs was like the sighing of a prehistoric beast. They leaned forward in anticipation.

Instead of addressing Mung and Iyeasu on the dais, Fujita Koin turned towards Saga. 'Will the Lord of Choshu allow me to speak for him?'

'Yes,' the little man answered. He smiled at Mung, his front teeth protruding over his lower lip.

Mung's head swivelled from Iyeasu to Hotta. The Fujiwara leader shrugged. He had no idea why Saga had relinquished his right to speak when all Tokyo waited to hear him.

The old man of Mito turned to the dais. Mung suddenly felt it was he who had been manipulated.

Fujita Koin wet his soft lips and said, 'My worthy brother, Lord Saga, and I have listened to our honourable colleagues in this most illustrious council. Each has expressed most eloquently those reasons to reject the barbarian's demands. I move to adopt a resolution adjourning this meeting, to allow these messengers,' he indicated Mung and Iyeasu, 'to inform the invaders of our decision.'

The Lords of Mito and Choshu snapped open their fans. Others did the same. The resentment, bitterness and anger built up during hours of debate swept the hall. All fans were open. With such speed was the vote taken that Mung realized it had been planned. Lord Crest's demands were rejected, the meeting over.

'Unanimous,' the master of protocol announced. 'This meeting is adjourned.'

Mung was confused. Why, if the vote had gone according to his plan, did he feel tricked? He and Iyeasu watched Saga and Fujita Koin leave the hall surrounded by supporters. 'Sonno joi! Sonno joi!' they chanted.

'To the Yoshiwara to celebrate,' the giant Danjuro roared. 'We shall wake the ladies of the Willow World and exercise their bottoms!'

'To the Yoshiwara,' the lords chanted, 'to the Yoshiwara!'

No one in the hall noticed Hideyoshi exit through a side door. Only Udo and Sandanj, waiting outside, saw him meet two hooded men in the shadow of the building, and leave with them.

'Sandanj,' Udo ordered, 'follow those three. Report back to me at Mung's villa.' He fell in step with Mung and Iyeasu, accompanied by a contingent of Fujiwara guards.

'Your father adjourned the meeting without Saga rallying the anti-foreign element into a call for war,' Mung said to Iyeasu. 'Why?'

'They did not have to. It is the tactics of Musashi. We were stunned into inaction and lost the chance to bring charges against Saga for agreeing to the three million pound indemnity. He walked out a hero.'

Mung remained silent for some moments. Then he said,

'Let them celebrate in the Yoshiwara. We have what we need for now. Tomorrow we meet the Englishman and present our counter-proposals.'

'I see no flaws in our plan,' Iyeasu said. 'Although my father is a master of strategy and Saga is unpredictable, as we have just seen.'

They reached the edge of Tamieka Pond. Mung shrugged. 'We have done our best.'

'Yes, and now I leave you to head for the Yoshiwara.'

'To celebrate with Saga?' Mung laughed.

'To find rooms. Being disowned presents its own problems.'

Mung looked into Iyeasu's sad eyes and said, 'My house is yours. Please honour my family with your presence.'

'No, thank you. Stripping and meditating is only one of my odd habits. I am an unconventional fellow.'

'My wife says that in some ways you and I are alike.'

'That is pleasant to hear. Most women consider me a waddling joke.'

Mung bowed. 'I am honoured to laugh with you, never at you. There are few men who have sacrificed so much of themselves. I trust we can call each other friend.'

'Let us begin now, Friend,' Iyeasu said in English, extending his hand western fashion. The two shook hands, then stepped back and bowed.

Iyeasu went off with the Fujiwara samurai, passing within ten feet of one of the hooded men who had met Hideyoshi. As soon as they were out of sight, the Golden Lizard stepped into the waning moonlight and pushed the cowl off his tattooed head. His golden scales shimmered in the faint light. He raised his hand and fifty armed men stood up from their hiding places amidst the trees.

At sight of the contingent of twenty armed Black Dragons coming from the villa to meet Mung and Udo, the Golden Lizard lowered his hand. He and his men melted back into the woods. He frowned as he watched Udo

161

speaking excitedly to Mung. The lizard-man gave whispered instructions to his aide for an attack on Mung's villa.

'I met the chief Yakuza of all Japan,' Udo said. 'He is ready to cooperate against the Golden Lizard. It was Wada Zenshichi's warning that prepared you for the attack on the river.'

'I do not care to deal with criminals,' Mung said, 'but I see no alternative.' He looked up at the star-studded sky. 'It could be worse. We have two hours until daylight and I need sleep before meeting again with Lord Crest.'

Udo reached out and held Mung's arm. 'I bring other news which is not so pleasant.'

'My son?'

Udo nodded. 'Yoshida is being escorted to Tokyo by Kyoto's leading physician. He would not reveal the nature of the illness. Rhee's description of Yoshida's condition sheds no light on the matter.'

'Where is Rhee?'

Udo pointed to the villa and Mung picked up his stride. He moved so quickly past the Black Dragon guards, they had to make a quick about-turn and run to catch up.

'Rhee!' Mung shouted from the porch.

Ukiko met him at the door and bowed. 'I am pleased to see you, my husband. Rhee sleeps. Have you received more information about our son?'

Rhee entered the room rubbing sleep from his eyes. 'Sire,' he said, 'Yoshida appears thin and strained but otherwise healthy. The physician would say nothing.'

There was a commotion on the porch. 'It is I, Sandanj!' a voice called out. The short muscular man struggled with two guards.

'Let him go,' Udo ordered.

Sandanj broke free and stumbled into the room. 'This house is to be attacked! I followed Hideyoshi and his hooded friends to the Yasukune shrine. The count was welcomed by the anti-foreign fire-eaters gathered there. I trailed his companions to the woods on the other side of Tamieka Pond. There were Yakuza waiting for them.'

'How can you be certain it is the tattooed men?' Udo asked.

Sandanj bowed to Ukiko. 'If the lady of the house would kindly bring tea?'

Mung nodded and Ukiko left the room. Sandanj held out his hand, palm up.

'What is that you are holding?' Udo asked.

'A tattooed ear. I took it from a lookout in the woods. The Yakuza almost attacked you two after Iyeasu left. I had to circle around back of the house to get here.'

'How many of them are there?' Mung asked.

'I saw twenty.'

'We have thirty Black Dragons here,' Mung said. 'The Yakuza want me.' He pulled his Colt and checked the cylinders. 'Udo, do you have your revolver?'

'Yes.'

'And I have this derringer,' Sandanj said.

'The Yakuza will find me prepared this time,' Mung growled. 'I can give them six lead presents for a welcoming gift. Sandanj, you take ten Black Dragons and lead Ukiko out of here the same way you came. The Yakuza will see you go and think we are weakened and unprepared.'

Standing in the doorway, Ukiko said, 'I will remain.'

Mung bowed to his wife. 'This time I must insist you do as I say.' He motioned to Sandanj and the guards on the porch. 'Take my wife to the imperial palace and send back help as soon as possible.'

Ukiko was swept from the house, and Mung ordered the lights extinguished. It was the signal for the remaining twenty Black Dragons outside to divide into two groups. They crept into position at both sides of the house. Mung, Udo and Rhee, by the faint reflection of the moon in the pond, watched through the shutters.

* * *

163

The Golden Lizard raised his right hand and thirty men moved around the pond to attack that side of the house. He pointed with his left hand and two groups of ten Yakuza moved down towards the edge of the pond. The first ten, stripped and carrying long knives, waded into the shallow water.

'I see them,' Rhee whispered. 'Some are coming through the woods on our left. A few have entered the water.'

'There are many more than twenty,' Udo said.

'We will attack the ten coming from the water in front of us,' Mung ordered. 'With our guns we can blast our way through. Tell our men to follow us. Everyone is to make for the imperial palace.'

They watched the Yakuza wade through the shallow pond towards them. Mung put three extra bullets in each side of his mouth. Udo held an extra six in his left hand.

Rhee stretched the chain between two flailing sticks. 'They are bellied down in the water and will probably creep up the steps,' he said. 'We will not be able to see them until they reach the porch.'

'It will make our surprise more effective,' Mung whispered. 'When we charge out of here, go through the paper walls. Get ready.'

The three crouched, their weapons raised, no longer able to see the swimmers. Then they heard dripping water. The tattooed men were crawling up the steps.

'EEEEeeeIIIIIIIiiiiiiiYYYYyyyaaaaaaa!' The savage war cry came from thirty Yakuza charging the left side of the house. Two Black Dragon samurai were driven backward through the paper walls into the room. Mung spun around and saw three Yakuza jump through the openings. They stabbed the two samurai to death.

Rhee leapt up with lightning speed and charged the three Yakuza. He killed the nearest with a snap-punch between the eyes before the tattooed man could withdraw his sword from the body of the dead Black Dragon samurai. The

Okinawan crushed the skull of the second attacker with his flailing stick, and whipped the sword from the third man's hand with the chain as he delivered a front kick to his stomach. More Yakuza burst into the room and Rhee jumped to face them.

'We are overrun,' Udo shouted.

'The porch,' Mung shouted.

Ten wet, painted bodies came screaming up the steps brandishing long steel knives. Mung and Udo fired. Two Yakuza fell. Both pistols roared again. 'I will hold them. Get away,' Rhee shouted. His flailing stick sang a bloody tune, keeping back the Yakuza fighting their way into the room. Mung aimed and killed two more tattooed men trying to circle Rhee. Then, from the other side of the house, ten Black Dragons charged through the walls and joined the Okinawan.

Udo killed two attackers on the porch. He dropped the bullets in his left hand and pulled Mung through the wall, the two of them firing, killing three more Yakuza, opening the way. They leapt from the porch and cleared the stone steps, landing on their knees in the water. Three Yakuza dived after them. Mung turned in time to block a knife-thrust with his left arm. He pushed the muzzle of the Colt against the tattooed head and fired.

Two painted bodies pressed Udo underwater. He pushed his pistol up against the stomach of one attacker and pulled the trigger, but the gun was empty. His head broke the water and a long Yakuza knife slashed his shoulder. Mung fired and killed the attacker. The second Yakuza was raising his knife to kill the wounded Udo, and Mung was out of bullets. He dived over the water and brought the steel barrel of the Colt across the shaven skull. The tattooed man dropped like a stone.

Mung reached down and helped Udo up. He was spitting water and dripping blood from a wide gash in his shoulder. 'I am out of bullets,' he gasped.

Mung tucked the pistol under his left arm. He spat three bullets into the palm of his right hand and gave them to Udo. He spat out two more and loaded his own weapon. They backed across the pond, watching helplessly as the Yakuza slaughtered the remaining Black Dragons.

Only Rhee remained alive and the tattooed men turned their attention to him, ringing the Okinawan chief. He was a blur of motion with his flailing sticks, flying kicks and punches. Then suddenly he went down. Like a pack of dogs, the Yakuza were on him.

'You cannot help him,' Udo shouted to Mung, tugging at him to cross the pond. Udo was weak. Mung had to support him.

They were waist deep in the middle of the pond when Mung saw the Golden Lizard, arms folded across his muscular chest, standing on the far shore. Ten more Yakuza came out from the trees behind him and entered the water. Mung looked back at the house. The battle there was over. Twenty Yakuza, some with torches, all with bared blades, moved down the stone steps and into the water.

'I am going to try to kill the lizard-man with a long shot,' Mung said. 'Udo, can you stand?'

Udo nodded, and Mung released his grip. 'Pass me your gun if I miss.' He raised the Colt, aiming over the heads of the oncoming Yakuza. He steadied his right hand with the stump of his left arm, and fired. A branch snapped off a tree above the lizard-man's head. Mung expected the Yakuza leader to crouch or run, but he did neither. He spread his arms wide, presenting the best possible target, daring Mung to shoot again.

'I will kill that brass balls son of a bitch,' Mung growled. He looked down the barrel, centred the yellow body in his gun sight, and squeezed the trigger. The gun bucked in his hand. The lizard-man spun and fell face down on the ground.

'You got him!' Udo shouted.

The lines of Yakuza wading out from both shores stopped. Two men splashed back to their leader. He struggled to his knees and they helped him stand. Blood flowed from a shoulder wound.

A high piercing whistle from behind the villa cut the night. Other whistles to the left and right joined the first. Their shrieking sounds hurt the ears. The whistles stopped and torchbearers rounded the building. A deep-throated cry erupted, 'Yaaaaaaa-kuuuuuuzzzz-aaaaaa!' A hundred armed men rushed to the water's edge.

An imposing figure stepped forward and took a place at the top of the stone steps. He threw off his kimono, revealing an intricate design of mystical tattooed beasts on his body. 'I am Wada Zenshichi, chief Yakuza of all Japan!'

Sandanj appeared at the Yakuza's side and pointed to Mung. 'And that is a minister of the government of Japan,' Sandanj said. 'A personal advisor to the Emperor.' He stalked down the steps and into the water, straight for the line of the Golden Lizard's men. They stepped back, allowing Sandanj through. He and Mung helped Udo out of the pool.

Wada Zenshichi pointed at the tattooed men still in the water. 'Kill them!'

The chief Yakuza's men charged into the pond, quickly overwhelming the Golden Lizard's followers. The water became red with blood and choked with bodies. The lizard-man had disappeared. Only a pool of blood remained at the place he had been.

Wada Zenshichi and Mung bowed to each other, but neither man spoke. Mung nodded. He owed a great debt to the leader of the tattooed men, and Wada Zenshichi's face told Mung he knew he had a claim of honour on one of the most powerful men in the empire – the Black Dragon.

Chapter 17

Light from the rising sun illuminated the destruction in and around the villa. Udo was propped against a wall, his wound bandaged. He seemed to be resting comfortably. Mung searched for Rhee's body. He found it under three dead Yakuza.

Another man has given his life for me, Mung thought sadly. He gazed at the body and suddenly his heart jumped. 'Blood is pumping from his leg!' he shouted. 'Rhee is alive! Sandanj, get more material for bandages.'

Sandanj tore clean towels into strips. 'He has so many wounds I do not know where to begin.'

'We must stop the blood from leaking out of him. He cannot have much left.' They worked over the unconscious Okinawan chief.

'Did Ukiko reach the palace?' Mung asked.

'When we left here I realized there were more Yakuza moving in on the house than I had estimated. I sent her ahead with the escort and raced to the bonsai shop for help. I assumed the Fujiwara were too busy enforcing the curfew with Lord Maeda's troops. The imperial guard would not leave the Emperor's side under the foreigners' threat to attack.'

'You reasoned and acted well,' Mung said.

'Someone comes.' Sandanj pointed through the torn walls. 'It is Jiroo.'

Mung went to meet his senior aide.

Jiroo looked at the carnage surrounding them. 'In the name of Buddha and all the spirits, what happened here?'

'Time for that later,' Mung said. 'How is Yoshida?'

'Your son appears better today. The physician maintains the boy is ill but will not discuss it.'

'Where are they?'

'Resting in a honjin nearby. We arrived last night. There were bands of trouble-making ronin and samurai roaming the streets. I came here at first light.'

'Bring the physician as quickly as possible. Rhee has lost a great deal of blood, and Udo is wounded.'

'I have closed the wound in the young samurai's shoulder,' the physician said. 'He will recover soon.'

'And Rhee?' Mung asked.

'The Okinawan lives, although how I do not know. He has eighteen cut and stab wounds, a number deep and serious. I gave him a strength restoring tea containing a sedative. If he wakes in a day or two, that will be the best sign you can hope for.'

Mung looked at the body swathed in bandages. It resembled a picture he had seen of an Egyptian mummy. 'Tell me about my son, Yoshida.'

The elderly physician removed his spectacles. He cleaned them on his obi and blinked at Mung. 'The boy is two people, himself and another.'

'I do not understand.'

'Your son's body has become the residing place of a second soul. Two personalities within the one body break the harmony of nature. They weaken the physical and spiritual balance of yin and yang.'

'How do you know this?'

'I have spoken to Yoshida and Musashi.'

'Musashi!' Mung went cold.

'More and more the ancient Sword Saint dominates your son's personality. Did you or your wife notice Yoshida behaving strangely before he left for Kyoto?'

The vision of Yoshida shouting Musashi's name and

killing the Yakuza on the river with the wooden clapper, flashed through Mung's mind. He could not bring himself to speak of it. 'What else can you tell me?' he asked the physician.

'From the moment your son arrived at the school in Kyoto, his teachers knew something was wrong. He had difficulty reading, his eyes were constantly moving, and he isolated himself as much as possible.'

'How is it his teachers in Kagoshima did not observe this behaviour?' Mung asked.

'I am certain they must have. But you are a high official and your wife was headmistress of the school. We Japanese are loath to upset a superior. I must tell you there are other specific signs. His pulse is sunken and soggy. The Mu pressure point near the heart is extremely weak. His kidneys and the tips of the twelfth ribs are tender. All are classic symptoms.'

Mung tightened his stomach muscles to allay the weakness he felt there. 'Has your diagnosis been confirmed?'

'Yes.'

'There is no room for doubt?'

'None.'

Mung walked onto the porch. He looked out at the blood-red pond, the floating bodies, and those strewn around the villa. 'How will their fathers and mothers feel?' he asked aloud.

The physician came out onto the porch. 'I cannot explain man's cruelty or the indifference of the gods. I only repair as much of the damage as possible.'

'Can you repair the damage in my son's mind?'

There was no response.

'What is the course of treatment?' Mung asked.

'Your son's x-hen force is disturbed. It exhausts the jing, which is the vital flow of energy located in the kidneys.

Did Yoshida ever have a period of illness when he ran a high temperature for longer than three days?'

'Yes, when he was thirteen. We thought he would die. The fever lasted a week.'

'That must be when his kidneys were infected by the Cold Wind. I must try to expel it with a combination of herb teas, breathing exercises, and the ministering of a faith healer. I have arranged a place for Yoshida to stay during the treatment.'

Mung looked startled. 'Yoshida should remain with his parents who love him. He can be treated at our home.'

The physician sighed. He put on his spectacles and looked carefully at Mung, judging that the man in front of him could be told the entire truth. 'The prognosis for such an illness is not good. If the treatments are ineffective, a gradual weakness could lead to death. Or there could be madness, a complete possession by the second soul. Your son is extremely ill. With your permission, I would like to remain here and treat him. He and I are on good terms when he is Yoshida. I will apply my skill as an acupuncturist and, in addition, try a new method we developed in Kyoto to strengthen the original soul. It entails daily meditation in which I guide the patient to confront his acquired soul, and then have him write a diary of each encounter.'

'How successful have you been with this new treatment?'

The physician hesitated, then said, 'There is hope.'

Mung walked the length of the porch a number of times before he spoke again. 'I want my wife to be with me when we see our son. I shall prepare her. But the meeting should be under the best possible conditions.'

'I will take him to the rest home today. You can see him there.'

'I cannot come to see Yoshida just yet. I am in the midst of important negotiations. There are just three hours before my meeting with the foreigners, and I must get some sleep before then. Can you prescribe a stimulant for when I awake?'

The physician rummaged in his wicker case, then handed Mung a cachet. 'Make tea with this. I shall take the Okinawan with me for treatment. You cannot sleep in this place.'

'I will take Udo home and sleep at his house,' Mung said. He led the physician to the end of the porch, away from the others. Lowering his voice, Mung said, 'During the battle I was holding bullets in my mouth and I swallowed one.'

'What is a bullet?'

Mung showed the physician a bullet and described its makeup.

'It really explodes?' the physician said.

Mung picked up his pistol. He reloaded and fired, and the physician jumped at the noise. 'Everyone in Kyoto is talking about these foreign inventions,' he said, shaking his head. 'There are too many new things to learn.'

'Do you think it will kill me?' Mung asked. 'If so, I must make preparations.'

The physician looked around at the dead bodies stiffening from rigor mortis. 'If this is part of your life, you should always be prepared for death. I do not know how your stomach acid will act on the bullet casing. My feeling is it will not eat through the metal before you expel it. If it did explode in your stomach . . . Well that would be it.' He spread his hands. 'If it explodes on re-exposure to the air, you would probably lose part of your rectum. Let us hope you pass this bullet without incident. If so, I would like to examine it and write on the subject.' He pointed to three dead bodies on the porch with bullet wounds. 'I fear we physicians will be dealing with many more cases involving bullets.'

Chapter 18

Sandanj crouched over the hibachi in Udo's house, brewing the stimulant while Mung dressed. 'I informed your wife of your safety,' he told Mung. 'She asked when it will be possible to see Yoshida.'

'What did you tell her?'

'As you instructed. After your meeting with the foreigners and your report to the Emperor, you and she will see him together. She prays for your success.' Sandanj nodded at the adjoining room. 'Is Udo still asleep?'

'Yes.' Mung was struggling to make his limbs work. 'I wish I was too. I am so tired, my bones hurt. Did you report to Lord Hotta and Baron Iyeasu?'

Sandanj handed Mung the tea. 'Baron Iyeasu will meet you on the governor's barge that takes you to the British warship.'

Mung drank the tea in one gulp and screwed up his face. 'I hope this stimulant works better than it tastes.' He gritted his teeth.

'Jiroo should come soon,' Sandanj said. 'He has been reassigning our Black Dragons and arranging a Fujiwara escort for you to the port.'

'Twenty Black Dragons died last night,' Mung said. 'Membership in our society is becoming fatal.'

'To die for the Emperor is the highest honour a man can aspire to.'

Mung looked searchingly at the twenty-five-year-old Sandanj, wondering if he gave any thought to those he killed. Then Mung recalled killing for the first time in the California gold fields, and again outside Kagoshima. In the battle of the Hakusar Valley I ordered my riflemen to fire into the massed ranks of the shogun's samurai, he thought. Hundreds were killed. I never thought of their parents, wives or children. Is it my age or Yoshida's illness that is influencing my values?

'Sire,' Sandanj said, 'Jiroo comes with the escort.'

Mung's heart was beginning to beat more quickly. His face warmed with a rush of blood as the tea took effect. 'You remain with Udo,' he told Sandanj.

'Sire.' Jiroo bowed. 'You are looking far more fit than I expected after last night's ordeal.'

'To the port,' Mung said. 'There is no time to waste.' He stepped out briskly.

Jiroo moved to catch up with Mung. The guards fell in around them. 'Sire,' Jiroo said, 'those Black Dragons who returned from abroad have begun to arrive in Tokyo.'

'Good. Use them to replace the men we lost.'

'Unless you allow them to discard their western dress, their efforts will be in vain. They have been chased and threatened by samurai and ronin out looking for foreigners to punish.'

'They have permission to wear traditional dress,' Mung said. He felt strong as he strode towards the port, his eyes bright with the stimulant. 'But when this anti-foreign reaction has passed, they are to carry out my orders to influence the people of Tokyo towards western things.'

Mung and Iyeasu sat alone in the bow of the governor's barge. Thirty oarsmen rowed the large craft to the HMS *Nemesis*.

'I went to see what remains of your house,' Iyeasu said. 'They were still fishing bodies from the pond. The imperial groundskeeper has been ordered to restore the place.'

'I will never live there again,' Mung said. 'Tamieka Pond will always be blood-red when I look at it.'

'How you three survived is a wonder.'

'Rhee may not survive, but it was Sandanj who saved us. He saw Hideyoshi meet the Golden Lizard, and followed them. He warned us in time before the attack.'

'Sandanj did not report that to Lord Hotta or to me.'

'He was following my orders. I had to be certain of your innocence.'

'Are you now?'

'You would be dead if I were not.'

'And my brother?'

'I plan to bargain for his life with your father. No one will know of Hideyoshi's involvement if your father supports our proposals in the Rujo.'

Iyeasu looked up at the sky. 'I spent most of last night watching the moon and thinking.' His round face was wistful. 'The situation of being disowned is difficult to become accustomed to.' He looked square into Mung's eyes. 'Be careful. If you threaten Mito, my father will destroy you.'

'I am depending on his desire to keep your family from being shamed, and his second son alive. If Sandanj testifies, it is the end of Hideyoshi.'

The barge nudged the *Nemesis* and the British bosun piped the two ministers aboard. Mung and Iyeasu were received in the stateroom.

'I have requested that you alone hear our counterproposal,' Mung said to Lord Crest. 'You are the leader of this expedition. Where you go, the others will follow.'

'Sir,' the Englishman said, 'I do not intend to bargain. What is the decision of your government?'

'Rejection of your demands,' Mung said.

'Then it is war.'

'Only if you fire the first shot,' Iyeasu said. 'You must accept modification of your original requests. The art of

175

statecraft is to satisfy the needs of both sides. I suggest you listen to Mung.'

Edward Crest moved behind his large gold inlaid mahogany desk. He fingered the writing quills laid out before him. 'Mr Mung, I had hoped to use these to sign a treaty. Please do not waste my time trying to haggle.'

Mung had played high stakes poker and taken chances before, but never with the fate of his country. Yet he felt confident. Whether it was the stimulant or his perception of the situation, he had decided to press on. 'If you truly desire to be prime minister of England, the road to that position begins here in Japan.'

'You-little-yellow-turd!' Edward Crest spat out the words between clenched teeth. He turned red from his gold-braided collar to the roots of his steel-grey hair. 'How dare you speak to me in such a manner! I could have you clapped in irons and buried in the bilge of this ship!'

Iyeasu looked over at Mung. His face was as flushed as the Englishman's. A muscle twitched in Mung's right foot, betraying his anxiety, but he glared back at Edward Crest.

'Please, Lord Crest,' Iyeasu said, 'sit down and hear what Mung has to say.'

The big man stepped back from his desk. 'I choose to stand.' He watched Mung.

'Last night seventy men died because of your presence,' Mung said. 'The attack was on me in my home because I met with you, the barbarian.'

Lord Crest flushed a deeper crimson. His eyes glared and he clenched his fists. 'Barbarians, you call us!'

'I am trying to shock you into understanding the situation,' Mung said. 'You spoke of burying me in chains as if I represent some local island tribe. Japan may be technically backward, but our society is as sophisticated as any in the West. If you cannot grasp this, it is impossible for you to consider the proposals I have to make.'

'And if we barbarians choose to see Japan as one large tribe,' Edward Crest taunted, 'then what?'

'You will have to kill forty million of my people. And while you are kept busy accomplishing that, someone else will become prime minister in your place.'

'Duty comes before political aspirations.'

'What if there were another solution?' Mung asked.

Edward Crest clasped his hands behind his back and chewed his upper lip. He looked out from under bushy eyebrows and said, 'Courtesy and the responsibility of my position require me to hear you out, Mr Mung.'

'I want to tell you what will happen if we cannot agree on modifying your demands,' Mung said. 'The moment you bombard Tokyo, I and Baron Iyeasu will be relieved of duty. The city will be evacuated and the war begun. It is a war Japan cannot win, but the baron and I will not live to see the destruction.'

'We will be expected to kill ourselves,' Iyeasu said. 'That is a samurai's duty when he is disgraced by failure. The Emperor has already prepared orders for all Japan to fight you until death if we fail in this mission. In ten days there would be a quarter of a million fighting men in Tokyo. Half a million in twenty days, and one million warriors within a month.'

'They will have to swim to reach us,' Edward Crest said.

'Mung has already stated that the most optimistic of our generals knows we cannot defeat you. But neither can you come ashore in Tokyo.'

'Japan accepts the responsibility for Lord Saga's actions at Shimonoseki,' Mung said.

The Englishman stepped back to his desk. 'What of the three million sterling indemnity?'

'To be paid,' Mung said. 'But not in cash, and not via Europeans levying our taxes or dispensing our justice.'

'How then?'

Mung pressed his foot to the floor to stop its jumping. 'Your lordship, Japan does not have three million sterling, but we do wish to modernize. Britain has already recognized this by agreeing to help us build the Yokohama shipyard.'

'That was a political decision by the British Foreign Office, which will cost my country dearly.'

'Britain will earn back ten times as much in as many years on commissions,' Mung said. 'In addition, your people will control the docks and shipworks for at least two decades until we Japanese learn to operate the facilities. Your country can achieve peacefully what you demand by force. Use the Yokohama shipyard as an example.'

'What is your proposal, Mr Mung?'

'To offer Britain and her allies many more financially lucrative projects.'

'Where will Japan get the funds?'

'Some we shall borrow,' Iyeasu said. 'Of course, as a debtor nation we would be under the influence of those from whom we borrow. I have already received favourable reactions from the consuls of France, Russia and Holland.'

'It seems their foreign offices, like ours, are out of touch with their military,' Edward Crest huffed. 'I am no banker but I know they always want their investments protected by guns and cold steel. Again I ask where will the money come from to modernize your country?'

'For two and a half centuries the merchants of Japan have been a despised class,' Mung said. 'However over the years the wealth of our country has slowly but steadily been flowing into their hands. Their recent elevation to the status of peasant was the first step in putting that wealth back into circulation. They are being given an opportunity to invest in industrializing their nation.'

'To change generations of custom and tradition will take

longer than our European bankers will wait,' Lord Crest said.

'Not so,' Iycasu said. 'The Emperor is prepared to order specific merchant families to invest in certain international projects.'

'They would do that without governmental guarantees?' Edward Crest asked.

'With pride,' Iyeasu answered. 'They were hardly recognized as human beings until Mung helped change the law. The honour of serving the Emperor is as great as a Japanese can conceive. For a merchant, probably beyond belief.'

'Tell me more of these long-term projects you propose,' Edward Crest said, sitting back in his chair. He waved for Mung and Iyeasu to be seated.

Mung's foot had stopped twitching. 'Britain will be the model and supplier for the Japanese merchant fleet and navy,' he said. 'The victor of the coming Franco-Prussian war will train and equip our army. The French are interested in constructing an ironworks at Yokosuka to support the British shipyard in Yokohama. The Germans and Dutch will be asked to set up universities and technical colleges. The Americans to establish agricultural colleges and elementary schools.'

'How can my allies benefit by educating your people?'

'By participating in the building of 50,000 elementary schools. The Emperor will order it.'

'Where will that money and the teachers come from?' Edward Crest asked his questions in unabashed amazement, for he was being influenced by what he was hearing.

'The local councils in each village and city will be responsible,' Iyeasu said. 'People may starve, but the Emperor's wishes will be carried out. The teachers will be trained by European instructors whose governments will be compensated for this service.'

Edward Crest steepled his fingers and leaned forward

179

over his desk. 'If the Emperor is so powerful, why doesn't he order the anti-foreign factions to cease their opposition to your plans of modernization?'

'When it comes to ordering the aristocratic class, it is not simple,' Iyeasu said. 'The kings of England have had similar problems through the ages. There are as many legal fictions for circumventing the code of Bushido as there were to avoid the medieval knights' code of chivalry.'

'Sir,' Mung said, 'Europeans will be asked to help us build roads, rail lines and bridges. Many of our lords remember their first train ride with Commodore Perry, and the other demonstrations he gave. They want a telegraph service and steel mills for Japan. Our people must learn the efficient use of water power, and steam power for engines. Lord Crest, Europe will control us because of our needs, not yours.'

The Englishman sat upright and put his hands flat on the desk. In a subdued voice he said, 'You, Mr Mung, are trying to bring the ship of Japanese state around on a 180 degree turn with all your sails rigged. You may very well capsize. If you manage to keep afloat, the new course you have plotted will take your people into unfamiliar waters. Your ship of state could founder.'

'Japan will sink into historical oblivion if we do not bring her around,' Mung said. 'Reassure your bankers these islands will never disappear, and any debt assumed by the government of Japan will be repaid. It would dishonour our ancestors if we reneged on a debt.'

'I must still ask how you intend to pay the indemnity.'

'Each project undertaken by a foreign government will be allocated certain profits over and above the usual margin. This amount will be applied against the outstanding debt of three million sterling.'

'At three per cent interest per annum,' Edward Crest said.

'I beg your pardon, your lordship,' Iyeasu said, 'but von Bismarck of Prussia recently negotiated a ten million sterling loan from England at one and a half per cent.'

'That is quite true. Since the rampagings of Napoleon Bonaparte, England will always pay the Prussians or anyone else to keep the French looking in another direction. Two per cent interest, seven new ports in which we collect taxes, and extraterritoriality.'

'The Rujo will not accept your administration of justice over Japanese nationals, nor the collection of taxes for our government,' Mung said. 'And the original request regarding missionaries is impossible. We could not protect them if they were allowed to roam about the country.'

'Would you grant the priests freedom in the cities, allow Europeans to judge their own nationals, and allow a committee of Japanese and Europeans to collect taxes?'

'If I said yes,' Mung asked, 'would that satisfy you and your allies?'

'The seven new ports would have to be included,' Edward Crest said.

In Mung's plan of modernization, European presence in the major port cities was essential. His leg began jumping again. 'This would be your only objection to my proposals?' he asked.

'It is necessary for me to convince the six European captains.'

'Limit your missionaries to the port cities and I shall recommend our agreement to the Rujo,' Mung said.

'And I shall recommend it to my allies,' Edward Crest said. He bowed Japanese style, then put out his hand. The three men shook hands all around.

Edward Crest smiled. 'Our discussion has brought on a thirst. I can have lemonade or hot tea brought in. I do not allow strong spirits on my ship. Figures show whisky kills more English sailors than our enemies.'

'A favour, your lordship,' Mung said. 'My son is seriously ill. I request to speak with the ship's doctor about his affliction.'

'It is a Christian's duty to help his fellow man. I shall send for the ship's surgeon. Please wait here. Baron Iyeasu and I will take a turn around the deck while you discuss the matter. I do hope it goes well with your son.'

The ship's surgeon entered the stateroom appearing ill at ease, but relaxed when he heard Mung's fluent English. He nodded from time to time as Mung described Yoshida's symptoms.

'Mr Minister,' the doctor said, 'the condition you describe is diagnosed in different ways in Europe. Mostly by observation of unusual behaviour. The illness is treated by evacuation of the bowels, induced vomiting, and bleeding. Recently our scientists have combined with technicians and mechanics in a new approach. It involves total shock to the patient's physical and mental systems. There are a number of different devices, although none of them is available aboard ship.'

'If you could explain their workings, I might be able to have one constructed.'

'The purpose of the mechanical contraptions is to disorient the patient, thus separating the two personalities. All the devices have restraining jackets to hold the patients securely – in a spinning bed, whirling chair or hollow wheel. These are rotated at speeds of up to one hundred times per minute. It is an extremely stressful treatment, from which weak patients sometimes die.'

'Are any cured?'

'Not many.' The doctor cupped his chin in his hand. 'You know, before I left London there was a paper read at the Royal College of Medicine. It was written seventy years ago by an American, Doctor Benjamin Rush. He claimed

182

positive results by employing friendly companions to listen sympathetically to patients with this mental disorder. That may be worth a try.'

Mung thanked the doctor for his time. He departed from the *Nemesis* with a higher regard for Japanese medicine, and positive news for the Emperor. However, he held little hope for Yoshida's recovery.

Chapter 19

In the Emperor's presence, Lord Hotta questioned Mung and Iyeasu. 'If the foreign captains accept your proposals, will the Rujo agree?'

'My Black Dragons report war talk among the samurai and ronin,' Mung said. 'Many lords who were formerly uncommitted have taken up the "Sonno joi" battle cry. If Fujita Koin and Saga oppose us, it may never come to a vote.' Mung addressed the Emperor. 'Your highness, Fujita Koin is a proud man. He will do everything to protect his family and the honour of his ancestors. If we were to threaten Hideyoshi with public disgrace and seppuku, Iyeasu believes his father would listen to a special proposal.'

'Why would the Emperor order your brother to commit seppuku?' Hotta asked Iyeasu.

'He is responsible for hiring the tattooed men to kill Mung.'

'Is there proof?' Hotta asked.

'Yes,' Mung said. 'Hideyoshi was observed conferring with the Yakuza prior to the attack. Further investigation revealed he paid for the assassination attempt on Lord Maeda and me. There are witnesses.'

'We are three sons with the same father,' Iyeasu said, 'but Hideyoshi's mother is not mine nor Danjuro's. We call him the spider. He spins webs, leaving tacky spots here and there for his victims to be caught in. Then he comes out and destroys them.'

'The Emperor has already ordered that the person responsible for the assassination attempts should die and his family be disgraced,' Hotta said.

'The threat of family disgrace and Hideyoshi's death could be used to control Fujita Koin,' Mung said. He addressed the Emperor again. 'Your highness, I ask you to consider overlooking Hideyoshi's actions if the Lord of Mito will influence his allies to vote with us in the Rujo.'

'There is still Lord Saga to consider,' Hotta said.

'If the Emperor would call the Choshu lord before him,' Mung said, 'I will charge Saga with causing the foreign threat to Tokyo by unauthorized hostility and agreeing to the three million pound indemnity. We could give him the choice of committing seppuku or backing our proposals.'

'Mung,' Hotta said, 'you are beginning to think like a first rate Japanese statesman, but neither of these men fears death.' He looked to the Emperor. 'Your highness, they do respect you and would do much to avoid disgrace.'

'What will happen if these two lords decide to revolt?' the Emperor asked.

His three advisors were shocked. 'No Japanese would disobey your direct order,' Hotta stammered. 'Especially these two noblemen. But they may do everything to avoid receiving your message. That is why they should be summoned before they expect it.'

'Isolate Saga,' the Emperor said. 'He will appear before me after Hotta has dealt with Fujita Koin. Tell the Lord of Mito that an Emperor does not go back on his word. If I receive official proof of Hideyoshi's wrongdoing, the houses of Mito will be destroyed completely and forever.'

Mung and Hotta conferred, and agreed upon their roles as accuser and prosecutor. If a judge was needed, the Emperor would be called. Iyeasu requested not to be present at the appearance of his father and two brothers before Lord Hotta.

* * *

185

'The houses of Mito are charged with crimes against the Emperor,' Hotta said.

'Never!' the old man of Mito exploded.

'Have you relinquished your title as Lord of Mito?'

'I have not!'

'Then you are responsible for the actions of your "remaining" two sons.'

The old man's face crimsoned. He gummed his soft lips and glared at the Fujiwara lord. 'I have accepted responsibility for them since they came out of their mothers' wombs.'

'I accuse Hideyoshi Koin of hiring assassins on two occasions to kill my family and me,' Mung said.

'You must have proof,' Hideyoshi sneered.

Mung opened a silk purse and shook out the shrivelled tattooed ear. 'This belonged to the Yakuza guard who accompanied you and the Golden Lizard from the Hall of a Hundred Mats to the Yasukune shrine.'

Hideyoshi recoiled from the ugly, foul-smelling thing on the mat before him. 'It proves nothing,' he said.

'At the shrine you incited the samurai and ronin against the policy I, as personal representative of the Emperor, brought to the Rujo,' Mung said.

'The Rujo had already rejected the Emperor's policy,' Hideyoshi snapped.

The breath whistled in through Fujita Koin's fluttering lips as he touched his head to the floor. 'Lord Hotta, I ask you to forgive my son's choice of words. He spoke in haste. This accusation by a commoner against a noble has shocked him. No person would ever decline the Emperor's wishes. It was the demands of the foreigners that were rejected.'

'The count is forgiven,' Hotta said, 'but be warned – the accusation stands. If Hideyoshi is found guilty of consorting with an organization of common criminals, he will be publicly disgraced, ordered to commit seppuku, and the Lord of Mito held responsible.'

Mung saw Hideyoshi shift nervously and look to his father. The crime of having consorted with those beneath his class was considered worse than the assassination attempt.

'It is the word of a fisherman,' Hideyoshi said.

'There are others,' Mung said. 'The person who removed this ear from its owner's head survived last night's attack on my house. He observed Count Hideyoshi consorting with the Golden Lizard, and will testify that it took place only minutes before the attack.' He looked at Fujita Koin. 'It is the second time your son has ordered common criminals to kill me.'

'Be careful,' Fujita Koin warned. 'Now it is you who threaten my family.'

'Your son has disgraced you and your ancestors,' Mung said.

'Your word and some non-existent witness are not enough to convict a person of noble birth,' Hideyoshi said. 'There are different laws for Japan's aristocracy than for peasants like you.'

'Is there further proof?' Danjuro asked Mung.

'Does the name Wada Zenshichi mean anything to you? He is chief Yakuza of all Japan. The Golden Lizard has been using the money supplied by your brother for services rendered, to challenge Zenshichi's leadership of the tattooed men. It was the chief Yakuza who warned me of the attack on the river in Kagoshima. His men saved my life last night. Wada Zenshichi will provide witnesses that Hideyoshi paid for the death of Lord Maeda. That is an offence against another aristocrat.'

'Tell them it is a lie,' Fujita Koin said aloud.

There was silence in the room. Slowly the old man

turned and looked at his second son. 'Tell them it is a lie and I will stand with you.'

Danjuro addressed his brother. 'If common criminals testify and you are found guilty, Mito is disgraced. Speak the truth.'

Hideyoshi's pockmarked face was livid with rage. He pointed at Mung. 'This peasant has been influencing the Emperor to give up the throne to foreigners. I believe he is a spy for America. He lived there. Many years he lived there. He wants to bring barbarians to rule our country and change our ways.'

'Did you consort with the Yakuza?' Fujita Koin demanded of his son. 'Did you commission the attacks? Are you responsible for Lord Maeda's death?'

The sharp tone of his father's voice snapped Hideyoshi around so he and the old man were eye to eye. Mung saw fear in the pockmarked face. Hideyoshi's father recognized the truth.

'To save Japan,' Hideyoshi whispered. 'Father, it was to save Japan. With Satsuma and Saga as our allies, we control the largest military force in the empire. We can restore the shogunate. You will be the shogun. The title will remain in our family for generations. We can bring power and honour to the houses of Mito.' The fear in Hideyoshi's face was replaced by conviction. 'We shall restore the Emperor to his traditional role as it was before the fall of the shogun. Under our leadership Mito shall achieve the glory you have always desired for our family.'

'You are not fit to lead Mito or anyone else,' Fujita Koin said. 'I have lived longer than most men and never violated the code of Bushido. Now I am disgraced by my son. I regret I lived to see this day.'

'I do not understand,' Hideyoshi pleaded. 'I thought you wanted Japanese tradition to continue. You fought on the side of the shogun.'

'I was wrong then. You are wrong now.' Fujita Koin twice opened his mouth to continue, but could not speak. He lowered his head until his chin rested on his chest, and remained silent.

'During the shogun's reign, the Emperor only sanctioned government,' Danjuro said to his brother. 'Now he rules, and Mito supports him. We are against foreign customs, but not their knowledge.' The Mito giant spoke simply but with great emotion. 'Brother, you are a liar. You have broken your oath of Bushido. You deceived everyone. You wish power for yourself, not Mito.'

For a moment Mung feared the old lord of Mito was dying. His face turned chalk white. Suddenly he fell forward, banging his head on the floor, and prostrated himself full length before Lord Hotta. His voice was like dry gravel. 'I was born the servant of the Emperor and wish to die his servant. My son has disgraced the houses of Mito. I am responsible. Order me and I shall obey.'

Mung saw Lord Hotta shudder. A tear formed in the corner of his eye. It teetered there but did not spill over. 'Fujita Koin,' Hotta said, 'the Emperor vowed that when he learned who ordered the assassinations, that person would die and his family's name would be obliterated from man's memory.'

Fujita Koin sat back on his heels, looking a hundred years old.

'Through the centuries Mito and Fujiwara have been allies and enemies,' Hotta said. 'But there was always respect between us. I offer this alternative. Your vote and those of your allies for any resolution put forward by Mung regarding the foreigners. In return, I will not officially inform his imperial majesty of your son's misdeeds.'

Fujita Koin could not believe his ears. 'Hideyoshi's actions will be forgiven?'

189

'And forgotten.'

'Will Mung swear not to take revenge on Mito for my son's plots against him and his family?'

'I do so swear,' Mung said. He thought to add that the boy from the fishing village had acted more honourably than a nobleman, but the despair on the old man's face silenced him.

In a thin, shaky voice, Fujita Koin said, 'I disowned the wrong son.'

Soon after the Lord of Mito left the palace, the Emperor returned to his place in the reception room. He nodded, and the master of protocol announced, 'Lord Saga of Choshu.'

The wiry little man wriggled across the floor faster than anyone Mung had ever seen. He bowed to the Emperor, adjusted his wire-frame glasses, and smiled with his big buck teeth.

'Is it true you agreed to pay a three million pound indemnity to the foreigners?' Lord Hotta asked.

'Who accuses me?' Saga asked.

'I do,' Mung said.

'Are there witnesses?' Saga asked. 'If you have witnesses, you should have accused me in the Rujo.'

'Fujita Koin closed the meeting sooner than expected.'

A faint smile crossed Saga's lips. 'It is wise to learn the rules before playing the game.'

'Lord Saga,' Hotta said, 'this is no game. The witness against you is the American consul, Townsend Harris. You admitted to him that you agreed to pay the indemnity.'

'Ah yes. Yes indeed I did. I must be more careful in the future. Do you not agree, Mr Minister of Maritime Services?'

Mung sensed the little man was more confident than he

should be. 'The American consul is of high enough rank to testify against you in our court,' Mung said.

'The Emperor has decided to allow you the opportunity to preserve your family honour and avoid seppuku,' Hotta said.

'I will always do what the Emperor wishes.'

Mung scrutinized Saga's face. He appeared prepared to accept the situation.

'If that is so,' Hotta said, 'the Emperor wishes you and your allies to support any resolution put forth by Mung regarding the foreign demands. Fujita Koin will also vote in favour.'

'The man who runs with the river goes furthest,' Saga said. 'He who bucks the current, wearies and drowns. Will my mistake at Shimonoseki be forgiven?'

'And forgotten,' Hotta said.

'You will have a unanimous vote in the Rujo,' Saga said.

Mung's elation at having manipulated two of the most powerful men in the empire was suddenly offset by his desire to see his son.

Chapter 20

Hideyoshi lagged behind the guards escorting his father's kago. Taking care Danjuro did not notice, he dropped out of the procession and made for the Shimbara quarter.

In the commercial rabbit warren of winding lanes, streets and alleys, Hideyoshi entered a mat-maker's stall. A few minutes later he left by the rear entrance, accompanied by a tattooed man. They hurried along, behind houses, shops and restaurants, to an abandoned storehouse.

Hideyoshi descended through a trapdoor to an underground room where the Golden Lizard lay on a tatami mat. The blood-stained bandage wrapped under his arm and over his shoulder contrasted sharply with his golden scales. The hooded eyes flashed at Hideyoshi. 'How did they know we were coming?' he hissed. 'They were waiting for us.'

Although wounded, the lizard-man still frightened Hideyoshi. He took a step backward. 'One of the Black Dragons saw us meet outside the council hall. He followed us to the shrine, then you to your men. How bad is your wound?'

'The bullet tore a hole in my shoulder and broke my collar-bone. I will not die, but Mung will. In addition to the Tokyo police, he has set his Black Dragons and Wada Zenshichi's Yakuza on me.'

'Do you think you can travel?'

The lizard-man sneered. 'My dear benefactor, what are you up to? You do not trust me and I certainly do not trust you.'

Hideyoshi ignored the remark. 'There is a law which

prohibits a father from issuing a ban if his son is not present. He must wait six months before legal renunciation. If I stay away from my father, he cannot disown me as he did my brother. I have made arrangements for a boat to the south. There is a place for you on the boat if you wish.'

'I am wounded. My men are dead or in hiding. I cannot fulfil our contract and kill Mung just yet.'

'The fisherman can wait. I prefer my brother, Danjuro, dead before him.'

'Ha!' The Golden Lizard laughed, and grimaced with pain. 'Hideyoshi, you are evil enough to be a great man.'

'Will you come?'

'I can arrange to have your brother killed before we go.'

'No. It must wait until my father dies and I am certain he has willed the lordship to Danjuro. That should not be long. My father looked like death itself after the meeting with the Emperor.' Hideyoshi reached down and helped the lizard-man to his feet, trying to feel with his fingertips if the texture of tattooed skin was different. 'When Danjuro dies, I will be Lord of Mito. You can benefit from that.'

'I will kill your brother and Mung.'

At the conclusion of his audience with Mung and Hotta, Saga made directly for the Yoshiwara. Hurrying along the gaily decorated streets, he was oblivious to the laughter and music of the pleasure-quarter.

At Hatcho Street, Saga entered the House of Four Heavenly Queens. In a private room overlooking the garden, he told the madam, 'Bring your best pigeon.'

She soon returned with a white and black speckled bird, an inkstand and a long, thin strip of rice paper. Saga sat at a low table and wrote his message, 'Hita wa ichida na wa matsudai. Man is mortal, fame immortal.'

He tied the cylinder to the bird's leg and released the pigeon over the garden. It circled once, then winged away into the setting sun, carrying the signal that would set in motion a series of events to change Japanese history.

It was not far from the Emperor's reception hall to Mung's apartment, but the effects of the stimulant had worn off. Ukiko started to bow, took one look at her husband, and rushed to support him.

'Yoshida is very sick,' he said with tears in his eyes, aware that exhaustion had allowed his emotions to surface. His tongue felt thick and fuzzy. It was as if he had just now heard the news. 'I do not know how to help the boy.'

'Will he die?' Ukiko asked, supporting her husband to the sleeping pad.

'I do not think he is in immediate danger, and I have learned the Kyoto physician knows as much as anyone about the illness.'

Ukiko undid Mung's obi. He felt the last bit of strength leave his body, and rested his head on her shoulder. He heard her soft, reassuring whisper, 'Sleep, sleep, sleep, my beloved.' Gently she lowered him onto the pad. She bent over and kissed his cheek. 'Rest, my husband. Together we shall find a way to help our son.'

'Who is making all that noise out there?' Udo called from his pallet.

'These porch steps are uneven,' Sandanj called back.

'Get in here,' Udo said.

The door slid open and Sandanj crawled through.

'Why are you coming in on your hands and knees?' Udo asked.

'Because someone keeps adding an extra step to your porch.'

'You are drunk.'

'You are correct and I am going to stay this way. I have

been drinking all afternoon and evening, and I will continue to drink all night. Do you have any saké?'

'I want you to stop drinking,' Udo said.

'That is not nice. That is not nice at all. I have not been allowed to drink for sixty-eight months, and now my restrictions have been lifted.' He rose up on his knees and pounded his chest. He toppled over backward and lay there laughing. 'I have been drinking like a fish and eating like a pig. I am planning to fornicate like your bunnies.'

'Good,' Udo said, 'I will help you. We shall go to the Yoshiwara together. I need your help because I am still weak from my shoulder wound.'

'In the Yoshiwara,' Sandanj giggled, 'everyone helps himself.'

'You sot.' Udo laughed. He reached down and pulled Sandanj to his feet. 'I am in love and you are going to help me sneak in to see Gin-ko.'

'You are serious?' Sandanj staggered back to take a better look at his friend. 'Do you really love her? And what about your shoulder? Is it still painful?'

'All I needed was a good sleep. You need to sober up.'

'Ha! Now that you are rested and your golden rod is pointing towards the Yoshiwara, you think it is love. Have you ever been in love before?' Sandanj shouted.

'You do not have to speak so loudly. I have had many women. I trained them for other men and pleasured them for money. Many loved me, but I never loved.'

'How do you know this is it?'

'My heart is too large for my chest when I think of her. And she is all I can think of. I know I love her.'

'It sounds like the way they say it should be,' Sandanj said. 'Does it disturb you to think about all the men she has pleasured?'

'No. Only about those she may still have to pleasure.

That is why I must see her tonight. I want to talk with her, buy her contract, marry her.'

'Buying a Yoshiwara contract would cost a fortune. To marry her, you need permission from Mung. He is not only your father. Every wife must be approved by the Black Dragon.'

'I have already sent a message to Kang Shu in Canton for the money,' Udo said. 'It will be enough to buy the entire Yoshiwara district. And a present for you will be sent from Canton.'

'You would buy a present for Sandanj?' He hung his head and shook it from side to side. 'That is the most beautiful thing you could do.' He began to sniffle.

'Why are you crying?'

'I am so happy. I have been eating and drinking. Soon I will be fornicating, and you are going to give me a present. What is it going to be?'

'Stop crying and I will tell you.'

'Nobody has given me a present since I was a very small boy. What is it?'

'A Chinese printing press,' Udo said.

'Oh.'

'By the look on your face I think you do not like the present.'

'What will I do with it?'

'You are dedicated to serving the Emperor, are you not?'

Sandanj threw back his shoulders and stood at attention. 'I am dedicated to serving the Emperor,' he said.

'Good. His imperial majesty wishes to influence the people to western ideas. You are going to start a newspaper with your printing press that can print a hundred times faster than anything in Japan.'

'I am honoured.'

'You will also offer to publish Princess Atsu's *Book of Good Deeds* without charge.'

'I am pleased to be of service.'

'Then you will publish your translated cookbooks and label them, "Published by Printer to the Royal Household." That should help sell them very well. The British do it with tea and whisky.'

'I am happy. My dream is coming true.' Sandanj broke out in a big smile and rushed to hug Udo. 'By all the gods, I swear you are the best friend a man could have. How did you think of these things?'

'Will you help me see Gin-ko?'

'I hope you have a better plan than last time.' Sandanj pointed to the painting leaning against the wall. 'Those four sphere-grabbers and that old hag with the snakeskin whip are mean characters.'

Udo had made his plan to coincide with the rising of the full moon. He believed Gin-ko had hinted when he should visit by saying she often moon-watched. He and Sandanj approached the back of the house through an alley, and Udo pinpointed her room.

Sandanj scouted down the alley to the front of the house. 'All clear,' he whispered on his return. 'It is very, very quiet inside.'

'Are you ready?' Udo asked.

Sandanj nodded solemnly, and took out his knife. They used razor-sharp blades to slit a three-foot line in the paper wall at the base of the floor, then coordinated slicing two lines three feet apart down the wall.

Udo pushed in the flap and peeked inside the room. 'It looks empty,' he whispered.

'What if she is not in the garden either?' Sandanj asked, fearing his friend might find the woman he loved with a client.

'I will wait until she returns to her room,' Udo said. 'You keep watch.' He handed Sandanj his swords and crawled through the opening into the dark room. He lay quietly, inhaling her scent and listening.

Through the open shoji screen door, Udo could see across the courtyard. The moon topped the peaked roof, illuminating the other side. The old woman and the apprentice girl sat in the lotus position, gazing up. Silvery light bathed their faces.

The moon brightened the courtyard as it continued its journey among the stars. Udo's heart sank. The four guards were seated near the old woman. Then a silhouette appeared on the porch of the room he was in. Gin-ko was seated with her back to him. He lay quietly and stared at her, his adoration so intense he thought she must surely sense his presence.

Udo inched his way across the floor, getting close enough to reach out and touch Gin-ko. She heard his breathing and started to turn. 'Please do not move,' he whispered.

Gin-ko froze. Then casually she reached up and pulled a butterfly hairpin from her coiffure. 'Who is it?' she whispered.

'Udo.' He knelt directly behind her so that those looking across the courtyard would see only one silhouette.

'What do you want?'

The sound of her voice made him weak in the stomach and strong in the heart. 'I love you,' he whispered.

'Many men love me.' She replaced the hairpin, appearing to relax.

'Not anymore. I want to marry you.'

'Who are you?'

'It is me, Udo. Ukiko's stepson. Will you marry me?'

'The son of a government minister marry a courtesan?'

'There are samurai and nobles, even a shogun, who married courtesans. I see no disgrace. The shame would be yours for not allowing me to show my love.'

Gin-ko turned around, kneeling face to face with Udo. He could taste her sweet breath in his mouth. She reached out with long tapered fingers and caressed his cheek. Her soft hand slid down his neck. He thrilled as she probed the knobs of his spine. Suddenly a lightning bolt shot through his body. She had touched the pressure point and immobilized him. He could hear her. He could feel her touch and smell her. He loved her but could not say so.

The old woman spoke from behind him. 'I saw you remove the hairpin and thought you might be in trouble.'

'No,' Gin-ko said, 'you taught me well.'

'Release the lovesick puppy. I am surprised he returned so quickly. A squeezing of the spheres usually reduces the golden rod to a melted candle for some time.'

Gin-ko removed her hand from Udo's neck. He felt a tingling sensation throughout his body. Movement returned to his limbs. Then he heard a whistling sound, and the snakeskin whip wrapped around his neck. He gasped for air, clutching at the scaly thong on his throat. He fell on his wounded shoulder and thrashed on the floor like a fish out of water. He felt his chest would explode from the need for air. His eyes dimmed and he arched from head to toe.

The old woman flicked her wrist and the snakeskin uncoiled. Udo collapsed on the floor, gulping great mouthfuls of air, sucking it down into his starved lungs. 'There is blood pouring out of his sleeve,' he heard Gin-ko say. He felt her cradle his head in her lap and he looked up into her face. Their eyes met and held for a moment. 'I love you,' he said, but it came out as a croaking sound from his injured vocal cords. He gazed up at her, wishing she would never let him go. His eyes rolled up into his head.

'He has passed out,' Gin-ko said.

'Guards,' the old woman ordered, 'bandage his wounds

and call the police. I should cut off his golden rod before they come.'

'I will bandage him,' Gin-ko said. 'And you are not cutting anything off him.' She looked up at the old woman. 'He said he wants to marry me.'

The old woman cackled, hobbling closer. 'They all say that when they do not want to pay.'

'I wonder how it would be if I did marry him,' Gin-ko said. Had she looked into the rheumy eyes of the hag, she would have seen fear.

'You would be barefoot, bowlegged, and on your way to bearing ten children in between planting his rice, cooking his food, and sewing his clothes. Then you would wait at home for him to return from the Yoshiwara where he would go for his pleasure.'

'He is the son of a government minister.'

'The adopted son of a minister who is not an aristocrat and has more enemies than a dog has fleas. Mung will not survive long in Tokyo politics. When he is gone, there will be nothing for the adopted son to inherit. Take that giant Danjuro, he is a catch. He will be the next Lord of Mito.' The old woman waved Gin-ko away. 'You have finished bandaging lover-boy. Go to your room.'

Gin-ko disregarded Little Mother's command and remained with the unconscious Udo. When the police arrived, the guards carried him to the front door and deposited him in a cart. He was trundled off to the municipal jail.

Gin-ko stepped out of her shoes and backed into her room. She slid the screen door closed.

'Psssst! Pssst!' The noise was behind her. She spun around. Pulling a butterfly pin from her hair, she hurled it. The dart buried itself in the paper wall just above Sandanj's head peeking through the flap.

'What are you throwing?' he whispered.

'Who are you? I will call the guards.'

'No, please, not those sphere-grabbers again.'

'Are you Udo's friend?'

'Yes. I fell asleep and was awakened by a commotion. Where is Udo?'

'Do not move. The dart I threw is poisoned.' Gin-ko pulled it out and knelt. Her face was close to Sandanj's. 'What is it you want?'

'You are just as dangerous as your old mother,' he said.

'She is not my mother.'

'Where is my friend, Udo?'

'On his way to the municipal jail. He is wounded.'

'Lady, if you hurt my friend you will have to answer to me. All he wants is to love you.'

'That is what all men want.' Gin-ko's eyes saddened and her head lowered.

'Not like that.'

'Is this his first love affair?'

'Are you joking?' Sandanj looked up with pride. 'My friend pleasured many women in China. He was in charge of one of the finest bordellos in Canton.'

Gin-ko raised her head. 'You mean his body was paid for as mine is?'

'Yes. And he was very good at his work.'

Gin-ko reached out to help Sandanj. 'Come in, please. Tell me more about Udo.'

'Another time. Right now I have to get him released from jail.' Sandanj wriggled backwards out of the room.

Chapter 21

Jiroo had come to see Mung but Ukiko insisted he wait until Mung had bathed, dressed and eaten before they spoke. When Mung appeared, Jiroo said, 'Your adopted son spent last night in jail. I had him released this morning. He broke into the house of a Yoshiwara courtesan he claims to be in love with.'

'My friend, Gin-ko?' Ukiko asked, and Jiroo nodded.

'Dip him in cold water and send him to me,' Mung said.

'Besides love sickness, Udo is suffering from fever and weakness. His shoulder wound opened during a scuffle with her guards. I was able to persuade the mistress of the house and the police not to press charges. But I must tell you, he is determined to buy the lady's contract and marry her.'

'Where is he now?' Mung asked.

'Bedded down on the outskirts of the city. The Love Lion has torn him tooth and nail. I suggest we do something to keep him away from the Yoshiwara. His body and heart both need a rest more than a courtesan.'

Mung nodded. 'Send him out to the *Kanrin Maru*. Keep him isolated until the ship leaves for Prussia. He will be studying von Bismarck's intelligence network. I am told it is the best in the world.'

'May I see him before he leaves?' Ukiko asked.

'Jiroo will arrange it,' Mung said, thinking to please his wife and distract her from thoughts of Yoshida. 'What is the situation in the city?' he asked Jiroo.

'The samurai and ronin are more agitated than before. They have focused their anger on the foreign gunboats in the harbour. And I received two separate reports of a plot to capture the Emperor.'

'Do you believe that?' Mung asked.

'I doubted anyone would conceive such an idea, but the captain of the palace guard reminded me it would be the simplest way to gain power in Japan. No Japanese would attack a force holding the Emperor hostage for fear of harming him. The captain has doubled the Emperor's guard.'

'Hideyoshi Koin and the Golden Lizard could conceive such a plot,' Mung said.

'Wada Zenshichi sent word that Hideyoshi and the lizard-man escaped his Yakuza in a boat heading south.'

'What about Fujita Koin and Saga?'

'The Lord of Mito is a dispirited man. He has not risen from his bed since you last saw him. Saga went straight to the House of Four Heavenly Queens and probably rests between two of them at this moment.'

'Could Saga's army be near?'

'If his men followed the foreigners up the coast, our look-outs or the Tokyo Fishermen's Guild would have reported it.'

As the Black Dragon and his senior aide discussed the situation, 2,500 Choshu samurai in light marching kit trotted in formation down the Tokaido Road forty miles from Tokyo. Scouts raced ahead, taking out sentries and government toll stations along Japan's main trunk road. Thirty Choshu hawkers were positioned in a semicircle around the southern approaches to Tokyo, bringing down any bird that flew in a straight line. Saga of Choshu did sleep with his arms around two heavenly queens, content to let his commanders implement the first part of his plan.

* * *

203

Mung and Ukiko were received by the Kyoto physician. 'Your son is resting quietly,' the doctor said. 'You can see him when he wakes.'

'Doctor,' Ukiko asked, 'will Yoshida recover?' She began to weep. 'Will he die?'

The doctor adjusted his spectacles. He looked to Mung, who nodded. 'Madam,' the doctor said, 'much courage was needed to ask those questions. Unfortunately I cannot answer them until treatment has begun. After that we will be able to evaluate Yoshida's progress. You can help now by giving your son love and attention. He needs his parents' support.'

'Is he dangerous?' Mung asked.

'As Musashi he has already killed, as you know.' The physician was aware Mung had chosen not to tell him about the incident on the river. 'When the second soul enters your son's body, it sometimes gains complete control. When he is the Sword Saint he is the epitome of Bushido, and will react to any situation accordingly. Other times Yoshida is perfectly normal. There are also periods when his soul and Musashi's share the same body. It is then he is most agitated.'

Ukiko listened, gripping Mung's hand.

'I would like to know about Rhee's condition,' Mung said.

'Come,' the physician said, leading them to another room. 'Your retainer is still in danger, but not as close to death as last night. He has a strong will to live.'

'And our son?' Ukiko asked.

'He has two wills, one in conflict with the other.'

Rhee was swathed in bandages. A lovely young woman, stripped to the waist, was at his side. Her lithe torso stretched over him, her tight breasts standing out as she leaned forward to dampen Rhee's lips and forehead.

'Why the bare-chested maiden?' Mung asked.

'Most important to the recovery of the patient is his attitude. The crucial time to influence him is upon awakening. After violent injuries, patients often go into shock. We have found that when beautiful women are near, warriors recover more quickly. The stimulation of their sex glands seems to hasten the healing process.'

A burly young man appeared in the doorway. 'Doctor, Yoshida Ishikawa has awakened as himself and Musashi.'

'Watch him,' the doctor said. He turned to Ukiko and Mung. 'Perhaps you should postpone this first meeting. It may not be pleasant.'

'I must see him,' Mung said. 'My wife too.'

The doctor nodded. He led them from the house to a one-room cottage made of solid planked walls with one door and no windows. Fresh air entered through the space between the walls and the roof. Guards stood at each corner of the building. The burly attendant was peering through a viewing port in the wall.

As Mung and Ukiko approached, they heard their son speaking with someone. The second man argued in a harsh voice vaguely familiar to Mung.

'Who is that with Yoshida?' Ukiko asked the doctor.

'Your son is alone. He is speaking with his second self.'

'You must train in the Way!' the harsh voice shouted. With a start, Mung recognized the voice of his friend, General Ryochi Okuda, who had died years before. 'The Way requires total devotion to the strategy of the sword.'

Mung mounted the porch steps in a cold sweat. He and Ukiko heard their son's voice answer, 'I am ill-suited physically and mentally for the life of a warrior.'

The physician motioned the attendant away from the viewing port. Mung and Ukiko took his place. Their son stood in the centre of the room, fists jammed into his sides, head thrown back. He glared into space and growled, 'Listen to me, Yoshida Ishikawa. I, Miyamoto Musashi, from birth have been drawn to the Way. I will guide you in your search for honour. Together we shall climb Mount Fuji. There you will kneel before the great Buddha and pray to the gods of steel and thunder. They will grant you the courage to study with me. We shall travel the empire challenging all champions, and praise the Emperor wherever we go.'

Mung and Ukiko watched Yoshida drop his hands. His shoulders slumped and he spoke in his own thin voice, filled with desperation, pleading for his life. 'I have studied the laws of Buddha and the teachings of Confucius, not the chronicles of war or military tactics. Where Musashi takes up the sword, I raise the pen to find the true spirit of life.'

Yoshida's head snapped back. His eyes glared as he paced the room. 'Intellectual cowardice,' he shouted in Musashi's voice. 'It is mirrored in that sallow, scholarly face of yours.'

'Bunbu itchi. The pen and sword in accord,' Yoshida replied to his second self. 'I am the pen and you the sword, Master Musashi.' He bowed.

Mung watched, and heard his son speaking with two voices, fighting for his identity, his sanity, his life. Mung trembled in fear for the young man.

Ukiko moved so quickly, no one stopped her. She threw open the door and cried out, 'Yoshida!'

The young man froze in place. Surprise, then happiness spread over his face at sight of his mother. Suddenly fear took hold. He drew back and jammed his fists into his hips. 'Who is this woman?' Musashi's voice demanded.

'My mother,' Yoshida answered.

'Musashi allows no distractions from studying the Way of the Warrior.'

Ukiko reached out to her son. She saw beads of perspiration cover his face. He began to quiver like a frightened rabbit. 'I want my mother,' he said.

Ukiko embraced Yoshida, but he stiffened and shook so violently she could not hold him. He would have fallen had Mung not rushed to lower him to the sleeping mat in the corner of the room.

'He will rest now,' the doctor said. 'These seizures exhaust him.'

'May we remain here?' Mung asked.

'Of course.' The doctor backed out of the room.

Mung saw a shadow cover the viewing port in the wall and knew the attendant was there. He spoke to Ukiko in whispers. 'I feel so helpless. All my power is not enough to command my son to be healthy.'

Ukiko patted his hand. 'Once the treatments begin, his condition will improve.' She brushed Yoshida's close-cropped hair with her finger tips. 'He had his hair cut so he would look like you. He wants very much to be like his father.'

'Let him live and be well,' Mung said. 'He must be his own person. I had such hope for his future.'

'I wish to stay with him,' Ukiko said. 'Can you arrange it?'

'Yes, for both of us.' He held her hand and listened to Yoshida's deep, even breathing. 'There is so much I want to tell him. Japan is going to become an exciting place to live. We are going to build a new nation from the old. I wrote to John in Washington asking him to seek out the foremost American educators to help Iyeasu set up a free school system here. I would like to tell Yoshida about the past – my school days in Massachusetts, whaling, my time in Hawaii and the gold fields of California. I want him to know that it was not only because of my loyalty to the Emperor or to help Japan that I returned. I came back to father a son who would honour my ancestors, and me when I died.' Mung looked at Ukiko with tears streaming down his face. 'We may lose him before I can tell him how much I love him.'

Ukiko took her husband into her arms and they both wept. 'He knows,' she sobbed, 'he knows.'

After some time Mung stood up. 'I will talk to the doctor about a place for us to stay.'

He entered the main house and was speaking to the physician when a runner burst in. He bowed and spoke quickly. 'Sire, Jiroo requests you come at once to the foreign compound. One westerner has been killed and another wounded.'

'Doctor,' Mung said, 'I appreciate any assistance you can give my wife. Tell her I will return as soon as possible.' He hurried out of the door.

The foreign compound bristled with armed Europeans. Barricades were being erected, doors reinforced and windows shuttered. Mung was stopped at the entrance to the American consul's house by a bayonet pressed to his chest. 'I am Moryiama Ishikawa,' he said in English.

'That sounds about right,' the marine guard said. 'We've got to be careful with you murdering yellow bastards.'

Mung disregarded the insult. He pushed aside the bayonet and entered the house. Townsend Harris and Jiroo stepped back from a blood-covered figure sprawled on the couch.

'Who is it?' Mung asked.

'Heuskens, my translator,' the American consul said.

'How is he?'

'Dead.'

'Where is the wounded man?' Mung asked.

'This was he. Mr Richardson, Lord Alcock's aide, was also killed.'

'How? What happened?'

Townsend Harris took a deep breath, and answered, 'I

was with Richardson, Heuskens and some British staff officers as guests of the French aboard the *Armentise*. There was some drinking. Richardson proposed a tour of the port. The French captain sent his marines along for protection and to buy some fresh vegetables. I and Heuskens accompanied them ashore.'

'Weren't you stopped by the Fujiwara guards?' Mung asked.

'They challenged us but Heuskens, who is fluent in Japanese, told them the British had your permission to visit the Yasukune shrine.' The American consul looked at the bloody figure on the couch. 'I mean he was fluent in Japanese. Oh dear God, the man is dead!'

Mung pressed the American for further details, as much to learn what had happened as to take his mind off the dead man. 'Why didn't you reprimand Heuskens? I never gave permission for anyone to go into the city.'

'I didn't understand when he spoke Japanese. He was in his cups and didn't explain until the French marines were gone and Richardson had started for the Yasukune shrine to try and catch a glimpse of the Emperor on his return from morning prayers. A band of drunken ronin surrounded the two of us a hundred yards from this compound. Heuskens tried to reason with them but they were in an ugly mood. They slashed his arm, then came after me. Heuskens tried to protect me and they cut him down. He never had a chance. He carried no weapon.'

'How did you escape?' Mung asked, drawing the consul away from the bloody figure on the couch.

'Three of my marines saw the attack and fired over the killers' heads. They broke and ran.'

'And Richardson?'

'Lord Alcock stopped here before evacuating his family to the *Nemesis*. He told me Richardson and the naval officers met a contingent of Tosa samurai coming from the

209

shrine. The Tosa men demanded the right of way. Richardson refused. The samurai cut him down, pushed the others aside and marched on as if nothing had happened.' Townsend Harris shook his head. 'Lord Alcock left here with the intention of persuading Edward Crest to burn Tokyo.'

Mung felt sick. His worst nightmare was being realized. 'Do you think he will succeed?'

'I don't know.'

'Do you know where the French marines are?' Mung asked Jiroo.

'They were chased to their boat by another band of samurai from the Hikawa shrine. No casualties on either side. The Frenchmen were very disciplined. They could have used their rifles, but did not.'

'Thank the gods for that,' Mung said. 'Has Lord Hotta taken action?'

'More of his men and Lord Maeda's have moved into the port area,' Jiroo said. 'He instituted a search for those ronin who killed Heuskens, and demanded that the Tosa samurai who killed Richardson be handed over to him for punishment.'

'Mung,' Townsend Harris said, 'I did not understand the words passed between you and Jiroo, but I strongly suggest you see Lord Crest immediately. He will be under great pressure from Lord Alcock to avenge Richardson's death.'

'What about America's revenge?' Mung asked.

'According to the rules, we shall demand apologies and compensation. Heuskens wasn't American. He was a Dutch national I hired in Canton. I promised him adventure. We became friends.' Harris appeared about to burst into tears.

'How can I prevent Lord Crest from burning Tokyo?' Mung asked.

'Give him what he demands.'

Chapter 22

Mung held his emotions in check as he reported to the Emperor. 'All foreign warships are moving closer to Tokyo's municipal pier. Their guns will soon be in position to shell the city,' he concluded.

Iyeasu estimated the casualties and possible destruction from such a bombardment. Then Hotta spoke of plans for an evacuation of Tokyo's one million inhabitants.

'You must save the city,' the Emperor said. 'It is impossible to vacate the capital of Japan.'

Less than an hour later, Mung and Iyeasu were on the governor's barge heading for the *Nemesis*. 'Edward Crest does not have to make one concession,' Mung said, 'and he knows it.'

'We have Lord Hotta's apology,' Iyeasu said. 'It must be used to keep the missionaries restricted to the port areas.'

'It is going to be a gruesome business. I do not know if Lord Alcock will be satisfied by a display of Japanese justice.'

Iyeasu pointed at the *Nemesis* with her guns run out and battle flags flying. 'Edward Crest is the man who commands those cannon. He is the one we must convince.'

The barge moved alongside the frigate. Mung paused at the bottom of the boarding platform. 'Will your father honour his word and vote for whatever proposal we bring to the Rujo?' he asked Iyeasu.

'Yes, it is Bushido.'

'And Saga?'

'He is a shifty dog.'

They mounted the platform and were jostled by the

angry royal marines who escorted them, with cocked rifles and fixed bayonets, to the ship's stateroom. In the cabin, six stern-faced captains, three on either side, flanked Lord Edward Crest. The lord motioned for the two Japanese to come closer, and they were pressed forward by the marines.

'I will not ask you to be seated,' Edward Crest said. 'I demand an explanation for the unprovoked attacks on foreign nationals which resulted in the deaths of two consular employees!'

'Your lordship,' Iyeasu said, 'we cautioned the foreign consuls to restrict their people to the compounds. We requested that you keep your men aboard ship.'

'So you blame us for the murder of our own people? Is that your excuse for these cold-blooded killings?'

'No excuse could justify the loss of life,' Mung said. 'In Japan, samurai have always held the power of life and death without recourse to any court other than their swords. We are searching for those ronin who attacked the interpreter. It was Tosa samurai who killed Mr Richardson. Lord Hotta has ordered them disciplined.'

'And what will be their fate?' Edward Crest demanded.

'Your signalman will soon report activity on the municipal dock,' Iyeasu said. 'When he does, you and your entire fleet will see that Japanese justice is swift.'

'I have kept Lord Alcock from this meeting,' Edward Crest said. 'He wishes me to fire on Tokyo immediately. However, we are not the barbarians your people think. We come prepared to teach your countrymen how to behave in a civilized manner. We can improve the lives of your people by sharing our knowledge. But until the Japanese government acts in a way befitting a sovereign nation, we shall dictate our terms.' He leaned forward over his desk. 'Mr Mung, Baron Iyeasu, inform the Emperor and your Great Council that all our original demands stand. We

212

collect your taxes for you, control seven ports, and maintain extraterritoriality. A sum of money to compensate the two bereaved families, and a further three million sterling in addition to the three million which Lord Saga agreed to, will be included in the indemnity payment due. In addition, your counterproposal to have our countries involve themselves with projects relating to the modernization of Japan will be pursued with vigour.' Edward Crest waved a finger at Mung and Iyeasu. 'This is an ultimatum! There will be no negotiations. Tell your government that.'

A navy commander entered the stateroom, saluted, and said, 'Sir, officer of the deck reporting. We are receiving signals from the municipal pier but cannot read them. It appears something is about to take place there.'

'Is this what you referred to, Mr Mung?'

'Yes, your lordship. I respectfully request that you and the captains come topside to view Japanese justice. If you could equip everyone with a telescope? And invite Lord Alcock?'

Edward Crest looked around at the captains flanking him. 'Gentlemen, as this meeting is concluded, I suggest we adjourn to see what entertainment is being provided for us.'

From the quarterdeck of the *Nemesis* it was approximately one hundred yards to Tokyo's municipal dock. The western officers saw fifteen samurai march out to the end of the pier and kneel side by side facing the warship. With the telescopes, they could clearly see the dark, stern eyes of the warriors.

'What is this to be?' Lord Alcock demanded. 'A ceremony of public apology? If so, kneeling and kowtowing is not enough.'

'It is, as you say, a public apology,' Iyeasu replied, 'but of a kind you westerners are unfamiliar with. These are the

213

Tosa samurai who killed Mr Richardson.' He spoke in French so all would understand, his voice reflecting fierce pride. 'These samurai are the equivalent of your knights in King Arthur's time. The women moving onto the pier are the new wives of five of the kneeling samurai. The women have not yet borne children.'

Five young women moved gracefully out to the end of the pier. They knelt as did their husbands, side by side, but allowed a space of ten feet between the men and themselves.

'What is this about?' the French captain demanded.

'The men responsible for the death of Mr Richardson will commit ritual suicide,' Iyeasu said. 'The long sword you see them withdrawing is called a katana. The scrolls they wrap around the scabbards are their death poems.' He paused to wait for the next ceremonial step. 'They set both aside to be returned to their families.' He paused again. 'Now they meditate.'

'Is this called Japanese justice?' Lord Crest asked. 'Those men should be punished, but not forced to kill themselves. It is sacrilege.'

'Would you have another man responsible for their deaths?' Iyeasu asked. 'Why make butchers of the innocent by having them hang, burn or guillotine the guilty? These samurai requested this boon from Lord Hotta, rather than be executed as common criminals.'

'Monsieur, the ladies too?' the French captain cried.

'They were granted permission to join their husbands. It is called shinju – suicide for love. You see, when a samurai marries he presents his wife with a dagger, and the slogan, "Death before dishonour." These women have chosen their own slogan, "Life without my husband is dishonour." They will slit their throats with those daggers.'

'Baron Iyeasu,' Lord Alcock said, 'if I were to petition the Fujiwara lord to spare the lives of those poor wretches, would he take notice?'

'No. Killing your aide is not their crime. It is violating Lord Hotta's orders that foreigners should not be harmed.'

'But the ladies! You must save them. They are so very young.'

'If you shell Tokyo,' Mung said, 'fifty thousand young women will die.'

Lord Alcock looked at Edward Crest, who clamped his jaw shut and spoke between clenched teeth. 'Our demands remain.'

'Observe the first samurai on the right.' Iyeasu pointed. 'He opens his kimono to expose his chest down to his abdomen. He unsheaths the wakiyashi, the short sword. The big man coming out onto the pier is the strongest swordsman in Tokyo. The Tosa men requested his assistance.'

Danjuro stepped behind the first Tosa samurai. Mung looked at Iyeasu, who avoided his eyes and continued. 'The big man wields the long sword, an ancient one called a tsurugi. He will decapitate each samurai as soon as the man pierces his own stomach with his short sword. It is to prevent crying out and dishonour. It reduces pain.'

Mung saw that Iyeasu was shaking, barely able to control his voice. Yet he went on. 'Gentlemen, please raise your telescopes. The apology of the Tosa samurai is about to commence.'

The reluctant Europeans adjusted their scopes. They studied the faces of the warriors, expecting to see fear. There was only burning pride in the eyes of the stiff-backed men who knelt on the dock.

The leader of the Tosa samurai pulled his kimono open further. He unsheathed his short sword, grasped the hilt with both hands, and placed the point at the left side of his lower abdomen. His nostrils flared as he sucked in a long, deep breath, and puffed his cheeks. He hardened his stomach muscles and drove the point deep, then pulled the

215

handle across. Blood spurted out and Danjuro's long sword whistled through the air. It cut at the base of the neck, sending the samurai's head flying off into the water. Danjuro put his foot on the man's back and shoved the headless body into the bay. He moved to the next man, and the next, and the next. Not once did his blade falter, nor did he miss that exact point at the top of the spine.

Danjuro tracked bloody footsteps across the open space to the first woman. Mung shivered. He knew what Danjuro was about to say, and was certain of the young woman's answer.

'It is no dishonour for you to leave now,' the Mito giant whispered softly. 'Lord Hotta wishes it and I request it. I have never killed a woman. Please return home.'

The young woman looked up with large, frightened eyes at the big, soft-spoken samurai. 'Please hurry,' she said, 'my husband awaits me.'

'Put the knife to your throat,' Danjuro said. 'I promise it shall be painless.'

The woman pressed the dagger point into her soft skin. At the first speck of blood, Danjuro turned the ancient killing sword to the specially made blunt edge, and killed her with a stroke to the base of the skull. Swiftly he completed his task, killing all the women. Then, in a rage, he hurled the tsurugi out towards the *Nemesis*. He returned to the bodies of the young women and gently straightened their heads. He crossed their hands over their breasts.

Aboard the *Nemesis* and along the waterfront, there was silence. A lone sea gull hovered over the grisly scene.

'Lord Crest, all Japan will march against you prepared for death as those Tosa samurai were,' Mung pointed to the headless bodies in the bloodstained water, 'if you do not retreat from one demand – the unrestricted movement of missionaries. If you insist on that clause, we will have to fight you sooner or later. We cannot possibly protect your priests outside the port cities.'

A trembling Edward Crest looked to his pale-faced captains. 'Gentlemen, I have no stomach for more senseless bloodletting. I recommend that the Christian clergy in Japan remain within the port cities.'

All the captains nodded their agreement.

Edward Crest drew himself up. 'Mr Ministers, that was an amazing display of discipline. I greatly respect your people's bravery. But their sacrifice has not altered the situation. Bring back your government's approval by noon tomorrow or I shall be forced to burn Tokyo.'

Chapter 23

At a relentless ground-eating pace, Lord Saga's warriors continued towards Tokyo, the pulsating rattle of their armour filling the countryside. By the shadowy light of a hovering moon, the Choshu men appeared to be a mile-long dragon snaking its way to the capital.

Ukiko reluctantly left Yoshida's side after the physician assured her the young man would sleep for some time. With Sandanj as her guide, she went to see Udo. He lay pale and feverish in a small hut on the outskirts of the city. At the sight of her, he tried to sit up but did not have the strength.

'Rest,' Ukiko said. 'You have lost a great deal of blood.'

The whip mark was raw on his throat and his voice was hoarse. 'Ukiko, can a younger brother consult an older sister in matters of love?' he asked.

'Of course.' She dipped a cloth in a bowl of scented water and placed it on his burning forehead. 'That is why the gods created older sisters.'

'When you met Mung, did you immediately fall in love with him?'

'You must never tell anyone this because he was my sister's husband. I did fantasize about him.'

'When Saiyo died, were you driven to marry him because of love?'

'I did love him. I knew I would be a good mother to Yoshida, and a good wife. Over the years Mung has come to love me.'

The fever muddled Udo's thoughts and he babbled. Then

218

he said clearly, 'The first time I met Gin-ko, I loved her. She was standing in front of the florist shop. She turned and I fell in love with her. But she thinks me a prude.' His fevered eyes stared into space. 'Do you know what I worked at in Canton?' he shouted.

'No need to holler, old friend.' Sandanj pressed Udo back onto the mat.

'I must tell.'

'I am listening,' Ukiko said.

Udo closed his eyes and took a deep breath. 'I was a male prostitute. I trained women to pleasure men.' He moaned and rolled his head from side to side. 'A truthful courtesan is as rare as a square egg. How many times have I repeated that? Now I love a courtesan,' he moaned.

'Gin-ko is a wonderful person,' Ukiko said. 'She is my friend.'

'I taught girls in Canton to rub a flower against their cheeks to excite their clients. Gin-ko did it to me.'

'Her profession is to arouse men's passions,' Ukiko said.

'She touched my neck.'

'What does that mean?' Sandanj asked.

Ukiko shrugged. 'I do not know.'

Udo looked up with pleading eyes at Ukiko. 'I have no choice. I love her. Help me to win her.' His eyes fluttered closed and he began to recite,

> 'So forlorn am I
> My body like a floating world
> The roots unmoored
> I drift away.'

He sighed, his body relaxed, and his breathing grew deep and even.

'Sandanj,' Ukiko said, 'remain with him. See him safely aboard the *Kanrin Maru*. I must return to Yoshida.'

'Are there words of comfort he may take on his journey?'

'Tell him Gin-ko was not recruited to the Yoshiwara. She sold herself to extricate her parents from debtors' prison.'

'He will appreciate that.'

'Tell him I shall speak to Gin-ko about marriage. But he should know that Little Mother holds her contract and the old woman is very possessive.'

Sandanj nodded. 'I will tell him. I thank you for Udo, and pray Yoshida recovers soon.' He bowed.

Ukiko hurried away. Her rickshaw was stopped several times to allow passage of lords on their way to the Hall of a Hundred Mats. She knew Mung was there, and prayed the crucial vote would be in his favour. When the road was clear, the rickshaw man hurried on. She prayed that Yoshida and not Musashi would be waiting for her.

In the great hall lit by a thousand flickering oil lamps Mung and Iyeasu sat on the dais, confident they had avoided war. Black Dragon agents reported that both Saga and Fujita Koin had instructed their allies to vote for any proposal put forth by the two ministers. In less than one hour the Rujo accepted the terms of the foreign captains. The lords filed out of the great hall in angry silence, resentful of being forced to change the course of Japanese history.

Iyeasu went to his apartment in the Yoshiwara, and Mung to his wife and son. He was with Ukiko when Yoshida opened his eyes and said, 'Mother, I am hungry.' They embraced him so fervently, he gasped for breath.

'The most beautiful words,' Ukiko wept. 'The most beautiful, wonderful words you could speak. I will prepare something right away.' She ran through a list of foods he might want to eat and Yoshida made his choice. 'Oh, I am so happy.' She kissed Yoshida, then Mung, and hurried to the kitchen.

Alone with his son, Mung began talking in a way he had

220

never done before. It was as if he knew Yoshida was leaving soon and he wanted to tell the young man as much as he could. 'My father was a samurai in the service of an unfortunate lord. This lord displeased the shogun, who eventually confiscated the lord's property and disowned his samurai. That is how your grandfather became a ronin. There were many like him wandering the country without a lord to serve. Some became bandits. Your grandfather became the town clerk and teacher in the fishing village of Nakanohama. He married and had two sons. I am the youngest. When your grandfather felt my brother and I could support our mother, and that we both understood the importance of honouring his ancestors, he committed seppuku. The shame of being a ronin had never left him.'

'Father, you have told me of your brother's death in the shipwreck, and of your rescue and adoption by the American whaling captain. But I do not understand why you returned to Japan despite the death penalty.'

'Because I wanted a son to honour my grave and those of my ancestors.'

'I shall fulfil that duty,' Yoshida said.

'Yes, yes, my son.' Mung fought back tears. Yoshida was emaciated, his eyes sunken and dark. Mung feared the Sword Saint would leap out from behind the frail mask of his son's personality.

'Father, it seems to me that finding a wife and honouring your parents was not the only reason you returned.'

'That is true. I knew from my whaling experience and from my adoptive father, who was employed by the American government, that Japan could no longer remain isolated. The Americans' search for new markets, and the invention of the steam engine, were changing the world. The steamship negated the winds and tides that protected these islands for centuries. I returned to warn our people. My American parents had schooled me well for the task.'

Mung tapped his head. 'Harvard High School provided the best education possible in the United States.'

'How is it you remember everything and I forget the simplest things? Lately I often find myself in strange places. Then I do not remember how I arrived, or why I went.'

'Yoshida,' Mung said, 'I have never met another person with a memory like mine. Many have asked me to teach them, but I cannot. I never learned. The gift was with me from birth. I have come to believe the gods ordained my shipwreck and education in America. They endowed me with a perfect memory in order that I might bring my knowledge home.'

'Father, tell me again about how my American Uncle John helped bring down the shogun.'

'Since your mother, Saiyo, was killed by American raiders, my relations with your uncle have not been as warm as they were. But he was as important as anyone in bringing about the fall of the shogun. He fought side by side with us, and was made a Satsuma samurai in recognition of his service. When we signed the treaty with Commodore Perry, your Uncle John was there. He brought a steel plough as a gift from America to Japan. Before that we used steel only for swords, and horses only to carry warriors.' Mung smiled. 'Lord Takai harnessed two sumo wrestlers to pull the plough through rocks and weeds. Since then the manufacture of steel-tipped ploughs in Japan has opened up more land to cultivation. John and I also introduced fast ripening rice from China to Japan, resulting in two crops a year instead of one. Recently John wrote me about the use of chemical fertilizers and planned rotation of crops that result in higher yields per acre.'

'Do you consider the progress in agriculture more important than your establishment of Japan's maritime industry?'

'The most important thing I will ever do may soon

become a reality. Only three other men in the empire know of my plan – Baron Iyeasu, Lord Hotta and the Emperor. It is to establish a constitutional government.'

'But that would take power from the Emperor and give it to the Rujo. A government that operates to the will of one man most certainly would be more efficient than decisions made by a large group.'

Mung noticed a spark in his son's eyes and sensed Musashi lurking. He wondered if Yoshida's incisive questions were influenced by the Sword Saint. 'It appears so at first,' he answered, 'but facts disprove the effectiveness of absolute rulers. England, France and Germany are constitutional monarchies. America does not even have a king, and these are the four most powerful nations in the world.'

'Where does their strength reside?'

'Your questions make me proud of you,' Mung said, still wondering who he was talking to – his son, Musashi, or his dead friend, Ryochi. 'Once again I am angry with myself for not having spent more time with you. I tell you now what I will tell the Rujo. The strength of those countries rests with the people. The more that people participate in governing themselves, the more powerful the nation. France is drifting back towards monarchy, and becoming weaker. She will probably lose the upcoming war with Prussia because of it. America becomes stronger the further it moves towards democracy.'

'I should think a democratic government would be militarily feeble because it would be so slow to react.'

'The opposite is true. Quick reactions are often the wrong ones. To defeat a democracy, you must conquer the people. To defeat a monarchy, you need only kill, capture or control the king.'

'Our people would never accept a constitution that would reduce the powers of the Emperor,' Yoshida said.

'I will make you the fourth man in the empire privy to

my secret. I have persuaded the Emperor to make a gift of a constitution to the people. That way they cannot refuse, and the Emperor remains head of state.'

Just then, Ukiko entered carrying a tray of food. Yoshida began to eat with relish. Mung watched him, wondering if his son would live to see the constitution approved.

It was the hour of the hare, and still dark. Mung, Ukiko and Yoshida slept in the same room.

Jiroo entered quietly and woke Mung. 'You are needed,' the senior Black Dragon whispered. 'We have been warned there will be an attempt to capture the Emperor on his return from the Yasukune shrine. We have little time to prepare.'

Mung woke Ukiko and whispered to her. 'I must leave.' He looked at the still form of his son and heard his rhythmic breathing. He did not see the blazing eyes of Musashi searching the room for a way to escape and protect the Emperor.

Chapter 24

The Emperor's refusal to change the ritual of his morning devotions posed an urgent problem for Mung.

'Why can't his majesty pray at the Kanda shrine?' Iyeasu asked. 'It too is close to the palace.'

'It must be the Yasukune shrine,' Mung said. 'People remember too well the Emperor's move from Kyoto to Tokyo. Every mishap, calamity and cloudburst in the empire was blamed on his worshipping in different shrines along the way. Yasukune has been established as the imperial place of worship in the new capital. Any variation could cause more civil disruption.'

'My men are spread very thin,' Lord Hotta said. 'With the help of Lord Maeda's troops it is possible to control the city and port areas, but not the imperial shrine too.'

'My Black Dragons will guard the shrine,' Mung said, 'although we have been warned the attack will be made on the Emperor's return journey to the palace.'

'By whom?' Iyeasu asked.

'Mostly bandit ronin looking for trouble,' Mung said. 'There are also the Tosa samurai, friends of those who committed seppuku. They claim the Emperor is being misled by Lord Hotta and me.'

'How is it they have not accused me of misleading the Emperor?' Iyeasu asked.

'They continue to associate you with your father's policies,' Lord Hotta said. 'For the moment, that serves our purpose. I recommend you not to become involved in today's action.'

'It is my duty,' Iyeasu protested.

'With the information Mung's Black Dragons have provided, there is no doubt we can foil the attack,' Hotta said. 'But even an unsuccessful attempt to take the Emperor hostage will have unpredictable results. Mung and I are already involved. You must remain untainted. If anything happens to us, the Emperor will need you to advise him.'

Mung's senior aide entered the room. Jiroo bowed and reported, 'The Lord of Tosa knew nothing about the plot to capture the Emperor. He and I devised a plan by which he will imprison his men in his palace prior to the attack. He awaits your orders on how to dispose of them.'

'Let him wait,' Hotta said. 'How many ronin will we have to deal with?'

'There are three hundred, but forty are Black Dragons who infiltrated the group.'

'How could so few men expect to overcome the imperial guard and the Emperor's entire entourage?' Iyeasu asked.

Jiroo unrolled a Tokyo street map and pointed. 'The Emperor's carriage passes this crossroad on its return to the palace. The Tosa men were to have attacked from the intersecting street on the left, the ronin from the right. The people watching the procession will be prostrate on the ground as the Emperor's carriage moves by. The attackers plan to run right over them, and catch the imperial guard, facing inward, from behind. The imperial archers will be too close to aim their three-foot arrows. They do not carry swords and will be cut down.'

'Then what?' Iyeasu asked. 'The attackers will be surrounded by the imperial guard, the lancers, artillery and infantry.'

'But no Japanese will raise a sword if there is a chance of endangering the Emperor,' Jiroo said. 'The attackers intend to keep their backs to his majesty's carriage until a reversal of the decision to accept the foreigners' demands is effected.'

226

'The plan is brilliant in its simplicity,' Mung said. 'Hideyoshi was the architect. He inspired the ronin and convinced the Tosa men.'

'It does not sound like one of my brother's schemes,' Iyeasu said. 'His methods are usually more involved, his plots more intricate.'

The men in the room were silent for some moments. Then Hotta said, 'The ronin will hear about the imprisonment of the Tosa men.'

'No,' Jiroo said. 'The liaisons between the Tosa samurai and the ronin are Black Dragons. I have arranged for some of our people, fitted out in Tosa armour, to be in the right place at the right time. The ronin will believe their plan is in effect. It will enable us to entrap all the rebels in one place.'

'Good,' Mung said. 'Now here is my plan to stop the attack . . .'

Mung's scheme was well conceived. It so easily countered Hideyoshi's scheme that Hotta complimented him.

'Be wary,' Iyeasu warned again. 'If my brother is involved, watch out for a trap.'

'All possibilities have been considered,' Mung said. 'I have every intersection and potential place of ambush guarded. We are prepared.'

'Having succeeded through the benign influence of my imperial ancestors to the throne of lineal succession unbroken for ages eternal, and having assumed the power to reign over and govern the empire, I have performed with solemnity the daily ritual of invoking the spirits on behalf of the people. I ask they be allowed to maintain the rules of correct conduct, allowed to cultivate inherited virtues and continue intact the glorious traditions set by their ancestors.' The Emperor of Japan clapped once to send his prayer on its way. A bell chimed. He left the Yasukune shrine and entered his coach for the return trip to the palace.

Lord Hotta rode ahead of the imperial carriage, keeping his eyes on the people prostrated on the ground. He observed the fifty lords, their retainers, and the archers now armed with concealed short swords, roaming both sides of the carriage. The imperial guards in their blood-red uniforms were grim and tense. Today they did not giggle at the infantry slipping and stumbling through the warm horse droppings. The foot soldiers paid no heed to the road, but kept their hands on their swords and their eyes searching for an enemy.

Five hundred yards before the procession approached the street of the expected attack, Mung gave a signal. The commander of the imperial guard sent a company of his men rushing into that street, threatening everyone who did not flee. Panic-stricken people rushed away, towards the oncoming ronin. Before the would-be attackers could draw their swords, the Black Dragons in their midst began stabbing and hacking at everyone within reach. Mauled by the fear-crazed mob from without, gouged by the Black Dragons from within, and with the imperial guards pressing hard to reach them, the ronin broke and ran, straight into units of Lord Hotta's samurai waiting in the streets and alleys to cut them down. The fighting was short, brutal and bloody. The rebels were killed, as Mung had planned.

The imperial guard readjusted its ranks on either side of the route of march. All but thirty guards double-timed out of the main gate of the palace to fill in positions along the route closest to the gate. It was closed and barred until the Emperor's re-entry.

Mung signalled success to Lord Hotta, then turned and hurried away, directly to the nearest public latrine. He squatted, said a quick prayer, then took a deep breath and voided his bowels. His long sigh of relief was heard by a passerby who wished him good health over the screen. Mung looked down and saw the bullet in his faeces. He thanked the spirits it had not exploded inside him. He fingered his pouch of bullets and shrugged. The physician will not know the difference in bullets when I give him one as I promised.

Mung set out to see Yoshida and Ukiko, confident of his own health and the Emperor's safety. He prayed for good news about his son.

A short distance from the Kanda river, Lord Saga of Choshu reined in his war horse and watched his troops trot into view. More than half had dropped out on the eleven-hour run to the capital, but those who arrived, although weary and dull-eyed, responded well to the orders of their officers. They separated into two groups on the far side of the river.

The smaller contingent, two hundred of Saga's best men, trotted across the Suidobashi bridge. They ran directly to the Takebashi gate of the palace and easily forced it. Once inside they moved west through the imperial gardens at their ground-eating pace, catching the thirty remaining imperial guards at the main gate from behind. The struggle was brief. Within seconds the Choshu men had deployed, and signalled their success to Lord Saga outside the walls.

Saga threw his fist into the air. Seven hundred Choshu warriors began crossing the Kanda river at the Kahikawa bridge. Saga wheeled his horse right and left, herding his exhausted men into ranks opposite the main gate three hundred yards away.

A few Choshu stragglers were still on the bridge when the Emperor's procession came into view. The commander of the imperial guard, catching sight of the warriors standing in formation, assumed they were there for added security. He issued the familiar order to begin the formal entrance into the palace grounds. 'Column of twos,' he ordered the lancers. They trotted their mounts forward and formed a double file to the main gate. Fifty lords and their retainers proceeded forward and lined up behind the lancers. They stopped and waited for the royal carriage.

Sandanj, on his return from the *Kanrin Maru*, had by chance fallen in with the Choshu stragglers crossing the Kahikawa bridge. It struck him as odd they were dressed for battle. When he crossed the Kanda river and recognized Saga astride his war horse, Sandanj grasped what was taking place. He sprinted across the open area towards the imperial lancers. 'Stand to arms! Stand to arms!' he shouted.

The commander of the imperial guard galloped forward. Sandanj pointed. 'It is Saga and his Choshu warriors! Protect the Emperor!'

Lord Hotta, having seen the unusual troop formation along the river, halted the imperial carriage and galloped ahead to the commander of the guard.

'Sire, it appears the first attempt to capture the Emperor was a diversion,' the commander reported, motioning to Lord Saga. 'This is the real thing.'

Hotta, a battle-hardened veteran, took in the situation. 'Iyeasu was correct about his brother. He plans like a spider. But Saga has misjudged. If we take swift action, he will not have time to stop us. Use your lancers, the lords and their retainers to screen us. Deploy the artillery, archers and infantry. Unless Saga advances, do nothing until I return. Now see to opening the gates. I will lead the Emperor's carriage ahead of the procession into the safety of the palace.' He galloped away.

The commander of the guard spurred his mount between the column of lancers, shouting to them and the lords to move aside. He pulled his horse up short at the giant wooden doors and gave the familiar command. 'The Emperor arrives! Open!'

The gates swung back. Hotta galloped through the entrance pulling the bridle of the lead horse of the Emperor's carriage. The imperial carriage continued on but the Fujiwara lord was pulled from his mount by Choshu samurai. The gates slammed shut before anyone could follow.

Hotta pushed away the Choshu men helping him up from the ground. 'What is the meaning of this?' he demanded. 'What are you doing in here?'

'Sonno joi!' the Choshu commander declared. 'The Emperor is now protected by those who truly revere his imperial majesty, Japan and things Japanese.'

'You are saying the Emperor is your prisoner.'

'Not so.' The Choshu officer pointed to the Emperor being escorted from his carriage by his own house servants. Choshu samurai prostrated themselves on the ground before him.

'What is it you want?' Hotta demanded, silently relieved at the respect being accorded the Emperor.

'You are to meet Lord Saga outside the walls. You may inform him there have been no deaths inside the palace grounds. Saga will speak for us.' The commander slapped his fist over his heart. 'Sonno joi! Revere the Emperor and expel the barbarian!'

Hotta shoved the officer aside and stalked through the small door in the tall wooden gate. Outside there was mild confusion. The lords of the realm, lined in ranks behind the lancers, did not understand why they had been pulled aside by the imperial carriage racing into the palace grounds. Hotta disregarded their questions and summoned the commander of the imperial guard.

The commander rode up and reported, 'Sire, there are now eight hundred samurai with Lord Saga. They have made no attempt to move or communicate.'

'Get off that horse and follow me,' Hotta said.

He led the commander away and spoke quietly. 'The Choshu are inside. They hold the Emperor captive.'

The commander went white.

'Do not panic,' Hotta said. 'Get hold of yourself. I do not want the others to know what is happening just yet.'

'How can we keep it secret? Everyone awaits answers.'

'I will speak with that bucktoothed baboon Saga. Tell the lords this is a military exercise. Everyone is to remain in position.'

'Will they believe the Choshu are part of the exercise?'

'Tell them Saga and his men are protesting at the Rujo's decision to accept the foreigners' terms.'

'But he voted for the decision.'

'Say no more than I have told you.' Hotta waved for Sandanj to approach.

'Mung went to his son,' Hotta told Sandanj. 'Get him!' He shoved Sandanj up into the saddle of the commander's horse and slapped its rump. Then he strode to meet Saga.

The Choshu lord sat sideways in the saddle. His armour was too large, his helmet tilted back, and his wire-frame spectacles slipped down his nose. He looked a clown, but it was no comedian's voice that stopped Hotta ten paces away. 'Remain there!' Saga barked.

'Do you fear my sword?' Hotta sneered.

'Of course.' Saga bowed. 'Cut off the head and the body dies. Isn't that what we learned at military school? If our positions were reversed, I would kill you.'

'What do you want?'

'The barbarians out of Japan.'

'You voted to accept their terms.'

'I gave my word to vote yes, and I did. Now I tell you on my honour and that of my illustrious ancestors, I will die before I allow the round-eyes to rule Japan.'

Hotta motioned at the archers and lancers, then pointed

at the artillery. 'You and your men will be cut to pieces if you move a step.'

'Would you shoot the Emperor?' Saga leered down.

'You hold his imperial majesty hostage, not me.'

'Do not use the word hostage. Rather let us say my samurai have become the new guardians of the imperial presence.'

'You are kidnappers. Although I cannot believe you would harm the Emperor.'

'Believe what you will.' Saga gave a big toothy grin.

'As yet, your men inside the walls have killed no one,' Hotta said.

'That is good. I hope to achieve my goal without bloodshed, if possible. But if you make any attempt to reach the Emperor . . .'

'What will you do when the Emperor orders you to stand down?' Hotta asked.

'My men will not allow any message to or from the Emperor until this episode is settled. Convene the Rujo,' Saga ordered.

Hotta took a step closer. 'Tell your men to lay down their weapons or I will have you all slaughtered.'

The Lord of Choshu appeared to grow into his armour. He straightened in the saddle, threw back his shoulders and shouted, 'Kiii-oooootz-kaiii! Attention!' His face turned grim and he pushed his spectacles into place. 'My men inside the walls will hear your cannon. They have their orders.' He turned his head and bellowed, 'Prepare to advance!'

Hotta turned and saw the imperial lancers before the palace gate lower their long, steel-tipped shafts and gather their horses under them. The imperial archers strung their bows. The infantry unsheathed their swords. The canno-neers prepared to fire.

'Advance,' Saga roared, and eight hundred Choshu men stepped forward.

'Wait,' Hotta cried. 'Wait!' Sweat streamed from every pore in his trembling body. 'I would never have believed you capable of killing the grandson of the goddess Amater-asu-o-mi-Kami,' he gasped. 'No harm must come to the Emperor.'

'Halt!' Saga bellowed. He glowered down between his horse's ears at the shaken Hotta. 'I want the Rujo convened here. Out in the open before the main gate. While we await the assembly, I want food and water brought for my men. If anyone tries to reach the Emperor, we march.'

'I will need until noon to convene the Rujo.'

'You have until the sun reaches its apex. If the Rujo is not assembled by then, there will be darkness over the land of the rising sun.'

Chapter 25

Mung could see trouble in Ukiko's face. She and the physician awaited him on the porch of the main house. He looked to the cottage. There were six guards instead of four. Two wore fresh head bandages, a third favoured an injured leg. 'What has happened?' Mung asked.

'It will be easier if we talk in the house,' the physician said.

'I want to see my son.'

Ukiko bowed to her husband. 'Please hear the physician first.'

Mung allowed himself to be drawn into the main house. Over an untouched pot of tea, the physician explained. 'Yoshida's soul has succumbed to Musashi.'

'Permanently?' Mung asked.

'I do not know. Meanwhile I have ordered him restrained.'

Mung looked from the physician to Ukiko. 'It had to be done,' she said. 'I was with him when he became Musashi. He almost escaped.'

'Did he injure those guards?' Mung asked.

'I sent a fourth man home to recuperate,' the physician said.

'How could Yoshida who is thin as a reed do so much damage?'

'I saw it,' Ukiko said. 'He has incredible strength.'

'Did he hurt you?'

She bowed her head and sobbed. 'He did not recognize me, but I was safe because he acted according to the laws of Bushido. He fought like the historical accounts I have read of Musashi.'

'But Musashi was a sixteenth-century swordsman and Yoshida had no weapon.'

The physician poured tea. 'Your son rolled up a tatami mat,' he said. 'When the attendant brought in the morning meal, Yoshida used the mat as a battering ram. The results of how well he fought are too obvious. That is the reason he is bound and two additional guards stand watch.'

'Will he recognize me?' Mung asked.

'Yoshida would. Musashi will not.'

'I must see him. My presence may help bring his true soul back.'

The physician stood up. 'It can be no worse. I will arrange it.' He left the house.

'I am not prepared to face him again so soon.' Ukiko sobbed. 'Forgive me.'

Mung took her into his arms. 'Yoshida will recover,' he crooned. 'You do not have to come with me.'

'He is no longer Yoshida.' She lifted her tear-streaked face. 'When I saw him last he was truly a soul possessed. He attacked those guards with such ferocity they were even frightened by his shouts. I was terrified.'

Mung attempted to stem his wife's tears. 'Shhhh,' he whispered, 'shhhh.' He rocked her in his arms. 'I regret my work keeps me away from being with you through all this.'

Ukiko wiped her eyes and patted dry the tear-stains on Mung's kimono. 'You must never,' she wagged her finger, 'never, never put Yoshida or me before your duty. You serve Japan.'

Mung leaned his forehead against hers and remained silent.

'Go to your son,' Ukiko said.

He did not move. 'I have ordered hundreds of men on

missions that took them from their families for months, even years at a time. Not one ever complained or refrained.'

'They too swore an oath in the Black Dragon Society,' Ukiko said. 'They understand that their lives, as yours, belong to the Emperor.'

He touched his lips to her forehead, bowed, and went to Yoshida.

Mung squatted alone next to the sleeping figure on the tatami mat. Yoshida's back was towards him, his hands and legs bound from behind. As Mung's eyes became accustomed to the dim light he saw that the plaited bamboo cord had cut into the frail wrists. Like a delicate ruby bracelet, droplets of blood formed around the cord. Mung tried to loosen the knot but with his one hand it proved impossible. Had he been less anxious he would have seen that Musashi, while feigning sleep, was straining at the bonds, forcing them into his flesh.

The guard watching through the porthole rushed in. 'Do not untie him.'

'The bonds are too tight,' Mung said. 'His wrists are swollen. Release him now.'

'He is a most dangerous person,' the guard protested. 'I request you speak with the physician first.'

'Untie him,' Mung ordered. 'His feet are bound. That is enough.'

Reluctantly the guard bent to the task.

The moment his hands were freed, Yoshida mumbled, 'Water. Please give me water.'

'Hurry,' Mung ordered.

The guard turned and took the three steps to the water bucket. Musashi, his back to both men, heard the guard dip the wooden ladle into the water. He spun around, pinning Mung's good arm, pushing aside the stump of his left arm and searching for his sword. Mung had left the sword outside the room but he understood the intention.

He threw himself on top of his son's body, pinning him to the floor. The face that grimaced up was not Yoshida's. The crazed eyes glared, the bare teeth gnashed. Musashi punched the knuckle of his forefinger into Mung's temple and stars exploded in Mung's head. Musashi brought his bound feet up under Mung's stomach with a great heave that catapulted him across the room. Mung hit the far wall and slid down to a sitting position, too stunned to move. The guard came up behind Musashi and cracked him over the head with the wooden ladle. The young man fell backward onto the mat.

Two more guards rushed in. 'Are you well, sire?' the first one asked, helping Mung to his feet. 'There is a messenger for you.' He helped Mung out to the porch.

Sandanj waved the guard away, out of hearing. 'Sire, Lord Hotta needs you immediately,' he whispered. 'The Emperor has been taken hostage.'

Mung shook his head to clear it. 'The Emperor taken hostage,' he repeated aloud.

Inside the room, the two guards binding Musashi heard Mung's words. They looked at each other. 'I will finish tying his hands, you go and listen,' the first guard said.

The second guard hurried out of the room. The other leaned over to tie the knot. Musashi opened his eyes and brought his head up with such force it smashed the guard's nose. He sat back on his heels, dazed. Musashi struggled upright onto his knees and bashed his head against the guard's, again and again until the man lay unconscious.

Musashi twisted free of his bonds and untied his legs. With the cunning of the insane he crouched in the middle of the room, planning his escape. His eyes darted from the partially open door to the viewing slot. The guards outside were paying attention to the exchange between Mung and Sandanj. Musashi pulled himself up the interior wall and squeezed between the eaves. He lay on his stomach, balanced on top of the wooden wall.

'I am taking your horse,' Mung said to Sandanj. 'Follow me on foot.' He galloped away.

A guard entered the room to check on the prisoner. Seeing the empty mat and the unconscious guard, he shouted an alarm. Two more guards rushed in, and Musashi dropped to the ground outside the building in a crouch. Another guard rushed towards him with drawn sword in the classical two-handed overhead stroke. Musashi dived forward, driving his head into the man's stomach and taking him off his feet. He reached down and clutched the guard's windpipe with one hand. The mouth gaped. The face turned blue. He snatched the man's sword. 'It is not my duty to kill unskilled peasants. It is to save the Emperor.' Musashi let go of the limp figure. He turned and fled towards the imperial palace. Sandanj and four guards followed after.

Pigeons strutted on the naked stone walls of the imperial palace. Sea birds wheeled overhead, screeching at the two armed forces facing each other. A short distance from the huge wooden doors of the main palace gate, Mung and Hotta conferred in the shade.

'Noon brings with it two deadlines,' Mung said, 'Saga's and Lord Crest's.'

'The Rujo will soon be assembled in the great hall,' Hotta replied. 'I will inform them of Saga's demand to be heard by them here in front of the palace walls.'

'If we convene the Rujo out here at Saga's orders, it means he is in command and will obtain his demands.'

'Of course,' Hotta said, with an impatient wave of his hand. 'That little Choshu pimp holds the Emperor hostage.'

'I do not believe he will harm his imperial majesty,' Mung said.

'We cannot take that chance.'

'I think we can. According to what you told me, Saga never actually threatened harm to the Emperor. Last night in the vote, he kept his word according to the code of Bushido.'

'I tried to call his bluff,' Hotta said, 'and he ordered his men forward. That little four-eyed primitive interprets Bushido his own way when he wants to.'

'He did not want you to use the word hostage,' Mung said. 'You told me his men prostrated themselves before the Emperor. He has isolated himself from the Emperor for fear of disobeying his orders. He told you he would march forward, but did not say he would fight.'

Hotta punched his thigh as he strode back and forth, glaring over at the little man astride his war horse. 'He said he would see darkness over the land. If he kills the Emperor, Japan dies. That is what Saga meant. Eternal darkness.'

Suddenly a bedraggled figure darted out from the artillery formation, brandishing a naked long sword. His clothing was torn, his hair dishevelled. He looked from the imperial lancers to the ranks of Choshu samurai three hundred yards away, and appeared confused. An officer of the imperial guard strode out to challenge him.

'Yoshida,' Mung gasped. He watched the officer confront his son with a sword.

Musashi grinned with contempt for the guardsman. He whipped his own sword around in a lightning move, knocking the blade from the officer's hand. 'I am Miyamoto Musashi!' Yoshida barked at the officer. 'Return to your post or die!' He pressed the point of his blade into the officer's throat until blood ran down his neck into his armour.

'Do as he says!' Mung shouted. He started towards his son.

Musashi turned away from the officer and strode towards Saga astride his war horse. Sandanj and Yoshida's guards came up behind Mung, and Sandanj held Mung back. They watched ten Choshu samurai form a screen in front of Saga. Musashi moved sideways down the line like a fighting crab, crossing swords with each samurai. Using his blade like a snapping steel claw, he skittered by each one, engaging and disengaging the ten warriors with apparent skill. It became clear he was not attempting to inflict injury, but only testing their competence. Blades flashed in the morning sun, clanging over the ancient cobblestones. Musashi reached the last man in line and attacked with fury. He beat down the man's guard and struck him a killing blow to the forehead.

Mung struggled to free himself.

'Hold him back,' Hotta ordered Sandanj. 'Your son wears no uniform,' Hotta said to Mung. 'Saga may not consider it an attack by us. Think of the Emperor.'

'Yoshida will be killed!'

'Not if he continues to fight with such skill,' Hotta said.

Musashi skipped, danced and whirled, in front of, around and behind the nine remaining Choshu samurai. He killed one with a stroke between neck and shoulder. The next died from a two-handed thrust into the stomach. Before Musashi could withdraw his sword from the body, the others leapt to hack him down. But their blades cut air. He rolled backward on the ground and picked up the blade of the first fallen warrior. The remaining seven samurai divided into two groups determined to keep Musashi between them.

'Hold,' Saga ordered. He pointed at Yoshida. 'How do you call yourself, Warrior?'

'Guardian of his imperial majesty, the Emperor,' Musashi replied.

'You are a brave and skilful swordsman.' Saga bowed. 'I

wish to tell you this. If you should defeat these seven samurai, I shall withdraw my troops and commit seppuku before their blood dries on these stones.'

'Well said, my Lord Saga.' Musashi laughed. 'Prepare for death.' He leapt forward, feinting to the head of one Choshu man and cutting the throat of another. He fought with such skill that the men of both forces cheered him.

As Mung watched his son parry, strike and dodge the flashing blades of the samurai warriors, he suddenly realized that Yoshida was proving Saga's dedication to the warrior code. The Choshu lord would never kill the Emperor.

Mung recalled the battle of the Hakusar Valley. The shogun's army, certain of victory, had moved forward. Lord Nariakira sent his two sons to certain death leading a cavalry charge that brought the shogun's troops closer to Mung's hidden riflemen and his brother's artillery. Mung had seen how proud Nariakira was, even knowing his sons would die, and never understood until now. He felt the same pride as his son rushed, feinted and charged the remaining Choshu samurai.

Musashi continued to beat off sustained attacks, although he was weakening. His opponents were veterans of the blade. No matter what tricks Musashi tried, they kept him between them. He retreated, beating off chops, cuts and slashes with a series of defensive moves so adept both forces took up a chant to encourage him.

Musashi catapulted forward again, blocking one blow, ducking another, then thrusting for a samurai's throat. The point of his blade was turned by the warrior's armour. The man lowered his shoulder and drove it into Musashi's chest. The wind went out of him. He was thrown off balance. The samurai on his right levelled his blade and brought it around waist high. It bit deep between Musashi's

242

ribs. The remaining Choshu warriors recognized the death blow. They stepped back and bowed.

Mung saw Yoshida lean to his injured side and sink to the ground. He broke free of Sandanj's grip and ran to his son. Yoshida raised his head. The eyes were no longer mad. He smiled at his father and asked, 'Do you know how to catch flying fish?'

Mung sobbed. 'I love you.'

Yoshida nodded. He closed his eyes and leaned forward, his face in the crook of Mung's neck. Mung heard his son sigh, and felt his last breath. He embraced him.

Mung became aware of being helped to his feet by Sandanj and Hotta. Eight imperial guardsmen marched out from their formation. The commander addressed Mung. 'We respectfully request the honour of carrying this warrior from the field of battle.'

Mung looked at Yoshida's thin crumpled body, and then at the commander. His throat constricted into a knot. He opened his mouth twice but could not speak. He nodded his consent.

Four guards lined up on each side of Yoshida. They lay him on his back, folded his hands over his chest, then slipped their long swords flat side up, under his body. Each man held a point and a hilt. They lifted Yoshida and marched away. Mung followed. He saw the long steel-tipped shafts of the royal lancers dip in salute. The imperial archers, infantry and artillery slapped their right fists over their hearts. Fifty lords of the realm sat their mounts at attention as the body of Yoshida Ishikawa passed.

Saga of Choshu raised his fist in salute. His men threw their clenched fists in the air, chanting, 'Hai! Hai! Hai!'

Mung stopped and turned to look at Saga. 'I will see that man die,' he said, then continued walking. 'Sandanj, take my son to Ukiko. I want his body cremated. The ashes are to be buried in Kagoshima next to his mother. 'I do not know if I will ever see my wife again.'

'So it is ordered, so it is done.' Sandanj hurried off.

'Hotta,' Mung said, 'you attend to the Rujo.'

'Where will you be?'

Mung's face was livid. The scar across his nose was a slash of white. 'I am the Black Dragon. Saga will die. I swear it.' He held up his blood-covered hands. 'On my son's body, I swear it.'

Chapter 26

Mung stood alone before the seven foreign captains in the stateroom of the HMS *Nemesis*.

'Is it war or peace?' Edward Crest asked.

'The Rujo has voted to accept your terms,' Mung answered. 'But they are powerless to implement the treaty.'

'And pray tell us why that is,' Lord Crest said.

'Anti-foreign ronin hold the Emperor prisoner. Among them are those who killed the interpreter, Heuskens,' Mung lied. 'They are led by your former captive, Saga of Choshu.'

'He is a troublesome little man,' Edward Crest said. 'Where is Townsend Harris?'

'Barricaded in his house,' Mung lied again. He had ordered his Black Dragons to confine the American consul to his home.

'Why don't the imperial guard and whoever else loves the Emperor, free him?'

'Because no Japanese would dare raise a hand if it might endanger his imperial highness. He is to us what Jesus is to you.'

Lord Crest coughed and the captains shifted uneasily in their seats. 'You are assuming a bit much there, old son,' the British lord said. He cleared his throat. 'Now, Mr Mung, I see that you arrived here without Baron Iyeasu, and it is two hours until the noon deadline. Is there a secret proposal you wish to present?'

'Yes. I propose that you free the Emperor, which will earn you his gratitude and the respect of the Japanese people. It will guarantee your treaty.'

'If we move against those bandits and the Emperor is

harmed, we will earn the undying hatred of Japan forever, shan't we, Mr Mung?'

'Sir, I speak to you as a samurai and a gentleman. I have absolute proof Saga's men will not harm the Emperor.' Mung lied a third time. 'I have trusted agents among the bandits, who have informed me of this.'

'If so, why not use Lord Hotta's Fujiwara troops?'

'You must understand that no Japanese will take the risk.'

'You are taking the risk,' Lord Crest said.

'I have lived outside of Japan long enough to see beyond the veil of tradition. I wish to remind you that the killers of the American interpreter are with Lord Saga.'

'Revenge on Saga or for the American interpreter's death does not concern me as much as the future threat to all foreigners living in Japan. These villains must be taught a lesson. But, I will not put my men ashore. Our advantage is at sea.'

'How accurate are your cannon?' Mung asked.

'When properly ranged, my gunners can drop their shells within a fifty yard radius at five miles.'

'Saga's force stands in formation three miles away.' Mung unrolled a Tokyo survey map. 'The target is three hundred yards from the wall of the imperial palace. The Emperor is safe inside, but even the walls must not be hit by your shells.'

Edward Crest leaned over the map. He asked several questions, then plunked his finger down on the Kahikawa bridge. 'We could range our guns on the river and walk the barrage into the rear of Saga's formation.'

'How soon?' Mung asked.

'As soon as I am assured the treaty, as we have agreed, is approved.'

Mung removed a scroll from his sleeve. 'This is the original agreement signed by the Rujo.' He handed it to

Edward Crest. 'You will be presented with a copy at the formal ceremony. No one but you and my agents are aware of this. Have your interpreters examine it.'

'I will, you can rest assured of that. But now that I have it, what is to stop me from waiting until the situation calms and then simply implementing it?'

'So long as the Emperor remains in the hands of those anti-foreign bandits, that treaty is not worth the rice used to make the paper.'

Edward Crest turned to the six captains and spoke in French. The discussion was heated, but short. Then he faced Mung again. 'Only the *Nemesis* will be involved. I trust no gunners except my own. But it is not possible to destroy Saga's formation unless we have a forward observer to target the area in front of the main gate.'

'I am your forward observer,' Mung said.

Lord Crest frowned at Mung. 'It has been years since you were aboard a western ship. Did you ever use signal flags?'

Mung signalled the answer with his hands. 'It has been a decade and a half. But I never forget anything. If your signal officers will instruct me, I shall range your guns.'

The ship's bells behind him rang the eleventh hour as Mung hurried to the fifty Black Dragons awaiting him on the municipal pier. They followed him at a trot to the Hinze-mon gate. From the gate he sent a messenger to the commander of the imperial guard. He stationed his men in blocking positions across the road.

Mung entered the palace grounds and climbed to the top of the outer wall. He ran along the narrow pathway until he overlooked the imperial guard and could be seen by the lookout in the crow's-nest of the *Nemesis*.

Mung watched Lord Saga arrogantly walking his mount back and forth in front of his men. He would have preferred to avenge Yoshida's death by directing the first barrage onto the Choshu lord, but duty took precedent over revenge. And despite all, Mung held a grudging respect for the little man. Saga fought for what he believed in – tradition. It was for this same reason that Mung was certain Saga would not harm the Emperor, nor allow anyone else to do so.

Mung pulled the semaphore flags from his obi. Buckled to the stump of his left arm was a leather brace strapped on by the British signal officer. Mung placed one flag in the brace and gripped the second. He waited until he saw his messenger reach the commander of the imperial guard. As they spoke, Mung raised the flags over his head and wigwagged. There was a flash from the *Nemesis'* deck and a rumble. Then it sounded as if a loose tile was slipping down a slate roof. The shell passed and fell into the Kanda river. Its explosion geysered water, mud and rocks into the air behind the startled Choshu men.

Mung watched the commander of the guard gallop up to the base of the wall below him. 'What are you doing?' the commander shouted.

'Ride out to Lord Saga and tell him to surrender, or I will bombard his men to Hell,' Mung said.

'Lord Hotta commanded me to wait for the Rujo to assemble.'

'Those orders are cancelled.' Mung held out his right hand to show the scarab ring. 'When you were made commander of the Emperor's guard, his majesty told you the Black Dragon's orders supersede all others.'

The commander wheeled his horse nearer to the wall to examine the ring. He looked up at Mung. 'So it is ordered, so it is done.' He brought his horse around and galloped across the cobblestones to Lord Saga.

Mung watched the Choshu lord dismiss the commander with a curt wave of his hand. Saga turned in the saddle and shouted orders. His men stood to attention and drew their weapons. Mung raised his flags and wigwagged.

Those in front of the main palace gate heard what sounded like distant thunder out on the bay. Then the rattle of many wagons. The shells whistled in. The explosions on the near bank of the Kanda river were deafening. The blast knocked Choshu samurai from the rear rank through to the front rank. Saga's horse reared up, but the little man controlled the animal. He galloped up and down the line, bullying his men back into ranks, encouraging them. Mung whipped the flags again, signalling for a closer barrage.

The high explosive shells of the second salvo sailed into the rear rank of Choshu warriors. Men were blown to pieces. Bodies and blood flew in every direction. Saga's horse was knocked down but the little man leapt clear. The animal staggered to its feet and ran off in wild-eyed fright. The Choshu ranks were shredded.

Mung signalled to the *Nemesis*, 'Cease fire.' He hurried down from the wall to the captain of the guard and commandeered his horse, riding the jittery animal slowly through the dead and wounded to reach the Choshu leader.

'Saga!' Mung shouted down. 'I have but to raise my hand and there will be nothing left of you or your men. Do you surrender?'

Saga set his wire-frame spectacles straight on his nose and looked up at Mung. 'How could you be certain I would not harm the Emperor?'

'When you saluted my son, I knew there was honour in your soul. A man of honour would not violate the code of Bushido.'

'Your son was a fearless warrior to be immortalized in poems. But tell me who fired those guns.'

'The Europeans.'

'Aaahhhh. You went to them. I knew no true Japanese

249

could endanger the Emperor.' He cocked his head and smiled at Mung. 'Except you, of course. Yes, I made a mistake about you. But it proves my point. Living outside of Japan changes a man.'

'I serve the Emperor,' Mung declared.

Saga looked around at the carriage. 'How could the round-eyes fire so accurately? They cannot possibly have seen us.'

'That is one of the skills we must learn from them.'

'It would be a good thing to know. But alas you and I will not be here to see it.'

'If Lord Hotta agrees,' Mung said, 'I will recommend your seppuku.'

Saga nodded. 'Yes, Hotta will agree to seppuku for me. It cannot be otherwise. I am a lord of the realm. But you, my wily fisherman, will die by strangulation. You contrived with foreigners to kill Japanese.' He pointed at the fifty lords sitting on their horses. 'They are my aristocratic brothers, and noble witnesses. I can tell you that Fujita Koin of Mito will get out of his sickbed to vote you a commoner's death.'

By order of the Rujo, Mung was taken directly to Tokyo's municipal jail. There he was given a letter from the Emperor.

You stand accused of conspiring with foreigners against the people of Japan. There will be a trial, and you should prepare for the possibility of a negative decision. Use the enclosed writing material to advise me of your thoughts for the future, and to prepare your successor in the role of Black Dragon. Should you die, it will be Japan's loss.

Mung was lowered into a six-foot-square pit. It was hewn ten feet deep into bedrock and covered by a bamboo grate. In one corner stood a bucket for slops, in another a bucket of water. Two samurai stood guard over him.

I would have liked Yoshida to meet the Emperor, he thought. 'Yoshida is gone,' he said aloud. He drew his knees to his chest and curled up on the cold ground. He lay still, using his infallible memory to recall his son.

Yoshida was named for my friend who died trying to overthrow the shogun, he thought. Many died attempting to institute reform in Japan. Saiyo, killed by American privateers, Ryochi by foreign cannon, and Gompachi, my predecessor as Black Dragon, by those opposed to modernization. Now I will join them. Mung felt a weary sense of relief in that knowledge.

He lay for two days without eating or drinking. He floated out of his body, through the bamboo grate, up over Tokyo. But it was not actually Tokyo he saw. It was the busy port of New York as he remembered it, superimposed on the Japanese city. The bay bustled with passenger steamers, merchant ships and little fat tugs scurrying here and there. Mung swooped down to Yokohama where smoke stacks billowed black smoke into the sky. The orange glow of giant forges flickered, and golden streams of molten metal splashed along concrete gutters. Close by the foundry was the largest dry-dock he had ever seen. It was filled by an iron-plated battleship from whose fantail fluttered the rising sun.

Suddenly Mung was drawn down, down into the black smoke. He lost the sense of airy flight and found himself in a strangely familiar room. Slowly his eyes became accustomed to the coppery light. He saw scattered dead bodies – men, women and children piled naked on the floor, draped haphazardly over chairs and tables, and propped against the walls. Others were stacked in neat rows. This was the same dream he had after Saiyo's death. He tried to wake up, tried to free himself from the trance he had entered. But could not.

A diaphanous soul floated up from a body at the top of a neat pile. 'Yoshida!' Mung cried. Tears coursed down his cheeks. He sobbed like a child. 'I tried to dream of you. Please do not leave me.'

Yoshida floated to the door. He reached out to open it, then stopped and turned to say, 'You serve the Emperor. You must let me go on.'

'I need you,' Mung pleaded. 'Do not go.'

Mung opened his eyes. His mouth was dry and his teeth large in his gums. He tried to unfold his arms but could not. He straightened his knees and rolled on to his back. His arms came apart and fell limp at his sides. Pain began with the return of circulation. He crawled to the water bucket and drank.

'He is alive,' one of the guards said. 'Get some food down to him.'

In the days that followed, Mung heeded Yoshida's advice and dedicated his mind to the Emperor. He wrote day and night, in every waking moment in the brightly lit cell. It was forbidden for him to speak or be spoken to but Jiroo, who came every day to collect Mung's writings, always mentioned the weather, the date, and the Emperor's good health to the guards. From Jiroo's attempt to talk to the guards about Saga, Mung knew the Choshu lord still lived.

The more Mung recorded the activities of the Black Dragon Society under his leadership, the more he became aware of his personal imprint on the organization. His predecessors had been concerned exclusively with Japan's internal affairs, but he had posted agents in Europe, Asia and America. The world was coming closer to Japan. It also became painfully clear that under his direction the society had lost more men in less time than ever before. He acknowledged this fault in his report, warning his successor not to recruit hastily. 'Intellectual quality,' he wrote, 'will prove more productive than quantitative mediocrity.'

Mung wrote of his scheme, already in effect, to activate retired Satsuma generals loyal to him in an effort to regain control of the powerful fiefdom in the south. He reminded those Black Dragons who had been abroad that when the time was again appropriate, they were to influence Tokyo's population to adopt modern ways.

Mung's acceptance of the inevitability of his death unfettered his thoughts and his inbred restraint in the face of authority. It allowed him to make recommendations to the Emperor that he would have previously only hinted at.

'Your imperial majesty,' Mung wrote, 'I have couched my recommendations for the basis of Japan's constitution in non-abrasive terms so they will be readily acceptable to those aristocratic opponents of modernization.

1) Deliberative assemblies should be widely established, and all matters decided by public discussion.
2) All classes, high and low, should unite in vigorously carrying out the administration of affairs of state.
3) The common people, no less than the civil and military officials, should be allowed to pursue their own calling so there will be no discontent.
4) Evil customs of the past should be broken off, and everything based upon the just laws of nature.
5) Knowledge should be sought throughout the world so as to strengthen the foundations of imperial rule.

'Points 1 and 2 can be used to stress national unity and a democratic form of government with you at its head. Point 3 is meant to eliminate feudal caste restrictions. Recommendation 4 anticipates the eventual combination of Shintoism and Buddhism into a state religion, with the extensive religious land holdings reverting to the central government.

The search for knowledge, stated in point 5, is meant to replace the anti-foreign slogan, "Expel the barbarian".

'Acceptance of these five points would result in centralization of power in the hands of a constitutional monarchy. This, your imperial majesty, is the future of Japan.'

On the eighteenth day of Mung's internment, a ladder was lowered into the pit. Slowly, one step at a time, he climbed up. Two rungs from the top, a huge hand reached down and lifted him out. 'Can you walk?' Danjuro asked.

'If I am to be strangled, I prefer to be carried.'

'I am taking you for a bath and clean clothes.'

'If my legs agree, I will walk,' Mung said.

'I requested this assignment,' Danjuro said. 'I want you to know I do not agree with my father's policy.'

'If so, you could have joined your brother and me.'

'I may be physically bigger than Iyeasu, but I could never find the inner strength to go against our father as he did.'

'Neither could I.'

'Mung, you are a good man, and dedicated to your cause. Your son inherited those qualities. It was apparent in the way he fought. I wanted to tell you that.'

'Before I die?'

'It has not been decided yet. But I think you will die.'

'Am I being cleaned up for a trial or to be strangled?' Mung asked.

'I am certain you will be allowed to commit seppuku. But I doubt you will be asked to testify.'

'My guilt is so apparent?'

'You have a sense of humour.' The Mito giant laughed. 'Half of Tokyo saw you waving those flags at the round-eyes. Fifty lords watched you force Saga to surrender. The time to state your beliefs is just before you commit seppuku. It will have greater effect.'

Mung stopped and looked up at Danjuro. 'Why did you come for me? I stink and am unpleasant to look at.'

'There are rumours you have been writing day and night. They say your work will guide the Emperor in modernizing the country. I want to read what you have written. True I am not a scholar like you,' Danjuro said, 'but I know it will take brains to design guns and build factories, modern ships and other weapons. I was a boy when the Chiba food riots took place. I know that Lord Takai killed two thousand people and left them crucified until the bodies rotted off the wooden stakes. I was in the Rujo when you told the lords of the Kanto Plains that the people rioted because they were starving due to overtaxation. I saw you and your American brother demonstrate the use of the steel-tipped plough, and have seen the results of the fast-ripening rice you brought from China. If you die, we must rely on your writings.'

'And if I live?' Mung asked.

Danjuro signalled him to be quiet. He veiled Mung's face and walked him quickly to a closed palanquin. Mung was carried to the imperial palace. Once there, he was allowed to scrub himself clean, rinse, and dress in fresh clothing.

Danjuro waited for him, and led Mung to an apartment door. 'My father is near death,' Danjuro said. 'If by chance you do live, you will have the support of Mito when I lead it.'

Mung bowed to the Mito giant. 'If it is within my power, you shall see my writings. Contact your brother, Iyeasu, for advice, but beware of Hideyoshi. He wishes to lead Mito, and is in league with the Golden Lizard.'

'If they crawl out from under their rocks, I shall step on both of them.' Danjuro motioned to the door. 'I have taken the unauthorized liberty of bringing your wife here.'

Mung bowed more deeply. 'If I am permitted seppuku, will you stand behind as you did the men from Tosa?'

'It will be my honour.'

Mung nodded, and entered the apartment. The sight of Ukiko ripped open the wound of Yoshida's death. She had lost weight. Her eyes were red, her face drawn.

'Oh, my husband,' she sobbed, and touched her head to the floor. 'Yoshida is gone.'

Mung knelt and raised her up. They embraced. 'I know,' he whispered, 'I know. He died in my arms. He breathed his last breath on my neck.'

'I am so glad I did not see him die.'

'I accept your feelings,' Mung whispered, 'but I will always cherish those last moments. Being with him at the moment of his death has made up in part for all the times I was not there for him during his lifetime. He was not Musashi but our little Yoshida when he died. He joked about flying fish. Do you remember my question to him in front of the school?' Mung shivered, and sobbed. When he gained control of himself, he said, 'Since Yoshida's death I have not thought of sexual intercourse, and I do not now. But I did think often of your warm body in that cold cell. I have been so alone. May we lie together and touch?'

Ukiko sobbed with Mung. 'I have longed for you, and feared I would never see you again. We are all we have left. Come. We will comfort each other.'

Side by side, they lay naked under a quilt, reminiscing about Yoshida. They searched their memories to tell each other of incidents the other had not experienced. Mung found himself describing his son's last moments with pride. Some memories brought them tears, others laughter. And if they told the same story twice, neither interrupted.

Ukiko snuggled her chin down on Mung's chest and whispered, 'You have an erection.'

'I know.' He hugged her. 'I thought it would not be possible again.'

'Please, Mung.' Ukiko kissed his eyes closed. 'I want

you inside me.' She threw her leg over him and pushed herself forward. Mung entered her warmth and felt the chill of the cold stone cell disappear from his body. Locked in a lovers' embrace, they talked away her guilt at betraying her sister's trust by not taking care of Yoshida, and his remorse for being away from home so often.

A deep-seated biological urge arose in both husband and wife, such as neither had ever experienced – an urge more primeval than the desire for sexual gratification. Their bodies moved together in frenzied mating, their perspiration and life-giving matter mingling time and again in the furious act of creation.

Chapter 27

It was after midnight when Sandanj slipped into the apartment. 'Sire,' he whispered, 'you must come with me.'

Instantly alert, Mung asked, 'What is the Rujo's decision?'

'You must leave Tokyo immediately.'

Mung saw the worried face in the flickering lamplight. 'There is something you are not telling me.'

'Lord Hotta will explain.'

Ukiko sat up. 'Will I be permitted to accompany my husband?'

'I am forbidden to say more.'

'You will answer,' Mung said.

'Yes, sire,' Sandanj touched his head to the floor, 'but only if it does not conflict with orders from his imperial majesty.' He sat back on his heels and withdrew a scroll from his sleeve, holding it so the imperial seal was visible.

Mung and Ukiko bowed.

'After your meeting with Lord Hotta you are to read this, then destroy it,' Sandanj said. 'Now please hurry.'

Mung took the letter and bowed, touching it to his forehead. He motioned to Ukiko to remain in bed. As he dressed, he asked, 'How is Udo?'

'Udo sailed for Prussia three days after the treaty was signed with Lord Crest,' Sandanj said.

'It is done?'

'Without any more bloodshed, and the credit for that is yours. Please hurry. You are in danger.'

'Even in the imperial palace?' Ukiko asked.

'Anywhere in Tokyo.' Sandanj moved to the door.

Mung got down on his knees before Ukiko. 'You have a duty to perform. Return to Satsuma. Care for the resting places of our loved ones in the Kagoshima cemetery. I will send for you when it is safe.'

They bowed to each other. Mung followed Sandanj into the hall. He was hurried along by the commander of the imperial guard and ten Black Dragons. Outside Lord Hotta's apartment, the men took up defensive positions. Mung entered alone.

Iyeasu and Jiroo sat grim-faced before Lord Hotta. Mung took a place next to Iyeasu, and bowed.

'The Rujo has decided you shall live,' Hotta said. 'The Emperor wishes you to go north to Sapporo on the island of Hokkaido. From there you will direct the Black Dragon Society as you did from Satsuma.'

'Jiroo,' Mung asked, 'have you read my notes to the Emperor?'

'Yes, sire.'

'Then you are prepared to resume leadership in Tokyo?'

'Yes, sire.'

'Mung, the Emperor has withdrawn your title of Minister of Maritime Services,' Hotta said. 'You are appointed Inspector General of Hokkaido. His imperial majesty wishes the settlements on Hokkaido strengthened militarily, economically and culturally. Your agents in China report increased Russian movement from Vladivostok into the kingdom of Korea. Sapporo is only four hundred sea miles from that Russian port city. Russians have also been observed near Sakhalin island. It has never even been surveyed. In the coming years, we may well have to withstand Russian pressure. Since the British have blocked the Russians from a warm water port in India, the czar is now looking in the direction of Korea's southern peninsula. It points like a dagger at Japan's heart, the ideal place from which to launch an invasion of our islands.'

'Carrier pigeons are already on their way to Sapporo,' Iyeasu said. 'The governor and other community officials will be informed of your arrival. They will provide complete cooperation.'

'If I was found innocent by the Rujo, why is there such anger against me?' Mung asked.

'You were not found innocent,' Iyeasu said. 'Lord Hotta convinced the Rujo he ordered you to direct the foreign guns on Saga and his men.'

'It is not true,' Mung protested.

'Everyone in the Great Council knows that,' Iyeasu said. 'But no one was prepared to call the Fujiwara lord a liar.'

'I may have saved your life,' Hotta said, 'but now your supporters as well as your enemies are against you.'

'Saga and Fujita Koin would have enjoyed disgracing you,' Mung said. 'Why did they not speak?'

'Because,' Hotta said, 'I made a promise to Fujita Koin not to reveal his son Hideyoshi's involvement in the plot to capture the Emperor. With Saga, I made a different arrangement. He and I will commit seppuku together.'

'You do not have the right to sacrifice your life for mine,' Mung said. 'I planned and ordered the bombardment of the Choshu.'

'I should have done it,' Hotta said. 'Saga bluffed me. I am sacrificing my life for yours because it must be done. I have read your recommendations to the Emperor. You are ahead of your time. You envisage a future for Japan that I find hard to conceive. The Emperor and I believe yours is the correct course if we are to avoid foreign domination. I will slit my belly to save you, and hopefully Japan. Your concept of a central government will begin when Saga and I transfer our and Lord Maeda's samurai to the direct command of the Emperor. The transfer will establish the first imperial army since Kublai Khan invaded Japan. In one stroke, at the cost of Saga's life and mine, Japan will take the irreversible path to centralized government.'

'Sire,' Mung said, 'I have served my purpose. After my son's death, I find the thought of joining him a relief.'

'Japan needs you more than me,' Hotta said. 'Do not fail. That is an order from the Emperor and me. I shall shout it from the grave if you falter.'

Mung raised his head and looked into Hotta's eyes. The older man smiled. Mung placed his fist over his heart and bowed, holding his forehead to the floor to hide his tears. 'So it is ordered,' he sobbed, 'so it is done.'

'Sire,' Iyeasu said, 'Mung should leave now. The tide turns in an hour.'

'Jiroo,' Hotta ordered, 'see the Black Dragon off safely.'

Mung stood up. 'Hotta, Lord of the Fujiwara, I vow your sacrifice shall not be in vain,' he declared. 'When I rise, lie down and walk by the way, I shall devote my heart, my soul and my strength to the Emperor and Japan.' He backed out of the room with head bowed.

'Take care, Fisherman,' Hotta called. 'If I am privileged to meet your son, I shall send him your fond remembrances. What a warrior that boy was!'

Outside in the hall, Mung was again surrounded by Black Dragons and hurried from the palace. They moved quickly across the parade ground and out the Hinzemon gate. More of his men waited to escort him. They trotted through the empty streets to the port. He saw lookouts wave them on. Twice, groups of ronin paralleled their route like wolf packs. Jiroo and Sandanj saw them but made no comment.

A fire arrow streaked into the sky from the port area ahead. 'That is our signal,' Jiroo said. 'There are too many ronin waiting at the port. I have an alternative plan.'

They continued on for another hundred yards. Then Jiroo whistled. He and Sandanj whisked Mung from the

261

midst of the trotting warriors, into an alley where two Black Dragons waited. They were led at a run through the darkness, then stopped in a shadow. From the port area ahead, they could hear battle cries and the clash of weapons.

Jiroo described the location of a sampan waiting to take Mung five miles out to sea for a rendezvous with a ship going north.

'You are to be complimented for your thorough planning,' Mung said, 'however I have something to do before I leave Tokyo.' He held out the scarab ring before Jiroo could protest.

Jiroo bowed. 'What are your orders, sire?'

'Leave me with Sandanj. I shall contact you from Sapporo.'

Jiroo and the two Black Dragons bowed, and disappeared into the night.

'Take me to Tokyo's chief Yakuza,' Mung ordered Sandanj. He was aware the Yakuza's price would be high, but he accepted that as an added guarantee of his safety. He meant to keep his oath to witness Saga's death, and satisfy his need to observe Hotta's sacrifice.

Sandanj departed as instructed when Wada Zenshichi bowed Mung into the bonsai shop.

'How may I serve the Black Dragon?' the chief Yakuza asked.

'Two men will commit seppuku in the palace grounds tomorrow. I must be present at the ceremony but not be seen. Can you arrange that?'

Wada Zenshichi bowed. 'Yes. It takes place with the rising of the sun. I will make arrangements.'

'After the ceremony, I must travel secretly to Sapporo.'

'That too will be done.' The chief Yakuza bowed and left the shop, pleased to be drawing one of Japan's most powerful men further into his debt.

Alone in the damp, musty shop, surrounded by miniature trees, Mung read the Emperor's letter.

'From the Emperor Mutsuhito, son of Komei, descendant of the Sun Goddess, Amaterasu-o-mi-Kami.

'To Mung, Moryiama Einosuke Ishikawa, son of a samurai, adopted son of an American and the departed Yasuo Ishikawa.

'Men, like shooting stars, are brief flashes in the course of history. Fate chooses certain people to shine as a beacon for others. That the gods have chosen you to beam the light of modern knowledge into our land, is karma. Your son's death was also fate. To be plucked in the flower of one's manhood appears cruel. But each of us has been assigned certain tasks to fulfil on this earth. Yoshida Ishikawa achieved his mission and was taken. You have not yet completed yours. Living is often more difficult than dying.

'You have suffered much, yet served me well. I hereby confer on you the title of Shishi, Man of High Purpose. It is an ancient and private title bestowed by previous Emperors on personal champions sent forth to accomplish difficult tasks. Your mission is to modernize Japan. To strengthen the empire so we need never again bow our heads to any nation. I give my blessings and those of my illustrious ancestors to you. Like the golden light of the sun, you will dazzle your enemies and illuminate the minds of our people. Shishi, go forth!'

Mung finished reading and placed his finger tips on the imperial seal. 'Let me be worthy,' he whispered, touching the paper to his forehead. Then he put the letter into an earthenware pot and burned it. He curled up in the corner and slept.

Some time later, Wada Zenshichi returned to the bonsai shop. He handed Mung a bundle of old clothes that smelled of the sea. 'At the ceremony, you will stand with the fishermen and farmers. A place has been secured for you.'

'And the trip north?'

'You will journey overland to the port of Nigata on the inland sea, and from there travel by ship up the coast.'

'The overland route will take at least a month.'

'Many people search for you on the Pacific Ocean side. You will arrive in Sapporo before the bay freezes over. Anyone following will have to await the spring thaw.'

Mung nodded. 'How may I repay you?' he asked.

'License my Yakuza in the northern fur trade. Allow them exclusive rights to deal with the Chinese, Manchurians, Koreans and especially the Russian seal hunters working Sakhalin island.'

Mung knew that in Europe the demand for furs was great and the prices high. Wada Zenshichi's request was well thought out. 'It shall be done,' he said. 'In addition, I will pay for information. Especially about the Russians.'

'It will be an honour to serve the Emperor.' The Yakuza bowed, then clapped his hands. A guide appeared. 'It is time for you to leave.'

It was still dark, but the Ginza was crowded with people walking towards the palace. Mung was led through the main gate to the third row in front of a specially erected platform draped in white silk. It was surrounded by a low picket fence thirty-six feet square with entrances from the north and south. Four flags with inscriptions from the sacred writings were posted at each corner.

Mung looked away from the two buckets at the rear of the platform. They would be used to carry the severed heads. He was reminded of the public hanging he had witnessed in the California gold fields, with its picnic atmosphere. Men drank and women dressed for the occasion. Their children played and hawkers plied the crowd. In comparison, the mood here was sombre, the atmosphere tense. The people were edgy and nervously quiet.

Mung looked to the fat-bellied clouds in the distance, their bottoms illuminated by the first light of dawn. Suddenly the palace gates swung open. The commander of the imperial guard led a contingent of his men carrying furled flags. Their red capes and white plumes stood out in sharp contrast to the sombre, grey walls behind them. They marched to a position in front of the picket fence and halted.

A trumpet sounded its call, a second blared, and then a third. Kettledrums boomed. From the west, Lord Maeda's bannermen marched over the Kahikawa bridge. They came to a halt facing the imperial guards. From the right, Fujiwara bannermen converged. From the left, the Choshu marched with twenty-foot-long silk battle flags representing more than six hundred years of continuous tradition. The combined flags of the three fiefdoms fluttered gallantly. The bannermen reached their appointed positions in front of the imperial guard and halted.

At a signal from the commander, his imperial guardsmen marched forward and exchanged flags with the bannermen of the fiefdoms. The guards marched away and the bannermen unfurled their new flags, showing the rising sun and sixteen rays on a white background. The people bowed before the imperial ensign. The drums ceased and the bugles sounded. The imperial guards did an about-turn and led the bannermen into the palace. The formal act of establishing the first units of the modern imperial Japanese army was concluded.

A Shinto priest playing a reedy tune on a bamboo flute and a Buddhist priest tapping a hand drum, appeared at the palace gate. They led 270 lords, each dressed in the ceremonial armour of his fiefdom. The people bowed. The procession passed close to Mung, then wheeled left and formed ranks in front of the picket fence. Six of the lords entered the enclosure through the southern entrance. They were seated on the ground before the white platform. These were the official witnesses.

The music ceased. All eyes turned to the main gate. Lord Hotta and Lord Saga stood in the entrance to the palace grounds, wearing pure white robes with black obis. Slowly they approached, Hotta on the side closest to Mung. The people bowed. Mung raised himself sooner than the others, and stared at the Fujiwara lord, willing Hotta to see him. Their eyes met. Mung saw surprise, then pleasure in Hotta's face.

Suddenly Mung was knocked to the ground from behind. An imperial guard jammed his foot between Mung's shoulder blades and growled, 'Stay there until the procession passes!'

When the guard allowed Mung to rise, the two lords had mounted the platform. A murmur ran through the crowd as Danjuro strode out of the palace and climbed the platform steps. Hotta spoke to Danjuro, then Saga. They both nodded their agreement. All three looked to the witnesses, who bowed their assent. Danjuro stepped back and picked up the two buckets. He left the platform. A shudder rippled through the crowd. The Fujiwara and Choshu lords would perform seppuku in the old way – without assistance.

Hotta addressed the witnesses but spoke loudly enough for others to hear. 'I, Hotta, lord of the ancient fiefdom of Fujiwara, and my brother in Bushido, Saga of Choshu, perform this act for the Emperor and Japan.' He withdrew his long sword from his obi. He wrapped the razor sharp blade in rice paper on which he had written his death poem. He knelt, laid the sword before him, and recited,

'Life is a mountain stream
Man steps in and out again.
Man returns to the waters cold.
A different man
A different mould.'

He threw his head back and shouted,

266

'Fukoku kyhoii! Rich country, strong army!'

Saga placed his sword on the mat before him and recited his death poem,

> 'Learn the wisdom of the West.
> Resort to friendship when obliged.
> Fight when victory is possible.
> Fukoku kyhoii!'

Saga flung his spectacles to the ground. Both men undid their obis and tossed them away. They pulled open their robes and bared their torsos. Two witnesses came forward with trays holding unsheathed wakiyashis. Saga and Hotta rose up on their knees. Each one took a short sword by the hilt from the tray. With both hands they raised the swords over their heads, pointed skyward. The witnesses retreated.

Not a murmur, not a breath nor breeze disturbed the scene. All waited for the rising sun to top the palace walls.

Mung willed the sun to stop, but its light soon spread over the ancient stones. The polished steel tips of the swords caught the sparkle of the sunlight. The two lords looked up at their gleaming blades. Slowly, as if retaining the sunlight in the steel, they brought the points down and pressed them above their left hips. 'Fukoku kyhoii!' they shouted in unison, and drove their blades in, then drew them swiftly across their abdomens. Both doubled over.

'Fukoku kyhoii!' the people responded. 'Fukoku kyhoii!' They chanted to cover any cries the two lords might utter. 'Fukoku kyhoii!' Blood ran scarlet into the white silk. 'Fukoku kyhoii!' The people were pledging themselves to a rich country, a strong army, and were now prepared to learn from the West to one day defeat it. In an act of self-sacrifice, two men had changed the attitude of a nation.

Mung knew it would take time, but it was clear that

change was inevitable. He was first to kneel and touch his head to the ground. Others around him followed his example. It spread until even the lords of the realm bowed. When Mung looked up again the two bodies lay deathly still.

'Fukoku kyhoii,' he whispered, and set out on his journey north.

Chapter 28

September 1871, Vulcan, Siberia

A cruel wind whistled through cracks in the walls of the prison hut.

'This vodka is disgusting,' Baron Vladimir Benzowsky said. 'It must be distilled from horse piss and gunpowder.' He threw the bottle at his servant seated on the floor.

Boris caught the bottle and held it up to the flickering candle. A bit of vodka remained. 'Yes, master,' he answered. The greedy pink lips in his hairy face parted and he sucked the bottle dry.

'You stupid Cossack!' Benzowsky said. 'All Cossacks are natural-born liars, drinkers and fighters.' He strode over to his servant and knocked the empty bottle from his hand. 'You sound like that fat pig I'm going to screw. She grunts and snorts. God in Heaven, what have I done to deserve this?'

Benzowsky straightened up and banged his head on the ceiling. At six foot six inches there was not a roof in all the prison huts in the penal colony that allowed him to stand straight. He was wider than the door and brutally strong. The most hardened convicts in Vulcan feared the Russian baron. They said he had been born without a conscience.

Benzowsky rubbed the curly brown locks of his bruised head and glared down at Boris. 'You peasant swine! I know you are laughing behind that greasy beard of yours.'

Boris spread his thick, dirt-stained hands and rolled his soulful eyes.

Benzowsky took another bottle from a gunnysack on his bed and pulled the cork. 'Answer me! Why am I here?'

Boris knew the nobleman's temper and the answers he must give to humour him. 'Master, you were sentenced to ten years in Siberia because you diddled your uncles' wives.'

'I bedded some of my cousins too,' Benzowsky gloated. 'The ones I serviced never complained.'

'But your uncles are princes, related to the czar's family.'

'Half of Russia is related to the czars. They screwed more wedded women than I ever did. What would be the punishment of the Zaporasti Cossacks for screwing another man's wife?'

'We would cut off your balls, force you to eat them, then torture you.'

'How wasteful.' Benzowsky picked up his faded uniform jacket. The captain's epaulets had been removed three years before upon his arrival in Vulcan. 'If I had my balls cut off, I wouldn't be able to satisfy the commandant's pig of a wife. Without her favours we would starve, or freeze to death.'

'That is true.' Boris stared at the new bottle in Benzowsky's hand. 'Winter is here again.'

The baron plopped down on the bed and drank. 'I don't know if I can survive another seven months of ice and snow,' he lamented. 'The bay is almost frozen over. My brother said he would get me out of here in six months. That motherless bastard is not coming.'

'Master,' Boris said, 'why don't we listen to the commandant's houseboy. He and his Japanese friends hunted and traded furs in these waters before they were caught.' The Cossack grunted and stood up. Suddenly the hut became crowded. Although eight inches shorter than the baron, Boris was even wider, with massive hunched shoulders. He held his big callused hand out for the bottle.

Benzowsky ignored the outstretched hand. 'You and those Japanese peasants may be able to endure on the icy sea, but my aristocratic blood is thinner than a peasant's. It passes through the brain more often. Science has proved that.'

'Science.' Boris shrugged. 'About that I do not know. But the mail-boat leaves tomorrow and the bay will soon freeze over. If we capture that boat, the Japanese can sail it out of here. Vulcan would be frozen in behind us for another seven months before word could be sent out to look for us.'

'We would freeze to death in the Tatar strait.'

'Arima and his Japanese know the Russian trading posts and seal hunters' camps along those shores.'

'Idiot,' Benzowsky snarled, 'the traders would see we are escapees from a prison colony. They would kill us, freeze our bodies, and collect the reward next spring. I've heard that one escaped prisoner is worth a hundred sealskins.'

'Why can't we kill the seal hunters?' Boris asked.

'Stupid Cossack, they travel in fleets of at least five ships. All with a cannon or two and armed men. The mail-boat cannot hold more than twenty.'

There was a pounding on the door of the hut. 'Baron, Baron Benzowsky, it is time to go.'

'Stop breaking my house, you slant-eyed bastard,' Benzowsky shouted. He finished half the bottle of vodka in one pull and tossed it to Boris. He put on his enormous bearskin coat and hat. Pointing at his servant, the baron declared, 'That Japanese speaks Russian better than you.' He bent down and squeezed through the door.

Freezing wind whipped snow across the parade ground. Benzowsky watched it buffet the flimsy prisoners' huts and drift against the large stone barracks near the commandant's house, the only private residence in Vulcan. He shoved Arima ahead of him and trudged towards the big house.

'How long ago did the commandant leave?' Benzowsky shouted into the biting wind.

'Five minutes,' Arima called back. 'He will be gone three hours for his card game.'

'Interrupt us early. I can't stand being with his big-titted slob.'

'She may be fat, but she pays well in food and liquor.' Arima slowed his pace, dropping back alongside the Russian. 'The mail-boat leaves tomorrow,' he whispered. 'It is our last chance.'

'Go yourself,' Benzowsky said.

'Alone we cannot take over the boat. My men know how and where to sail it, but we know nothing about firearms.'

'Because you are ignorant savages.'

'Prisoners will freeze in their huts this winter. It has happened here before.'

Benzowsky punched the smaller man in the back with his mittened fist and Arima tumbled into the snow. The baron continued walking towards the big house.

Arima came to his knees in the deserted parade ground. No one ventured out at night when the temperature dropped below zero. Even the guards remained inside their towers. The commandant's wife had given the four soldiers outside the house their usual bottle of vodka to watch the building from the nearby barracks. Arima got to his feet. If he could not persuade the Russian to come with them, he would have to force Benzowsky into leading them out of Vulcan. He brushed the snow off his coat and ran to reach the front steps of the house first. He made a quick bow to the guard watching from the barracks' window, and opened the front door.

The big Russian stamped the snow from his boots and draped his fur coat over Arima's head. 'I will find my way upstairs.' He slapped his hat on the coat. 'Call me in an hour.'

With the clothing bundled in his arms, Arima bowed. He watched until Benzowsky entered the bedroom at the top of the stairs. He hung the clothes and went outside, so intent on his plan he did not feel the cold. His decision was made. He bowed to the guard in the window and hurried off to one of the smallest huts in the compound.

Arima crawled through the entrance and squeezed into a place around the fire with six other Japanese. All were Yakuza fur hunters and traders captured by Russian patrol boats around Sakhalin island and the Siberian coastline along the Tatar strait. They waited for their leader to speak.

Arima pointed to one man. 'Inform the commandant his wife is ill.'

'The plan is on?'

'It is on,' Arima answered. 'And there is no need to be frightened. If we stay here this winter, we will die anyway. Go.' He reached behind, took some sticks from a small pile and put them on the fire. 'May as well use it all now. After tonight either we shall be aboard the mail-boat or dead.'

The messenger left the hut. 'The Russian giant would not listen?' another man said.

'I asked him and he struck me. We have no choice but to force him to lead us.'

'We leave together or die together,' another Yakuza said in their secret language. 'Not many in Vulcan will survive the coming weather.'

'This is the last time we go over the plan,' Arima said. 'I will signal you from the kitchen once I have killed the inside guard and the cook. Enter through the back way. You will not be seen from the barracks if you crawl. If I am not in the kitchen, you know what to do with the bodies.'

Four of the men nodded. The fifth said, 'I wait until you leave here. I count to one thousand before I go to take the Cossack to the main house. But I wait until after the

273

commandant arrives before I tell the Cossack he is ordered there.'

'That is it,' Arima said. 'We haven't much time. Start counting.' He crawled from the hut.

Leaning into the snow-laden wind, Arima returned to the big house. On the porch he bowed to the soldier in the barracks' window, and entered. He put on his servant's jacket and went directly to the kitchen. The cook and interior guard were playing Russian chequers.

'I need the vodka and food,' Arima said, rolling his eyes towards the bedroom above.

'Wait until I lose,' the cook laughed.

'I will lose first,' the guard said. He clapped his chequer down. 'You must jump twice.'

Arima heard the hall clock chime the half hour and his eye twitched. He took a deep breath. The commandant would soon be told of his wife's supposed illness. 'I do not understand a game in which you try to lose,' Arima said.

'Of course not.' The cook smiled. 'You do not understand because you are Oriental.' He tapped his head. 'Your brains work differently.'

The guard grunted his agreement. He made a move that would lose him his last three chequers to win the game. 'Let's open the storehouse for the little yellow fellow so we can get back to some serious playing.'

Both the cook and guard took keys from a large ring on their belts and led the way to the pantry. The cook opened the top lock, the guard the bottom. They unlatched the door. A room twelve feet by twelve feet was lined on both sides with shelves full of preserves, tinned beef and pickled vegetables. At the far end hung a full side of beef, smoked hams, ducks and chickens. Strings of sausage and preserved meats were looped from hooks in the ceiling.

Arima set down a tray on which the cook placed two

clear bottles of vodka, a tin of corned beef and a jar of pickled beets. 'For the gentleman upstairs.' He winked.

Arima had played this game many times before. He rolled his eyes upward, then looked at the bottles on the tray. It was a ritual he performed each time the baron visited. Now he would use it to kill the two smiling men in front of him.

The guard winked and the cook nodded for Arima to be off. 'Don't forget to wash those bottles,' the cook said.

Arima bowed and went alone to the kitchen. There, as usual, stood two glasses and a pitcher of water. He uncorked both bottles and half-filled each glass with vodka. This time, instead of replacing the vodka in the bottles with water from the pitcher, he removed a flask from his pocket and poured a clear liquid into each, filling the bottles to the brim. He then poured the remaining liquid from the flask into the two glasses. The cyanide in the flask had been made by and later tested on a Russian doctor who, in exchange for extra food, worked for a month to distil the bitter almonds brought to him by Arima.

The cook and guard returned to the kitchen. 'Would you care for a drink of water?' Arima asked.

The two men smiled knowingly. Arima splashed a touch of water from the pitcher into each glass and handed it to them. They raised their glasses in a silent toast, and drank. They returned the empty glasses to Arima, then sat down at the chequerboard, and died.

Arima pulled the table away to prevent their limp bodies from turning it over. He scooped up the fallen chequers and put them on the table. He ran to the back window, lifted the curtain and signalled. His four men started crawling through the snow towards the house. He put the glasses and vodka on the tray and hurried to the front of the house to look out of the window.

It was not long before three horsemen galloped across

the parade ground and up to the house. Arima's legs were shaking. He had hoped the commandant would come alone. He watched Vulcan's chief officer dismount, followed by his two aides. They clumped up the front steps and Arima opened the door. He took their coats and bowed.

'Is the doctor with my wife?' The commandant unbuckled his sword and gun belt and handed them to Arima. The Yakuza was so nervous he could not bring himself to speak. He pointed up the stairs and bowed again.

The commandant pointed to the bottles on the tray. 'Give my men a drink of that vodka! And close the damn door!' He started up the stairs. Through the open door behind the two officers, Arima saw the four house guards come running from the barracks – dragging their rifles, buttoning their tunics, trying to reach their posts before being discovered. Arima closed the door with his foot and quickly poured two drinks. He was shaking so hard the glasses rattled on the tray.

The commandant stopped in the middle of the staircase and called down, 'Be careful, boy! You'll spill that before my men have a chance to taste it.'

The two officers took the glasses and raised them to their commander. 'Your wife's good health.' They drank.

The commandant reached the bedroom door and opened it. He saw two bare bodies on the rug before the fireplace. 'What the hell is going on?' His wife's long blond hair was fanned out over the carpet. Under her ample thighs was a pillow, and between them Baron Vladimir Benzowsky.

'You slime! You dirty slime!' the commandant shouted. He dashed in and struck Benzowsky a blow in the face, opening the baron's cheek. Benzowsky saw his own blood splatter the quivering white belly of the woman under him. The smooth handsome face turned into a vicious mask of rage. He rose as the commandant struck another blow. He took the punch on the top of the head and grabbed hold of the commandant's tunic. He pulled himself up off the woman and smashed his fist into the red angry face above him.

'Do not hurt him!' the wife screamed. She reached up to claw Benzowsky's bare chest. He backhanded her so hard across the jaw, she was knocked unconscious.

'Help! Guards!' the commandant shouted, spitting blood and broken teeth.

Benzowsky towered over the man. He grabbed the commandant around the throat with both hands, and strangled him. Arima appeared in the doorway just as Benzowsky dropped the lifeless body. Stark naked, the baron crouched, prepared to attack.

'Is she dead too?' Arima asked.

'Where is the house guard?' Benzowsky hissed.

'I poisoned him and the cook. Get dressed.'

Benzowsky grabbed his clothes. As he buckled his trousers, understanding dawned on him. He started for Arima. 'You sneaking son of a bitch. You planned this.' He looked down with disgust at the purple face of the commandant. The swollen tongue protruded from bloody lips.

Arima levelled the commandant's pistol at the big Russian. 'I need you to take over the mail-boat.'

Benzowsky pulled back and glowered at the small Japanese.

'We have little more than an hour,' Arima said.

A pounding at the front door caught the attention of both men. 'Guards,' Benzowsky whispered.

'Finish dressing,' Arima said. 'I sent for your servant.' He tucked the pistol away and ran down the stairs. He dragged the two dead officers behind the front door, then opened it and bowed.

'These two say they were summoned by the commandant,' a guard with cocked rifle said. He stepped back and pointed to Boris and the Yakuza at the bottom of the steps.

'Only the big one,' Arima said. 'The other can leave.'

From the corner of his mouth the guard whispered, 'Are we caught?'

Arima glanced over his shoulder as if to be certain he would not be heard, then whispered, 'No, but the commandant found the baron with his wife. He will want to question all four of you.' He waved Boris up the steps and into the house, then slammed the door in the guard's frightened face.

Boris gaped at the two dead officers behind the door. 'Mother of God!' He crossed himself.

'Shut up!' Arima shoved the Cossack towards the stairs. 'Get up there to the first room on the right. Hurry, the baron is waiting. We are going to escape from here.'

Arima ran to the empty kitchen. The pantry door stood open. The bodies of the cook and guard were sprawled on the floor and the four Yakuza cowered inside. Arima pulled and pushed the Japanese out. 'Carry the two bodies from the front door in here, and hurry.'

The back door of the kitchen opened and a butler entered from the servants' quarters. Arima pulled the gun and pointed it, but the butler leapt forward. Arima dropped the gun and turned sideways. He took the servant's weight on his hip and flipped him over, onto the floor. Throwing his right arm under and across the butler's throat, his left around the back, Arima pressured the head forward in a death-lock. The butler fought, he frothed at the mouth and kicked. Arima held on tight.

The other Yakuza, hearing the struggle, came running to the kitchen door. Through gritted teeth, Arima grunted, 'Get those two bodies into the pantry. This one is almost dead.' The butler slumped in his arms. Arima held the death-lock a moment longer.

Upstairs, a stunned Boris gawked at the dead commandant. Benzowsky shook him. 'Get hold of yourself, man.' He pointed to the naked woman. 'She is still alive.'

For the first time Boris noticed the white, voluptuous body on the carpet before the fire. The woman's head rolled and she was beginning to moan.

'Tie her up,' Benzowsky ordered. 'I will settle with that crazy houseboy.' He pushed Boris towards the nude woman.

The bearded Cossack stood looking down at her. She brought her hands up from her thighs and touched her full breasts. She turned, and cried out at the sight of her husband's body. Boris dropped his pants. He pushed the woman's legs apart, kissed her navel, and entered her with a brutal thrust.

Downstairs, Benzowsky watched four little Japanese dragging two Russian officers towards the pantry. In the kitchen Arima was tugging the butler across the floor. The baron grabbed the Japanese by the collar and lifted him up with one hand. 'How many have you killed?'

'Five,' Arima gasped. 'You will be six.' He pushed the revolver into Benzowsky's face.

'You informed the commandant,' Benzowsky growled into the gun muzzle.

'Put me down or I will kill you,' Arima said.

Benzowsky let him drop to his feet. The smaller man stepped back with the gun still levelled. 'If we do not escape now, we will all die. Vulcan is the most northern prison colony in Siberia. This winter will be one of the worst ever. Guards and prisoners will freeze to death. The last time it happened, the guards locked themselves in their barracks and cannibalized the prisoners and each other.'

'How do you know what the weather will be?'

'We were born in this climate. There are signs in the skies we have never seen before, but heard about in stories told by our parents. It is going to be bad.'

'If we take the mail-boat, where can we go?'

'South. And fast. The entire northern sea will freeze.'

'Can we make it to Japan?'

'No,' Arima said. 'It is the law in my country that all foreigners are to be killed upon arrival. And Japanese who have set foot on foreign soil or ships are put to death.'

'Then where, goddamn it?'

'We will become pirates,' Arima said. 'When we get enough men and boats, we will raid the Korean coast down to China.'

'Where will we get more men, you fool? Only twenty can fit on the mail-boat.'

'That is easy, if we live through the winter. We will raid other prison colonies.'

A deep bellowing moan from the Cossack upstairs was accompanied by shrieks from the woman. Arima followed Benzowsky who went up the steps three at a time. The baron held Arima back at the bedroom door. Boris pressed a knife to the woman's throat. Her breasts were bleeding from teeth marks and he was pounding his hips into her thighs. She screamed.

In mid-stroke, Boris snarled at the men in the doorway. 'If you try to stop me, I'll kill you. Just once more, that's all. Don't try to stop me.'

Without a weapon, Benzowsky was wary of the crazed Cossack. He shrugged his shoulders. What am I worried about her for, he thought. 'Finish,' he said, 'then kill her and come downstairs!'

The woman heard her fate pronounced and shrieked. Boris slit her windpipe. He climaxed as she died under him.

'Good,' Arima said, 'now we are all killers.'

Benzowsky turned and grabbed the pistol from Arima.

He drove his knee into the Japanese's stomach. He kicked him out into the hall. 'How did you plan to get by the guards around the house?' He pulled Arima to his feet and slapped him. 'You must have made a plan.'

'We invite them in one at a time,' Arima groaned.

'You cannot poison them all.'

'That is one of the reasons we need you and your servant. We Japanese are traders and fishermen. We do not know about firearms.'

Benzowsky glanced down at the pistol he had seized, and Arima shrugged. 'I only pointed it at people.'

Benzowsky spun the cylinders. 'It's loaded, you damn fool! You could have killed me without even meaning to.'

The hall clock chimed nine times and the four Japanese peered out from the kitchen. Boris lumbered down the stairs tugging his trousers into place. The men stared at each other.

'We have only one hour before the guard changes,' Arima said. 'By that time we must arm as many prisoners as possible.'

'Soldiering is my business,' Benzowsky said. 'If we give all those bastards weapons, they will kill us. Yet we cannot take the barracks with only twenty men.'

'There is no need to attack the guards,' Arima said. 'Only the ship. Then the guards will have to come to us.'

For the first time since he had arrived in Vulcan, Vladimir Benzowsky felt that he might leave it alive. 'We must capture the ship first, then spike the cannons of the shore fortifications so we can sail out of here unhindered.'

'I know nothing about spiked cannons,' Arima said.

'Boris and I know the men in Vulcan who do. Get your Japanese to start packing food from the pantry, and call the first guard in here. We are on our way out of this hell-hole.'

Chapter 29

As Mung travelled north to Sapporo on a Yakuza boat, Ukiko prepared for a trip south. She had remained in Tokyo to nurse Rhee that he might accompany her, but his progress was slower than hoped for. Now something so wonderful had happened, Ukiko could no longer delay her journey to Kagoshima.

Gin-ko and Little Mother had been Ukiko's companions since Yoshida's death and Mung's banishment. On this day, upon her arrival at the Yoshiwara house, Ukiko was surprised to be greeted at the door by Gin-ko. She was served tea in the garden by Little Mother. There were no servants, apprentices or guards in sight. The rooms surrounding the garden stood open and bare.

'We are leaving Tokyo,' Gin-ko said.

'Where to?'

'With you, whenever you sail for Kagoshima. That is, if you do not mind travelling companions.'

'Oh!' Ukiko clapped her hands with joy. 'I dreaded making the voyage alone. I came to tell you good news and you have brightened my life.'

'She has darkened mine,' Little Mother grumbled, sitting down with the two women. She pointed at the beautiful Yoshiwara courtesan. 'This girl could make a fortune every year for another five years at least.' She lit her pipe. 'She will throw it away for that lovesick puppy.'

'Udo,' Ukiko whispered with glee. 'Why did you not tell me?'

'Little Mother exaggerates. I promised my parents the moment I was no longer obliged to earn money in this way, I would change my life style. I trained to be a courtesan after my father and mother were sent to debtors' prison. I came to work in the Yoshiwara, paid their debts, bought back their home, and maintained them. But neither of my parents fully recovered from their experience in prison. Their passing within a week of each other two months ago, leaves me free to do as I wish.'

'Gifts keep pouring in.' Little Mother puffed her anger into a cloud of tobacco smoke that wreathed her head. 'The less this girl wants to do with her admirers, the more fascinated with her they are,' she grumbled.

'What is it you wish to do?' Ukiko asked.

'Some day to marry and raise a family.'

'With Udo?'

'He will make her bowlegged from bearing brats, bent from planting rice and wrinkled from washing his clothes,' Little Mother huffed.

Gin-ko ignored the old woman's grumbling. 'I have thought of Udo,' she said to Ukiko, 'but first I intend to enter a Buddhist monastery near Kagoshima.'

Ukiko gasped. 'As a nun?'

Tears streamed down Little Mother's weathered cheeks. She knocked her pipe clean on the butt of the snakeskin whip and sniffled. 'They will shave her bald as an onion.'

'You will accompany me, Little Mother,' Gin-ko said.

'They will not shave this old head.'

'Hush now, I am not entering as a novitiate. The honourable matron has granted permission for us to rest and meditate as long as we wish.'

Little Mother scowled. 'In exchange for a handsome contribution to the monastery.'

'How long will you stay?' Ukiko asked.

'At least until Udo returns. That should give me time to contemplate the future.'

'Do you wish to marry Udo?' Ukiko asked.

'He appears to be the person most suited to someone with my background. Sandanj told me about him, that he also was a professional pleasure-person.'

'May I write him that you will be in Kagoshima when he returns?'

Gin-ko blushed and lowered her head. 'That would be kind of you. But please do not mention marriage. Of that I am not certain. And Udo's infatuation with a Yoshiwara courtesan may dim when he sees me as a woman.'

'He sees you as a woman for certain,' Little Mother said. 'And if he ever turned you down, he would have to answer to me.'

'I would enjoy my son marrying my friend,' Ukiko said. 'I would become honourable mother-in-law. You know what they say about Japanese mothers-in-law.' She and Gin-ko giggled, and said in unison, 'The curse of the Japanese bride.'

'That is a good reason to marry Udo.' Gin-ko giggled again. 'At least I would be certain of having a benevolent mother-in-law.'

'You will see what a terror I am on the journey to Kagoshima,' Ukiko said.

'Might just as well,' Little Mother grouched. 'This house is sold and we are almost packed. When do you plan to leave?'

'I am pregnant,' Ukiko blurted out, and began to weep. 'That is the reason I must travel immediately.'

'How wonderful,' Gin-ko cried. She embraced Ukiko and both wept.

'What are you two bawling about?' Little Mother gulped.

Ukiko and Gin-ko spread their arms and drew the older woman into their embrace.

'The gods are replacing the son you lost with a new son of your own,' Little Mother sobbed. 'A person as good as you deserves happiness. Sometimes the gods do things correctly.'

'I never thought I would become pregnant,' Ukiko sobbed. 'I did not use any charms or potions. It just happened. If only I could tell Mung. But meanwhile I must journey to Kagoshima before I get too far on in the pregnancy.'

'How many monthly cycles have you missed?' Little Mother asked.

'One,' Ukiko whispered.

Gin-ko and Little Mother pulled back and stared at her.

'Oh, it has to be true.' Ukiko wiped away her tears. 'I am so regular, the month does not begin unless I have my cycle. The Kyoto physician thinks so too. He prescribed herbs for me, and told me to get to Kagoshima and rest.'

'Will the birth put you in danger?' Gin-ko asked.

A shadow crossed Ukiko's face.

'How old are you?' Little Mother asked.

'I am a healthy and happy thirty-nine year old woman whose only concern is to engage a guard to accompany us on our journey. I had hoped Rhee would be well enough to travel.'

'Do not worry,' Little Mother said. 'I will not let any harm come to either of you.'

'Just the same,' Ukiko said, 'we should look for someone.'

Gin-ko placed her hand on Ukiko's. 'Little Mother was sent by the chief Yakuza of Tokyo to protect me because I once saved his life by passing along information to him.'

Ukiko looked doubtfully at the old woman.

'Little Mother is a ninja,' Gin-ko said.

Ukiko's eyes flew open. 'A professional killer?'

'I am one of the few female practitioners of the ancient profession who has survived to retire.' The old woman preened, and patted her snakeskin whip. 'You two will be safe with me. Have no fear. But Gin-ko cannot enter a monastery now. She and I will look after you. That is, if you are truly pregnant.'

Ukiko missed two more monthly cycles before their arrival in Kagoshima. Her skin glowed, her cheeks blossomed and her stomach began to grow. The only unsettling part of the pregnancy was her lack of strength. The child within her drew all the energy from her body. Ukiko happily accepted her weakness. This was the answer to her years of prayer, wishes and dreams. The fortune-teller, the astrologer and Little Mother all guaranteed she would give Mung a male child.

In January 1872, Udo's answer to Ukiko's letter arrived from Vienna. He expected to return to Kagoshima in March. He congratulated Ukiko on her pregnancy, and looked forward to becoming older brother in the family. The letter included a formal request to Little Mother for permission to call upon Gin-ko.

No mail arrived from or went to Sapporo. No birds, boats or couriers could travel in the worst winter in memory. From the Tatar strait south to the Tsuguru strait, the Sea of Japan was one frozen mass of pack ice. Every port on the island of Hokkaido was closed in. On the Russian side of the sea, the coast was blocked by ice from Kamchatka in the north to three hundred miles south of Vladivostok at the North Korean port of Chongjin. Hundreds froze or starved to death on both sides of the Sea of Japan but the Vulcan escapees, led by Arima and Baron Benzowsky, had found a safe haven in the southern-most prison colony of Olga.

Chapter 30

4 March 1872

The gangplank was down yet Udo could not move from the ship. His throat tightened, his wide, unblinking eyes raked the Kagoshima pier. He felt relieved yet disappointed that Gin-ko and Ukiko were not there. They could not have known I would arrive on the mail-boat from Tokyo, he thought, wanting desperately to see them. It is probably better they have not come. I would have made a fool of myself. I will go first to Ukiko's house in the city, he decided. If they are not there, I will seek them in Mung's house on the side of the mountain. His feet would still not move. He was frightened. Thoughts of Gin-ko being married to someone else, or returned to the Yoshiwara, or with shaven head in a Buddhist monastery, immobilized him.

'Your baggage is on the dock,' the captain said. 'If you will be so kind as to give instructions to the porters.'

Udo walked stiff-legged down the gangplank. He directed the porters to store his belongings, and set off. He looked at people he passed to see if western clothes were in fashion as was the fad in Tokyo. They were not. He was dressed correctly in a traditional kimono made by the capital's finest tailor. Only his short-cropped Prussian-style haircut was pleasingly different. Joy and anxiety battled in his heart as he walked and thought of Gin-ko. He came to the older residential area of Ukiko's father's house. Neat well-trimmed hedges and fruit trees fronted carefully tended gardens on both sides of the street.

Udo stopped before Ukiko's house. He hummed, to be

certain his vocal cords would work if Gin-ko suddenly appeared.

'Sire? Sire, may I help you?' A servant girl standing at the front door was addressing him.

'Yes,' he mumbled, 'is this Madam Ishikawa's house?'

'Yes. May I ask who is calling?'

'Udo Ishikawa.'

'Oh honourable sir,' the girl bowed, 'everyone is waiting for you.' She hurried down the steps to lead him into the house.

'Is Miss Gin-ko here?' Udo asked.

'She and Little Mother are shopping. May I offer you tea?'

'Where is Madam Ishikawa?'

'The lady is resting. The doctor does not allow her to leave the house, you know. The seventh month is critical.'

'How long does she usually rest?'

'On and off through most of the day. One moment please, I will bring rice cookies and tea.'

'Thank you.' Udo smiled. 'They are my favourites. I have been so long away.'

'Is that Udo's voice I hear?' Ukiko called. Leaning heavily against the wall, she shuffled towards him. Her huge belly threw her off balance. The loose kimono protruded far out in front of her white tabi socks.

Udo hurried forward and took her hand. The servant girl took her arm. They led her to the sitting room and eased her to a seat on some pillows.

'The doctor warned you not to walk without assistance,' the girl said.

'Older sister,' Udo chided, 'are you disobeying the doctor?' He noticed the lack of strength in her movements, and the pale colour of her face.

'I am so happy to see you,' Ukiko said. 'Sit opposite me

and tell us everything about Berlin. Especially about Bismarck. You called him the Iron Chancellor in your letter. Is he so strong?'

'And as large as Danjuro, the Mito giant.' Udo laughed. 'I once saw him making love to a tree. It was late at night. Everyone was celebrating Napoleon III's surrender of the French armies. I chanced to look out the window and there was Otto von Bismarck hugging a large oak tree.' Udo saw colour return to Ukiko's face as he talked. 'At first I thought, what a strange sex habit, even for a round-eye.'

Ukiko and the servant girl giggled. Ukiko peeked over her fan with wide eyes that demanded he continue.

'I decided it was my duty as an observer to understand this western behaviour. In Japan we have many beautiful trees. Who knows what these barbarians might do to them in the dark of the night if they become sexually aroused.'

The two women giggled.

'As I approached the great man, his physician stepped out of the shadows and stopped me. "It is for the chancellor's health," the doctor said. "The tree has an aura of strength upon which he draws".'

'Aaaahhhh.' Both women nodded solemnly. 'The Shinto priests often speak of the spirits in rocks, trees and rivers,' Ukiko said.

'The chancellor overheard my conversation with the physician and invited me to join him in hugging the tree. We had the most enlightening discussion of my trip to Europe. He explained his policy of Realpolitik to me.'

'What is that?' the servant girl asked.

Udo winked at Ukiko and said, 'You will have to come out with me one night and we will hug a tree together.'

The girl blushed and giggled.

'The truth is that General von Moltke joined us,' he said. 'It was a large venerable tree with a great trunk and room for the three of us. We talked until people from the party came out to toast the Iron Chancellor's victory.' Udo sat back on his heels, enjoying the feeling. It was good to be home and seated on the floor rather than in a straight-back chair with stiff leather shoes on his feet. He enjoyed the familiar smells and the quietness of a Japanese house. 'Would you ladies like to hear about the concerts in Berlin? About the enormous amounts of beer, sausage and strudel those Prussians can consume? Or about the gilded paintings and colourful porcelain? There are marble floors so smooth I thought they were ice. Copper and bronze ornaments and alabaster statues are everywhere. They have halls just for dancing, other halls for music, and some halls for eating. There are fairylands of crystal chandeliers, sparkling fountains and exotic tapestries.' He stopped and looked at the two breathless women.

'You have described Heaven,' Ukiko whispered.

'I also thought so at first,' Udo said, 'but I soon realized that a Japanese has different tastes. There was too much food and too much furniture. The people come too close and touch you when they talk.' He paused, then asked, 'Is Gin-ko unmarried?'

The two women looked at him, then at each other.

'I hear voices,' the girl said. She rose and went to the front door.

'They have returned from shopping,' Ukiko whispered.

Udo strained to hear what was being said. From the suave, urbane raconteur, he became a nervous suitor. He looked down at the fan he held. All the ribs were either broken or twisted. Little Mother entered and fastened her rheumy eyes on him. Udo peered behind her to catch a glimpse of Gin-ko.

'I have sent her home,' the old woman said. She shifted the whip from her shoulder to her lap as she sat down.

Udo kept an eye on the whip and on the old weathered face. 'When will I see her?' he asked.

Little Mother scowled. 'If it was my decision, never!'

'What are your intentions?' Ukiko asked.

'Marriage,' Udo answered.

'Little Mother will act as nakoda,' Ukiko said.

'You do remember your Japanese?' the old woman taunted. 'I am to be the marriage broker. And if a wedding does take place, I shall be the godmother to your children. I shall referee disputes, but never will I allow a divorce. If you hurt Gin-ko . . .' Little Mother caressed her whip and glared at Udo.

He flushed with anger. 'Old woman, you used that snakeskin on me once, and you threaten me now. I warn you, married or not, never do either again.'

Little Mother removed her hand from the whip and cocked an eye at Udo. 'The lady Gin-ko was a gifted courtesan, but I never knew her to love anyone she entertained. I will not allow her to be hurt.'

Udo slowly bowed his agreement. 'If I am honoured to become her husband, I will protect her. Furthermore, since receiving my sister's letter, I have not been with another woman.'

'Haw!' The old woman guffawed. 'You have been at sea the better part of two months. I doubt there were female sailors to tempt you.'

'Little Mother and I worry that your past experiences in Canton as a brothel-keeper may affect the way you treat Gin-ko,' Ukiko said.

'I have also thought on this,' Udo said. 'It is known that Mung never entertained a concubine during his marriage to you or your sister. I vow to the best of my ability to emulate my father.'

'Your vow is respectfully noted, but it is the husband's privilege to receive concubines or visit the Willow World.' Little Mother bowed her head slightly. 'Too soon we speak of a marriage that has not been agreed upon. Gin-ko will not have one of those quick affairs where the groom steals the bride and away they flee. She will have a mi-ai.'

'The mutual viewing will take place here in this house,' Ukiko said. 'For that reason we have arranged for you to stay at the local honjin.'

'If after the mi-ai, Gin-ko does not wish to see you again,' Little Mother said, 'you must accept her decision.'

'So it will be,' Udo answered.

'One more thing,' Little Mother said. 'As your parents and Gin-ko's are all dead, and if a marriage does take place, I will live in the same house as you with the title of honourable mother-in-law.'

Udo's eyes grew hard. 'Is this a condition or a request?'

The old woman lowered her head and softly said, 'A respectful request.'

Scenes at the house in the Yoshiwara flashed through Udo's mind. He recalled the adoration in Little Mother's eyes when she looked at Gin-ko, and the fierce protective glare when she thought her beautiful charge was threatened. Udo bowed. He softened his voice and said, 'I agree.' He saw the faint glow of a smile crack the wrinkled face. For the first time since landing, Udo's heart lightened, and began to race.

Little Mother saw the glow of confidence spread over Udo's face. 'The mi-ai will take place in two days,' she said. 'All rules will be observed.'

Ukiko, as matron of the house, sat at the head of a low rectangular table at the mi-ai. Little Mother, as nakoda, sat on the other end. Udo, at the centre, watched anxiously for Gin-ko.

Ignoring his furtive glances, Little Mother asked, 'Do you agree that a Japanese maid is like a bright cheerful bird? That when married she resembles a dove, and when widowed, a crow?'

Udo barely glanced at the old woman when he answered, 'I have little knowledge of birds.' He still saw no sign of Gin-ko. 'How is my sister today?' he asked Ukiko.

She shifted the pillows behind her and smiled weakly. 'Fine. This happy occasion makes the sun shine, the air silky, and the sweets tastier.' She pointed at the rice cakes on the table.

Udo took a cake to fill his mouth so he would not have to speak. It would be impolite to inquire after Gin-ko. He took another rice cake and smiled at Ukiko. She was obviously very weak. Her face was pale and her hands limp at her sides. He gulped another rice cake when Gin-ko entered the room.

Udo stared. She was the most beautiful woman he had ever seen. Despite her colourful outer robe and exquisite obi, the beauty and calmness of her face dominated. Her long, glossy black hair fanned down her back in the old Kyoto style. She blushed and lowered her head at sight of Udo. Beneath layers of kimono, her slim shy body made its presence felt. She seated herself opposite. He found it difficult to breathe.

Gin-ko glanced up at Udo. He sat tall and square-faced. His powerful shoulder muscles sloped down from his neck. He had a sharp nose, high forehead and the piercing eyes of a fighting bird. She longed to be held by him.

Ukiko and Little Mother nodded to each other across the table. They made polite conversation about the weather, the price of pomegranates and the new national mail service.

Udo and Gin-ko gazed at each other. Neither spoke until Little Mother asked him, 'How would you support Miss Gin-ko if she were to consent to marriage?'

Udo reluctantly took his eyes from the beauty opposite him. 'My honourable father employs me at a gracious salary. In addition, I have investments in a newly opened

293

printing house, a newspaper, and a Chinese restaurant in Tokyo. They are managed by my friend, Sandanj.' Udo neglected to mention the House of a Thousand Delights, also managed by Sandanj.

Gin-ko whispered to Ukiko, who said, 'The lady would like to hear about Sandanj. He was her frequent visitor in Tokyo before she travelled south with me.'

'Sandanj told me he was well received by the lady and Little Mother,' Udo said. Sandanj had also told Udo about the butterfly darts, although Gin-ko was not wearing them now. She sat straight and still, yet the powerful force of love he felt emanating from her threatened to overwhelm him. He was giddy, and talked to hide his confusion. 'Sandanj has published Princess Atsu's *Book of Good Deeds*. It and his book on French cooking are best-sellers in the Ginza. The chef I brought from China who works in the restaurant, is helping Sandanj with another book called *The Secrets of Cantonese Cooking*. Oh! I told you this already.'

'Not about Princess Atsu and the cookbooks,' Gin-ko said directly to Udo.

Little Mother frowned at the impropriety, then relented. 'You may speak to each other, but loud enough for me to hear.'

Ukiko straightened the pillows behind her. 'You three should take a stroll. The sun is shining and the weather fair.' She addressed Udo. 'It would be respectful to show Gin-ko the graves of your father and brother.'

'Will Miss Gin-ko be pleased to walk that distance?' he asked.

'It is not too far,' she answered.

Udo felt his heart try to leap from his chest with every beat. To introduce a woman to one's ancestors was halfway to marriage.

Little Mother frowned at Gin-ko. She preferred to have Udo sweat for success.

'Older sister,' Udo asked, although realizing Ukiko was too weak, 'will you accompany us?'

'Thank you for the honour, but I shall rest. The servant girl will be here if I have need.'

Outside the house many people waited to see the handsome couple on their mi-ai stroll. The children found the old woman with the whip most interesting.

'Will Ukiko give birth to a healthy child?' Udo asked as they walked up the mountainside.

'At her age, giving birth is dangerous for mother and child,' Gin-ko said.

'What does the physician say?'

'Ukiko has decided to have the child at all costs.'

'The mi-ai is meant for you to know one another better,' Little Mother said. 'Do not worry about other people's problems. If you decide to marry, there will soon be enough of your own. Talk about your thoughts and dreams for life.'

They walked in silence for some minutes. The path grew steeper. Then their wooden clogs made clopping sounds on a small bridge. Gin-ko stopped and looked into the clear mountain stream that eddied around ancient boulders and flowed over smooth river stones. 'Sometimes I dream of a magic stream in which I could bathe away that part of my past I wish to forget,' she said.

'I rarely dream,' Udo said, 'but I too have wondered how to forget certain parts of my life.'

'Japanese literature glorifies the courtesan,' Gin-ko said. 'Most people do not know of the many suicides among women from the pleasure-houses. There is a special death-cart provided by the Tokyo municipality that moves through the streets of the Yoshiwara every night to pick up bodies of young women.'

'I know,' Udo said. 'I was taken to jail in that cart after I broke into your house.'

'Every night of my life in the Yoshiwara I sat and watched for that cart. Never quite sure if I wanted to be taken away in it or to be certain I was not already there.' Gin-ko sighed. 'I still rise at night and listen for the rattle of the wheels on the cobblestones.'

They remained silent. Then Gin-ko asked, 'Is there such a river that will wash away our pasts?'

'Neither of us would be who we are without our experiences. I love you,' Udo said. 'That is what matters.' He turned his dark eyes directly on her. Gin-ko felt them sear her heart.

'More than any man alive, I can understand your dream,' Udo said. 'What we were before may not be pleasing for us to remember, but we must not reject it. It has made us into the people we are today. More than most men on this earth, I am able to accept your past because I too have given my body to others for money. But never my soul or my heart, until now. I wish you to be my wife.'

Gin-ko did not respond. The two stared down into the stream. They did not see Little Mother holding onto the bridge rail for support. She brushed a tear from her eye.

Gin-ko and Udo turned to walk up the mountainside again. After a while she said, 'It is not for Japanese women to have opinions. In my former profession, I developed them.'

'In our home, you will express them,' Udo said. 'Outside I ask you to consider those around us. Great changes are sweeping Japan. We will dress differently, our professions and diet will be altered by the modernization of our country. Yet certain things will never change. The status of women, I fear, is one of them.'

Gin-ko nodded. They walked into the cemetery overlooking Kagoshima.

'The victims of the worst tidal wave in Japan were first to be buried here seventeen years ago,' Udo said. 'Later, those killed by the shelling of the American privateer. Ukiko's father and sister were among them.' He bowed to a well-kept grave site. 'Honourable father,' he said, 'please make the acquaintance of Miss Gin-ko and Little Mother.'

The two women bowed.

'My father died in battle while in the service of the Emperor,' Udo said. 'He was protecting Mung.'

Gin-ko and Little Mother bowed again.

'It is fitting that Mung is now your father,' Gin-ko said.

'He has been good to me.' Udo pointed at a smaller marker alongside his father's grave. 'This is in memory of my older brother, Uraga. His body is not here. He exploded a ship loaded with ammunition in Canton harbour. It killed over a hundred tong-men who were in pursuit of Mung.'

Gin-ko bowed to the marker, and asked, 'What are tong-men?'

'They are gangs, something like our Yakuza, but much more bloodthirsty.'

Gin-ko turned and looked questioningly at Little Mother. The old woman nodded her assent. Gin-ko drew up the embroidered sleeve of her kimono and held out her elegant arm. Near the crook of the elbow where two delicate blue veins parted, was the tattoo of a tiny yellow butterfly. 'This is a protective sign given me by Wada Zenshichi.' She watched for Udo's reaction. His expression did not change and she continued, 'I once saved his life by passing on information overheard in our house. There are no female Yakuza, but I am as close as a woman can be to the organization.'

Udo reached into his sleeve and produced an earring. 'This was given me by the most powerful tong chief in southern China. It saved my life in France. The chief of

Prussia's intelligence service took me on a spying mission behind French lines, all the way into Paris. While there, he was betrayed. We fled to the area in Paris known as Chinatown. This earring gained us the protection of my benefactor, Kang Shu, and we escaped.'

'Since everyone is making confessions,' Little Mother said, 'you should know that I am a ninja.'

The wind whistled through Udo's teeth as he sucked in his breath. 'Sandanj said you are dangerous. He told me about the poisoned hairpins, but not this. Did you teach Gin-ko to use the pressure point behind the neck?'

'I am sorry I paralysed you,' Gin-ko said.

'I deserved it. Many times I used that trick to control women.'

Little Mother moved closer to the couple. 'I suggest you two never again speak of your lives as prostitutes. The memories can only bring pain.'

Udo and Gin-ko made the vow with their eyes. They bowed to each other, then moved to the next graves. Udo introduced the women to Saiyo – Ukiko's sister and Mung's first wife – and to their father, Yasuo Ishikawa. Yoshida's urn was buried just forward and between the two graves.

The courting couple walked slowly around the area and gathered wildflowers. They placed bouquets of yellow and white blossoms on each of the graves, then left the cemetery.

On the return, Gin-ko stopped on the bridge. She removed two dried oak leaves from her sleeve and showed them to Udo. 'Udo and Gin-ko are to be married,' was printed on one. The other leaf was blank. She handed them to him. 'The spirits of the river, rocks and trees will grant the request of whichever leaf you place in the stream.'

'And what is your request?' Udo whispered.

'I cannot go against the will of the gods.' She looked

sideways at him. 'But before you decide, I must tell you that I know what the Black Dragon Society is. I am proud you are a member. I will never question your comings and goings. I hope my knowledge of your position is not a problem.'

Udo knelt on the bridge and gently placed the printed leaf on the water. It whirled away, dipping and ducking in the current. The couple looked into each other's eyes, and bowed.

From the corner of her eye, Little Mother noticed a shadow moving in the forest. When she turned to look, it had disappeared. She made no comment as she followed the young couple home to prepare for the second phase of courting, the exchange of gifts.

Chapter 31

The runner located the six hooded monks on the main road a hundred miles south of Kagoshima. He delivered a letter from Hideyoshi to the Golden Lizard.

'My father is dead,' Hideyoshi wrote. 'Make all haste to the capital. Do not take the time for your revenge on Mung's family. That will come later. My brother, Danjuro, must die before his installation as Lord of Mito.'

The Golden Lizard reread the letter, then crumpled it in his fist. He gathered the others around him. 'This message confirms the yuino has taken place in Kagoshima, and the astrologer has set the wedding date. Mung's adopted son and the whore will be married today. We are ordered to Tokyo as soon as we kill them,' he lied.

The five Yakuza were excited by the prospect of seeing the capital for the first time. 'We can make Kagoshima in four days if we stretch our legs,' one of them said.

'We shall be there in three,' the lizard-man snapped. 'In time for the sato-gaeri, the returning home ceremony. They will all be together on that evening.' He rubbed his scarred and misshapen shoulder. 'That is when we kill them.'

Clothed in white, the colour of mourning, Gin-ko was escorted by Little Mother to the house on the hillside. For the bride, white signified the severance of personal links with the past, and the resolve to leave her husband only as a corpse.

When the bride and nakoda were gone, Ukiko's house was scrubbed clean. A bonfire was lit at the front gate to purify the grounds, as if after the removal of a dead body.

In the house on the hillside, Little Mother helped Gin-ko change into the traditional flowered kimono. Her hair was arranged in the bunned Tokyo style to fit under the large white wedding hat. Her exquisite face was powdered a delicate, porcelain white.

Udo arrived first at Ukiko's house, wearing a black kimono and black haori, an outer jacket. He watched Gin-ko enter and sit across from him. Little Mother and Ukiko spoke but the silent couple did not hear. They gazed at each other. Although the bride and groom forced themselves to eat the wedding meal, neither tasted the food. The time came for the san-san ku-do, the three, three, nine.

As guest, for she arrived at the table after the groom, Gin-ko began the ceremony. She touched her lips three times each to three different cups of saké Udo had poured. He poured for himself, and repeated the procedure. Then they both left the room to change into more colourful clothing.

At the table again, Gin-ko poured for her husband and master, who raised the three cups nine times. They looked into each other's eyes as their lips touched the rice wine, and silently pledged themselves for life.

Udo withdrew a small dagger from his sleeve and placed it on the back of his hands. He presented it to Gin-ko.

She bowed, and accepted the blade, pronouncing, 'With this I shall protect my honour.'

Udo touched the two swords in his obi and intoned, 'With these shall I defend your honour.'

Gin-ko placed the dagger in her obi. The wedding ceremony was concluded.

The newlyweds, escorted by Little Mother, took leave of Ukiko and walked to the hillside house.

At the porch steps, the old woman bowed. In an emotion-choked voice, she said, 'I shall see you three days hence at the sato-gaeri in Ukiko's house.'

'We shall be there at seven p.m.,' Udo said. He and Gin-ko bowed, then entered the house together.

Little Mother sat down by the pond. She listened to the evening quiet itself into night, and prayed to the gods that the two professional lovers would find happiness in each other's arms.

Inside, Udo and Gin-ko stood uncertainly near the door. They looked around and both giggled.

'Shall I prepare tea for my husband?' she asked.

'No, thank you,' he said.

They admired the flower arrangements done by Ukiko's servant girl, and commented on the tasteful paintings, the cleanliness of the house and grounds. Neither could think of anything further to say. They stood silently.

'I will have tea if my wife joins me,' Udo said.

'I thank you for the honour.' Gin-ko bowed. 'Ukiko told me it is customary for the bride to prepare for bed while the husband enjoys his tea.'

Udo felt his stomach drop. 'Yes, that would be good,' he muttered. 'Very good.'

With the untouched teacup before him, Udo waited. When it seemed the sounds of Gin-ko's undressing had ceased, he entered the bedroom.

Soft lamplight played on Gin-ko's slim, naked back. Her arms were raised, her hands behind her neck undoing her shimmering hair. Suddenly it cascaded down the arch of her back and brushed her rounded buttocks. Udo drew in his breath. She turned and saw him. Her navel sucked in. Her small pointed breasts stood out.

Udo undid his obi and removed his clothing. Gin-ko watched the muscles in his back and shoulders dance and bunch as he bent to pull off his tabi socks. She felt a tenderness towards his nudity such as she had never felt for any man. They stood naked, facing each other, the magnetism of their bodies causing them to sway. They touched and both flinched, but neither stepped away.

302

Gin-ko knelt and pulled back the quilt. She moved gracefully into the bed. Udo lay down next to her. They stared at the ceiling without touching or speaking. Gone was the polish and self-confidence they once knew with others.

Gin-ko wriggled her fingers across the open space between them and found Udo's hand. He clutched at her fingers and she felt him tremble. Then she heard him sob. She raised up and saw a tear on his cheek. 'What have I done?' she whispered. 'Have I offended you?'

'I have been so lonely.' He wept, turning towards her.

The floodgates of Gin-ko's emotions shattered. She sobbed with great gasps. They held each other close, their teardrops mingling. 'My yearning for a soul mate has been frightful,' she sobbed. 'Hold me, my dear one. Hold me tight, my beloved. We shall never be alone again.'

They lay together in a tearful embrace, clinging one to the other. Then Udo whispered. 'This is our confirmation. The past we wish to forget is drowned in the river of our love. We are reborn. We begin anew.'

In the house on the side of the mountain, Udo and Gin-ko learned of true love. Like two adolescents, they expanded their affection to intimate warmth that raised itself to tender passion and flaming ardour. They spoke of their rapture, their yearnings, their need for each other, and expressed their love over and over again.

On the third day, Gin-ko and Udo presented a letter to the town elders stating the time and place of their marriage to be recorded. An official document was signed and sealed, then presented to Gin-ko. At seven that evening, they appeared at Ukiko's house for the sato-gaeri and the final ceremony. Gin-ko presented the marriage certificate to Little Mother who handed it to Ukiko.

The mistress of the house tried to hide the discomfort

she suffered from her swollen body. She motioned the newlyweds to be seated. 'You are such a handsome pair,' she said. 'You were beautiful before you left here and now even more so. It is the kind of elegant loveliness that shines from within and warms those around. I wish Mung was here to see you.'

Gin-ko and Udo both blushed. They bowed to hide their embarrassment.

'You are truly an exceptional couple,' Little Mother said, 'but even the gods must eat.'

The servant girl carried in the ceremonial meal: bean-curd soup, sweet boiled chestnuts with kamaboko – fish balls, rice, sashimi – raw fish in sauce, boiled lotus roots in soy sauce, broiled sea bass, and sea slugs in vinegar. After each course, Gin-ko and Udo expressed their appreciation of the tasty food. The dessert was sugar plums and sweet cakes.

When the meal was complete, Ukiko motioned with her fan. It was a prearranged signal for the servant girl to bring tea, then leave for the evening. Ukiko wished to discuss an important matter with the newlyweds.

A short distance from Ukiko's house, the Golden Lizard issued final orders to his five Yakuza. 'When the servant passes the fish pond, two will attack the house from the rear, one from each side. Use your steel hooks to slash through the walls, and your long knives to kill. Muso, you will approach the front with me after you kill the servant girl. There is only one man in the house. No bulge was seen under his obi, but take no chances. He might have that repeating pistol hidden somewhere. Kill him first.'

'We will not have a problem with the three women,' Muso said. He pulled out a double-barrelled muzzle-loading pistol. 'Just in case.'

'Each of you will cut off one head,' the lizard-man said.

'I will send them to Mung in a sack. I would like to be in Sapporo to see his face when he opens that sack.'

The servant bowed and took her leave. Ukiko turned to the others. 'I am getting weaker every day,' she said. 'It is possible I will not survive the birth.'

'Shush!' Little Mother said. 'Do not speak like that. It will frighten the child.'

'Please,' Ukiko said, 'I have known from the first it would be dangerous for me to give birth. The Kyoto physician told me so.' She turned to Gin-ko. 'You must promise to be with me at the delivery.'

Gin-ko nodded.

'Please hold him up quickly so I may see him,' Ukiko said.

'I promise,' Gin-ko said, 'but talk such as this is not healthy for you or the child.'

'Udo,' Ukiko said, 'if I die, your duty as older brother will become serious. Mung is away most of the time.'

Udo bowed but said nothing. Ukiko seemed weaker than ever. He feared she was speaking the truth.

'Why think these horrible thoughts?' Little Mother said.

'Death is not horrible,' Ukiko replied. 'To lose the child would be worse.' She shivered, then drew herself up. 'I had three portraits painted during the term of my pregnancy. They are for Mung. He would have enjoyed watching the child grow within me.'

A nightingale called from outside the house. Little Mother stood up and shrugged her shoulder. The whip slid down her arm into her right hand. A throwing knife appeared in the other. 'We have been watched for several days,' she said to Udo. 'Are you armed?'

'No. No swords, no gun.' He spread his empty hands wide.

'Take this.' Little Mother handed him the throwing

knife. She pulled a butterfly dart from her hair. 'I hired two ninja to guard this house. Let us hope they are able to do their job. That bird call was their danger signal.'

As the servant passed the fish pond, Muso stepped from behind a tree into the path and drove his long steel knife into her stomach. She looked down, not realizing she had been stabbed until she saw the blood spreading around the knife handle sticking from her kimono. She doubled up and fell, mortally wounded.

Muso leaned over to withdraw his knife and a dark figure armed with a hatchet sprang at him. The Golden Lizard stepped from behind the tree and swung his long steel hook, ripping out the ninja's throat. The man fell dead on top of Muso.

The two Yakuza working their way to the rear of the house, heard the nightingale call from behind. They knew night birds rarely call from the short grass. There were no trees nearby. Both turned to look back. Like a black hunting leopard, the ninja moved forward on all fours. They saw the shiny steel blade in his right hand, but not the fire-blackened knife that he drove into the first Yakuza's heart. As the tattooed man went down, he buried his hook in the ninja's leg. The other Yakuza slashed at the attacker with his long knife, severing an artery. The ninja dropped his second knife. He saw his life's blood shooting out in long red spurts, and the Yakuza positioning himself for a kill. The ninja plucked a bamboo tube from behind his ear. He put it to his lips and blew, sending a dart into the Yakuza's cheek.

The tattooed man pulled the dart out of his skin and looked at it. 'I am poisoned,' he said.

The ninja sank to his knees with a smile. Both men died on the blood-stained grass.

Two other Yakuza tore their way through the walls of

each side of the house. Ignoring the old woman crouched in the corner and the two women huddled by the table, they made for Udo. He hurled a pot of boiling tea into their faces but they shook off the hot liquid, advancing with hooks and knives in position. Udo, not knowing how to throw the small delicate knife he held, waved it before him, backing up to dodge the slashing hooks and stabbing knives.

Suddenly the snakeskin whip cracked. It whistled across the back of the first Yakuza, tearing open his kimono and burning his flesh. He writhed to the floor, screaming. Udo leapt on the fallen man and cut his throat. The butterfly dart Little Mother threw at the second attacker stuck in the shoulder of his kimono. He raised his arm to stab Udo and his feet were taken out from under him by the snakeskin lash. He crashed to the floor just as the Golden Lizard and Muso broke through the front door.

Ukiko and Gin-ko screamed at sight of the scaly human body. 'He is the one who attacked us on the river!' Ukiko cried.

Little Mother coiled her whip with a snap of the wrist. She estimated the distance and cracked the whip in the face of the lizard-man. The leaded tip opened a six inch gash down his cheek. She snapped the whip again and wrapped the snakeskin around his throat.

Muso levelled the big double-barrelled pistol and pulled both triggers. The roar inside the house was deafening. Little Mother was knocked three feet back, landing in a heap on the floor. She tried to sit up and throw another butterfly dart, but her strength was gone. Her hand slumped and the poisoned dart stuck into her own leg.

Muso dropped his weapon and struggled to release the whip from around the Golden Lizard's throat. Udo, gripping the throwing knife, started for Muso's back. He took two steps and was dropped by a kick from the Yakuza on

307

the floor. Udo dropped the knife. The Yakuza jumped up and raised his knife, but felt something bounce off his back. Gin-ko's small dagger fell harmlessly to the floor. The Yakuza turned to face his new attacker and saw the two women crouched in the corner. He laughed, then clutched at his shoulder. Little Mother's dart had worked its way through his kimono to his skin. He staggered towards the women and tried to strike Gin-ko. She ducked away and he collapsed across Ukiko's abdomen with his full weight. Udo snatched a hook from the floor and jumped up to face the lizard-man. He and Muso were gone.

Ukiko screamed and sat up with such force the dead Yakuza was thrown off. Her face was a mask of pain covered with beads of sweat. 'Save the baby!' she gasped.

Gin-ko crawled to Ukiko and touched her large stomach. 'The child is about to be born. Get the doctor. Get the midwife.'

The physician came quickly to Ukiko's side. 'There is no time to wait for the midwife,' he said. 'No time to move those bodies away. Gin-ko, you will help me. The birth is progressing too quickly.'

Ukiko spat a gag from between her clenched teeth. She felt warm blood flowing down her legs. 'Save the child, Doctor! We have spoken of this before. Save the baby!'

'Madam, you are haemorrhaging. It is a breech delivery. I cannot guarantee its life or yours. I must be allowed to make the decisions.'

Ukiko tried to speak but another wave of pain racked her body. She clamped her jaws so tight on the gag that blood oozed from around her teeth, but still she shook her head no. She thrashed back and forth and screamed. Her body twitched. Gin-ko and Udo held her.

Ukiko fought to remain conscious. Her eyes pleaded

with Udo. Then she whispered to him, 'Save the child. Without it I do not want to live.'

Udo reached out and grasped the physician's shoulder. 'You will save the baby at all costs.'

The doctor looked down at Ukiko. 'Very well, madam. Keep that cloth between your teeth and invoke the blessings of the gods.'

Ukiko looked at Gin-ko. 'You promised to hold him up.'

Gin-ko embraced her friend.

The awful silence between the ear-splitting screams was no relief to those within hearing. The delivery seemed to go on forever. The physician had no choice but to work quickly to save the child. Finally it was born.

A shaky Gin-ko performed the duties of a midwife according to the doctor's directions as he worked at trying to stem the flow of blood from the mother. Gin-ko cleared the mucus from the baby's mouth and nose, and massaged its back until it gasped its first breath. She touched the infant to the floor to signify earth, the root of all men. She held the baby out to Udo. 'Put your hands on the child so he will know humanity.'

Hesitantly Udo placed both hands on the wrinkled, bloody little body. He and Gin-ko gazed at the child, then at each other.

'Hold him as high as possible,' the physician instructed. 'To the length of the umbilical cord towards Heaven and obedience to the Emperor.'

Gin-ko brought the baby down. In swift motion the physician cut and tied the cord, then returned to the task of trying to staunch the flow of blood from Ukiko.

The baby wailed and Ukiko's eyes fluttered open. She tried to raise her head. Udo supported her neck and Gin-ko held the baby for her to see. Ukiko focused on her son. Her eyes widened and colour returned to her cheeks. She sighed. 'It is a boy child. They were right. He is the most beautiful baby.' She smiled and slumped in Udo's arms.

The doctor seized Ukiko's wrist. He touched the large vein in her neck, then sat back on his heels. 'I pray this child will have half the courage of his mother. She is dead.'

Chapter 32

'Mung should receive the letter soon,' Udo said. 'I sent it a month ago.'

Gin-ko shifted the baby in her arms. She knelt and placed a sprig of wisteria on Ukiko's grave. 'Child,' she said, 'your mother's spirit will always watch over you. She loves and will protect you.' Gin-ko nuzzled the baby. 'Say goodbye to your mother. Tomorrow we leave for Tokyo.'

The infant gurgled and tried to suck Gin-ko's cheek.

'Bow to your mother's grave.' Gin-ko dipped the child's head. 'Now to your grandfather and your Auntie Saiyo.' She bent lower. 'Now we give a very great bow to your brother Yoshida who rests between them.' She straightened and handed the child to the wet-nurse. 'It is not right to call the boy, Child,' Gin-ko said to Udo. 'We should give him a yomo, an infant's name. We may not see Mung for years.'

'You are correct. As older brother I will name him. Mung can always change it.'

'May I suggest your father's name,' Gin-ko said.

Udo came to her side. 'I want our children to carry his name and my brother's.'

'It is already two months since our wedding and I have just had my monthly cycle again.' She frowned.

Udo put his hands on Gin-ko's arms and looked deep into her eyes. 'We shall just have to keep trying day and night to make a baby. This is the sacrifice of a husband.'

Gin-ko giggled.

'Shimatzu would be a good name for the little one,' Udo said. 'Shimatzu Nariakira was Lord of Satsuma. He saved

Mung's life when Mung returned to Japan. He raised Mung to samurai rank and then to Scholar of Satsuma.'

'It is a strong name,' Gin-ko said. 'I think Mung will approve.'

Udo took the child from the nurse. They made another round of the family graves to introduce him as Shimatzu Ishikawa. Then Gin-ko placed the snakeskin whip on Little Mother's grave at the end of the row, and said a prayer for her.

'We do not have much time to perform the naming ceremony,' Gin-ko said. 'We will buy prayer notes for Shimatzu's name on the way home, and have the Shinto priest pin them on the torii gateway of the shrine. Then we will burn incense in the Buddhist temple and give an offering there. Come. We must hurry.'

After the worst winter in history, the warm winds of spring and the rolling sea were freeing the land of ice. Pack ice cracked and boomed in Sapporo harbour. The eight-month freeze was finally over. Gentle breezes unlocked the coves and inlets along Hokkaido's western coast. The inland sea was already navigable, and fishermen waited restlessly for the harbour to clear.

Mung moved slowly in the frenzied crowd along Sapporo's waterfront. Every person who could walk or be carried was present. The first mail-boat since October lay bobbing at the mouth of the harbour just beyond the undulating field of ice.

A great cheer went up from the north end of the dock where Sapporo's seal hunters were setting out. They scampered from ice floe to ice floe, when necessary using their fifteen-foot poles to vault across the ice packs. They pushed or paddled miniature icebergs with their poles, drawing closer to and finally reaching the mail-boat. The people cheered and chanted encouragement to the daring men clearing a path and leading the boat back through the floating ice to the dock. No crew ever received a warmer, more joyous welcome than did the one bringing the mail.

The lone passenger limped down the gangplank and through the crowd. 'Where can I find the inspector general?' he kept asking along the way.

Before long he stood before Mung on the dock. He removed his large fur cap and bowed. The sun glinted on the copper skewer through his topknot. People were shocked to see the inspector general embrace an Okinawan chief in public.

With a big smile, Rhee handed a sack to Mung. 'Letters from your family, dispatches from Iyeasu, and reports from Jiroo. There are pigeons aboard the boat for the more immediate replies.'

As they walked to Mung's house, he listened carefully to the verbal messages Rhee had brought. Then Mung said, 'Tell me about yourself. I never thought to see you alive. I noticed you limp. How is the rest of you?'

'I lost an ear.' Rhee turned his head to show Mung the gruesome scar. 'But I can hear,' he said. 'I do my karate exercises every day. I can still be useful as your bodyguard.'

'And so you will be,' Mung said. 'As long as we both shall live.'

'Thank you.' Rhee bowed. 'I regret I was not with you when Yoshida died.'

'There was nothing you could have done. He was ill.'

'He died a warrior's death.'

Mung did not reply.

'I went to see a play performed about Yoshida and his final battle,' Rhee said. 'The imperial guards honour the spot where he fell.'

Mung shrugged. 'Tell me what is happening in Tokyo. Did Udo and the delegation return from Berlin? Who won

313

the war in Europe? Has the Emperor instituted more changes?'

'Udo had not returned when I left four months back. I picked up the mail-boat a week ago. Much of my information comes from the newspaper managed by Sandanj Prussia won the war. The Emperor has established a National Assembly in place of the Rujo. He issued what is called the Charter Oath, a strange document that reaffirms the power of the Emperor. Most people were not quite certain of its meaning, but all swore to it. Shortly after it was issued, the Emperor abolished the old system of lords owning land. The land tax is now paid directly to the government in Tokyo. The Emperor avoided a confrontation with the lords by raising their yearly stipends. In addition, he appointed them as governors over the same property they previously ruled. So now they earn more money, and are responsible to the National Assembly, which is responsible to the Emperor.'

'That is the biggest difference in the world,' Mung said. 'I can smell Iyeasu's strategy in all this. Some day in the not too distant future, when all lands revert to the Emperor, social rank and inherited privilege will also be abolished. The Emperor will make a gift of the constitution to the people. They will not be able to refuse, and a democracy will be established. But where did the money come from to pay the lords?'

'They were paid with a new currency called yen. The government borrowed money from the French, British and Germans, and the Emperor permitted the large merchant houses to participate in the economic reforms by loaning the government money. The merchants were so happy to be recognized, many gave huge gifts of cash.'

'Was there no opposition to the change?'

'Tosa and Hinzen marched on the capital, but they were defeated by the new imperial army. That persuaded others not to try. The retired generals you activated in the south, supported the imperial army with their Satsuma warriors. When the Emperor took ownership of the lands from the lords, Mito incorporated its troops into the imperial army. All this, according to Sandanj's newspaper, ensures the success of what he calls the Meiji Reformation.'

'How is it Mito supports a central government?'

'Fujita Koin died. Danjuro now leads Mito with the advice of his brother, Iyeasu.'

'Danjuro helped me when I was in prison,' Mung said. 'He is more intelligent than most give him credit for.'

'There was an assassination attempt on his life just before his installation as lord. Rumour says it was an outlaw band of Yakuza paid by his brother, Hideyoshi. Danjuro survived and the three brothers sit on the National Assembly, but the oldest and youngest do not speak with Hideyoshi.'

'Tell me about the people in the capital,' Mung said.

Rhee shrugged. 'You would never believe what is happening in Tokyo. People are copying everything western. The leaders of style are mostly those Black Dragons who returned from abroad, and Sandanj is their idol. In addition to directing the most influential newspaper in Japan, and his best-selling cookbooks, he manages the finest Chinese restaurant, and the House of a Thousand Delights in the Yoshiwara, where he gathers information for Jiroo.'

'That must be Udo's idea,' Mung said.

'Ukiko wrote me from Kagoshima that Udo wanted to court a woman friend of hers. She approves of the match.'

'Is it Gin-ko?'

'Yes, that is her name. I seem to remember she worked in the Yoshiwara,' Rhee said.

Mung nodded. 'She was a well-known courtesan. I had ordered Udo to investigate her because I suspected she had a connection with the Yakuza. I did not think he would want to marry her, but if Ukiko approves so do I. What

315

else have you heard about Ukiko? She was supposed to travel to Kagoshima.'

'I spoke with her the day before she travelled south some months ago,' Rhee said. 'The doctor advised her to go early in her pregnancy.'

Mung dropped the mail sack. He grabbed Rhee's arm. 'What did you say?'

'The Kyoto doctor confirmed her pregnancy,' Rhee said. 'I received two letters from Kagoshima. She wrote she was large as a house, and the baby was certain to be a boy.'

'When? When will the birth be?'

'May.'

Mung used his fingers to count the months. 'May. This is May.' He danced in a circle, then snatched open the mail sack and pawed through the letters.

'She would not have given birth before the mail-boat left Tokyo,' Rhee said. 'Maybe word will come by pigeon.'

'I will line up the letters according to date,' Mung shouted, throwing the mail bag over his shoulder with such force he was pulled off balance. He plopped down on his buttocks, laughing. 'We can drink a barrel of saké while I go through the mail.'

Rhee helped Mung to his feet.

'Ukiko must be so happy,' Mung said. 'It is the thing she wanted most in the world. You do not know how many good luck charms and amulets I had to sleep with because she wanted to become pregnant. The worst was the potions she slipped into my tea, which I was not supposed to notice.' He laughed. 'Some of them tasted so terrible you would not believe it.'

They reached Mung's house and he forgot about the saké in the rush to read his wife's letters.

The gods have seen fit to take Yoshida's life, but they are giving us another. Sorrow and joy are what living is made of. Let us look at the happiness and beauty of this gift from Heaven.

Ukiko wrote of her joy at feeling the child grow within her, and regret that Mung could not share her happiness. She revealed her innermost thoughts to her husband, and he treasured every one.

Ukiko's final letter made Mung feel as if dark grey clouds of winter were returning to close him in. The ink marks were shaky, the characters askew. Ukiko wrote about the future of their son as if she would not be there. Mung remembered Saiyo's premonition of her own death. He shivered.

The last letter from Kagoshima was from Udo:

Honourable Father,
    It is with joy and sorrow that I write you. Joy, because you have sired a healthy son. Sorrow, because in realizing her most fervent wish to bear your child, Ukiko gave up her own life.
    She was in a weakened condition from the beginning. While still in Tokyo the physician from Kyoto warned her the pregnancy would be dangerous. But Ukiko insisted that at all costs the child's life should take precedence over hers. Then the birth was brought on prematurely by the Golden Lizard's attack on us in your home.

Udo went on to tell of his marriage to Gin-ko. He completed the letter with an official report of his trip to Berlin, and the Black Dragon Society's activities in Tokyo and Kagoshima.

Mung put the report aside. He handed Rhee the letter. 'I have a son,' he said in a dead voice.

As the Okinawan read, Mung felt a sudden chill. His body began to tremble violently. By the use of sheer willpower he stilled his convulsions and sat erect. The edges of his mouth turned down. 'She had no right to die!' he exclaimed. 'Damn that child! I want her, not him. She never understood.' He snatched a flask of saké and drained it, waiting for its warmth to spread through his cold body.

317

The warmth did not come. He remained seated, straining to keep his muscles under control.

Rhee looked up from the letter. 'Sire, I regret your loss, but am pleased at your gain. The Christian missionaries say God gives and God takes back, blessed is God.'

Mung's brittle black eyes speared Rhee. 'Do not ever blabber to me about gods! Especially the Christian god. I forbid you to listen to that drivel again. The Christian minister who converted me . . .' Mung saw Rhee's eyes widen. 'You did not know I was once a Christian,' Mung sneered. 'Nobody in Japan knows. I learned their ways and know their priests are as big a group of liars as our priests. That minister told me the righteous man's head is the seat of the god. I have tried to be good. I have tried to do right. And the gods sit on my head and stamp my heart to a pulp.' He stood up and grabbed his coat. 'To hell with them!' he shouted on his way out.

Mung walked the rocky coastline under the setting sun, and wandered under a full moon. For many hours his mind and heart battled to rule his body. His mind struggled for self-discipline, demanding work and dedication to forget the pain. His heart desired death. He stepped to the very edge of a steep cliff, letting the wind sway him over the crumbling earth beneath his feet, hoping to fall. But he did not.

Mung stumbled along a high rocky outcropping overlooking the ice-flecked sea. His hair had turned grey at the temples. Lines on both sides of his cheekbones were like gashes in his gaunt face. He watched the sun rise over the cold waters, its purple glow in the heavens giving way to gold. The orange fireball crested the skyline.

Mung held the stump of his hand up to the sun. 'Amaterasu-o-mi-Kami,' he shouted, 'goddess of the sun, mother of earth and the Emperor! Look what you have done! You took my father when I was a child, my hand

318

when a young man, my first wife, my first son, now my second wife. So many have died around me. Now you have given me a second son to love. I was not a good father to the first. I do not have enough strength to love this child and serve Japan. You curse me with the choice I never gave my Black Dragons.' Tears streamed down his ravaged face. He raised both arms up. 'Dai Nippon banzai!' He choked, and fell to his knees, arms still upraised. 'Dai Nippon banzai!'

From early morning until late in the afternoon, a glum-faced Mung sat with his scribes and read the official correspondence. He did not eat. He grunted his orders.

Rhee knelt at the door, then crawled into the room in response to Mung's summons.

'Have you ordered the crew of the mail-boat to stand by for their return to Tokyo?' Mung demanded.

'Yes, sire, although they would like more time ashore.'

Mung frowned. 'I take it they are complaining. If they open their mouths again, have them killed and another crew put aboard.'

Rhee bowed, avoiding Mung's bloodshot eyes.

Mung signalled a scribe to take his dictation. 'To Udo Ishikawa. You are to set up a spy network similar to that you described as used by the Prussians, and concentrate on Korea, northern China and Manchuria near the Russian border. You will leave the Korean trade mission when negotiations are completed and travel to Vladivostok. One of our boats will wait there until just before the freeze in September and bring you to Sapporo. You are to map major roads, and establish trade with those cities and provinces you pass through. You will ascertain the results of the sale of Russian Alaska to America, and why the czar wishes to negotiate ownership of Sakhalin and the Kurile islands with Japan. I am ordered to meet Count Muriev of

319

Vladivostok this June on the island of Senhoshi. I need information about his bargaining position. That is all.' Mung turned to Rhee. 'You have enough pigeons prepared to fly?'

'Yes, siro.'

'Send a bird reminding Jiroo of the no-second-thought order to kill the Golden Lizard. He is to send Danjuro here to Sapporo. The Mito giant helped me once. Now I will save him from his brother, Hideyoshi.'

'Why not kill Hideyoshi?'

'I promised his father I would not take revenge. Iyeasu must find his own way to restrain his brother.'

Chapter 33

In the month and a half after the mail-boat's arrival, reports of food shortages, the drowning of a child, the loss of an entire fishing crew, all appeared to leave Mung unmoved. He did not leave his house. The few who saw him said he never blinked, that his voice had the hollow ring of a cold, dark cavern. Only the Okinawan was permitted to come and go freely, but even he was kept at a distance by the man who ruled Hokkaido. The people of Sapporo called him Ishi-gokoro, Stone Heart, instead of Ishi-kawa, Stone River.

For Mung, the weeks of May and into mid-June were a time of intense preparations for his meeting with the Russians. He selected the brightest men from the governor's staff to accompany him. He sent Yakuza fur traders to scout Senhoshi where the meeting would take place. Sapporo seal hunters were ordered to reconnoitre the Kuriles, and local fishermen to observe Russian activities on Sakhalin. Mung studied every map, read every scroll, and questioned the sea captains of Sapporo about the geography of the northern islands.

Although forty-five years old, Mung could still recall and draw in detail the first maps he had seen when rescued by William Whittefield as a boy of fourteen. His geography classes in Harvard High School and three years as mate and captain aboard American whalers from Boston to the Bering Strait, had given him the ability to fill in those large blank spaces on old Japanese maps decorated with sea monsters. He sat alone, drawing his own charts and tables of tides, winds and currents based on the more accurate method of western cartography.

The memory that never failed him also peeked uninvited into his personal past, recalling with pain and heart-rending sorrow his loved ones. On those occasions, he turned to face the wall and meditate. He ate little, spoke less, and met only with those it was necessary to be in contact with.

The bi-monthly mail-boat brought Mung instructions from the Emperor, letters from Iyeasu, a packet of mail from his adoptive brother in America, and Jiroo's reports on the Black Dragon Society. That same day five pigeons flew into Sapporo bearing more recent messages regarding the Sakhalin and Kurile island negotiations.

Jiroo wrote,

Count Muriev, Russia's representative, is a worthy adversary. He is a devout Christian. A shrewd but honest negotiator, who makes a virtue of being inconspicuous until it is time to act. Recently he appeared secretly in Tokyo as third secretary to the newly appointed Russian ambassador. It is said Count Muriev avows his sweat will bring honour to the czar and glory to Russia.

Iyeasu wrote,

The Emperor has complied with your request and ordered my brother, now referred to as Lord Danjuro, out of Yedo for his safety. Danjuro was told he will be military commander of Hokkaido. This should reduce your burden of administration.

Be wary of Count Muriev. He is one of those rare round-eyes who views the Oriental as an equal human being. Like the American Commodore Perry, Muriev recognizes the true potential of Japan and the Japanese people. He is not blinded by racial prejudices. This clever man, with only one poorly armed ship, bluffed the Chinese government in Peking into ceding Russia a large part of Manchuria along the Amur river, plus the maritime provinces for a thousand miles on the Pacific Ocean from the Korean border to Kamchatka peninsula. Be cautious.

Udo wrote,

322

My information was gathered by Kang Shu in Canton, at The House of a Thousand Delights in the Yoshiwara, and by Tala Derzhavin, the wife of the new Russian ambassador to Tokyo . . .

Mung recalled the woman's name. Udo had reported her as a sexual deviate in Canton to whom his Black Dragons still supplied drugs. She was such a rich source of information that Mung had never voiced his disapproval of Udo's methods with the woman.

The information sent by Udo, combined with John's accounts from Washington – of world politics, of advances in science and technology – put international events into perspective for Mung. All the western powers in the Americas and Europe had been expanding, except Russia. In fact, the czar had sold Russian Alaska. Under these circumstances, the Russian diplomatic move towards Sakhalin became clear. Count Muriev wanted the thirty thousand square mile island for Russia. Mung saw the possibility of a large advantage for Japan. Udo's information was invaluable.

The personal note at the end of Udo's letter disturbed Mung.

I am leaving now with the trade delegation for Korea. Gin-ko and Shimatzu are to accompany me. You will see your son in the fall after we embark from Vladivostok.

Mung crumpled the letter. He would send a pigeon with orders for Udo to leave the child and Gin-ko behind. Then he realized it was too late. They would already be on their way. Mung gathered his papers, turning his thoughts quickly to something else. Danjuro had not arrived. He would face Muriev alone in the preliminary negotiations.

Senhoshi was located between Hokkaido and Sakhalin. Except for several log cabins and a council hall used seasonally by fishermen and sealers, the island was barren.

Both Mung and Muriev had allowed their subordinates to conduct the first three meetings. Now, in the rustic council house, the two men faced each other from opposite ends of a rough hewn wooden table. Interpreters stood next to each of them. Four of Mung's samurai sat opposite four Russian naval officers.

'You are a difficult man to meet,' the Russian count said. 'Why do you allow your juniors to conduct negotiations when it is you who will decide Japan's policy?'

'I am here on behalf of my government as a polite gesture of respect for you,' Mung said.

Muriev changed from speaking Russian to German, confusing his interpreters. 'Most international negotiations are made difficult by small men who wish to appear more important than the issues at hand. I have inquired about you, Mr Mung. You are not one of those little people.'

Mung answered in the guttural language of the Netherlands. 'Pardon my Dutch but I am sure you, as most German-speaking people, will understand it. I agree it would be easier if we discussed the major issues in private.'

Muriev answered in French. 'I have been told you are a well-travelled, cultured person whose efforts in the service of his country have not always been fully appreciated.'

Muriev's knowledge of his background confirmed for Mung some of the information he had received prior to leaving Sapporo. He understood that Muriev was purposely changing languages in order to impress his subordinates with Mung's intellectual ability and sophistication. Mung reinforced the impression by responding in fluent French, causing the eyes of the Russian officers to open wider. 'Is it true that when Czar Alexander II appointed you governor general of Siberia, he added, "and whatever other lands you find out there"?' Mung said.

Muriev laughed and his officers shifted uneasily, for he was a taciturn man rarely given to levity. 'Mr Mung,'

Muriev said, 'if we continue speaking French, I have the advantage. It is a language of the Russian aristocracy, which my officers understand. I take it your samurai do not.'

'Dismiss your men and I shall send mine out,' Mung said.

Muriev nodded, and the room was cleared. The building remained surrounded by samurai and Russian soldiers.

'You had this island scouted long before our meeting,' Muriev said.

'If my men were observed, yours were also here,' Mung replied.

'Then we have found our first point for agreement,' Muriev said. 'That it is preferable to familiarize oneself with the road to be travelled prior to departure. But it is only fitting for me to have done so, since Senhoshi is part of Sakhalin and rightfully belongs to Russia.'

'An island belongs to those who inhabit it,' Mung said. 'Japanese settled Sakhalin in 1547.'

'A hundred or so people banished from Honshu do not constitute a settlement policy by a government of forty million,' Muriev countered. 'Since 1760 there have been, and are now, more Russians on the northern end of Sakhalin than there were on the entire island in all its history.'

'Are prison colonies considered settlements by international law?' Mung asked. 'My government feels there is peace between our countries and on Sakhalin. Let the island remain divided for another two hundred years. We prefer to allow the present situation to continue. If legal ownership was put to the test, our rights would be established. Sakhalin is a natural extension of Hokkaido that broke off during volcanic eruptions.'

'You speak of events that occurred before man was created,' Muriev said, lighting a cigar. 'But your argument is faulted, Mr Mung. You assume Hokkaido is a natural

325

extension of Japan's main island of Honshu. But the depth in the Tsuguru strait separating the two land masses is too great. The flora and fauna differ. Even the indigenous people are racially opposite. They are Caucasians, the hairy ones you call Ainu. Russia has more claim to Hokkaido than Japan does.'

In addition to being clever, the Russian has prepared himself well for this meeting, Mung thought. 'Are you saying that Hokkaido is to be negotiated?' he challenged.

'No, but I prefer not to waste time. Sakhalin has no value to Japan. It is too far from your population centres.'

'That is true,' Mung said. 'Weather conditions restrict crops and the fishing season. I plan to remedy the situation by introducing a new strain of winter wheat developed in the north-west territories of America. If only the fishing season could be extended . . .'

Muriev blew on the tip of his cigar. 'Your government sent you north to develop Hokkaido where others have failed. What would it cost to resettle three thousand Japanese from Honshu to Hokkaido and develop its wheat and livestock capabilities?'

'Japanese do not raise livestock. We do not eat meat.'

'Because of the Black Current on the eastern shores of Hokkaido, it is warmer than our side of the Sea of Japan. If you were to raise sheep and cattle, my people in the maritime settlements would buy all you could provide. Give me an estimate for a resettlement programme.'

Mung shrugged, and named what he considered an exorbitant sum. 'Forty million yen.'

Muriev scribbled on a sheet of paper, and reflected silently. Then he said to Mung, 'That amounts to three million roubles. I could do it for less with Russians.' He dropped his quill and leaned forward. 'Can you make the decision for your country?'

'Every bit as much as you can,' Mung answered with a

steady eye on the Russian. 'I too must receive approval from my government. I do have full confidence the Emperor will support my recommendations.'

'And I am confident of the czar's confirmation. So I make you this offer. Japan will receive an interest free loan in the amount of forty million yen to resettle pioneers on Hokkaido. The loan is to be repaid during the next ten years by produce exported from Japan to our maritime provinces. In addition, Russia will cede the Kurile islands in return for Japan's recognition of Russia's sovereignty over Sakhalin. We will send experts to teach your people animal husbandry, and in return would expect to participate in the experiment with the new American winter wheat.'

Mung felt drained. He sensed Muriev's eyes watching him closely. He had prepared for every eventuality but this, an offer that far exceeded any he had hoped for. The National Assembly clearly wants to retain some rights to Sakhalin, but they do not have the information available to me from Washington, he thought. The Russians conceding the Kuriles makes the difference. The resettlement plan would establish Hokkaido as the strongest buffer possible against a Russian incursion into northern Japan. The loan of such a great amount of money to implement resettlement, indicates the czar's government has no wish for a confrontation with Japan. From Udo, Mung knew Muriev would soon be recalled to St Petersburg. I do not want to have to negotiate with someone else, he thought.

Mung was about to ask for a recess when Rhee entered the council house and began serving tea. Mung stared at the Okinawan's topknot. It and the copper skewer reminded him of a month-old communiqué from the commander of the new imperial army, which referred to the importance of the Ryukyu islands in the defence and economy of southern Japan. An idea dawned on Mung.

He addressed Muriev in French. 'My body servant is from the Ryukyu islands. For three centuries, the fiefdom of Satsuma in the south of Japan has governed them. The Chinese continue to claim sovereignty over the islands, and collect a symbolic yearly tribute from the Ryukyu king. My country will soon press the Chinese to recognize Japan's rights to these islands.'

'I am governor general of Siberia and the north,' Muriev said.

'Did not Czar Alexander refer to the north and whatever else is out there?'

Muriev leaned back. He puffed at his cigar, watching the grave-faced Japanese with the hard, pain-filled eyes.

Finally Mung said, 'If Russia would champion Japan's claim to the Ryukyu islands, I would be prepared to sign a treaty guaranteeing the czar's sovereignty over Sakhalin.'

Without taking his eyes from Mung, Muriev dismissed Rhee. The Russian count stood up and began pacing, puffing his cigar and considering the alternatives. His tobacco smoke hazed the entire room. I expected these negotiations to continue for years, Muriev thought. That I would be in St Petersburg long before an agreement was reached. My offer to this Japanese was a bluff, trying to frighten him with a legitimate proposal to be decided upon immediately. He tingled at the thought of returning to the czar with the border communities guaranteed free from starvation. His mind raced. Because the czar's treasury was depleted by the Crimean War, he sold Russian Alaska to the Americans. A treaty with Japan would save the national treasury ten times the amount of the loan. If the winter wheat is successful in Hokkaido, Siberia could become the breadbasket of Russia, with enough left over for export to China.

Mung coughed. He could barely make out the features of the Russian count through the cigar smoke. Muriev turned and said, 'Mr Mung, I can transfer three million roubles from the Siberian treasury with no signature but my own. I can guarantee international recognition of Japan's rights to the Kurile islands. What I cannot do is speak for my government regarding your claims to the Ryukyu islands.'

'You are asking me to sign away 30,000 square miles of Sakhalin for 1,200 square miles of the Kuriles,' Mung said. 'The Ryukyu islands are only another 600 square miles. It is not too much to ask.'

'You are correct,' Muriev said. 'When I return to Vladivostok I could order the Russian ambassadors in Korea, China and Japan to support your claims unless they hear otherwise from the czar in St Petersburg. Furthermore, they can use their influence on other European powers to do the same.'

'How long would it take for St Petersburg to make a decision to countermand your orders?'

'A year. If that is satisfactory, I am open to exploring the implications of what we have said.'

Mung nodded gravely, then asked, 'Would you support Japan's request to end the unequal treaties with the European nations?'

It required seven weeks of discussions, map-making, negotiating fishing rights, and clarifying hunting grounds, trading privileges, exchange rates and repatriation of Japanese held in Russian prisons, before agreement was reached. During those forty-nine days, Mung watched every ship arriving from Vladivostok with anxiety. He feared the arrival of news of international events would render Sakhalin unimportant to the Russians.

At the end of August, Mung and Muriev met for the last time. After the ceremonial signing, the two men left the celebration and walked the beach together.

'You are a dour man,' Muriev said. 'Negotiating with you has been like taking a daily dose of vinegar.'

'It was never my intention to be rude or discourteous,' Mung said.

'You have not been either. These negotiations are the smoothest and most straightforward I have ever been involved in. If I had not come to respect, even like you, I would not mention this. But, Mr Mung, you are dried up. There is no juice in you. I am known as a solemn man, but you surpass me.'

They continued walking silently. Muriev is right, Mung thought. I feel dried up. I seek safety in silence. I am even now yearning for the solitude of my cabin. I am bitter because of the deaths of Yoshida and Ukiko, but I did not think it was so obvious to others.

'Mr Mung, I sense you have suffered greatly, but you must believe that you will find happiness again,' Muriev said. 'God gives hope to all.'

'I think it may have been Satan who gave man hope,' Mung said. 'Hope makes man suffer pain, starvation and untold indignities he would never stand for if hope were not drawing him on. In the end man dies after being degraded, hurt and humiliated. He could have died in the beginning without all the trouble.'

'I taste vinegar.' The Russian count shook his head. 'Before we return to the others and say our farewells, I regret to inform you of a problem which could affect your people in the north. A Baron Benzowsky, who was exiled to the penal colony of Vulcan, led a revolt there last winter. All the guards and most of the prisoners were killed. Benzowsky's pirates captured a mail-boat just before the freeze, and sailed south. They attacked the prison colony of Olga and wintered there, using it as a base to gather more outlaws and capture more boats. Since the thaw, they have raided and raped ten settlements in the maritime provinces.'

'Why should that affect my people?' Mung asked.

'Benzowsky has Japanese sailors, who were also prisoners in Vulcan, as guides. He has a fleet of five well-armed sailing ships manned by the worst cutthroats in the world. They force each new member of their band to practise cannibalism before being accepted. They survived starvation by using the prison guards at Olga as cattle. Twice they attempted a breakthrough south to China. Our patrol boats, with the aid of the Korean navy, turned them back. They now have a force large enough to sack a city. Benzowsky is a military man and he is desperate. On the return journey to Vladivostok, my fleet will sweep the Tatar strait. If Benzowsky slips by us, he may use his Japanese sailors to guide him across the sea to easier targets on Hokkaido, or even Honshu. You had best fortify your coastal towns.'

'It is too late,' Mung said. 'It is almost September.'

'Then pray we catch those bastards.'

Chapter 34

Amidst the smoking ruins of Samarga on the Manchurian side of the Tatar strait, officers of the Vulcan fleet gathered at a long table on the beach. Drunken pirates, stumbling to and from the surviving women prisoners, served as a background for the strategy meeting.

Vladimir Benzowsky sprawled in a large ornate chair. Behind him stood Boris, Cossack hat pushed back on his shaven skull, long black beard hiding the crossed bandoleers over his massive chest. He gripped a double-barrelled shotgun in each huge hand.

'Nobody has gold in these parts,' an officer said. 'Their wealth is in furs. Like the other towns we raided, they sent their pelts to Ga-van.'

There was grumbling and muttering around the long table, but no one raised his voice nor touched his weapon. A signal from Benzowsky, and Boris would kill. The two huge men controlled the band of cutthroats by fear.

The baron, now heavier by two stone, his nose large and purple-veined, closed his glassy eyes and drained a crystal champagne glass of vodka. 'I do not want you gentlemen to think I plan to winter six empty ships and seven hundred hungry men in this Godforsaken hole. They would have us for dinner.'

Arima refilled the champagne glass. Despite his drunkenness, the baron's officers were aware that when the Russian giant spoke precisely and politely, he was most dangerous.

'If anyone is inclined to leave the Vulcan armada, it would be foolhardy.' Benzowsky stood up, dwarfing Boris. 'If I did not find and kill you, Count Muriev would.'

'Is the Russian navy finally coming after us?' a captain asked.

Benzowsky motioned for Arima to answer. 'Twenty-one ships of the northern fleet are moving up the coast,' the Japanese said. 'Their orders are to find and destroy us, sail to Ga-van, pick up the furs stored there, and return to Vladivostok in time for the last convoy to Russia.'

'How does the little Jap bastard know so much?' the officer shouted.

'This Oriental gentleman has just returned from a trip up the Samarga river with a Russian navy steamboat in tow.' Benzowsky allowed time for his words to sink in. 'Arima captured some of the *Czarina*'s crew. He and his yellow friends questioned them until they revealed their innermost secrets.'

The men closest to Arima clapped him on the shoulders. A few others congratulated him, but most remained silent. Although he was a captain in the Vulcan fleet, Arima and the other Yakuza were not trusted by most of the Russians.

'How many guns on the steamer?' someone called out.

'Two,' Benzowsky said. 'Both twenty-pound swivel guns with rifled bores, exploding shells and new sighting equipment. They are mounted fore and aft.'

'Sweet bloody Jesus!' another captain said. 'The latest model twenty-pounders on a steamer!'

Everyone sat in awed silence. Most had never seen a steamship. All assumed there was not another in the maritime provinces.

Benzowsky took a deep breath, puffing himself up. 'This one ship and its guns are the keys to Ga-van's treasure house, and our way out of the north to China.'

'But Ga-van is a city, not a piss-arsed village like this.' An officer jerked his thumb at the smouldering remains of Samarga. He drank from a bottle, then added, 'Ga-van has two or three thousand people and regular soldiers.'

'We have seven hundred fighting men, two twenty-pounders and a steam warship,' Benzowsky said. 'And I have a plan to take their furs from them and make for China.'

'With Muriev and his fleet looking for us?' The officer lurched to his feet and took another drink. He pointed the bottle at Benzowsky. 'We've tried twice for China and been turned back both times. What difference will a steamboat make against twenty-one ships of the line?'

Boris swung the shotguns to bear, but the man ignored the Cossack and continued talking. 'If the Russian fleet is after us and there are only two hundred miles to manoeuvre between this hellhole and Sakhalin, those shotguns are only going to do Muriev's job for him. Ga-van could be a trap.'

Benzowsky motioned for Boris to lower his weapons. 'It is a trap,' the baron said. 'The men aboard the captured steamer informed Arima of that. The *Czarina* was waiting for Muriev to lead the Russian fleet in finishing us. Muriev made Ga-van the central storage point to lure us there. But now we have his steamer. This is not a paddle-wheeler. It has a screw type propeller and double mast for sailing. It will help us get through the northern end of the Tatar strait and into the Sea of Okhotsk.'

'That's close to the Arctic Circle,' the drunken officer said. 'It could already be frozen.'

Benzowsky nodded at Arima. 'The Jap and his friends know the area. They've hunted there. And this winter won't be as bad as last. I want the Russian fleet to follow us north. They don't have a steamship. While they're kept busy tacking east and west to move north after us, I'll be aboard the *Czarina* towing your ships through the Narrows and into the Sea of Okhotsk. We then make a right turn and sail around Sakhalin. The north wind will be at our backs and we'll run south ahead of the freeze.'

The officer, disregarding warnings from his mates, went

on. 'I served in the czar's navy, not with a bunch of little lake sailors like these. You're talking about travelling a thousand miles through the coldest seas on this earth. If we survive the breakout through the Narrows and the icebergs in the Okhotsk Sea, we will starve to death before reaching the southern end of Hokkaido.'

Benzowsky pointed at the officer. Boris brought up one of the shotguns and pulled both triggers. At twelve feet, the lead shot cut the man in half. Some of the pellets ripped away the cheek of the Mongol captain sitting next to him. The Mongol jumped up, cursing. 'You stupid Cossack son of a bitch!' Blood poured between the fingers clutching the mangled face. Boris brought up the second shotgun and fired one barrel. The Mongol fell over backward with a gaping hole in his chest. Boris reloaded.

Benzowsky smashed the table with his great fist, making the wooden boards jump. He swept the shattered champagne glass away and pointed around the table. 'The next time someone complains, the men nearest should kill him.' He snickered. 'Boris does not aim well.'

No one moved. Benzowsky pointed at the first dead officer. 'Everything he said is true. If we are not killed at Ga-van, and Muriev doesn't get us, and the ice doesn't break our ships apart, we could starve. What the former officer in the czar's navy did not say is that we have no choice. Muriev wants our blood. The only way to prevent him from getting it is to follow my directions. There is a large Japanese city near the southern end of Hokkaido. It has ten antiquated muzzle loaders in dirt forts which guard the harbour. We'll go there to reprovision. We'll holiday with Sapporo's women, take what the town has, then head into the Sea of Japan and on to the Yellow Sea where we'll be free to raid the China coast for the rest of our lives.'

Arima caught Benzowsky watching him. He froze his emotions at mention of the city of his birth. He had heard rumours of Boris' torturing of two Japanese prisoners found in Samarga prison while he was up-river.

Benzowsky was still talking. 'Arima will remain on the mail-boat. Most of his crew will join mine, including the other Japs to act as guides. I'll make the *Czarina* my flagship.' He unrolled a map and motioned Arima closer. 'Tomorrow I lead our armada north. You follow until fifty miles past Grosevichi. Take a position there and watch for the Russian fleet. If you see them, set off three green rockets at one-minute intervals, then catch us up. Except for the steamer, the mail-boat is the fastest we have.'

Benzowsky was lying and Arima knew it, but the two dead men were grim reminders to remain silent and do as he was told.

In the Tatar strait, Count Nicolas Muriev moved his fleet north in classic naval formation – ten cutters fanned out in a fifty-mile wide semicircle. They were scouting for five frigates and six sloops of war, all ships of the line, with not a steam driven vessel among them.

As the Vulcan pirates descended on Ga-van five hundred miles further north, the Russian scout ships were reporting the destruction of Samarga.

'Sir,' a young lieutenant said to Count Muriev, 'the town of Samarga is devastated. Corpses everywhere. Only a few people escaped to the surrounding woods. There was torture and rape. We found partially eaten human bodies in roasting pits.' The lieutenant choked.

'Get hold of yourself,' Muriev ordered. 'Was this your first time ashore after a pirate raid?'

'Yes, sir.' The young man nodded. 'I will get used to it.'

'I hope not,' Muriev said. 'What else is there to report?'

'The *Czarina* was taken intact by the Vulcan pirates.'

Now Muriev wanted to choke. The steamer was crucial

to his plan for capturing the pirates. He would have to press on to protect Ga-van.

'Sir,' the young officer said, 'the captain of the *Czarina* is here. We found him and the remainder of his crew scavenging in the ruins of Samarga.'

Muriev waved the captain in. He watched the man gather his last bit of pride, straighten up, tug his stained tunic into place, and salute.

'Report how your ship was stolen,' the governor general commanded.

'Sir, I had no reason to believe we were in danger. Fuel was low and I wanted to be prepared for your arrival, so I led a wood-cutting party ashore. I left a skeleton crew aboard the *Czarina*. It was afternoon when the work was done. I gave permission for the shore party to bathe and wash clothes along the river-bank. When one of our Russian mail-boats came up-river we waved, and they waved back.' The officer's shoulders slumped; his body began to shake. 'The pirates came over the rail so fast my men did not have a chance. They were slaughtered, the anchor was cut and the steamer towed off before we could reach it.' The captain began to weep. 'We chased it along the shore.' He sobbed and spread his hands in a futile gesture.

'Did they use the steam engine?' Muriev asked.

'No, they towed it until we lost sight of them.'

'I understand there are bodies to be buried in Samarga,' Muriev said. 'You and your men will dig those graves and remain to tend them for the next five years. Get out of my sight before I hang you. Now I must try to prevent another massacre.'

Nicolas Muriev knew there was no other armed steamship north of the thirty-eighth parallel. The twenty-pound cannon were the best Russian make, and could outshoot anything between Vladivostok and Alaska. He unrolled a map of the Tatar strait and put his finger on the Narrows. 'Benzowsky,' he growled, 'if you try to break out at the northern end, you are in for a surprise. I sent word to the Amur trading colony to fortify the Narrows. Now I will order the fleet north to Ga-van at all speed. You are trapped.'

Among the seven hundred Vulcan pirates, there were enough who had served on Russian navy steamships in the Baltic fleet to crew the *Czarina*. Early on the morning of September 8th the *Czarina*, flying the imperial colours and towing three sailing ships, appeared at the entrance to Ga-van harbour. Her canvas was down. Bogus prisoners on deck stood under the eyes of uniformed guards. A signal gun was fired from the quarterdeck of the steamer. Signal flags requested entry into the harbour.

The commander of the guard reported to Ga-van's provincial governor. 'Sir, it is the *Czarina*. I was told to expect her and the entire northern fleet, but she is not flying Count Muriev's flag.'

'Yes, yes,' the governor said. 'I have had my telescope on them. Those ships in tow are converted merchantmen. I'll wager Count Muriev drove the pirates north and the *Czarina* captured them. Give them a ten-gun salute. Wake the town. Have the church bells rung. There is little enough for our people to celebrate in this place.'

A puff of smoke appeared from both signal towers above the main gate of the wooden stockade fronting the city of Ga-van. Flags fluttered up the signalmast granting permission to enter.

'We tricked them,' Boris said. 'They are saluting us.'

'Head us in,' Benzowsky ordered the *Czarina*'s helmsman. 'Gunners, mark those cannon on the stockade wall.

338

And you idiots in uniform, stand at attention like the czar's sailors. No one moves until I give the order.'

The *Czarina* made a slow half circle towing the three sailing ships. She headed into the harbour under the muzzles of the cannon on the cliffs at the entrance. Men from the gun emplacements on the heights came out of their positions and waved.

'Steady, you no good bastards!' Benzowsky shouted. 'Smile and wave. They have telescopes too. Wait until we are almost to the dock. I want the harbour guns behind us. They usually can't be turned more than ninety degrees.' He could hear church bells and see people streaming out of the stockade gates. Soldiers waved from the top of the wooden parapets. Benzowsky waved back.

'Smile,' Boris shouted. 'Think of their wives you'll screw and their vodka you'll drink.'

The Cossack leaned forward and Benzowsky wrinkled up his nose. 'What is it?'

'We are very close.'

'You are too close to me and you stink.' Benzowsky looked behind and up at the harbour guns on the heights. The *Czarina* was almost ahead of their line of fire. The gunners on the parapets in front of the town had not reloaded their cannon after the salute. He pulled out a white handkerchief and waved it. 'Go to it, you motherless sons of Satan,' he shouted. 'Kill! Kill for your freedom! Kill for the wrongs they've done you! Kill for the hell of it!'

Pirate captains aboard the three sailing ships in tow saw the handkerchief. 'Helmsman, hard about,' each one ordered. 'Axeman, part the line.'

Men hidden in the bow cut the towing cables. The bogus prisoners on deck jumped to their primed cannon, and the uniformed pirates discarded their jackets. The *Czarina* and the sailing ships came around broadside to the dock. People cheered their manoeuvres.

Benzowsky gave the signal to fire and the two twenty-pounders roared. The two gun towers above Ga-van's main gate disintegrated in smoke and splinters. The three sailing ships unleashed accurate broadsides that put all but two of Ga-van's fifteen guns on the city walls out of action. Those two were destroyed by the twenty-pounders. The imperial Russian flag aboard the *Czarina* dropped and a large black standard unfurled – the blazing sun supported by a thunderbolt.

People on shore fled towards the main gate in terror.

At the first shot from the *Czarina*'s cannon, the garrison commander leapt twelve feet from the stockade wall to the parade ground where his men were formed up as an honour guard. 'We've been tricked!' he shouted. 'It's the Vulcan pirates. Swing the artillery around. There's no time for the horses. Put your shoulders to it.'

They wrestled five artillery pieces towards the main gate. The commander had his shoulder into a harness pulling the first gun through the gate when the fear-crazed mob fleeing the Vulcan's guns came charging through. The commander and his men were trampled. People tripped and fell over their bodies; they piled up over the gun. They blocked the entrance trying to climb over one another.

'Load with grapeshot,' Benzowsky ordered. 'Depress your guns.' He pointed at the pandemonium around the main gate. Five hundred lead Minie balls were packed in each canister slipped into the breeches of the twenty-pounders. The *Czarina* was only 150 yards from the target.

'Fire!' Benzowsky shouted.

The guns roared, echoing through the hills, followed by deep, ugly silence. Men and nature waited for the gun smoke to thin. Then moans and screams began to fill the eerie void. The mass of humanity had been shredded into a pile of bloody meat. Here and there an arm or leg was raised. A child staggered off, dragging her intestines. An old man tried climbing the pile of mangled bodies and kept slipping back. He had no legs to hold himself up.

'The city is ours!' Boris shouted. He and Benzowsky ducked as a shell whistled over their heads and exploded on shore.

'Stupid goddamned Cossack!'

'On the heights,' Boris said.

'How the hell did they turn those guns around?' Benzowsky shouted.

Boris pointed. They saw men outside gun emplacements on the heights digging furiously with pick and shovel. They were widening the aperture of the gun that had fired in order to traverse the weapon further. They were reloading for a second shot when Benzowsky commanded his men, 'Aft gun, take that target above the harbour entrance on the left.'

A shell from above roared, blowing away ten feet of the *Czarina*'s bow rail and some decking. Then the twenty-pounders responded. Manned by experienced deserters from the czar's navy, the shells arched up and into Ga-van's defensive positions. The other three pirate ships elevated their guns, and the unequal battle was ended. The harbour guns were silenced. The Vulcan armada had received only minor damage, with few losses.

Those people who succeeded in fleeing from Ga-van on the only road, were met by the crews of the two Vulcan ships which had landed ten miles below the city and marched inland to attack from the rear. Women and men were separated, the males above the age of twelve forced back to the city. They were needed to load the bales of fur from all

341

the northern colonies onto the pirate ships. Flogged if they fell, and killed if they did not rise, the men of Ga-van finished the work quickly. Then they were herded into the now empty warehouses.

'Eight hundred prisoners and about as many dead,' Boris reported.

'That means half escaped into the forest,' Benzowsky said. 'No matter. Without weapons or shelter, they'll starve or freeze. Use that stupid Cossack brain of yours to kill every man, woman and child we've captured in a way that will make Muriev and his men crazy mad to follow us up the Tatar strait. I want them so angry they can't think. Enjoy yourselves,' he added, 'but first send me two women.'

Arima awoke with a start. It was an hour before dawn on the mail-boat he had anchored in a cove near Grosevichi. His crew of Russians had drunk too much and were sleeping. He dressed against the cold and walked up on deck. Darkness surrounded the boat. He looked up and sucked air through his teeth. Contrary to his orders, the lookouts on the cliff had a fire burning. To Arima in the cove below, the glow resembled a lighthouse beacon. Cursing, he ordered a messenger up the cliff to extinguish the fire.

It was an hour before the man returned. 'They're still sleeping up there,' he gasped. 'The bastards got drunk. We've been spotted.'

Arima gripped the messenger's heavy jacket. 'What do you mean, spotted?'

'The whole goddamned Tatar strait is full of blinking signal lights. The Russian fleet is closing in on us.'

Arima pushed him down the stairs into the crew's quarters. 'Get them out! Out! Everyone out!' He screamed until his voice cracked. 'Cut the anchor! Up the sail!'

Arima was beside himself with rage. He screamed at the mate, 'Your stupid pig-faced friends were drunk again. They made a fire. We've been spotted by Muriev's fleet. We have to give warning to Benzowsky.'

The first mate looked up at the cliff, then out into the dark sea. 'There's no fire and no signal lights. It will be morning soon. Then we'll know for certain.'

Arima jumped up and down. He pulled his pistol and fired a shot between the mate's legs. 'Get us out of here!' he screamed.

The mate leapt away and pointed to the cliff. 'What about them?'

Arima shoved the gun in the mate's face. 'Cut the anchor and up sail, or I'll kill you. The hell with them! It's their fault we've been spotted. We were ordered to watch for Muriev before he saw us.'

'The captain's right,' the man coming up from the crew's quarters said. 'I saw the fire and the signal lights. They're coming for us.'

The mate backed away, glaring at Arima. 'Make sail,' he ordered his men. 'Cut the anchor line.'

Arima retreated to the fantail, still pointing the pistol at the mate. He backed to the three rockets standing ready. 'Helmsman, give me the matches.'

The big helmsman looked to the mate for orders and Arima waved his gun. The mate nodded and the helmsman handed Arima the packet.

With the sails set and the ship moving, Arima sent off the first rocket. He waited a minute, crouching with pistol in one hand and matches in the other, then fired the second rocket into the sky.

The ship was picking up speed. Arima could not light the third match without protecting it from the wind. With his eye on the mate twenty feet away, he rested his gun on the deck. He cupped his hand and lit the fuse. The mate nodded and the big helmsman let go of the wheel. He grabbed Arima by the back of the neck and flung him over the rail into the sea.

From the quarterdeck of his flagship, Count Muriev saw the three green rockets light up the sky. 'They are not ours,' he said.

'No, sir,' the captain of the flagship said. 'It has to be the pirates. Let us hope it is from the *Czarina*.'

'Order every ship to block her escape,' Count Muriev said.

Signal rockets soared into the sky. The men of the Vladivostok fleet ran to their battle stations. Twenty-one ships encircled the cove.

Arima clawed his way out of the cold water onto a large rock in the centre of the cove. By the light of the new dawn, he saw rocket trails crisscrossing the sky. Although shivering, his teeth chattering, he giggled at the sight of two Russian scout cutters blocking the mail-boat's escape. It warmed him to know the mate and his friends were about to be captured. He watched the mail-boat heel over to starboard and swing back on a radical turn that buried her railing. As she came about, her three port side cannon fired on the Russian cutters, and missed. The cutters held their fire as they moved quickly towards the mail-boat. They drew up on both sides of her stern, and hailed. When there was no answer, they both fired warning shots in front of her bow.

Every Vulcan pirate knew that capture meant death by hanging. The mail-boat raced past the rock, heading for shore. Arima could see the mate at the wheel. He is probably going to beach her and try to escape inland, Arima thought. He watched the two cutters separate. They swung to port and starboard, firing explosive shells as their guns came to bear.

The mail-boat shuddered. Fire broke out on the deck. It was still making headway towards shore when the main-mast crashed down. The sail caught fire, trapping men underneath.

All the ammunition for the six cannon was stored on deck. Arima slid around to the opposite side of the rock. He ducked his head just before the ship exploded and disintegrated, showering the cove with wreckage and broken bodies.

'Sir,' the captain of Muriev's flagship said, 'there is only one survivor, an Oriental. No one can speak to him. From the hand signs he makes, I assume he was a houseboy. Shall I hang him?'

'No. The son of Hokkaido's inspector general will be in Vladivostok when we return. I ordered him to be delayed. He can question the Oriental. Now what do we do about the Vulcan pirates?'

'I suggest we press on, sir. Those three rockets were a signal to the main force. They cannot be too far ahead. We dare not lose them in the winter weather that is due.'

Aboard the *Czarina*, Benzowsky asked Boris, 'What time was Arima's signal?'

'Just before dawn.'

'I didn't think Muriev could make it this fast. We have only a seven-hour head start. It's not enough.' Benzowsky's bloodshot eyes flicked from side to side. He shifted his weight back and forth while his alcohol-soaked brain struggled to think of a way out of the trap. 'It will take two hours to pick up the crews of the four ships in the harbour.'

'Five hours for the others to go back overland and get underway,' Boris said.

'That is the answer, you stupid Cossack!' Benzowsky grabbed him by his beard. 'Who else knows about the signal?'

'The lookouts. They're up on the heights.'

'Leave the bastards there. Tell everyone that Muriev is a day behind and coming fast. Get them back to their ships. Tell them to grab what food they can and hurry. Do not mention how close the Vladivostok fleet is. The two crews that travel overland will be caught in a running fight with the Russian navy. That will give us more time.'

Boris looked around the empty room for fear of being overheard. 'If those two crews learn of this, they'll murder us.'

'And if we do not get underway, Muriev will hang us.'

'Take the steamer and run,' Boris mumbled.

'You're thinking like the arse of a Cossack horse,' Benzowsky said. 'With the *Czarina* alone, maybe we could make it. But what would happen when we reached Sapporo? We need men and guns to take that city. There's enough fuel to get us there and furs to make us rich in China.'

'But not enough food for the trip,' Boris said. 'We only loaded the pelts.'

'Gather the crews of the ships in the harbour. Tell the two other crews we will rendezvous ten miles outside Gavan harbour.'

'There won't be enough food,' Boris warned again.

'Stupid Cossack, there are always two-legged deer.' Benzowsky shoved Boris towards the door. 'We've eaten man-meat before.'

Chapter 35

September 1872, Vladivostok

'This cabin is ours until Count Muriev returns from chasing pirates,' Udo said. 'Then we will be given permission to leave.'

Gin-ko shifted Shimatzu in her arms. 'I thought we arrived in time to catch the boat to Sapporo.'

'Yes, but it sailed without us. The count wants to speak with me.'

'This is the first Occidental house I have ever been in. Are they all so cluttered with rough furniture?'

'Tables and chairs in Europe are of finer quality, so they heap even more of it in. The smell of the people is what bothers me,' Udo said.

'But so did that of the Koreans and Manchurians who hosted us. It could be the different wood they burn and the foods they eat.' Gin-ko shifted the baby again.

'Is anything wrong? You appear a bit on edge.'

'It is the possibility of being frozen in for the winter.'

'The garrison commander says the bay will not freeze until November. He should know.'

'I do hope there is a good doctor here,' Gin-ko said.

'Do you feel ill?'

'If we do get frozen in, a good midwife would do.'

'Pregnant,' Udo whispered. 'You are pregnant?' He knelt before her.

Gin-ko nodded. She saw the wonder and happiness in her husband's face and her eyes brimmed with tears. She placed Shimatzu in a fur-lined crib and Udo took her in his arms.

'Do you feel well?' he asked.

'I feel wonderful, although I prefer the child to be born in Japan. He is due in February.'

Udo counted on his fingers. He counted again, and frowned. 'You were pregnant before we arrived in Pusan.'

'Yes.' She smiled. 'We were quite active if you remember.'

'On the entire trip up the Korean coast into Manchuria, you did not tell me.'

'You would have worried.' She drew Udo back to her. 'I wish to be with you. To travel with you. We will have many children. You promised.'

Udo nodded his head. 'Yes.'

'Please do not make my pregnancies an excuse to leave me behind.'

'I love you.' He choked. 'I am frightened because of what happened to Ukiko.'

'Ukiko was ill. The Korean physician said I am healthy enough to bear many children.' She looked up at him from lowered lids and began opening her robe.

Udo stopped her hands. 'You are pregnant.'

'I have been pregnant for some time.' She took his hands and placed them on her breasts. She ran them up and down her body. 'Pregnancy makes some women extremely sexual.'

'I love you with all my heart,' he said.

At Udo's request, the military commander of Vladivostok released an Oriental prisoner into his custody to do housework. Doihara was a young Japanese fur trader arrested five years before. He had bright, intelligent eyes and a confident air.

Udo watched Doihara carefully for two weeks. Then he took the young man for a walk away from the settlement.

348

'Your wife is Khalkha Mongol with family near Harbin,' Udo said. 'Do they accept you as her husband?'

'I am welcome in their yurt.'

'You were imprisoned for illegal trading with the Russian outposts along the Amur river. Do you speak their language, and that of your wife?'

'Khalkha Mongol is a most popular tongue among the tribes. I learned it for business, as well as Russian.'

Udo nodded. 'The other Japanese in Vladivostok will travel with me back to Japan, but you shall remain.'

'They will be killed for having been out of the country,' Doihara said.

'The Exclusion Edict is no longer in effect. Japan now seeks trade with foreign countries.'

'I wish to return to see my family.'

'Do you have a wife in Japan?'

'No. If allowed, I will take my Mongol wife and children with me.'

Udo shook his head. 'That I cannot permit. They must remain here with you.' He watched Doihara's reaction. The young Japanese bowed to the samurai's order.

'You shall remain in Vladivostok and become the most successful legitimate businessman in this region. I will see you are issued permits for trade and travel. Every spring you are to visit your wife's family near Harbin, then trade for furs on the way back through the Mongol tribal lands to the Amur river. Your real business will be gathering information for the Emperor. You are one of the few chosen to spy for the Son of Heaven.'

Doihara looked into Udo's eyes and realized he was speaking the truth. He fell to his knees and prostrated himself full length. 'For this honour, I would die.'

Udo remembered how he and his brother had thrown themselves down and answered the same way to Mung when they were recruited as Black Dragons. It seemed all

Japanese were taught the same lessons of obedience and loyalty to the Emperor by parents and teachers. He ordered Doihara to stand. 'Live to serve the Emperor. You will set up a shop called The Happy Dragon. People will bring you messages for me at the shop, and on your spring travels.'

'How will I know them?'

'By certain signs and words that I will impart to you. You will relay urgent messages to me by pigeon, or on the bi-monthly trading ships that are soon to move between Sapporo and Vladivostok.'

'I am truly honoured.' Doihara bowed. 'It will take money to begin a business, and what will I sell?'

'You shall have the necessary funds,' Udo said, 'but your success will be determined by the information you send, not the merchandise you move. I wish you to pay more and charge less than any other trader in Manchuria.'

Doihara bowed again. 'I shall endeavour to be worthy of the honour you have bestowed upon me and my family.'

'Take a private teacher and learn Mandarin Chinese. More people speak that language than any other. It will also help you to become familiar with the different religions in the area.'

'I am already a Christian,' Doihara said. 'The Russians spared my life because of my conversion.'

'Good,' Udo said. 'Be a Christian in Vladivostok. Among the tribes and the Chinese, believe whatever they do. It is common sense if you are going to live with and learn from them.'

Udo's words were so simply correct, Doihara apologized for not having thought of it himself.

On Count Muriev's first evening in Vladivostok, Udo was his sole guest at dinner. They conversed in German and French.

'You have inherited your father's knack with languages,' Muriev said.

'Mung is my adoptive father,' Udo replied, 'but fully responsible for the educational advantages I have received.'

'How is it you travel with your father's son?'

Udo told Muriev of Ukiko's death. He told of the Korean trade mission and the extended trip as a honeymoon.

'It was clear Mung was grieving during our negotiations,' Muriev said. 'Although I must say he did not let that affect his mission. Your father is a brilliant, honest man. Both attributes are rare in statesmen. I would prefer to lighten his burden, but alas can only add to it.'

'Is this why I was ordered to await your return?'

'Yes. I hoped to come back with Benzowsky's head on the bow of my flagship and the Vulcan pirates hanging from the rails, but unfortunately too many escaped our trap. I would have preferred prisoners but my men took none after they saw the atrocities at Samarga. We destroyed two large ships and killed many, but Benzowsky escaped with four hundred men aboard three sailing ships and an armed steamer.'

Udo listened to Count Muriev's description of the attack on Ga-van. The governor general concluded, 'Tomorrow I am sending you, your family and the Japanese from this prison compound to Sapporo on our fastest cutter. There will be five ten-pound cannon aboard for the defence of the city, and enough explosive shells to blow Benzowsky to Hell.'

'I understood you to say you expect he will be trapped in the Narrows at the northern end of the Tatar strait.'

Muriev crossed himself. 'Pray to the Almighty that I am correct. Benzowsky leads a band of hellions. Many are Russian-trained military men. With that steamer and those twenty-pounders, they can do a great deal of damage

351

wherever they go. Tell your father that if Benzowsky does come to Sapporo, the *Czarina* must be sunk first.' The count sat back and lit a cigar. 'We do have one captured Oriental pirate named Arima. Perhaps you would question him. We think he was a houseboy. If he has any useful information, please inform me. You may take him with you to Sapporo. My men will kill him if he remains.'

'I will question him before we leave,' Udo said. 'There is a Japanese prisoner named Doihara who married a Mongolian woman. He wishes to remain and set up a business in Vladivostok. I am thinking of making him our first Japanese business agent in this outpost.'

'I shall arrange for the necessary papers and permits,' Muriev said.

A north wind whipped out of the Arctic Circle and over the Sea of Okhotsk, funnelling through the Narrows to gale force strength into the Tatar strait. Only twelve miles of navigable water stood between the rocky shores of Sakhalin and the northern coast of Manchuria.

The lookouts at the Amur river settlement were posted to watch for the Vulcan pirate fleet, in temperatures of thirty degrees below zero Fahrenheit. Every night men stood twenty-minute watches, then staggered into the cabins with frozen cheeks. In the last month two had died of the cold, four had had their toes amputated. The men drank vodka to keep warm, and more vodka for courage to brave the cold.

Knowing it was impossible for sailing ships to navigate the twelve-mile wide passage while the north wind blew, by unspoken consent on both sides of the Narrows the lookouts spent less and less time ouside. During the last week of September, no one at all watched from dusk to dawn. No message had reached the settlement regarding the capture of the steamship, *Czarina*.

* * *

Vladimir Benzowsky, with the aid of his Japanese guides, put the three sailing ships in tow and steamed through the Narrows unseen. His men chopped ice from the deck housings, spars and rails to prevent the ships from capsizing from the weight of frozen saltwater. The Japanese guides turned the *Czarina* to starboard into the Sea of Okhotsk and around the northern point of Sakhalin. The armada headed south with the polar wind at its back. The temperature was down to sixty below zero.

Theirs was a long torturous journey through icebergs and floes. They used explosives to free their ships from ice that blocked their path. The steamer pulled the sailing boats into open water and towed them when there was not enough room to manoeuvre by sail. When one sailing ship's hull suddenly cracked like an eggshell under pressure from the ice, its food supplies, ammunition and guns were transferred to the other ships. Benzowsky ordered sixty men to be disarmed and left behind on an ice floe to die.

Towards the end of October, with food lockers empty and temperatures plummeting, the *Czarina* towed the remaining two sailing ships through the Soya strait. The fifty-mile gap between the southern end of Sakhalin and the northern tip of Hokkaido led into the Sea of Japan. There, Benzowsky called a meeting of his officers.

The men at the table had wild flowing beards, gaunt hungry faces, and fear in their eyes. Boris stood next to Benzowsky with both shotguns levelled. The body of a junior officer lay dead on the floor.

Benzowsky pointed at the body. 'I ordered Boris to shoot him in the head so no one will break their teeth on the pellets when we eat him. You've been signalling about the shortage of food. Now you know how to solve it.'

'Should we have the crew draw lots?' a captain asked.

'Idiot!' Benzowsky growled. 'You would have a mutiny. Decide how many bodies you need for another week. Kill and butcher the belligerent and useless from your crews. The Japs say we should make Sapporo in a few days. Tell that to your men! Food, women and whisky will be theirs for the taking. Now get back to your ships and follow my orders.'

Chapter 36

30 November 1872

The cartilage under Mung's bent nose appeared about to break the skin. Severe furrows ran from his high cheekbones to the corners of his mouth. The once silky black hair at his temples had turned pure white. His hollow voice chilled Udo. 'Why did you not inform Count Muriev of Arima's past?'

'In Berlin I learned from Bismarck that today's friends are tomorrow's enemies.'

'But Arima is a confessed cannibal who disgusts me. When I asked how he could do it, he answered he only ate white flesh. He is unclean.'

'In the spring we can send him to St Petersburg as a student spy,' Udo said. 'Meanwhile, he speaks fluent Russian and knows Benzowsky's tactics. He can be useful against the Vulcan pirates.'

'If they appear,' Mung said. 'They may have starved, frozen to death, or attacked somewhere else.'

'Arima reminds us Benzowsky will cannibalize, so there is no threat of starvation. He is too experienced to freeze, and would find no other settlement, except Sapporo, large enough for four hundred men.'

'If they do attack,' Mung said, 'there can be no negotiations. No surrender. This mild weather will change and the temperatures drop. Our people would die in the cold if we evacuated Sapporo. Make certain the lookouts are alert.'

'They are at half-mile intervals fifteen miles up the coast. Danjuro drills the riflemen. He positioned the four French cannon he brought, and Muriev's five. Nine ten-pounders firing explosive shells should surprise this Benzowsky. The tailors and women of Sapporo have finished repairing the balloon after your test flight.'

Inwardly Mung cringed at the mention of the observation balloon. He had been forced to leave his house for the first time to draw the plans from memory of those he studied when a foreign observer during the American Civil War. He had to supervise those who constructed the balloon. If the *Czarina* did appear, he would direct Sapporo's nine guns at the pirates from above.

'The people call it Colourful Frog.' Udo smiled. 'When you were in the air, the women enjoyed pointing out their kimonos that make up the balloon's body. Children have made ice sculptures of it. There is a holiday atmosphere in Sapporo.'

'The people should be preparing for a possible siege.' Mung's thoughts flashed back to his inspection of a nearby fishing village. The people there were so much like those in Nakonohama where he was born. The youngsters bowed and looked at him as he once looked with fear and awe at the occasional samurai passing through his village.

'We have taken all precautions,' Udo said. 'Will you be safe in the balloon? Possibly I could go aloft instead.'

'I still do not believe the Vulcan pirates will come. Tell me about the trade mission to Korea. Why did it go wrong?'

'Will you see your son?' Udo asked.

Rhee, sitting behind Mung, flashed a warning glance at Udo.

'No.' Mung frowned. 'I prefer you not to mention it again.'

Disregarding Rhee's warning and the anger in Mung's voice, Udo pressed on. 'Should we continue to call him Shimatzu?'

'Wife-killer would be more appropriate,' Mung snapped.

'I do not want to hear of him.' He turned to Rhee. 'Bring Mistress Gin-ko. I wish to thank her for helping Ukiko.' He looked back at Udo and repeated, 'About Korea.'

'The trade delegation consisted of twenty lords and nobles,' Udo said. 'Hideyoshi Koin was among them.'

'How did the aristocrats reconcile their new positions as men of commerce?' Mung asked.

'By ignoring the obvious relationship to merchants. Actually they never had an opportunity to speak of business. Our first mistake was landing in Pusan. It is two hundred miles from the capital, Seoul. We were treated as beggars pleading for recognition from a superior power. That alone was enough to infuriate our people. The Koreans made fun of those of our lords wearing modern western dress. On the third day, the delegation was ordered home by a minor civil servant. When I left them to come north, every member of the delegation was committed to war with Korea. Hideyoshi had the most to say. Many supported his plan to raise an army for invasion.'

'I doubt Japan could win a war with Korea,' Mung said. 'My conversations with Muriev and the information from Tala Derzhavin indicate the Koreans have a larger, more modern navy than ours.'

'They do,' Udo said, 'but only because half their ships are manned by Russians. The other half have Russian instructors aboard. Count Muriev has an unwritten agreement to aid Korea against foreign incursions.'

'Would Muriev actually risk a confrontation with European countries?' Mung asked.

'He did against the Americans. The Yankees made the same mistake of landing at Pusan to establish diplomatic relations with the royal Korean court. There was an inconclusive battle in the harbour, from which they retreated. They believed they were fighting Koreans when it was actually the Russian navy.'

Mung made a mental note to inform John in Washington. It would be part payment for the information which helped him conduct the negotiations on Sakhalin and the Kuriles.

'Why would Muriev take such a risk?' Mung asked.

'Russia is desperate for foreign currency and a warm water port on the Pacific. Muriev wants trade with southern China, Korea, Japan and the Pacific islands, in that order.'

'That is why he felt the Kuriles and forty million yen for Sakhalin was worth securing Russia's northernmost borders on the Pacific.'

'If you yield Sakhalin to the Russians, there will be an uproar in the National Assembly.'

'Then someone must give the assembly a geography lesson, and inform them of the new advances in steam technology,' Mung said. 'Do the Russians have formal trade relations with Korea?'

'Yes. That was granted in return for military assistance. The Korean court is playing two sides of a dangerous political game. They pay tribute to China for its military protection, and have agreements with Russia for its armed assistance.'

'The Emperor must forbid an attack against Korea,' Mung said. 'It would violate what you wrote was Bismarck's formula for military success – isolate one's enemies from their allies before a confrontation.'

'Bismarck's strategies are greatly respected in Tokyo,' Udo said. 'Our army has taken Prussia as its model. But superior strategy may not hold back those lords and samurai itching for a fight. Many nobles, led by Hideyoshi, are out to avenge the Korean insult to Japan's honour. Most people in the government have come to believe Japan must modernize, that imperialism is a most important sign of progress. They want to start by annexing Korea.'

Mung shook his head. 'It seems impossible that only months ago we opposed those who were against western style progress. Now I am in the position of holding them back.'

'The Black Dragons you ordered to set up self-improvement societies have been successful, although I think some of the western fads are getting out of hand.'

'Do you think there will be war with Korea?'

'Either China or Russia will dominate them unless we do,' Udo said.

'Then you are for invasion?'

'Not at the present. You once said the Korean peninsula points like a knife at Japan's heart. Even Iyeasu works for a military strong enough to stop European domination of Korea.'

'Iyeasu too,' Mung mused. 'He is a deep thinker. Do you see a possibility of defeating the Koreans?'

'In time, yes. What I observed when I travelled through their country was that even in the largest cities, there is no desire for modernization. Their schools teach classical literature, and no one ever speaks of political or economic reforms. Modernization of the military is restricted to the navy, and there they utilize Russians.'

'Do we have agents in the Korean court?' Mung asked.

'Kang Shu has had agents there for some time. On my journey I placed our spies there, as well as in China and Manchuria. Wherever I found Japanese living among foreigners, I enlisted them in the service of the Emperor. Not one refused or asked payment for serving. I have named their organization Genoysha – the Black Ocean Society – separating it from our better trained and selected members of the Black Dragon Society. I also hired foreigners. In addition to military and political information, these people will send reports on economic opportunities for our merchants.'

'You learned much from the Prussians,' Mung said. 'To win in war and fail in commerce, negates the victory. Since your return, the export of Japanese silk has increased a thousandfold. It has replaced lacquerware as our leading export. All Black Dragons abroad will begin to report on business opportunities as well. To gain the respect of the West, we must develop a superior economic system.'

Udo refrained from informing Mung he agreed with Iyeasu's premise that international respect could only be earned by superior military power. 'While travelling with Prussia's chief of intelligence, I learned of a blight to mulberry trees all over Europe,' he said to Mung. 'The silkworm needs those leaves in order to produce.'

'Hopefully our people will establish themselves in that industry before the European mulberry trees recover.'

Rhee entered and announced, 'Sire, Mistress Ishikawa.'

Mung watched Gin-ko enter the room. For the first time since his arrival in Sapporo, Udo saw Mung's face soften. Although big in the belly, she knelt graciously at her husband's side and bowed. 'I greet my honourable father-in-law.'

'You are one of those women who becomes more beautiful as her pregnancy progresses,' Mung said. 'Ukiko often spoke of you. Udo tells me you tried to protect her from the Golden Lizard. That you cared for Ukiko until her death.'

Rhee had cautioned Gin-ko not to mention the child, but she ignored his warning. 'My honourable mother-in-law wanted so much to give you a son. She knew from the beginning that childbearing was dangerous for her.'

Mung's face hardened. 'Did my wife suffer?'

'Not at all,' Gin-ko lied. 'She simply went to sleep.'

Mung saw a brief shadow pass over Gin-ko's beautiful face and was grateful for the lie. He waited as she presented three scrolls.

'Ukiko had a premonition of her death,' Gin-ko said. 'She did not fear it. Her thoughts were for the well-being

360

of your son. She commissioned these portraits during her pregnancy because she knew you would enjoy watching her grow big with child. I promised to give them to you.'

Mung lowered his eyes and did not move. When Gin-ko's outstretched hands began to tremble, Rhee came forward and motioned the husband and wife to leave.

Udo, and Gin-ko still holding the scrolls, backed to the door, then bowed. Mung's hollow voice held them. 'My greatest sorrow is that I could not be with my wife when she died. She may have told you death held no fear for her, but I know differently. I will always be indebted to both of you. Gin-ko, I have recommended to Princess Atsu that upon your return to the capital you take Ukiko's place in compiling the next *Book of Good Deeds*. You, Udo and Little Mother will be included in the second edition for your actions in Kagoshima.' He bowed low, touching his head to the floor.

'Thank you,' Gin-ko said. 'I respectfully repeat the fact that Ukiko was not afraid to die. It may be that knowing she bore a healthy son, gave her strength. To this I will swear, when she saw his manhood she smiled.'

Gin-ko thought Mung was about to raise his head, but his body quivered and his shoulders shook. Rhee ushered them out.

A roaring fire warmed the log cabin.

'This is not an ordinary child,' Danjuro said, hefting Shimatzu up and down in the palms of his hands. The baby's eyes shone, and he gurgled with joy at the Lord of Mito.

'I worry about Mung going up in that balloon,' Udo said. 'Will it work?'

'Yes.' Danjuro handed the baby to Gin-ko. 'I saw them inflate it with Mung aboard. It floated like the ones we used in training with the Prussian army instructors in Tokyo.'

'Did you really go up in a balloon?' Gin-ko asked.

'I am too heavy, and Mung may never have to go up again either. I doubt the cannibals are coming.'

'Arima thinks they are,' Udo said. 'And if they come, it will be with four hundred fighting men. You have only fifty samurai and three hundred fishermen.'

'And the inhabitants of Sapporo,' Danjuro said.

'Armed with sticks, knives and stones,' Udo countered. 'I doubt we can win with that.'

'The fifty samurai are Mito men,' Danjuro boasted. 'Each carries an American Henry pump rifle that fires fifteen bullets without reloading. Eighty of those fishermen are tough seal hunters. They swing their long poles like a samurai uses his sword. Last but not least, those flesh-eaters do not know we are waiting for them.'

'The women have armed themselves with pointed sticks,' Gin-ko said. She brought out her small dagger. 'No Japanese will be taken alive by those devils.'

Hearing the passion in his wife's voice made the danger more real to Udo. He looked at her large stomach, at her beautiful face, and remembered Arima's warning. The Vulcan pirate ships out-gunned Sapporo's nine modern cannon four to one, without counting the *Czarina*'s twenty-pounders. Now he understood the importance of the balloon. It was the only way of destroying the Vulcan armada. The defence of Sapporo was based on the surprise of directing the nine cannon accurately against the *Czarina*.

Chapter 37

Two months after their departure from Ga-van, all the men of the Vulcan fleet had three things in common: scurvy, frostbite and a pact with other men to cannibalize and defend themselves.

The *Czarina* and the two sailing ships were trapped. One hundred and fifty miles from Sapporo, they had ventured into Otsaru bay to hunt seal. The temperature dropped thirty degrees in six hours, the seals swam to safety, but the vessels were frozen in. Twenty-three days had passed.

On the two sailing ships, all discipline was gone. Men banded together in different sections of the ships, sallying out only to murder or tear firewood from the hull.

Aboard the *Czarina* there was restraint. Benzowsky and Boris had butchered ten of their crew and portioned out the flesh every day to prevent rebellion.

Boris' black straggly beard now reached down to his belt. His dark, sunken eyes twitched repeatedly. 'Master, the meat is gone.'

'Does the crew know?' Benzowsky grumbled. His bulbous nose was a raw open wound from frostbite. He dabbed it with the back of his gloved hand. 'Stupid Cossack, did you hear my question?'

'They'll know at supper-time.'

'We'll turn the twenty-pounders on one of the other ships and scavenge her,' Benzowsky said through gapped teeth and cracked lips. His bloody gums were soft and spongy from scurvy.

'When?' Boris asked.

'About four in the afternoon. We have six hours to get our men ready.'

About noon in Otsaru bay, one of those freak climatic changes that often rescue the flora and fauna from the arctic cold, took place over the northern seas. The polar gale ceased. Clouds disappeared and a warm west wind from the Pacific Ocean filled the vacuum. The sun shone and the temperature shot up ten degrees an hour. Seals poked their heads through cracking ice and climbed out to sun themselves.

Benzowsky himself fired the signal gun. He sent Boris across the ice to order the men out of the ships to hunt seal. Thirty animals were killed within an hour. Fresh meat was soon roasting on the decks.

Benzowsky held a conference with his two captains. 'We cannot sail the goddamned ships because you two bastards lost control,' he said. 'Your men used everything but the masts for firewood.'

'If we're here another week, my crew will burn the entire ship,' the first captain said.

'Mine too,' the second mumbled from a toothless mouth.

'Our Japs predict we'll soon be able to move,' Benzowsky said. 'Before the ice breaks up, I want your crews to chop off the masts, cut them up for firewood, and bring all of it to the *Czarina*.'

'They'll fight that,' the first captain said. 'Those masts have become like the holy crucifix for them, the only way out of this ice. They won't trust you not to leave them behind.'

'Idiots!' Benzowsky shouted. 'I'll cut the *Czarina*'s masts first. Your crews have burnt their sails, rope and most of the spars. What the hell good are the masts?'

'Nobody would trust you not to leave them,' the captain repeated. 'The *Czarina* doesn't need a sail.'

'I would leave my mother if I didn't need her,' Benzowsky roared. 'I need your men to take Sapporo. Our Japs say it is only 150 miles away.'

Boris raised his shotguns, but Benzowsky shook his head. 'No. These two bastards will do what I say.' He pointed at Boris. 'Go topside and train the twenty-pounders on the two ships. Load them with canisters of grapeshot. If their men go near a gun, fire! If they do not start cutting the masts down, fire! And if they don't start bringing the goddamned wood over the ice, blow them to Hell!' Benzowsky grabbed the captains by the collars and pulled them out of their chairs. 'You tell your men I will tow both of your ships to Sapporo because I need them. We're only two days away from more women than they can screw in a year. More whisky than they can drink in a month. And vegetables, dried fruit and bread to last us until we get to China.' He threw both men out of the cabin door.

By noon the following afternoon, the *Czarina* had the two ships in tow and had broken free of the ice. They were on the way to Sapporo. Of the 400 men who left Ga-van, 280 remained, including three Japanese who were the most hated men in the fleet. They had cannibalized, but were themselves always free from that danger. They were under guard for their personal safety aboard the *Czarina* because they were needed as guides.

On the way out of Otsaru bay, the three Yakuza huddled together. They had decided to flee rather than lead Benzowsky into Sapporo, Japan's largest northern city.

During the second night, one Japanese leapt over the side of the ship into the icy sea. At first light, while rounding Otsaru point in sight of land, the other two lowered themselves from the moving ship onto an ice floe.

'Men overboard!' came the lookout's cry.

The three crews watched the two Japanese jump from ice floe to ice floe, making for shore.

'The bastard Japs are escaping,' the lookout shouted.

Benzowsky needed the Japanese to lead them into Sapporo, but he also had to boost the morale of his men. 'Gunners, you need practice before we get to that Jap city. Let's see how good your aim is.'

The crews cheered at the booming of the twenty-pounders. The second shell hit the ice floe and the two Yakuza slid off into the water. The crews laughed and cheered as the two men floundered and splashed. Finally they stopped struggling and slid below the surface.

'That's what's going to happen to all of us unless we tear the hearts out of those Japs in that city,' Benzowsky roared. 'We're fifty miles from paradise, so get your weapons ready.'

The fire of the twenty-pounders alerted the Sapporo lookouts along the coast.

'They should reach us by mid-afternoon,' Danjuro said. 'The steamer is reported to be pulling two sailing ships. None of the boats have masts.'

'It is the fourth ship that worries me,' Mung said. 'According to Arima, Benzowsky always sends men to attack from the rear.'

'I've just spoken with Arima,' Udo said. 'He now believes the fourth ship may have been scavenged by the others. Our lookouts are twenty miles down the coast with good visibility, and there is no report of a landing.'

'If Arima is correct, they are desperate,' Danjuro said. 'This is my plan.' He unrolled a map in front of Mung, Udo and Rhee, who moved closer. 'Looking out from Sapporo, the left shore of the harbour falls away to the south. In that area I have positioned seven of the old muzzle loaders to draw the attention of the pirates. Four of the ten-pounders are also hidden there. They will not fire until Mung, from the balloon, ranges the old guns and gives the signal. Now the north shore of the harbour comes in straight with high cliffs. The three muzzle loaders on the heights will verify the range for the five cannon below to do their work.'

'Where are your fifty samurai?' Mung asked.

'They and the Sapporo sealers will be at the dock just below your observation balloon. We will keep the fishermen on the south shore and the townspeople behind the buildings as reserves.'

'Good,' Mung said. 'I shall ascend when the pirates enter the bay. The weather is still fair, with little wind. The three of you should be able to hear me when I use the megaphone. I will signal the guns with a flag. Go to your positions.'

'So it is ordered, so it is done,' Udo, Danjuro and Rhee chorused.

Under a cloudless sky, the *Czarina* steamed into Sapporo harbour towing two ships. It was three in the afternoon, fourteen hours since the last of the seal meat had been eaten. The Vulcan pirates strained to see the houses, temples and thatched roofs of the quiet port city nestled between hills.

'Sail ho!' came the call.

'Where away?' Benzowsky called.

'On land dead ahead.'

'Crazy son of a bitch!' Benzowsky raised his telescope. 'The scurvy is making everyone a raving lunatic. How the hell can there be a sail on shore?'

'There it is,' Boris said. 'Look at all the colours.'

'It's a goddamned rainbow with a basket underneath,' Benzowsky said. 'Sweet Jesus, it's a hot air balloon. I saw them demonstrated for the czar's artillery.'

'What does it mean?' Boris asked.

'They see us.'

'They knew we were coming.'

'Stupid Cossack, shut up. The man in the basket under the balloon is waving a flag.'

'They had to know we were coming,' Boris said.

'There it is.' Benzowsky pointed to the south shore. 'I count seven puffs of smoke. Gunners, mark those targets!' he roared.

The old Portuguese cannon sounded more impressive than they were effective. Six iron balls splashed short of the *Czarina*. The seventh skipped over the water and bounced off her hull. But the old smooth bore cannon had accomplished their mission. Two hundred feet above Sapporo in the balloon, Mung had gauged the range.

'Those Japs were right,' Benzowsky said. 'All they have are outdated muzzle loaders.'

Boris rolled his soulful eyes. 'But they were waiting for us.'

'You stupid Cossack. What difference does that make? The weather is bound to turn worse. If we don't get ashore, we'll die out here. When the engine stops, there won't be enough wood to start it again.' Benzowsky roared to the gunners, 'Destroy those popguns!'

The two twenty-pounders took fifteen minutes to silence the seven dirt forts.

'Still no sign of life ashore except for that man in the balloon,' Benzowsky said. 'Watch the ice,' he warned the helmsman. 'It's getting thicker as we get further into the harbour.' He grabbed the speaking tube. 'Engine room, halve the speed.'

'There is no more fuel,' came the voice from below. 'The engine will soon stop of its own accord.'

'When it does, arm your men and bring them topside.'

From the cliffs above the harbour's north shore, three

muzzle loaders fired down on the Vulcan fleet, their iron balls splashing short of the *Czarina*. Mung adjusted his ranging figures as the ten-pounders aboard the sailing ships ripped the old gun emplacements apart. Dirt black smoke drifted up from the old forts on both sides of the harbour. The bay was still again.

'That was ten guns we put out of action,' Benzowsky said, keeping his eye to the telescope. He scanned the shore and the city. He shouted to his lookouts for reports.

'No sign of life.'

'I don't see any movement.'

'Then why the hell is that monkey still up in the balloon?' Benzowsky shouted.

They were closing in on the shore. 'He must have more guns,' Boris said.

Benzowsky stared at the Cossack as if he had grown another head. 'Stop engine!' he shouted, shoving Boris towards the stern. 'Signal those captains behind us to drift onto our port and starboard sides. We'll shell the city from here until someone comes out.'

Despite only gentle rocking in the basket under Colourful Frog, Mung's stomach was queasy. He thanked the spirits for holding back the north wind. Burnt craters marked the positions of the dirt forts. The men in them had given him the range of the pirate ships. He hoped they had abandoned their weapons in time.

About to signal the new guns, Mung saw the *Czarina* stop dead in the water. The two other ships drifted forward on either side, masking her from the cannon on both shores. Mung whipped the flag across his body to signal 'hold fire', and leaned over the side of the basket. 'We wait until the steamer is in the clear,' he shouted through the megaphone.

Danjuro and Udo waved to Mung that they had heard.

He looked down, at the sealers and samurai, at the fishermen behind the dunes on the south shore, at Sapporo's inhabitants armed with sticks and clubs behind the houses near the shore.

The *Czarina's* twenty-pounders boomed, startling Mung so that he nearly knocked over the fire brazier that sent heat up into the balloon. The sailing ships fired one broadside after another. Mung helplessly watched the shells falling into the city. No place was safe. He could see dead and wounded in the streets. A group of children fled, like a flock of frightened birds. Screaming women chased after them.

Danjuro, Udo and Rhee were shouting and waving to him, but Mung could not hear over the noise of explosions. He assumed they wanted him to give the order to return fire, but then realized they were warning that the balloon was descending. He threw more oil-soaked wood on the fire and worked the bellows. Colourful Frog began to rise again.

The shelling had ignited several fires in the town. It was being destroyed. Mung saw people dying. Without shelter they cannot survive the winter, he thought. If even one of the food storehouses is destroyed, there will be famine. He raised his flag over his head.

The nine ten-pound artillery pieces fired in unison. Mung counted four direct hits and two close misses on the sailing ships. He signalled an adjustment in elevation. The second barrage was more accurate. Shells exploded on both ships. The Japanese gunners slid their third shells home before the Vulcan fleet could re-arrange its weapons. Mung was elated, although he realized that with only the one flag to signal and the two ships screening the *Czarina*, the steamer could not be destroyed.

The Vulcan pirates aboard the sailing ships found the range and returned fire. Aboard the *Czarina*, Benzowsky screamed at his gunners, 'Shoot that son of a bitch out of the sky!'

Mung heard the boom of the big guns, then a WHAP WHAP! Shells had passed through the balloon without exploding. He saw them burst on the outskirts of Sapporo. Suddenly the bottom of the basket dropped from under his feet. He was almost thrown out. He saw men hauling on the lines to prevent him from crashing onto the houses behind the dock, but it was too late. He let go the flag, grappled with the brazier until he pushed it over the side, and sank to the bottom of the basket. There was a loud thump that shook his teeth, then blackness.

'He is not in the basket,' Mung heard Danjuro shout. 'He has got to be somewhere near.'

'Keep looking,' he heard Udo call.

Mung spat out snow but could not move his limbs. 'I am here,' he called into the dark.

'Where in Buddha's name is that?' Danjuro shouted from close-by.

Mung realized he was in the darkness of a snowbank. 'Damned if I can tell you.' For the first time in months, he laughed, then worked at sitting up, angry at himself for having laughed.

'Here,' Danjuro shouted, 'I have found him.' He brushed snow off Mung. 'Are you hurt?'

'I do not think so. What happened?'

'I saw the basket hit a chimney and bounce off a few roofs. You must have fallen out and rolled down into the snow drift.'

'How long since I came down?'

'Ten minutes or so,' Danjuro said. 'You could not have stayed up any longer even if they had not shot you down. The weather is changing. The wind is coming in from the north and the temperature is dropping like a rock. People think the noise of the cannon changed the weather.'

'Will someone give me a report on our guns?'

'They are out of action,' Udo said.

Rhee came limping up. 'One of their ships is sinking and another is on fire. The pirates are fighting each other to get aboard the untouched *Czarina*.'

'Bring Arima to me,' Mung said.

'He is gone,' Rhee said. 'I saw him walking out on the ice towards the ships.'

Chapter 38

In the darkness, Arima and a seal hunter stood on a large ice floe drifting a hundred yards from shore. The sealer rested his long pole and looked towards the *Czarina*, clearly visible in the eerie light of the burning ship to starboard. To port only the bow of the second ship remained afloat, held in place by its anchor.

'Well,' Arima asked, 'can we slip up astern of them?'

'No. The tide is running out. The water will be clear of ice for some distance behind the ships.'

'Inspector General Ishikawa must be made aware of their strength,' Arima said. 'All Sapporo's cannon are destroyed. If those pirates defeat the Mito samurai, every person in the town is dead.'

The sealer looked towards his home on shore, then to the pirate ships. 'Do as I tell you,' he said. 'If you fall in, do not cry out. You would die from the cold even if I could pull you from the water.'

'What if you fall in?'

'Then we are both dead. You would never make it alone.' The sealer studied the ice floes around them. The outgoing tide was taking them south of the *Czarina*. He looked for a small floe they could manoeuvre. 'There!' He backwatered with his pole. 'When that floe touches ours, step on to it. Keep walking until you find the centre. Use your pole for balance. When I hop on, you will feel the ice tip. Do not move. I will keep it upright. Get ready.'

Arima hefted his fifteen-foot pole chest high. The smaller floe touched theirs. He stepped across and it sank under his feet. His heart skipped a beat. He walked until the ice

373

tipped the other way, then stepped back and turned. His inexperience had pushed the ice floe away. The gap widened. He was alone. The sealer cannot leap such a distance, he thought. But he saw the man move back, trot forward, plant his long pole in the ice, and gracefully vault the watery gap. Arima felt the ice tip and automatically stepped back.

'Do not move!' the sealer called, nimbly sidestepping until the floe stabilized. 'Now watch me. When I take a step towards my edge, you take one towards yours. Until we are in position to·pole ourselves to the *Czarina*.'

The ice floe teetered, rocked, then balanced.

'If we approach towards the bow, they are certain to see us,' Arima said.

'According to you, if we do not find out what they are planning we will die anyway.' The sealer dipped his long pole and rowed towards the ships. Arima copied the movements. Although it was zero degrees, both men heated up from the effort.

They heard shouts. 'I hope those bandits are killing each other,' the sealer said.

As they approached, Arima saw thirty men standing on the bow of the sunken hull. There were men on the ice in front of the *Czarina*'s bow, others in lifeboats at her stern. She seemed untouched by Sapporo's guns, her decks packed with armed men preventing the others from climbing aboard. The two twenty-pounder cannon fired and, although a quarter of a mile away, Arima was stunned by the muzzle blast. He saw the shells explode amidst the lights of Sapporo.

The familiar voice of Vladimir Benzowsky echoed through a megaphone. 'We cannot take all you bastards aboard or we'll sink. You'll be fed in shifts. Those who finish eating will take their turn on the ice. Don't worry. You'll all be in a warm bed before dawn. In the meantime,

374

we will shoot the cannon every fifteen minutes to keep the Japs worried.'

Arima and the sealer were less than a hundred yards from the *Czarina* when Boris' voice came through the megaphone. 'If you want to eat, fetch up more bodies. They have to be butchered and cooked.'

Arima translated Boris' words and the sealer retched. 'Remain strong,' Arima said. 'They will attack before morning. We must return and warn the inspector general.'

'At least the return will be easier,' the sealer said. 'Backwater with your pole. We walk over the ice floes as they come towards us with the tide. The trick is in selecting the right ones. This time I go first.'

'If the people of Sapporo douse their lights, it will be more difficult for Benzowsky to see where to shell the city,' Arima said to Mung. 'I have returned to warn you they are about to attack.'

'So you did not desert us.' Mung motioned Arima forward to warm himself at the fire. 'Rhee, have the town criers make certain no lights show in the city.'

'Why would the pirates attack in the dark when they could shell more accurately in daylight?' Danjuro asked.

'You destroyed two of their ships. The survivors are out on the ice and would freeze before morning. The steam engine is not functioning. The only fire is that of the burning ship. To cook their dead, they are burning the railings and decking of the *Czarina*.'

'They are filthy beasts!' Danjuro spat into the fire.

'How many men do they have?' Udo asked.

'About two hundred.'

'Only one ship and half their men,' Danjuro said.

'Do not underestimate them,' Arima cautioned. 'They are devils in a fight. They may not have repeating weapons but each one carries four or five handguns and a rifle. If they get by the Mito samurai, they will slaughter the fishermen no matter how outnumbered.'

'Against the shogun's army, I commanded the Satsuma rifles,' Mung said to Danjuro. 'With your lordship's permission, I will lead the samurai tonight.'

'My father was with the shogun. He told me how effectively you used the riflemen. Where do you wish to position me?'

'Out on the ice with the sealers. I want your men to draw the pirates in front of the riflemen so we can catch them on the flank.'

'It shall be done.' Danjuro bowed.

'Udo,' Mung said, 'you remain with the fishermen. If we cannot stop the pirates on the ice, you must overwhelm them on shore. Tell the people of Sapporo there are to be no prisoners. Send everyone home to eat and keep warm until called.' Mung turned to Danjuro. 'Position ten sealers out on the ice to warn of the attack. Arima and Rhee will remain with me.'

'There aren't enough boats for everyone,' Boris said.

'Goddammit!' Benzowsky said. 'The men are half dead from scurvy and half frozen from cold. How can we take that Jap town without enough boats to get all of us ashore.'

'Tow the *Czarina*,' Boris said.

'Idiot,' Benzowsky shouted. Then he looked at his servant, wrinkling his forehead. He rubbed the black crusted wound on his nose. 'You mean the longboats should tow us with their oars? For a stupid Cossack, you surprise me.' He shoved Boris to the door. 'Tell the captains to get the tow underway. Lower the *Czarina*'s longboats and take everyone else aboard. Give out all the weapons we have. I want our men armed to the teeth.'

* * *

It was after midnight when the arctic wind brought polar clouds that blanketed the earth with snow. Two hundred yards from shore the ice was rock solid. Three hundred yards beyond that, ten sealers formed a picket line of lookouts on the ice floes. They heard the Vulcan pirates before they saw them – angry voices carried forward on the cold night wind, towing the *Czarina* closer to shore through the thickening ice.

Gin-ko, with Udo at her side, waddled from one wounded person to another in the log cabin. A number of men comforted injured wives and children. Everyone stopped at the sound of the town crier's clapper. Gin-ko grasped Udo's hand. They were jostled by men on their way out to face the enemy. They looked into each other's eyes. She placed his hand on her swollen belly, then released her grip. They bowed, and Udo filed out with the others.

Gin-ko pointed around the room at several older women. 'You will tend the wounded. I go to help my man.' She donned her heavy fur coat and tied it closed over her large stomach. Taking one of the sharpened sticks standing near the door, she went out into the storm. Other women followed. From every house in the city, men, women and children trudged down to the dock through the drifting snow to face the attack of the Vulcan pirates.

'Arima,' Mung asked, 'should we expect any surprises because of this early attack?'

'I believe not. They have no scouts out and no second force approaching the city from behind. They will be surprised when their boats are stopped by solid ice two hundred yards from shore.'

'Then my plan remains. Danjuro and Udo, take your positions. Rhee and Arima, come with me.'

Mung led the fifty Mito samurai out on the ice at an

angle towards the south shore. He selected a place where the ice ridged up and positioned his men behind it, shoulder to shoulder. 'Keep your rifles under your clothes or they will freeze up.' He waved to Danjuro filing by with the sealers.

The Vulcan pirates, weakened by disease and frostbite, struggled to row, to tow the *Czarina* through the thickening ice. They shouted curses at the cold, the ice and snow, and most of all at the people of Sapporo.

Danjuro and the sealers moved from solid ice on to the floes. They pushed forward into the snow-laden wind that carried sounds of the pirates' approach. The visibility was poor, and suddenly the sealers found themselves facing longboats. The pirates, sitting backward at their oars, were unaware they were blocked by pack ice. The sealers fired their muskets, but most of the weapons jammed from the cold. Danjuro stood still, shaking his gun and cursing. Those armed with long poles charged into a hail of bullets from the more experienced pirates.

Aboard the *Czarina*, Benzowsky ordered the bow gun to fire ahead. The shell whistled harmlessly overhead but the blast frightened five sealers into the freezing water.

'Retreat!' Danjuro bellowed. The sealers were being massacred. Their mission was to lure the attackers across Mung's field of fire. 'Retreat!' he shouted again, hating the word.

From the bow of the *Czarina*, Benzowsky roared through his megaphone, 'If they can walk on the god-damned ice, so can we. Everybody out of the longboats. Everyone off the *Czarina*.' He grabbed Boris. 'Get them over the side and attack.'

'What about you?'

'Stupid Cossack!' Benzowsky shoved Boris. 'Move!'

Led by the two captains and the big Cossack, the Vulcan pirates abandoned their boats and scrambled over the floes on to solid ice. They knelt and fired into the backs of the fleeing sealers. With the fierce north wind pushing them on, the weakened pirates stumbled after the retreating sealers.

Mung, crouched behind the ice ridge, watched Danjuro shepherd the remaining sealers in front of the Mito riflemen and on to the shore. He saw the first of the pirates coming out of the storm, led by a huge man with flowing black beard and a shotgun in each hand. The Mito samurai withdrew their weapons from under their clothes and pushed up to the top of the ice ridge. They removed their right mittens and took aim. Mung reached inside his coat and pulled his revolver. He focused on the leader, and fired. The Henry rifles at his side cracked in volley after volley. The Mito riflemen pumped round after round into the chambers and poured a devastating fire into the bewildered enemy. Some pirates dropped to their knees and returned fire. Others simply huddled against the blizzard of bullets, until most were struck down.

'Cease fire,' Mung ordered.

Danjuro and Udo led the sealers and fishermen out on the ice, chanting in unison, 'Dai Nippon banzai! Dai Nippon banzai!' They dragged dead and wounded pirates to the edge of the ice and pushed them into the freezing water.

Boris and several others struggled up the ship's ladder and onto the *Czarina*'s deck. Benzowsky grabbed his servant by the collar. 'What happened?'

Boris winced. Mung's .44 bullet was embedded in his shoulder. The bone was shattered and blood pumped out of him. 'I am wounded,' he whined.

'Stupid Cossack!' Benzowsky punched Boris to his

knees, and ran to the bow gun. Figures were approaching over the ice, too agile to be his men. He jerked the lanyard and the gun roared, but the shell exploded beyond the moving figures. 'Retreat to the quarterdeck!' Benzowsky shouted at the gun crew 'Prepare to repel boarders.'

On solid ice under their feet, Udo held Mung back at the bow of the *Czarina*. Their men ran by and climbed on to the ship. There was gunfire overhead. 'You are the inspector general,' Udo said. 'Danjuro and Arima are there. I will go up and report back to you.'

'You are soon to be a father,' Mung said. 'You remain here.'

'You are a father.'

Tucking his pistol into his belt, Mung flashed an angry look at Udo and ran for the boarding ladder.

The Mito samurai knelt on the deck firing up at the last of the pirates on the quarterdeck. Slowly the shooting ceased. Men stood up on both sides – out of ammunition or holding frozen weapons.

Danjuro spotted the big Russian leader Arima had called Benzowsky. Behind him stood eight pirates. The Lord of Mito called out a challenge. He drew his long sword and strode to the bottom of the quarterdeck ladder, waving his sword at Benzowsky. The former captain of the czar's army drew his sabre and came down the steps. Danjuro, with total concentration, grunted as he changed the position of his feet. He shifted his grip to the classic position for attack. The two giants circled each other.

The Mito samurai moved back, one of them stumbling over a body sprawled on the deck.

Mung saw the big, blackbearded Russian, with blood soaking his fur coat, rise up and bring a shotgun to bear on Danjuro. Benzowsky looked at the shotgun, he looked at Boris and their eyes met. 'Shoot the bastard!' Benzowsky cried.

The black beard parted in a twisted smile. Boris' last effort was to swing the twin barrels to bear on Benzowsky. 'Dycki Cozzak!' he shouted, and pulled both triggers.

The blast caught the Russian baron in the neck and face. He stumbled backward on the rail-less deck and plunged over the side, breaking through ice into the water. The Mito samurai charged the quarterdeck, and the fight was finished.

Mung looked over the side at Benzowsky. His bloody head bobbed in the water between ice floes, held afloat by the air trapped in his clothing. His arms were raised in a plea for help, and the water of Sapporo bay poured into the bloody hole of his mouth. An ice floe banged into his head, and he sank.

'Arima,' Danjuro called, pointing to Boris, 'what did he say before he pulled the trigger?'

'Stupid Cossack,' Arima replied.

The ground was frozen too deep for burial. Sapporo's 160 dead were cremated in a mass funeral that blackened the sky. In the coming months, the inhabitants of Sapporo undertook rebuilding their city, trying to forget their pain in the exhausting work.

Mung left his house every day to supervise the reconditioning of the *Czarina*. He had served aboard a steamer on his way to the California gold fields. He and Rhee had their experience with the *Little Grape*, the small steam tug purchased some years before in Canton. Arima worked at translating the Russian operations manuals for the steamer. The fishermen kept the *Czarina* from being damaged by ice. Carpenters replaced the rails, furniture and parts scavenged from the hull. Sapporo's chandlers supplied rope and sail. Masts and spars were cut from the tall trees in the hills behind the city.

Danjuro set about establishing a militia, training Sapporo's young men to be part-time soldiers. Udo instructed the fishermen and sealers in identifying foreign ships. He taught them to draw maps and log tides, winds and currents.

During December and January thirty-two more people died of wounds suffered in the pirate attack. As February approached, Udo spent more and more time close to Gin-ko.

Although Mung regularly worked and spoke with others, he had not seen his son. Rhee made certain a runner informed Gin-ko to keep Shimatzu inside when Mung was about in the town. He was still referred to as Ishi-gokoro, Stone Heart.

Chapter 39

Sapporo, 1 February 1873

Udo reached out under the blanket and Gin-ko was not there. He sat up. Ah, there she was, silhouetted by the fireplace.

'Is it time?' he asked, embracing her from behind.

'Not yet.'

'You are shivering. I will get the quilt.'

'No, do not take your arms away,' Gin-ko said. 'I am afraid.'

'Of giving birth?'

'No. I keep hearing the death-cart in the Yoshiwara.'

'You have not listened for it in many months.'

'I dread our return to Tokyo. I could bring dishonour to Princess Atsu, to Mung, and especially to you. Your enemies will remember my former profession.'

Udo knelt before her. 'I swear that none of your fears will be realized. There is an old saying my father often repeated. If you see ten troubles coming down the road, do not fear. They will all disappear before they reach you. And it is true. People will know you as the aide to the Emperor's sister, the daughter-in-law of Hokkaido's inspector general, and my wife.' He rested his head on her great stomach, devising a plan to ensure her favourable reception in Tokyo, and protect her future. He would send a carrier pigeon to Sandanj with instructions. 'Oh!' He lifted his head. 'The little bugger kicked me in the ear.'

Gin-ko smiled. 'The baby is active. It could be born any day.'

'I worry about the strain on you of caring for two infants,' Udo said.

Gin-ko smiled. 'We have a nurse. And you agreed to having many children. I feel as if Shimatzu is ours. I wish for Mung to be his father, but not take the boy from us.'

'I doubt Mung will ever see his son. He is a bitter man.' Udo placed his hand on her stomach. 'Do you know that from the moment I felt the baby move inside you, I loved it. Perhaps if he had felt Shimatzu inside Ukiko, he would love him.'

'Rhee says Mung is like a drowning man. The weight of the child in addition to his work would pull him under.'

'Mung has so much to give this boy. Even before he adopted me, I felt close to him. He taught my brother and me to swim. He sent us to the first modern school in Japan. He taught us English, geography and history of the West. His first wife, Saiyo, was our teacher in western mathematics.'

'Our children will study in the most modern school, but I want them to know the old ways too,' Gin-ko said.

'Hurry and give birth so we can register our first child. I become nervous every time you roll over and sigh, or grunt.'

'I do not grunt.' Gin-ko pouted.

Udo laughed. 'Probably the baby is making all that noise.' He helped her up and back to bed.

Two days later, during a morning lecture to the captains of Sapporo's fishing fleet, a woman beckoned to Udo from the rear of the room.

'The birth is starting,' she said.

Udo would have run into the twenty below zero cold and frozen had not the captains held and dressed him first.

Out of breath, he burst into the cabin. The large front room was empty. He heard a woman's voice in the other

384

room chanting the same words Gin-ko had used at Shimatzu's birth. Like a sleepwalker, he went to the door. Ginko's sweat-streaked face was pale, but more beautiful than ever. He watched the midwife with a bloody little body. She touched it to the floor, held it out for the assistant to lay her hands on, then raised it towards Heaven and the Emperor. The assistant cut the umbilical cord.

The child made no sound. Udo grasped the wall for support. His stomach sickened. He watched them clean the infant and could not bring himself to ask if it was alive. They wrapped and placed it in its mother's arms.

Gin-ko raised her head and saw her husband. 'Father, come see your child.'

Udo knelt by her side. The midwife's assistant took off his fur coat and hat. His arms were limp, his hands weak. He opened his mouth but no words came out.

Gin-ko smiled. 'I am fine. The birth was not painful. When the midwife told me to push, I did, and the baby slipped out easily.'

'I was so afraid of losing you,' he whispered.

'He has an organ like yours to make babies with.'

The child cried. Udo looked at the squinty red little face and saw his son. He sobbed.

Gin-ko held out the infant. 'This I can give you. This, and my love forever.'

From sheltered fishing holes far out on the ice in Sapporo harbour, they heard the boom of a signal gun. The sound came from the west, echoing over the fog-shrouded ice floes in the Sea of Japan. Again the gun boomed. Men poked their heads from sealskin shelters. The air was white with wind-driven snow. There was as yet no sign of spring on this day in late March.

Several fishermen drew their muskets and fired in the air. A runner was sent to the military commander.

'The mail-boat has arrived a month and a half early,' Danjuro told Mung. 'I have sent sealers over the ice to make contact.'

Five hours later, Mung informed Danjuro and Udo, 'We are ordered to Tokyo. The National Assembly has summoned me to face charges of dereliction of duty in negotiating Sakhalin to the Russians.'

'Hideyoshi is responsible,' Udo said.

'Yes. He is also raising an army to invade Korea. For that reason they sent the mail-boat for us. The Emperor and Iyeasu are finding it difficult to withstand pressure for the Korean venture. The invasion is scheduled for June. We leave immediately on the *Czarina*.'

'How can we? The bay is frozen solid.'

'I have a plan for the steamer. Udo, from Tokyo you will go to Canton and northern China to sell the furs we found aboard the ship.'

'You may need me in Tokyo.'

'He is correct,' Danjuro said. 'You have enemies other than my brother and the Golden Lizard. Some may still resent Lord Hotta's sacrifice for you.'

'Neither have I forgotten Hotta, or his last words, "Fukoku kyhoii – rich country, strong army",' Mung said. 'We must not fail.'

'If the assembly votes against your negotiations, you will be expected to perform seppuku.'

'There is a saying in the American game called poker – to have an ace in the hole. When I informed the Emperor and Iyeasu of the Sakhalin agreement, I purposely asked them to hold back certain information. My ace in the hole is Muriev's verbal commitment to help us abrogate the unequal treaties with the western countries and support our claim to the Ryukyu islands.' Mung turned to Udo. 'Your main task in China will be to purchase warships and weapons for our military. Training with the new equipment should placate the hotheads. I will seek Russian assistance in negotiating a trade treaty with Korea.'

'Buying enough weapons to keep the army and navy busy will cost millions,' Danjuro said. 'Where will the money come from?'

'The sale of the furs and twelve million yen from the Russian loan. We already have the *Czarina*.'

'Does it matter who I buy weapons from?' Udo asked.

Mung held up a letter. 'John has arranged with the American and English consuls in Canton for you to purchase three warships. He assures me they will be available. The question is price. Do as well for the Emperor as you did for the Black Dragon Society on the contract labour transaction with the Germans. You will have another thirteen million yen for bribing Chinese officials to support our claims to the Ryukyu islands, and to encourage the Koreans to trade with us.'

'Do not forget you did inform the National Assembly about the resettlement of three thousand Japanese on Hokkaido,' Danjuro said. 'And you agreed to raise cattle to conduct trade with the Russian maritime provinces.'

'All that can be covered with one-third of the loan. Muriev agreed to three times the amount necessary. I look forward to facing the National Assembly.'

Udo rocked the baby in his arms. 'We all stared at Mung,' he told Gin-ko. 'He actually used the Sakhalin negotiations as a means for the assembly to recall him to face charges. He may have been severely hurt by the deaths of his wife and son, but he is still the Black Dragon. I believe he will satisfy the assembly, stop the Korean invasion, and gain international recognition of Japan's rights over the Ryukyus. He could also possibly achieve the cancellation of the unequal treaties with the West.'

'I am impressed,' Gin-ko said. 'But he has still not shown a bit of interest in his son or ours.'

'He granted permission for you and the two children to travel with me to China. We sail tomorrow for Tokyo.'

'But the bay is frozen solid.'

'Mung has mobilized the entire population of Sapporo to burn and chop a channel through the ice to make a path for the *Czarina*.'

Gin-ko, about to protest her inability to have the children ready and her things packed in time, held her tongue. If she wished to remain at Udo's side, she must become accustomed to his sudden moves. She bowed.

At dawn the following morning, Gin-ko and the children were aboard the *Czarina*. Except for Rhee and the black gang in the engine room, everyone was on deck.

'You wanted this ship renamed to change her luck,' Mung whispered to Danjuro, 'so you tell those priests to hurry. The channel will not remain clear forever.'

The Shinto and Buddhist priests circled the deck swinging incense burners, waving pine branches and chanting prayers. They stopped before the quarterdeck, looked up at Mung and called out the name *Sapporo-kan*. Mung nodded. It is better to rely on the old traditions in some instances, he thought. Kan, fighting ship, instead of maru, a term of endearment, is more fitting for this gunboat.

The priests circled and called the name twice more. Then Danjuro pressed money into their hands and hustled them down onto the ice. 'All clear,' he shouted to Mung, and went forward to man the bow gun.

Mung looked out to sea as he waited for the twenty-pounder to be loaded. Ahead of the ship, a watery lane a half mile long had been cut through ice over a foot thick. The two thousand people who had laboured through the night stood on either side of the channel, waiting to see the ship move without a sail.

Mung bowed to them. They bowed to him. He blew the steam whistle. 'Stand by to get underway,' he ordered. He picked up the speaking tube. 'Rhee, how is it down there?'

'Very well, sire. We have the warmest place in all Hokkaido.'

'Give me slow ahead. Remember this ship is much bigger than the little tugboat. Be prepared to stop or reverse quickly. There is a lot of ice floating out in that sea.'

'Slow ahead it is,' Rhee said.

The propeller turned. Mung felt the surge of power under his feet. It entered his hands through the big wooden steering wheel. 'Lookouts, keep a sharp watch for ice in the channel,' he called.

Men, women and children crowded around ice sculptures they had carved to honour the heroes of Sapporo – intricate crystal statues of flowers, trees, houses and animals. They had tried to inflate Colourful Frog but the balloon was too badly damaged. Instead it lay spread on the ice, the women who had contributed their kimonos and labour standing around it.

On the opposite side of the channel was a twelve-foot statue of the Mito giant wielding his long sword. Beyond that, the scene of a pregnant Gin-ko leading the women of Sapporo to defend the city. There was Udo with a slim Gin-ko carrying a baby. Mung realized the emotional and physical effort put into these tokens of praise. He bowed to those standing near each of the ice statues. The last one the *Sapporo-kan* passed was of him holding the hand of a small boy. He looked away.

'Ice dead ahead!' came the cry from aloft.

The waves had cracked a large chunk of ice at the end of the channel. The wind had turned it, blocking their exit. They were too close to stop in time. Mung pulled the steam whistle. He grabbed his megaphone. 'Shoot it,' he roared to Danjuro.

The Mito giant cranked the elevation handle on the twenty-pounder. He waited until the centre of the ice floe came into the sights, and jerked the lanyard. The shot echoed over the bay. A cloud of smoke and ice from the explosion obscured the steamer's bow,

'Brace yourselves,' Mung ordered. 'Stand by for a ram.'

There was a cheer from the people on the ice. The sealers raised their poles in salute as the *Sapporo-kan* slipped safely into the Sea of Japan. Mung was returning to face his enemies in the National Assembly.

Chapter 40

Five hundred miles north of Tokyo, the *Sapporo-kan* put into the port city of Sendai for fuel and supplies. Before the first basket of coal was taken aboard, Udo had rented two Tokyo carrier pigeons. The birds flew south with messages for Sandanj and Jiroo.

Five days later, thirty miles outside Tokyo bay, the *Sapporo-kan* was hailed by a merchantship. The boarding ladder was lowered and a short Japanese in tuxedo and top hat climbed onto the deck of the steamer. The man doffed his tall hat in a sweeping European bow.

'Sandanj!' Udo could not believe his eyes. 'I would never have guessed it was you.'

The squat little man rose and flicked his lapel. 'The latest fashion from London. I have the Tokyo concession to rent and sell evening clothes.'

Udo clapped his friend on the shoulder. 'I told Gin-ko you are an original. What a grand surprise!'

'I brought suits for you, Mung and Danjuro. There is a western dress for Gin-ko and clothes for the children.'

'Whether she will wear the dress is the question,' Udo said. 'Have you arranged the reception?'

'One of the largest ever seen. You must wear the European fashions. I have five seasick tailors aboard that merchantship. We have been waiting for two days.' He pulled a large cheroot from his vest pocket and handed it to Udo. 'Have a cigar.'

'I do not smoke.'

'You will learn. To be a real western-style man, you must get used to smoking these without coughing.'

Udo suddenly frowned. 'Is there anything wrong that you came out to meet us?'

'Not at all.' Sandanj lit his cigar. He sucked in until Udo thought his eyes would pop. The little man blew out a long stream of smoke. 'I came to prepare you for your arrival in Tokyo.'

'You had best explain to Mung and Danjuro what to expect. Be warned, Mung has changed. There is little humour in him these days.'

Sandanj flipped the cigar over the side and followed Udo. In the cabin below deck, he tried not to stare at the Black Dragon. Mung was emaciated, his face like a ruddy cast iron statue, with eyes to match. Sandanj bowed from the waist.

'Have you forgotten your manners along with your kimono?' Danjuro said.

'Excuse me, sire.' Sandanj knelt and touched his head to the floor.

'Why have you come?' Mung asked.

'To prepare you for your entrance into Tokyo.'

'I sent word from Sendai by pigeon,' Udo explained, 'ordering Sandanj to publicize the heroic defence of Sapporo led by you and Lord Danjuro.'

'Why was I not consulted?' Mung demanded.

'You once told me if you do not wish a negative answer, do not ask the question.'

Danjuro glared at Udo, believing he had overstepped the bounds of his authority and Mung's patience.

'If public opinion can influence the Emperor into not preventing Hideyoshi from raising an army for the invasion of Korea,' Udo said, 'the National Assembly can be swayed to honour the heroes of Sapporo, ratify the Sakhalin treaty, and put off the invasion.'

Mung fixed Sandanj with a cold eye. 'Tell me what you have done.'

The little man's Adam's apple bobbed, his bow tie wiggled. 'Sire, Jiroo and Iyeasu are in accord with my plans. The Black Dragons will influence a large turnout of people for your arrival. The self-improvement societies that you initiated to introduce modern ways have become a powerful force in the capital. Many western dignitaries will come to see the *Sapporo-kan*'s arrival, the first foreign prize of war in three hundred years. Iyeasu and other high ranking Japanese will be guests at a ceremony the day after your landing. The lords are cautious, and concerned there will be trouble over your having taken a Russian warship in battle. But they will see there are no repercussions to fear. In fact, the Russian ambassador will also be present at your arrival.'

Udo saw the frown still on Mung's face. 'I know you prefer anonymity,' Udo said. 'For that reason I did not request your permission. In order to stop the Korean invasion and influence the validation of the Sakhalin agreement, you are obliged to assume a prominent public position. My instructions to Sandanj and Jiroo were to make that position as firm as possible prior to your arrival in the capital.'

'You instructed Jiroo too, my senior advisor?' Mung blazed. He turned to Sandanj. 'Where and when will this reception take place?'

'The first part will be on your arrival in the port. I have signal rockets aboard the merchantship to alert Iyeasu and Jiroo to proceed with our plans. First there is a reception by high-ranking western officials at the dock, with musicians. That will be followed by a kite-fighting contest. There will be a reception for high-ranking Japanese guests the following day, with a poetry tournament, an ikebana – flower arranging – exhibition and bonsai display. Our newspaper has been full of your valiant exploits in conquering the Vulcan pirates. Gin-ko is already a legend.

There is a play in production at the Kabuki theatre about her part in the defence of Sapporo. The foreign papers have also translated the stories. If I may be allowed to precede you on the merchantship,' Sandanj said, 'I will host the foreign dignitaries who greet you.'

Mung's eyebrows raised, furrowing his brow. 'You are a busy fellow. Where do you get all the energy?'

'Have a cigar.' Sandanj produced a cheroot. 'They say it is good for your health.'

Mung waved off the cheroot. 'Russian Ambassador Derzhavin will be there?'

Sandanj stuffed the cigar back into his pocket. 'Yes. He is so pleased you put an end to the pirates and gave him this chance to make the first good public impression since the Sakhalin agreement, he will present you with a medal.'

'Are you serious?' Mung asked.

'Yes. I supply Tala Derzhavin and her female lover with opium. She told me. Sire, if the Russian ambassador grabs you and kisses you on both cheeks, do not pull back.'

'I am familiar with that European custom,' Mung said. 'Tell me, why did you wear evening dress to meet us at sea?'

'Sire, you ordered the Black Dragons to encourage western ways. These are my everyday business clothes. Tokyo has changed. I promote western dress with articles and advertisements in the newspaper and with everything I do. Many Japanese of importance wear tuxedos to all official functions.'

'I prefer a kimono,' Danjuro said.

'The Emperor wears a tuxedo and top hat similar to mine,' Sandanj said.

There was a moment of awed silence before Danjuro blurted out, 'Who ever saw his imperial majesty dressed like that?'

'Every morning he is seen by the people on his way to

and from the Yasukune shrine. He greets foreign dignitaries in that manner also.'

'You mean common people see the Emperor?' Danjuro said.

'His majesty has taken the lead in setting the modern style. The imperial archers no longer surround him. He travels in an open carriage. It is part of Iyeasu's plan to convince foreigners that we Japanese can modernize and run our own affairs. There is a great deal of pressure in the assembly to cancel the unequal treaties with the westerners. It is one reason many lords support Hideyoshi's invasion plans. They want Japan to become strong enough to defeat the Europeans.'

'Have the round-eyes been influenced by this change of clothing?' Danjuro asked.

'It is no longer polite to call the Europeans barbarians or round-eyes. The Emperor has also forbidden his subjects to prostrate themselves to any man. This offends the foreigners. A short bow is now the fashion.'

'Why did you kneel and touch your head to the floor?' Mung asked.

'Because Lord Danjuro told me to. In private, old habits are difficult to ignore.'

'There is no law requiring me to wear that baboon suit,' Danjuro said.

'If the Emperor wears a tuxedo,' Mung said, 'I suggest we all do so.' He stared at Udo, rocking back and forth. After some moments, he said, 'Very well. I would not have chosen the same method of stopping Hideyoshi, but I agree that influencing public opinion has merit.'

Udo suppressed a sigh of relief. His main purpose of protecting Gin-ko by making her a revered figure no one would dare criticize, would also benefit his country.

* * *

The Golden Lizard's head was permanently tilted left from the improper healing of his shattered collarbone. It exposed the scar made by Little Mother's whip, which had damaged his vocal cords. His laboured voice rasped. 'Your brother, Danjuro, will soon be here.'

'He must die in a way that will not cast suspicion on me,' Hideyoshi said.

'He dies and you inherit the lord governorship of Mito. What do I inherit?'

'Wada Zenshichi's role as leader of Japan's Yakuza. That was our agreement.'

'A promise you failed to keep. You did not have the power then, and you do not have it now.'

'The one who leads the Korean invasion will govern Japan,' Hideyoshi said. 'I intend to be that man.'

'Mung's recall is not only to answer for the negotiations, but to stop your plans for war.'

'You vowed to kill him,' Hideyoshi said.

The Golden Lizard fingered his scarred, twisted neck. A mad light shone in his eyes. 'I would kill you if I benefited from it. Mung! He is responsible for my disfigurement.'

'Allow me to finish Mung for you.' Hideyoshi giggled. 'I can do it so easily.'

'It will not be simple to approach the heroes of Sapporo.' The lizard-man pointed at the window. 'Take a look outside. The people are flocking to see the conquerors of the Vulcan pirates.'

'I can destroy Mung. Do not be concerned about that. But this Sandanj and his newspaper must be disposed of too. He influences people to change their minds like a Kabuki actor changes costumes.'

'How can you destroy Mung?'

'With a newspaper.' Hideyoshi giggled again and pulled a dated English language newspaper from his sleeve.

'What does it say?'

'What is printed here will cause Mung to commit sep-puku. The disgrace will cause that spawn of a fisherman's whore to slit his own belly.' Hideyoshi leaned closer to the Golden Lizard. 'My snakeskinned friend, if you kill Dan-juro and silence the newspaper, I promise Mung's death and guarantee Wada Zenshichi's power to you.'

The *Sapporo-kan*'s decks were holystoned to a creamy white. Her burnished brass reflected the morning sun and her crew stood at attention as she charged into Tokyo bay at flank speed. Smoke trailed flat behind the ship and white water curled at her bow. Danjuro fired blanks from the twenty-pounders and Udo blew the steam whistle. Mung stood at the wheel.

'There is our signal.' Udo pointed at a green smoke rocket arching into a clear blue sky from a new cement pier.

Mung called into the speaking tube. 'Rhee, halve the speed!'

'Yes, sire. I wish to recommend a week of baths for the black gang.'

'They will be my guests at the House of a Thousand Delights. Now prepare for docking as we practised it at sea.'

Mung looked to the southern end of the bay, seeing the red brick chimneys of the Yokohama iron foundry. Smoke from the big twin stacks drifted over the British-built shipyard. In the bay were many more steamboats than he would have imagined possible. Some were western ships, but most were converted Japanese junks. He looked to the waterfront. There was a new lighthouse. Buoys paraded up to new concrete piers and western style warehouses.

'Should you begin to turn?' Udo said.

So engrossed had Mung become in the new sights, it was necessary to alter course dramatically. 'Halve the speed

397

again!' he called to Khee. 'Prepare to stop engine. Close it down and bring your men topside. You too are among the heroes of Sapporo.' Mung turned to Udo. 'Bring your wife on deck and take her to the bow, with Danjuro.' He blew the whistle, spun the wheel and the warship came about alongside the new concrete pier. The engine stopped and the ship drifted gently towards shore. The westerners on the dock applauded the seamanship. Japanese on shore bowed as the mooring lines uncoiled neatly in the air and the ship was tied up.

Cheering erupted on the pier when people recognized Gin-ko with the baby in her arms moving forward with Udo. Mung was quietly proud she had chosen to remain in traditional dress. To him, western women appeared harsh in their corsets and bustles. Gin-ko and Udo turned to allow sailors securing the lines to pass. Udo held an older child in his arms. Mung grasped the quarterdeck rail for support. It was the first time he had ever seen his son.

Sandanj hurried onto the ship and up to the quarterdeck. 'Are you well, sire?' he asked Mung.

Mung shrugged. 'I have become used to the rolling deck under my feet.' He tugged at his tuxedo jacket. He touched his bow tie and stretched his neck, looking beyond the foreign visitors crowding aboard, but could no longer see Udo or the child he carried. Mung bowed to the western consuls and merchants introduced by Sandanj.

'Sire,' a newspaperman said in French, 'I would like to introduce the Russian consul and his wife, Ambassador and Madam Derzhavin.'

Mung bowed to the tall, angular blond woman. Behind her stood the beautiful Eurasian and Tala's stocky, pale-skinned husband. 'I am honoured,' Mung said.

'It is I who have the honour to express the gratitude of Czar Alexander and the people of Russia,' Vitaly Derzhavin said. 'The elimination of the Vulcan pirates was a service to society, similar to the successful removal of a malignant tumour. When I think of the people of Sapporo at the mercy of two thousand cannibals with ten heavily armed ships, it makes me shudder. Sir, if you had not stopped them, they would have ravaged the coast from Korea to southern China. In the name of Czar Alexander, I salute you!'

Mung flashed a hard glance at Sandanj, who said in Japanese, 'An Englishman helped me, sire. It is a modern innovation called creative journalism.'

Tala Derzhavin pressed forward and looked Mung square in the eye. 'Is it true the lady Gin-ko led the women of Sapporo out on the ice with only sharpened sticks against the Vulcan cannibals? That she and her followers were responsible for killing hundreds of men?'

Again Mung glared at Sandanj, who whipped out a cheroot and offered it to Madam Derzhavin. 'Have a cigar. Allow me to escort you to meet the lady Gin-ko in the bow of the ship.'

'I have come to confer the Georgian Cross on the inspector general of Hokkaido,' the ambassador said loudly, watching his wife and the Eurasian going to the bow. He turned back to Mung and slipped the ribbon over his head, then centred the medallion on Mung's chest and clicked his heels. 'For your actions against the Vulcan pirates in the northern seas!' He kissed Mung on both cheeks, and rushed off after his wife.

Photographers took pictures of the heroes of Sapporo on the bow. Mung went below to his cabin and changed into his Japanese clothes. He and Rhee left the ship unobserved.

Chapter 41

Udo sat Shimatzu next to him on the bunk bed of the ship's cabin. Gin-ko lay Yaka down. She brushed a wisp of her hair into place. 'I never had so many people touch me. The foreigners all shake hands. And they patted my shoulders.'

'It is their custom,' Sandanj said.

'That Russian woman especially made me nervous.' Gin-ko shuddered. 'She stood so close, and did not want to let go of my arm. Her Eurasian servant appeared quite disturbed.'

Udo exchanged an anxious glance with Sandanj, who deliberately changed the subject. 'Tomorrow the party will be only for Japanese. I am the host. You, dear beautiful lady, will be guest of honour with Mung and Lord Danjuro.'

The Mito giant bowed to Gin-ko. Then he opened his tuxedo jacket and ran a finger under his celluloid collar. 'I have a request,' he said to her.

Udo and Sandanj went to Danjuro's side. Gin-ko could see mischief in their eyes.

Danjuro shifted from foot to foot. 'There is a kite contest about to take place as part of the celebrations. We know it would not interest you, but Udo should come with us.'

'You mean kite fighting,' Gin-ko said.

'Oh no!' Sandanj shook his head. 'These are sophisticated aerial manipulators whom I invited to display their skills. I have offered the largest cash prize of the year. Teams are here from as far away as Shizuoko and Kawasaki.'

'And Mito,' Udo said. 'It would not be fitting if I did not accompany the Lord of Mito to encourage his team.'

'I will fly the children's names on the Mito kite,' Danjuro said. 'Of course Yaka's father must be there to send his prayers aloft too.'

'I think I would enjoy seeing the kites in the air,' Gin-ko teased.

The faces of the three men fell.

'No, on second thoughts,' she said, 'it would be too crowded for the children. Are we to remain aboard ship?'

The three faces lit up. 'Transportation is arranged to an apartment in the imperial palace,' Sandanj said.

'Kite fighting can be a rough sport,' Gin-ko said.

'Oh no!' Sandanj said. 'I invited only the gentlest kite fliers to this contest. Only the most respectable teams were considered.'

Gin-ko swallowed to keep from giggling. 'Go and enjoy yourselves. Fly the children's names boldly.'

Udo and Danjuro bolted through the door, with Sandanj close behind. He stopped short and turned back to hand Gin-ko his top hat and a fistful of cigars. He bowed, and ran after the others.

Gin-ko turned to the children. 'Your father and his friends have gone out to play.'

Mung and Rhee stood in the crowd on the pier, commenting on the transformation – the new buildings of western architecture, the multitude of rickshaws, steamships cris-scrossing the bay. Mung felt a sense of pride for having influenced some of the changes.

His eye was caught by three men in tuxedos on the *Sapporo-kan*. They moved stealthily towards the fantail, avoiding the western sightseers amidships. The three came over the stern rail and slid down the mooring line. With coattails flying, they came running up the pier. Mung turned his back as they approached. He started to follow, but five young, hard-looking men surrounded him. He reached for his Colt, then relaxed at the sound of a familiar voice. 'Sire, these are Black Dragons,' Jiroo said. 'It is not safe for you to walk unguarded in Tokyo. The Golden Lizard has recently met with Hideyoshi here in the capital.'

'Why is that son of a serpent not dead?'

'He is supported by those Yakuza in Tokyo who wish to challenge Wada Zenshichi. The lizard-man has a hiding place which has been impossible to locate. He surfaces, then disappears completely.'

'After this business with the National Assembly, I shall personally lead the search for him. Meanwhile, it feels good to be back in Tokyo. But what do you suppose those three were up to?'

'Half of Tokyo has come to see the heroes of Sapporo and the kite fighting. They are probably on their way to watch the contest.'

'I have not seen a good aerial battle in years,' Mung said.

Two hundred thousand people gathered on the windswept dunes at the north end of Tokyo bay. A hundred fighting kites lined the beach facing into the wind, the smallest kite ten feet square. Their bright coloured rice paper had been stretched and layered, then shrunk drum-tight over hand-crafted green bamboo struts. As many as forty men held the guide lines hanging from the edges of the big kites. Twenty to fifty men held the main lines, which stretched a third of a mile back to large spools.

Crowded behind the spools, the people waiting for the contest to begin stomped the ground in unison. 'Wasshoi! Forward! Wasshoi! Wasshoi!' They chanted and cheered. They sang, waved flags, and bought prayers for their favourite teams from wandering priests.

An official sounded a trumpet and one hundred team

captains moved ahead of their spools, straddling the main kite lines. A hush settled over the enormous crowd.

'Where is Sandanj?' the official called. 'He is to start this contest.'

'Sandanj! Sandanj!' the people chanted.

Udo and Danjuro broke through the crowd carrying the little man under the armpits, his tuxedo collar askew, his jacket buttons popped off. Sandanj acknowledged the cheers with a wave of his hand.

The people roared and the official accepted Sandanj's wave as the signal to begin. 'Winner take all!' he shouted, and fired off a star rocket that burst in multicolours overhead.

A thousand men grabbed their kite lines. They charged in the direction of the crowd, chanting as they came, 'Wasshoi! Wasshoi!' Their cries flowed like a rush of wind along the beach. The people fell back as the men trotted towards them pulling the fighting kites up, up, into the air. The colourful fliers climbed into a cloudless blue sky.

'Warrior of the Wind!' Danjuro pointed to a yellow and red kite. He pulled Udo and Sandanj by their jackets to the Mito team captain, who bowed to Danjuro.

'Pay attention to your duty,' Danjuro ordered. 'There is no rank during a kite fight. How can we help?'

The captain looked at the horde of oncoming line-pullers. He glanced back to his spool-man reeling in the line of the soaring yellow and red Mito kite. 'In a minute there is going to be a mass of snarled lines. At the beginning it is more luck than skill who stays aloft. You can help by taking the spool further back, ahead of the others and out of the tangle.'

'But it is a rule violation to move the reel into the crowd,' Sandanj said.

'There is only one rule in a war,' the captain said. 'Win!'

'Wasshoi!' Udo shouted. They dashed back to the reel.

At sight of the three men running towards him, the spool-man reached down and brought out a club.

'It is Lord Danjuro,' Sandanj cried. 'Your captain ordered us to carry the reel.'

Danjuro lifted one side of the big reel by himself, Udo and Sandanj lifted the other. The spool-man dropped his club and lifted the front. They charged back into the crowd. People screamed, laughed, cheered, heckled as the Warriors of the Wind teammates broke away from the mad mêlée of crisscrossed lines. The quick action sent their kite up faster and higher than any other on the beach. At a whistle signal from their captain, they set the reel down. The yellow and red kite, twelve square feet of bamboo and paper, crafted by a fifth generation kite-maker, flew high and steady.

The Mito captain, his eyes continually darting across the sky on the watch for an enemy, came back to the team at the reel. 'Twenty kites are already down. They either crashed into one another or their lines tangled so badly, they fell.'

'Look out,' Sandanj shouted, 'an attack!'

'I see it,' the captain said, 'the Yokohama kite.'

Udo saw a blue and gold kite come out of the throng to challenge Warrior of the Wind. The Yokohama kite was a sturdy fourteen-footer with a larger team on the lines than theirs.

'This should give us good exercise,' the Mito captain said. 'Let out a hundred feet of line.'

The spool-man allowed his reel to spin, but a sudden gust of wind whipping up the beach took the line whistling out of control. With both feet, the spool-man jumped on the wooden brake block. Smoke spiralled up and Warrior of the Wind sailed higher and higher. 'Water!' the spool-man shouted. 'We left the buckets at the starting point.'

Danjuro reached into the crowd and grabbed a jug from

404

a passing vendor. He poured the sweet liquid over the smoking brake block and line.

'It holds!' Udo shouted.

'Who will pay?' the vendor cried.

'I will,' Sandanj answered. 'Stay with us. Keep that jug filled and I will pay you for twenty jugs.'

'Yokohama attacks!' Danjuro called.

'Their line is crossed with someone else's,' the captain said. 'We wait to see if it can reach us.'

Udo watched the Yokohama kite soar upward after Warrior of the Wind. The Mito kite held its position with majestic aplomb. The Yokohama blue and gold was rising fast, then suddenly it stopped. Its tangled line could reel neither out nor in.

'That is what I have been waiting for.' The Mito captain dashed forward.

Udo, Sandanj and Danjuro sat on the spool and watched their captain direct his men on the guide lines. The yellow and red Warrior dived and looped up sideways into the stationary Yokohama kite, ripping a five-foot gash in the blue and gold paper. The Yokohama line was hopelessly tangled, with no ability to manoeuvre. The Warrior attacked with its sharp pointed shoulder, tearing pieces out of the blue and gold kite, until it spiralled down in tatters.

'Come with me,' Danjuro said, leading Udo and Sandanj forward to the captain. 'How is our position?' the Mito giant asked.

'Excellent. We are the highest fliers on the beach. While others fight to stay out of the water or the sand, we wait up there for another challenge.'

'I wish to put two names on the kite,' Udo said.

The captain whistled. His guide-men pulled on their lines to avoid a wounded, erratic flying kite on its way down.

'If you write the names on a piece of cloth,' the captain said, 'I will send them up.'

Sandanj produced a small writing kit from his torn jacket. Udo pulled out his shirt front and tore off two strips. He carefully lettered the names, Yaka and Shimatzu. The captain plucked a strand of fibre from the kite line and tied each piece of cloth to an end. He looped it over the main line and the wind took the two white strips of cloth fluttering up towards the yellow and red kite. Udo whispered a prayer for both children.

Suddenly the line went slack and the kite dipped. 'Linemen, pull!' the captain shouted. 'Pull! Pull the line taut!' He turned to Danjuro. 'There is an attack on the spool. Protect it.'

Danjuro, Sandanj and Udo sprinted into the crowd, following the kite line. People fell back to let them pass. Ten men dressed in black, wearing white headbands, surrounded the untended Mito reel. The spool-man sat on the sand holding his head.

'Chiba skunks!' Danjuro shouted. 'Charge!'

Udo's tuxedo jacket was torn off in the first rush. Sandanj lost his trousers and was dumped next to the spool-man. Danjuro's jacket, shirt and tie were torn clean off his body by the five Chiba men who dived on top of him.

Mung, Rhee and Jiroo caught sight of the uneven battle. Mung's days of kite fighting on the beaches of Nakano-hama were nothing like this. The shouts of the crowd and the need of his friends sent his blood racing. 'One hundred yen on the Mito kite,' he shouted.

A Tokyo dandy came running. 'I take one hundred yen against the Warriors of the Wind.'

Mung pulled his pistol.

'By the gods,' the dandy cried, 'are you going to shoot the opposition?'

Mung handed the Colt to Jiroo. 'Take care of this. And cover my bet.' He pulled Rhee with him. 'Wasshoi!' he shouted, launching himself at the men smothering Danjuro. He pulled two off and the Mito giant stood up, knocking the others aside. Rhee threw a forward snap punch and a spinning kick, felling two more Chiba men. The others fled into the crowd.

Udo and Sandanj helped the spool-man back to his place. Danjuro was bare-chested, Sandanj bare-legged, and Udo missing both sleeves of his torn shirt.

'Do not bow to me,' Mung cautioned them.

Danjuro slapped Mung on the back. 'This is the way those westerners greet people. I never thought to see Moryiama Ishikawa helping Mito in a fight.'

'I never thought to see the three of you in such a condition,' Mung said. 'Reel in the slack. We are far from victory.'

A Mito runner came through the crowd. 'Watch our flag,' he said. 'When the captain raises it, take in more line. When it drops, stop and come forward quickly. When you break free of this crowd, follow the yellow and red headbands. We will guide you through the other kite lines so you do not tangle.' He ran back through the mass of people.

The spool-man stood on top of the reel. 'The flag is up,' he shouted. 'Reel in.' Udo and Sandanj cranked furiously. 'It is down,' the spool-man shouted, leaping to the ground.

'Wasshoi!' Danjuro yelled. They picked up the reel. Spectators fell back as they charged forward. Clear of the people, they followed a flying wedge of Mito men through the maze of pulling lines, guide lines, and hundreds of kite fliers. Other teams tried to block their path or cross lines with them, but they fought their way through. Danjuro, at the point of the flying wedge, threw people left and right.

Suddenly they were in the clear, on the good footing of

hard sand near the water. At the captain's command, they raced a little further, then lowered the spool and sank to the beach.

'Good work,' the captain said. 'We beat off three challenges while you defended the spool.'

Mung looked up at the yellow and red Warrior. 'Except for a few small tears, she is sound,' he said. He saw only seven other kites in the air. Some lines were tangled. The teams were working themselves to exhaustion, running back and forth to produce the sawing motion that could effectively cut another line.

An enormous black kite with a single white parallel line across her face, dwarfed all others in the sky. 'That is Chiba's,' the captain said. 'I watched that black monster knock down a dozen others today.' He pointed. 'There, she attacks again.'

The giant kite swung in between two smaller kites. It dipped left and its top corner cut through the rice paper of the first small flier, ripping out half the bamboo struts. The small kite crumpled in the air and fell to the ground. In a quick move to the right, the big kite tucked its shoulder, then shot up and impaled the second smaller kite. For some minutes the little kite hung helplessly on the top corner of the bigger one, until its struts broke apart and the wind tore it to pieces. It dropped to earth like a deflated sack.

'They did that so quickly,' Mung said, 'it must be more than just the size difference.'

'They are expert,' the captain said. 'Now there are only three others besides ours and theirs.'

'What do those flags mean?' Sandanj pointed to three white flags going up the lines of the smaller kites.

'They have surrendered,' the captain said. 'We are the only ones left to fight the giant Chiba.'

'Why would the others surrender without a battle?' Mung asked.

'Money. Their sponsors are those who sent their children's names aloft with prayers for health, happiness and future prosperity. Those kites have already won great honour. Next year the teams will double their fees for sending names aloft. If they crash now, it would be considered bad luck.'

Udo pointed at the yellow and red Warrior. 'See those two pieces of cloth fluttering up there? Your son's name is written on one, mine on the other.'

'Before we make a decision to fight or not, allow me to tell you the odds are not good,' the captain said. 'The Chiba kite is eighteen square feet larger than ours. More than twice our size. They have three times as many men and have not been defeated in five years.'

Mung looked up at both kites. 'Can you win?'

'I came here to fight.'

'Karma is karma,' Mung said. 'The children's or ours.' He looked at Udo. 'Your son's name is up there. His future is also at stake.'

'Fight!' Udo said.

'Fight!' Mung repeated.

Danjuro's grin covered his face.

'Wassshoiiiii!' the captain cried. His men took up the chant. They came to their feet with lines in their hands. The captain blew a series of whistle signals and his men stomped their feet in cadence, alternately tugging on the guide lines, making Warrior dance its challenge in the sky. A roar came up from the spectators. Downed teams gathered on the dunes to watch the final battle.

The giant black raised its great head and shook it angrily from side to side. An awe-filled sigh came from the crowd. A hundred and fifty Chiba men shouted their war cries as they trotted forward. The people moved after them up the beach.

'We can beat them!' the Mito captain told his men. 'Follow my signals.'

'Wasshoi!' the Mito kite fliers answered.

The captain held them in check, letting the Chiba kite pullers cross the greater distance through the soft sand.

The closer the black kite came, the less confidence Mung had. It was enormous, the pulling line twice as thick as any he had seen. Fifty guide lines dangled from its sides.

The captain whistled and the Mito team leaned forward on their lines, whispering the chant, 'Wasshoi. Wasshoi. Wasshoi.' With each step forward, the chant grew louder. 'Wasshoi. Wasshoi.' Mung heard their bare feet pounding the hard wet sand in unison. 'Wasshoi! Wasshoi! Wasshoi! WASSHOI!'

The captain blew another series of whistles and suddenly Mung grasped his earlier tactic. Now, advancing into the wind gave the advantage of manoeuvrability.

'Dragon attack,' the Mito captain ordered. His men began wending their way forward, singing the dragon fighting song. The snake-like approach confused the Chiba team. They had no idea which side Mito would cross on.

'What is your strategy?' Danjuro shouted to the captain.

'The tiger and the buffalo. One is larger, the other quicker. You, sires, may rest yourselves now. I have trained my team well for this day. Wasshoi!' he cried.

The Warriors of the Wind dashed forward, slipping under the big black kite on the ocean side. The yellow and red shot up in front of the black. With a quick shake of its square shoulders, it cut two holes in the big kite's cheeks, then skipped forward out of harm's way.

Mung saw the Chiba captain being hoisted up on the shoulders of two men so as better to direct his large team. He appeared unperturbed by the Mito kite's preparation to repeat the previous manoeuvre. Then suddenly he signalled. His one hundred line-men swung to their right, crashing into the less numerous Warriors of the Wind. Some Mito line-men were knocked down and trampled. The big black kite swooped up above the yellow and red. It dipped, dropping the air from Warrior's face and falling on the smaller kite, smothering it. By quick thinking and swift action the Mito captain was able to disengage, but not before two upper struts were broken. The Mito men reeled in furiously, but the Chiba captain sent his team crashing into the Mito line-men again, driving them towards the water. The big black kite dropped on the smaller Warrior once more.

'We lost another strut,' Mung said.

'Yes,' Danjuro replied, 'but every time Chiba uses that tactic, it takes another tear in its own body. It requires more and more strength from its men to manoeuvre.'

'They have three times the men and more than twice the flying surface,' Udo said. 'They can afford that tactic. We cannot.'

'If they keep charging into our men,' Sandanj said, 'they will push them into the bay. Look, now they are chasing our team up the beach.'

The five men hurried to help the Mito spool-man. The crowd followed close behind.

Both spool-men were parallel when the Mito captain signalled, 'Stop. Out line.' The Mito spool-man released his brake. The yellow and red kite soared straight up.

Mung watched the Chiba team stop, sending the big black up after the red and yellow. Both reels spun so quickly, they whined. Sandanj, seeing the drink vendor gaping at the two kites shooting up into the sky, grabbed the jug and filled it with sea water. He reached the Mito spool-man just as he jumped on the brake block with both feet. The line screeched like a wounded animal. The reel shook. Fire danced around the wooden block. Sandanj poured sea water on the man's bare feet, the flaming block and smoking line. Steam billowed into his face. 'It is coming to the end!' Sandanj shouted.

Mung, Udo, Rhee and Danjuro dived onto the reel as the line ran out. The force of the kite's pull when the line hit its end, somersaulted the spool-man high into the air. The line twanged and fifteen Mito men were thrown off the pulling line. The others, including four Black Dragons, were dragged thirty feet through the sand before the kite stopped its rush.

'To the rear!' the captain thundered, driving his men up onto their feet. 'To the rear!'

They heaved, pulling the kite back almost parallel to the Chiba spool. Its line was approaching the end.

'Charge right!' the Mito captain shouted. His men crashed into the Chiba line-men, knocking many of them down.

The Chiba line reached its end on the reel and the remaining men did not have enough weight to stop the giant in the sky. Their line-men and spool-man were dragged a hundred feet along the beach before they could control it.

'Rest,' the Mito captain ordered. 'You will all need your wind for the next clash.' He spoke softly to Mung. 'The Chiba team is good, but I am better.'

'You mean your team is better.'

'That is what I tell them. The truth is, an army is only as good as its commander.'

'Here they come,' Udo called. The Chiba team came trotting up the beach, with discipline and determination to finish the fight.

'Good.' The Mito captain smiled. 'They have not rested.'

He waited until the Chiba spool was almost parallel to his, then ordered line to be let out. The yellow and red kite crashed sideways into the big black, ripping a three foot gash and breaking two enemy struts. But Warrior's left shoulder was crushed and flapping. It had lost some speed and manoeuvrability.

The crowd cheered the valiant Warrior. Mung glanced at the grim-faced Chiba captain. His eyes shot fire. He spat orders in rapid succession. His men rushed the Mito team harder than before, crashing and driving them towards the water. Again and again the larger Chiba team charged into the Mito line-men. Each time, the giant Chiba kite dived and soared to the right, trying to strike Warrior with its big square shoulders. The Mito men were knee deep in water.

Mung and the others ran to the team captain. 'How can we help?'

'I need a few more minutes to win. Look at them.' He pointed to the Chiba team. 'They have been running, pulling and manoeuvring the big kite for twenty minutes through the soft sand without a rest. Many of their men have fallen off the line. Just a few more minutes.'

'In less than that you will be under the waves,' Danjuro said.

Mung grabbed Danjuro, pointing with the stump of his left arm at the Chiba team captain. 'If an army is only as good as its commander, then let us take theirs off the battlefield.'

'Wasshoi!' Danjuro led the five man charge into the Chiba ranks. He bulled his way up to their captain and tackled the two men on whose shoulders he rode. The captain was dumped onto the sand, but Danjuro was immediately pounced upon by six Chiba men. Udo and Sandanj darted in, grabbing the captain under the shoulders and trying to drag him away. They were beaten off. Rhee drove in with fists flying, but was smothered by Chiba men.

The shaken captain stood up, face to face with a tall, one-handed samurai. Mung set his feet as he had been taught by the Harvard boxing coach, and threw a straight right cross. It landed square on the side of the captain's jaw. Mung heard the crack of his knuckles on bone and saw the Chiba captain stiffen. His eyes rolled up and he fell over backwards.

Suddenly Mung was doubled up over a fist in his stomach, then straightened by a knee to the forehead. He was lifted, rushed to the water's edge, and thrown into the waves. He tumbled, rolled, swallowed water. When finally he dragged himself out, the Mito team was waist deep, still trying to fight their kite. He also saw that the Chiba team was leaderless. With no one to drive them, they stood spraddle-legged, panting, hanging on to their kite line, not advancing.

'Attack!' Mung shouted to the Mito team. 'Their leader is down.'

'Warriors of the Wind,' the Mito captain bellowed. 'Attack! Attack!'

With their last bit of strength, the Mito men charged out of the water, pulling the yellow and red kite to do battle. It dived at the motionless Chiba kite. It slashed and backed into the big black. It dipped its good right shoulder and crashed into the monster kite again and again.

'Her struts are thicker,' Mung shouted at the captain. 'You are killing your own kite.'

The Mito captain's eyes were glazed with the fire of battle. His face glowed. He raised his fist in the air and shouted, 'Banzai! Dai Nippon banzai!' His men renewed their furious attack.

The leaderless, exhausted Chiba men looked up with tear-filled eyes at their big, black beauty being torn apart by the fiery yellow and red tiger.

'Wasshoi!' the Mito captain called.

'Wasshoi!' the Warriors of the Wind answered, moving forward at the cadenced attack pace.

414

The crowd had been stunned into silence by the turnabout, but now took up the Mito chant. They roared and stomped the ground in time with the Mito men. The beach trembled.

High above, Warrior went forward with its good right shoulder and sliced a fifteen-foot gash across the face of the big Chiba kite. Desperately the black flier fought to stay aloft. It quivered and struggled upward; its breath slipped out through the large gaping hole. It hung motionless, striving to stay in the air. Then, in a final gasp, the Chiba flier shivered and fell to earth, tail down.

For a moment, no one moved. Then 200,000 people rushed forward to congratulate the winners, to seize a piece of the Chiba kite for luck. It had fought valiantly.

Just before they were engulfed by the cheering crowd, Danjuro shouted out, 'Warriors of the Wind, you are my guests tonight for dinner to celebrate this victory.'

People swarmed around them and someone fell up against Mung. He reached out to help the man get his balance, and touched a knife handle protruding from his back. A dagger fell from the tattooed hand. Mung whirled and saw another tattooed man behind Danjuro fall to his knees with a blade in his back.

Few people in the frenzied crowd realized what had happened. Udo, Sandanj and Rhee, surrounded by Black Dragons, led Mung and Danjuro off the beach, and hurried to the imperial palace.

Chapter 42

The Tokyo fish auction was jammed with more visitors than buyers. Many holiday-makers had drifted in after the kite fighting contest. Earlier, the day's catch of octopus, sea bass and blackfish had been sold in lots, the shellfish and crabs by the basket. For the past thirty minutes, the more exotic shark fins, abalone and bonito had gone over the block individually.

The crowd held its breath as the senior auctioneer mounted the stand. He netted a three-pound brown fish with a flat white bottom and buckteeth. It wriggled in his hands. He leaned over the wooden table and thrust the fish towards the audience. They cried out, jumped back and giggled.

The Golden Lizard, a hood covering his head, drifted nonchalantly to the rear of the noisy crowd. Muso edged closer to the auctioneer.

'Fugu,' the auctioneer announced. 'Since there are many visitors today, among them quite a few who have never seen fugu, I will explain that this little fat fellow is the most deadly fish in the ocean. His liver has enough poison to kill 1,233 men. How do we know this? It was proven by a fun-loving Chinese emperor who experimented on 1,234 Mongolian captives.' The auctioneer cupped his hand to his ear and leaned forward. 'Did someone say this fish is not fat?' He tickled the white belly and the fugu ballooned into a ball. He flipped it from one hand to the other, then bounced the live fish on the bidding block.

'Stop the theatrics,' one of the many chefs standing close-by said. 'Put it up for bid.'

'I wish I was being paid by the size and not the weight of this fish,' the auctioneer lamented. He lifted up the living balloon. 'There are only five fugu for sale today, all this size. The sixth and last is a tiger fugu that weighs six pounds.'

'Six is bad luck,' a chef called out.

'Double six is terrible luck,' the auctioneer retorted, 'but you are not going to frighten the price down. Every one of your culinary cousins standing with you will be bidding for these little puffers. So let us begin, and find out who will win the bid to enjoy the exotic adventure of tasting death. I remind you of the famous poem,

> He who has seen Fuji but not tasted fugu has not lived.
> He who has tasted fugu may never see Fuji.
> Ahhhh, what a sight!'

He looked around at the crowd. 'Who will give me the first bid?'

Cautiously people began to shout out their bids, taking the price up to five yen. The professional buyers quit at ten, leaving it to the Tokyo chefs. The bids moved at a quarter of a yen each.

It soon became obvious there was a secret buyer contesting the price on each fish. No matter which chef bid, the auctioneer, without hesitation, jumped the bid.

'Sold for twenty yen!'

'Sold! Eighteen yen.'

'Sold! Twenty-three yen.'

The fifth fish was sold for twenty yen, and the angry chefs rushed the auctioneer's platform, shouting at him,

'We will put you in the wooden tub with the remaining tiger fugu.'

'Who is the bidder?'

'Are you raising the price with a fictitious buyer?'

The auctioneer struggled free. 'Please! Please!' he pleaded. 'A little decorum.' He looked towards Muso standing in the crowd. 'Would the person bidding please identify himself. If I point you out, my career as an auctioneer is ruined.'

'If you do not we will make you eat the tiger fugu, liver and all!' the closest chef threatened.

'The last fish cannot be sold,' the auctioneer said. 'Not unless the bidder raises his hand.'

People looked around. One or two young sports raised their hands and quickly withdrew them. A few giggled nervously. Tension grew.

Muso had earlier instructed the senior auctioneer, 'You have my bid on every fish as long as I do not raise my hand.' Muso had no wish to identify himself now but the last fish, the deadliest, was necessary for the plan. Looking towards the back, he saw the hooded figure of the Golden Lizard climb up the bamboo scaffolding at the rear of the fishmarket shed and nod. Muso raised his hand.

The auctioneer let out a sigh. 'Thank you.' He pushed the chefs off the platform. 'It is good fortune the quality of restaurant food does not depend on the nature of those who prepare it.' He scooped out the last and largest fish. Its silvery body was covered with black tiger stripes from head to tail. The large front teeth clicked and snapped at the hushed crowd. 'Of all the species of fugu, the tiger is the most deadly.' The auctioneer sang out his sales pitch, 'Who will start the bidding at twenty yen? Who will buy this beauty?'

With his rapid patter of bids and filler words, the price was soon taken to thirty yen, then neared forty. Only three restaurateurs remained in contention when the price reached fifty yen.

'Seventy yen,' Muso called, not caring if he bid the

418

highest price ever for a single fugu. He was not spending his own money.

'Last call at seventy,' the auctioneer shouted. 'Do I hear another bid? All in? All done? Sold!'

The three restaurateurs approached Muso as he collected his fish. 'We have pooled our money,' their spokesman said. 'We would like to purchase all six fish at a higher price than you paid.'

'It would be a pleasure to make a quick profit,' Muso said, 'but my employer is a connoisseur. He wishes the tiger fugu for himself. The others are presents for the heroes of Sapporo who will be at tonight's victory celebration of the Warriors of the Wind.'

'Ahhh.' The three bowed in admiration.

'May I introduce you to the chef who is in charge of the food for tonight's affair?' the spokesman asked.

'It will be an honour,' Muso replied. 'I would have sought him out myself.'

An older man was brought forward. He bowed. 'I understand the five fugu are to be presented to the guests at the banquet tonight.'

'Yes. My employer wishes to remain anonymous and I must show him what I have purchased with his money. I will bring the fish to you before the celebration begins.'

'He must be a person of quality to be served by one as diligent as you,' the chef said, bowing again.

On a sampan not far from the fishmarket, the Golden Lizard placed the six live fish on a wooden plank. He slit the belly of the tiger fugu. He parted the rough white skin and pricked the liver with a needle, then repeatedly punctured the back of the fish. He wet the body and smoothed it to see if the needle holes would show. They did not.

'The other fish will die before we can deliver them,' Muso said.

'No. They are immune to this poison,' the Golden Lizard said. 'Now put the cat up here.'

Muso lifted a wicker basket on to the wooden plank. The lizard-man sliced a portion of silver and black skin from the fish's back and cut a thin strip of snowy white flesh. He offered it to the animal. The cat ate. It nuzzled the bars of the basket, shivered, stiffened, and fell dead.

The Golden Lizard looked triumphantly at Muso. He dipped the needle back into the liver of the tiger fugu and proceeded to puncture the other fish.

'Cancel this evening's banquet,' Iyeasu said to Mung. 'If the lizard-man sent men to kill you and my brother in daylight at the kite fight, he will certainly find a better opportunity at night.'

'Your brother, Hideyoshi, is in league with the Yakuza,' Mung said.

'I know. So you must be doubly careful.'

Mung immersed himself in the heated tub. He felt the stiffness drain from his muscles and the pain wash out of his bruises. 'Udo and Sandanj have convinced me publicity is necessary to save the Sakhalin agreement. I do not enjoy being with people, but for now I must.' Droplets of sweat formed on his troubled face. The deep worry lines appeared to smooth slightly. He closed his eyes and rested his head back on the edge of the wooden tub.

'I do not agree with your desire to walk to the restaurant through the Ginza,' Iyeasu said. 'I can tell you about the changes that have taken place in the capital.'

'Certain things must be experienced,' Mung said. 'I cannot allow Hideyoshi, or anyone else, to imprison the Black Dragon with fear.'

'If you insist on observing for yourself, at least use a rickshaw.'

'Why not cage me in a closed palanquin. People would not see me and I would not see anything.'

'A palanquin is too conspicuous,' Iyeasu said, not understanding Mung's sarcasm. He rested his round body against the wall. 'They are out of fashion. The Emperor has set the mode in modern dress and transportation. He wishes us to impress the foreigners by our adoption of western ways as a prelude to their abolishing the unequal treaties.'

'Your tone of voice suggests you do not agree.'

'I have always advocated military strength to implement political change. The Europeans will give us only what we are strong enough to take.'

'Are you in favour of a Korean venture?' Mung stepped from the tub.

Iyeasu dropped his robe and entered the steaming water, grunting as he settled in. 'I was quietly for it until I read your articles in the newspapers.'

'So the articles are effective,' Mung said. 'Have they influenced others?'

'Some of our military men are impressed with your argument that Korea is not worth a clash with both Russia and China. However, everyone agrees that sooner or later Japan must avenge the Korean insult to our Emperor and our government.'

'Later is better,' Mung said. 'The situation may well change. When do I face the National Assembly?'

'In two days. I hope you understand that although you are a guest in the palace, you will not meet with the Emperor until you successfully defend your policy in the assembly.'

'And if I do not succeed?'

'You will be disgraced and your life forfeit.'

'What chance do I have?' Mung asked.

'If you can give the military some hope of future action, and convince our lords the world does not end a few miles

421

north of Sakhalin, you have a good chance. There is one restriction. You cannot tell the assembly about the forty million yen loan being used to buy warships and bribe Chinese officials regarding the Ryukyu islands. That could offend the foreigners. I personally think your plan is brilliant and will impress the Europeans. The Emperor does not.'

'May I explain the resettlement programme and trade agreements?'

'By all means. But you should know that Muriev is dead. He died suddenly a month after returning to St Petersburg.'

Mung leaned closer to Iyeasu. 'He was a good man. Did he confirm the treaty before he died?'

'In its entirety. The written and the verbal. His replacement, Count Reznov, affirmed everything, although his actions in the north are disturbing. He has ordered the expansion of seventy settlements along the Amur river, from Russia eighteen hundred miles through outer Mongolia and Manchuria to the Tatar strait. Your spy, Doihara in Vladivostok, reported this. Furthermore, this Doihara has spoken with surveyors who are building a road that entire distance. He questions their ability to maintain such a road in the cold weather, as it bypasses many of the outposts.'

'They cannot.' Mung reflected silently, trying to understand Reznov's reasoning. 'My god,' he finally said, 'a railroad across Siberia! The Russians want to copy the transcontinental railroad across America. They are building a trans-Siberian railroad.'

'Can they do it?'

'The Americans spanned three thousand miles and reduced the travelling time from New York to California from six months to six days.'

'You are guessing about the building of a trans-Siberian

railroad,' Iyeasu said. 'I suggest you do not tell anyone. It would hurt your cause.'

'I disagree. It can only help,' Mung said. 'This Reznov has compounded Muriev's mistake. It is a reaction to the czar's sale of Alaska to America. The Russian hierarchy wants to copy the imperialism of other European nations.'

'I and other Japanese wish to be imperialistic too,' Iyeasu said. 'If our population is to grow, it cannot be supported by the arable land available in Japan proper. The new agricultural methods you introduced fifteen years ago are barely supporting our growing population today.'

'The main source of our food comes from the sea,' Mung said. 'The Kurile islands stretch like a chain from the northern tip of Hokkaido across the Okhotsk Sea to the Russian tip of Kamchatka peninsula. They are a string of effective blocks to the Russians in the Okhotsk Sea, which also give us fishing rights to the entire northern Pacific. All the way to the west coast of America and up to Alaska.'

Iyeasu wiped the sweat from his beet red face. 'Muriev gave up that part of the world because it is frozen and cannot be sailed most of the year.'

'That is the mistake Muriev made in our negotiations. Reznov has compounded it. Only a deep water sailor would understand. John sent me the information from Washington. The combination of iron hulls to withstand the ice, and the newly invented steam converters to drive propeller-equipped ships, makes them three times faster. Fishing fleets will be able to remain in the ice area longer, and enter earlier. They may even be able to work during the entire winter. The cannibal, Benzowsky, proved it with a wooden-hulled, propeller-driven steamer.'

'I thought iron and steam would only be used for warships,' Iyeasu said. 'Not fishing vessels.'

'I was present at the treaty signing on Kanagawa beach with Commodore Perry. John presented Lord Takai with a steel-tipped plough. The Fujiwara lord believed steel was only for samurai swords. With that plough, we opened up thousands of new acres for cultivation. Soon we will use iron to build fishing ships.'

Iyeasu closed his eyes and rocked back and forth, sending water over the side of the tub. Finally he said, 'We could use the Yokohama foundry to produce iron, the shipyard to lay the hull of the first metallic fishing ship. Do you think there is another in the world?'

'You will never find the answer in that tub. Come, I want to see the changes in Tokyo.'

'But in a rickshaw, please. If not for your sake, then for mine. I am not inclined to long walks or other athletic events.'

Chapter 43

Jiroo had positioned one hundred Black Dragons along the route Mung and Iyeasu were to travel. Udo and ten men surrounded the rickshaw.

'Before you enter the Ginza,' Iyeasu said, 'I would like to show off the new Tokyo railroad station. Along the way you can enjoy English as she is Japped.' He pointed to a sign over a shop door.

> ENGLISHMAN, HAVE CARE ON YOUR BIG HEAD.
> LOW DOOR.
> THIS TAILOR SHOP IS A MEN AND LADIES OUTFATTER.

'When was the rail line completed?' Mung asked.

'Six months ago. It is only eighteen miles long, but it reduces transportation costs by seventy per cent from the port to the ironworks and shipyard in Yokohama.'

'Was the construction of a commercial port in Yokohama considered?'

Iyeasu shrugged. 'The British wanted to build a railroad. Our lords now desire to modernize everything, so they accepted it. There is also a telegraph line.' He pointed to an egg and milk shop. The sign in English read,

> EXTRACT OF FOWL
> PEST MILK IN TOKYO.

The barber sign next door read,

> HEAD CUTTER WITH PERFUMING WATERS FOR ANTI-FLEAS.

'Are there so many English speakers in Tokyo?' Mung asked.

'It is the result of your twenty-four Black Dragons and Sandanj with his books and newspaper. The western oriented self-improvement societies are quite influential, although sometimes, as you can see, misleading. Our people learn a little and act as if they know a great deal. They think all Europeans who use Latin letters can read English.'

'Certainly not the way our merchants write it,' Mung said. He pointed to a bold laundry sign,

WE MOST CLEANLY AND CAREFULLY WASH OUR CUSTOMERS
WITH CHEAP HALF PRICES
LADIES RECEIVE SPECIAL ATTENTION.

Iyeasu smiled. 'I have timed our visit with the arrival of the evening train.'

'Do they run on schedule?'

'Quite. Sometimes to the detriment of passengers and freight. A recent letter to Sandanj's newspaper complained of a coffin being taken away while the mourners remained on the platform.'

A whistle sounded and a train rolled into the station. The steam engine pulled six passenger cars and five freight cars loaded with cast iron farm implements.

'I never thought to become excited about farming tools,' Mung said. 'It is a sure sign of progress.' He pointed. 'What are those white stripes across the windows on the passenger cars?'

'We have to protect the country folk who come for the ride. Most of them have never seen glass before. They try to poke their heads through without opening the windows.'

'I would have done the same,' Mung said. 'Glass was one of the few things I brought back from America. I never saw it in my village.'

A stiff-backed Englishman helped his wife from the passenger coach. 'I am sorry, my dear,' he said. 'These Orientals act like pigs. No sense of decency whatsoever.'

The woman's face was beet-red. She tried to answer but words did not come. Her husband hired a rickshaw and they were whisked away.

Mung motioned Udo forward. 'Find out what happened to the English couple.'

'Look at that one,' Iyeasu said. 'Many strangely dressed people march up and down the Ginza showing off their western clothes. The Americans call them Ginza Gallivanters.'

Mung saw a graceful, petite Japanese woman in kimono and obi of gentle colours get off the train with a companion. He wore a flat American straw hat, striped jacket bound by an obi, and two swords. He held a bamboo cane, wore wooden clogs and long red underwear.

Udo returned with a smile on his face. 'In order to be in style when he reached Tokyo, the man in the straw hat changed from his traditional clothes in the railroad car. The Japanese in the car did not mind his nakedness, and the English couple sitting close-by tried to ignore it. But, when the train passed through a tunnel, he was thrown off his feet and fell naked into the English lady's lap. He lay sprawled on the floor in front of her, apologizing endlessly.'

'The clash of cultures cannot be helped,' Iyeasu said. 'If we are to copy the West, we must rub shoulders with them.' He directed the rickshaw man to the Ginza. 'Do you find any of this amusing?' he asked Mung.

'Yes.'

'Then why are you so solemn? You will not offend me if you laugh from the belly and show your teeth. I am accustomed to it.'

Mung barely smiled. 'I would not have returned to

Tokyo, nor be on the way to this banquet, if I could have avoided it. Lord Hotta's sacrifice, Ukiko and Yoshida's deaths, have taken the enjoyment out of my life. Duty is what I live for.'

Iyeasu shifted to look Mung in the eye. 'Your new son can bring you happiness.'

'He killed Ukiko,' Mung said sharply. 'It would interfere with my duties.'

'By it, you mean the child. Your wife gave her life that you might have him. She was proud to bear your son.'

'I needed her, not him. Children take your attention. They take your time. And your love.'

'Do you fear losing Shimatzu as you lost Yoshida?'

'Yes,' Mung whispered, and clamped his mouth shut.

The rickshaw reached the Ginza. Bright coloured lanterns and happy sounds evoked a gay atmosphere. Mung saw young blades parading the wide street in trousers, tails and stovepipe hats, the clothes usually too large for the small-statured Japanese. The sleeves and trousers of their suits were rolled up. Men wore ties without collars, or collars without ties. Several petite Japanese women stumbled in stiff leather shoes with high heels, trying to swing their corset-encased hips and satin-covered bustles.

'The wives of your Black Dragons have formed the Society for Asiatic Ladies, to promote western styles and fashions.'

'My god,' Mung exclaimed, 'look at that pair!'

Two men strode down the centre of the Ginza with absurd conceit. People bowed appreciation of their exceptional modern dress. One man wore an old tricorne hat, a ruffled lace collar tucked into his kimono, knee length silk stockings and wooden clogs. The second wore clogs, a tuxedo, and on his head a highly polished, dented, old metal diving helmet. As he swaggered along, the front glass piece swung open and shut in his face.

428

'This pair gallivant the Ginza every night,' Iyeasu said. 'Sailors told them the stockings, lace and hat belonged to George Washington, and the diving helmet was Thomas Jefferson's head armour. Americans are much admired.'

'Do you remember your father's story about the people in Kyoto imitating the Portuguese?' Mung asked.

'Every time I come here. It would not surprise me to see a pantalooned samurai swagger down the street wearing a wide-brimmed hat with a large ostrich feather. It could not be any more ridiculous.'

'I think I am ready to join the anti-western faction,' Mung said.

'You would now be in the minority.'

'Let us sit at one of these outdoor cafés and watch the gallivanters.' Mung summoned Udo. 'After you pick up Gin-ko, meet us at the banquet hall.'

Udo was about to enter his apartment when an imperial guardsman approached. 'I am here to inspect the rooms. Princess Atsu will soon enter.' The guard opened the door and strode in.

Gin-ko came from another room. 'What is this?' she asked.

'He says Princess Atsu is on her way here,' Udo replied.

The guard moved to enter the other room but Gin-ko barred his path. 'My children are asleep.'

A plump young woman with bright intelligent eyes entered the apartment. 'That will be all,' she told the guard. 'You may leave.'

The guard bowed, and backed out of the room. Gin-ko and Udo knelt, then lay flat on the floor.

'My brother has discontinued that form of the bow,' Princess Atsu said. 'It is not the modern way.'

Udo and Gin-ko rose on to their knees. The short woman with apple cheeks was smiling at them. 'Please

429

come closer,' she said. 'I am happy to meet the heroes of Sapporo. Is it true the enemy were cannibals?'

'Yes, your highness,' Udo said. 'Prior to their assault, they ate some of their own dead.'

The princess's cherry cheeks paled. 'Did the inspector general really go up in a balloon during the action?'

'Yes, to direct our artillery. He was shot down, but landed safely. Then he commanded the Mito riflemen in finishing the pirates.'

'Did the lady Gin-ko lead the women of Sapporo to battle against the cannibals?'

Udo looked at his wife and Gin-ko lowered her eyes. 'Yes,' she said, 'but the newspapers greatly exaggerate my role in the battle. We women never struck a blow. And there were two hundred pirates, not two thousand.'

The princess smiled. 'Your honesty will be helpful to me in verifying and compiling the second *Book of Good Deeds*. I came here to discuss our future relationship before you leave for the banquet. There is a pressing matter I must speak of.'

Udo reacted swiftly to the obvious suggestion. 'I beg your highness's pardon but it is necessary for me to arrange our transportation to the party.'

'You are excused.' The princess waited until Udo closed the door behind him, then turned to Gin-ko with an impish smile. 'Why do you suppose I came to visit so soon after your arrival?' she asked. 'You may speak freely.'

'To see if I am suitable to take Ukiko's place in arranging a marriage between you and Iyeasu.'

The princess nodded. 'Ukiko told you. She spoke of you with great respect and affection. She wrote me of your marriage to Udo the day before she died. Are you happy?'

'Yes, your highness.'

'Yours is a true love match. I love Iyeasu, but my position forbids me to express it. My brother may even

430

wish to marry me off to someone who is a political asset. Most men do not find me attractive, but I know I could make Iyeasu love me. I so admire his brilliant mind and sense of humour. And I am reasonably bright. I think we would enjoy each other's company.'

'May I have the honour of speaking to Iyeasu on your behalf?' Gin-ko asked.

'It must be done soon, and in a most delicate manner. Iyeasu Koin is an honourable man.' The princess sighed. 'He would perhaps say yes from respect for my position. Then again he could say no and commit seppuku. If he killed himself, I would join him in death.' The plump young woman began to weep.

'Princess, you must not talk of death,' Gin-ko said. 'We shall find a way, and soon.' She handed the princess a rice paper tissue to dry her tears.

'You and I shall be good friends,' Princess Atsu said.

'I will share a personal secret with you to seal our friendship. No one knows yet, not even my husband. I am pregnant,' Gin-ko whispered.

'Again,' the wide-eyed princess gasped. 'How wonderful! I wish to become pregnant with Iyeasu's child. How does it feel to have a little person growing inside of you?'

'As if I have fulfilled the entire purpose of my humanity,' Gin-ko said.

'May I touch your stomach?'

Gin-ko took the soft, pudgy hand and placed it on her abdomen. 'It is only three months. You will not feel anything yet. Allow me to show you the result of my first pregnancy.' She took the princess by the hand. 'Come, we shall look in at the children.'

Chapter 44

At the banquet hall, Danjuro and Iyeasu introduced Mung to several influential lords. The politically powerful men had been invited by the brothers in the belief they could be persuaded to support Mung in the National Assembly. It became clear to Mung that the festive meal was more to promote him and the Sakhalin agreement than to celebrate the kite fighting victory. Danjuro's apparently spontaneous invitation had been well-planned in advance.

Sandanj bowed to Udo and Gin-ko at the entrance. 'May I speak with your husband for a moment, my lady?'

'I shall be at the goldfish pond,' Gin-ko said.

'What is the problem?' Udo asked.

'Tala Derzhavin demands that her husband be killed.'

'Again!' Udo paced back and forth. 'Can you imagine the uproar if a European ambassador was assassinated in Tokyo? The westerners would have us in their debt for eternity.'

'She claims to know how Hideyoshi will destroy Mung.'

Udo spun around.

'I believe her,' Sandanj said. 'She did not request more opium. In addition, her Eurasian lover slipped me a note that Hideyoshi held two secret meetings with Ambassador Derzhavin. Tala wants you at her servants' entrance just after midnight.'

'Gentlemen,' the owner of the hall said, 'please enter. The speeches are about to begin.'

In the dining hall, the head table formed the closed end of an inverted U. The Warriors of the Wind sat on both sides of the two long low tables. Everyone wore traditional dress.

Danjuro, at the head table flanked by Mung and Iyeasu, raised his hand. 'Dai Nippon banzai!' he exclaimed. 'Long live a great Japan!'

'Dai Nippon banzai!' the guests responded.

'Warriors of the Wind, I salute you!' Danjuro's big fist boomed like a bass drum over his heart.

The kite fliers raised their fists. 'To the Lord of Mito!'

The team captain approached the head table. 'Lord Danjuro,' he said, 'on behalf of the Warriors of the Wind, I am honoured to present you with this token of our esteem.' He bowed and handed the Mito lord a thick piece of bamboo. 'It is the top strut of our kite. We disassembled the kite in order to share the memory of this day with all those who made it so glorious.'

After Rhee and Sandanj were presented with pieces of bamboo, the team captain stepped before Mung and bowed. 'Sire, your strategy of removing the Chiba captain helped us win the day. Yet I and the other men of the team felt that our kite fought with a life of its own. It was valiant beyond its construction and our skills. We believe this is because it was guided by the souls of two young warriors. If you will kindly hold out your hand.' The captain draped the two white strips of cloth over Mung's palm. 'Your son, Shimatzu, and grandson, Yaka, were with us in the sky.' Mung looked at the strips of cloth and swallowed hard.

The captain bowed before Udo and Gin-ko. 'How could we lose with a family like this!' He handed them each a piece of bamboo. 'Wasshoi!' he cried.

'Wasshoi! Wasshoi! Wasshoi!' the guests chanted.

Sandanj stood up. 'Sires and lady.' He bowed. 'It is my pleasure to proclaim the Warriors of the Wind the winners of today's kite flying contest. The inspector general of

Hokkaido will present the grand prize of two thousand yen.'

Mung made the presentation with words of praise for the team, the judges and the organizers. He was followed by a series of speakers who lauded the Warriors of the Wind, the heroes of Sapporo, and portrayed Mung as the leader in both ventures.

Danjuro concluded the evening's speeches. 'Tonight I will share with you a most exquisite gastronomical delight. A delicacy enjoyed only by those who are daring enough to take risks.' He tapped his iron fan on the table.

The hall's owner led the chef and his assistants up to the front table. He stepped aside for the display of five live fish on a pine board.

'Fugu,' the owner declared. 'Donated in honour of the heroes of Sapporo by an anonymous admirer.'

The guests sucked wind through their teeth. The proprietor unrolled scroll after scroll attesting to the training, apprenticeship and licensing of the chef to prepare and serve the deadly fish.

'I have eaten your prepared puffers many times,' Danjuro said. 'I accept your credentials.'

The chef bowed, and motioned his helpers to exhibit thirty different keen-edged knives used in the ceremonial preparations of fugu. The proprietor bowed and retired with his staff.

'The chef has assured me the fugu will be sliced in such a manner there will be a portion for everyone who desires it,' Danjuro announced. 'Tasting fugu is not mandatory. Sharing this victory meal is. Wasshoi!'

Waiters entered the hall and began serving. A relish dish was followed by bean-curd soup, cold vegetables, pickled eggplant and cabbage. Talk flowed easily around the tables and smiles were frequent. Warm saké accompanied each course. Faces glowed as different foods came and went.

Then all dishes were cleared and new places set before each guest. The waiters stepped away and the chef entered with a large, pale green ceramic platter. Arranged in concentric circles were exactly one hundred pure white, petal-shaped slices of fugu, so thin the ceramic colour tinted the fish. Interspersed between the delicate segments were bright red peels of radish.

'Fugu.' The word was whispered around the room. The chef displayed the enticing flower sculpture to the side tables, then to the front. He set it down before Danjuro. 'My lord,' the chef said, 'the highest award in the empire is the Order of the Chrysanthemum. In the name of the proprietor of this humble establishment and myself, this award is bestowed upon you, the inspector general of Hokkaido, and the heroes of Sapporo.'

'Wasshoi! Wasshoi! Wasshoi!' the Warriors of the Wind chanted.

> 'We will fly with you.
> We will eat with you.
> We will die with you.
> Wasshoi!'

Danjuro held up his hand and there was silence. 'The samurai is born and bred for war, but women are not.' He looked to Gin-ko. 'If a woman displays courage in battle on one occasion, a man could think her heroism an instinctive reaction. The lady Gin-ko Ishikawa, daughter-in-law of the inspector general, has shown exceptional courage on two occasions. I declare this Order of the Chrysanthemum to be rightfully hers.'

Every man in the room tapped his fan in agreement.

Udo's thoughts had been on Tala Derzhavin until Danjuro began to speak. Then he listened, pleased that the Lord of Mito had made it almost impossible for anyone to mention his wife's past in public. Gin-ko had become a living legend.

The chef, about to take the tray and bring it to Gin-ko, stood still when she spoke. Her voice was soft, yet heard by all. Her beauty such that young and old were drawn to look at and listen to her. 'Lord Danjuro,' she said, 'in Japan there is a movement to westernize our society. I fervently support this desire to modernize so that we may soon take our rightful place among other nations. But, I also believe we Japanese must never forget our heritage. To precede the Lord of Mito in being served would be a violation of tradition. If after you have tested the fugu I may, it shall be my treasured memory forever.' Gin-ko bowed her head. The guests tapped their fans.

Danjuro bowed to the beautiful woman, then picked up a pair of eating sticks. He gently pinched a rind of radish between two snowy white slices of fugu and raised them to his lips. 'Now you may serve the lady,' he told the chef.

The platter was placed before Gin-ko. She positioned her eating sticks in dainty fingers.

Danjuro chewed the soft delicate meat and swallowed, feeling a familiar warm tingle expand outward from his chest and stomach. The tingling sensation raced through his arms and legs and returned to his abdomen. He shuddered, experiencing the anticipation of a sexual climax. The eating sticks dropped from his hand.

Udo heard the clatter of the sticks on the table. He turned and saw Danjuro's lips quiver, then turn blue. Udo flung out his right hand, knocking the sticks and fugu from Gin-ko's grip. 'Do not eat!' He jumped up, shouting, 'No one is to leave!'

The Black Dragons in the room quickly blocked all exits. The guests silently watched the Mito giant pale in trying to force his muscles to obey him. His breathing was laboured. By supreme will and superhuman effort, he rose to his full height. He heard Mung order Rhee to pound his back. He saw the Okinawan swing his arm and heard the noise, but felt nothing. Rhee slammed his back again and Danjuro began to topple. He could not feel his legs. The table was coming up to his face.

Mung and Iyeasu pulled the Mito giant over on his back, feeling for a pulse. There was none. Mung put his ear to Danjuro's chest. There was no sound. 'Your brother is dead,' Mung said.

Iyeasu looked up at the chef. 'Did you prepare this dish with your own hands?'

'According to everything I was taught, the fish should be safe.' The man trembled. 'I always take extra precautions.'

'Eat it,' Iyeasu ordered.

The chef dropped the eating sticks twice before he could raise a piece of the fugu to his lips.

'Stop!' Mung said. 'It is certain this platter is poisoned. I want to know about the others.'

Four more platters, decorated with the exquisite designs of a crane, a deer, a turtle and a pheasant, were brought out.

'Select a tray,' Mung ordered the chef. He pointed at the proprietor. 'You too.'

Both men appeared comforted they were not to eat from the green platter. They took up new eating sticks, tweezered the fugu and ate, relieved to be able to prove their innocence. Their faces relaxed as they swallowed the fish. The owner opened his mouth to speak. He stiffened. The chef staggered against him. Both men fell dead on the floor.

'Hideyoshi is responsible for this!' Mung said. 'If I had not sworn an oath to your father, I would order him dead.'

'Hideyoshi is now lord governor of Mito, one of the most powerful men in the empire,' Iyeasu said. 'Your life, mine and the Sakhalin agreement are in more danger than ever before.'

'Sandanj,' Udo ordered, 'escort Gin-ko to our apartment.' He looked at his wife. 'You will remain in the imperial palace. It is safe there. I have work to do.'

Udo looked around the hall. No one had moved. Iyeasu and Mung knelt by Danjuro's body. 'Team captain,' Udo called, 'have your men carry Lord Danjuro to the imperial palace.'

Jiroo and twenty Black Dragons burst into the banquet hall. They surrounded Mung and Iyeasu in a protective circle.

Udo took Jiroo's arm and pulled him aside. 'I have confirmation Hideyoshi is responsible for this. He must die.'

The senior Black Dragon glanced towards Mung. 'He has vowed not to harm the viper.'

'I will do it,' Udo said. 'Will you help me kill Hideyoshi?'

Jiroo looked down at the frozen face of the Mito giant. 'Yes. Be at my apartment in the palace at two a.m.'

Udo stepped into the kitchen through the servants' entrance. The Eurasian beauty turned up a lantern. Tala Derzhavin stepped in front of her. 'I was surprised to see you on the *Sapporo-kan* this morning,' Tala said.

'Your warning came too late,' Udo said. 'Lord Danjuro died tonight instead of Mung.'

For a moment the tall angular woman lost her poise. 'How?'

'Poisoned by fugu at a banquet.'

Tala sighed. 'It was not Mung they were trying to poison. The newspaper will get rid of him.'

'What do you mean?'

'Will you kill my husband?' she challenged Udo.

438

'How can a newspaper kill a man?'

'According to Hideyoshi, Mung will do that himself.'

Udo's eyes blinked. 'So you know the pockmarked little slug.'

Tala smirked. 'Prove you will kill my husband and possibly you can prevent your father's death.'

The woman knew more than Udo thought possible. He had frightened her once before by swift violent action against the Eurasian. He moved quickly past the Russian woman and grabbed the Eurasian's hand. Pulling her forward, he spun her around with her arm bent up behind her back. She cried out and Tala Derzhavin gasped. Udo drew out his Arkansas toothpick and pressed the sharp edge against the exquisite throat.

'Do not do that,' Tala pleaded, her hands and eyes begging.

Udo's knife drew blood that trickled over the steel blade and into the beautiful bosom. The Eurasian trembled violently.

'She is bleeding,' Tala sobbed.

'I will kill her to save my father. I have never lied to you, nor pressured you by withholding opium. I will kill your husband if you save Mung's life.'

'You are cutting her. She is the only thing I love.'

'Your husband will die, if you help me.'

'The newspaper is an old one from Hawaii,' Tala said. 'The front page tells about Mangiro, a Japanese fisherboy who was rescued and adopted by an American whaling captain. It tells how John Mung, the same person, was taught Christianity by sailors, converted by a Reverend Damon, and baptized in Honolulu's Seamen's Chapel. Hideyoshi assured my husband that a public disclosure of Mung's Christian conversion would cause him to slash his belly.'

Udo withdrew the knife and Tala rushed forward to

embrace the Eurasian, covering her with kisses while dabbing away the blood on her neck and breasts. Tala stepped in front of her lover and faced Udo like a lioness protecting her cub. 'Will you keep your part of the bargain?' she demanded.

'Yes.'

'How soon?'

'I must think.' Udo had no doubt it was true the newspaper story would finish Mung. 'Why would Hideyoshi come to your husband? How did he speak with him?'

'Through an American sailor named MacDonald who speaks Japanese and French. It seems that sailor and Mung were prisoners in Nagasaki some twenty years ago. Mac-Donald was in port and wanted to see Mung again. Hideyoshi paid him to leave after they met with my husband.'

'But Hideyoshi wants to attack Korea, which will mean a confrontation with Russia,' Udo said. 'Why would he come to your husband for help?'

'Hideyoshi wants power. That means control of the imperial army. If his older brother is dead, he is the Lord of Mito. With modern weapons, he will take over the army.'

'I do not understand how he used the newspaper to bargain with the ambassador.'

Tala Derzhavin sighed. 'Hideyoshi has threatened to destroy Mung and the Sakhalin agreement if my husband does not supply him with arms. Hideyoshi promised if he did get the weapons, not to mount an invasion of Korea. My husband's orders from our government are to keep the peace with Japan. Anything less would be considered failure. That is the reason he awarded the highest medal our country has to your father. He wants peaceful ties between Russia and Japan.'

Udo was stunned. Hideyoshi had spun a web of intrigue that everyone was falling into. Danjuro was only one victim. 'How does Hideyoshi intend to take over the imperial army?'

'That is not my concern. When will you fulfil your promise?'

'Did your husband agree to Hideyoshi's terms?'

'He will deliver the weapons and ammunition if the Sakhalin agreement is ratified by the Japanese National Assembly. Hideyoshi said it was guaranteed if he voted for it. He also promised Russia preferential trade agreements.'

'I will kill your husband after the assembly votes in two days,' Udo said.

'I would like to see the disgusting bastard twitch his life out and know I was watching,' Tala Derzhavin said. 'Can that be arranged?'

Chapter 45

'You and Muso deserve special consideration,' Hideyoshi said. 'Pleasures of the flesh?' He grinned.

'Fulfil your part of our bargain,' the Golden Lizard hissed. 'Danjuro is dead, the newspaper about to be destroyed, and you will be lord governor of Mito.'

'I will destroy Mung for you. However his death and the fulfilment of our agreement must await the approval of the Sakhalin treaty.'

'When will the Golden Lizard become chief Yakuza?' Muso asked.

'Not until we receive the Russian weapons. In the meanwhile, you have the list of names as security.'

'Right here.' Muso patted his obi.

'My giving you that list was an act of faith. They are all former Mito samurai, loyal to me, who are now officers in the imperial army.'

'Do not talk of faith,' the Golden Lizard said. 'We both know either one of us would sell the other for an advantage. That list is my guarantee you will not go back on your word.'

'When I take over the imperial army, Wada Zenshichi's Yakuza will swear loyalty to you or die. How many men do you have now?'

'Thirty here in Tokyo.' The lizard-man watched Muso fill three saké cups, and took the first one. 'The French raise their glasses and toast like this.' He raised the cup. 'To Mung's death!'

Hideyoshi raised his cup again. 'And to our success.'

'What about that bonus?' Muso said. 'We have been living a celibate life since we arrived in Tokyo.'

'I have arranged a full day for you in a new pleasure house on the edge of the Yoshiwara. Two young women starting out on their own.'

'We would be identified by our tattoos,' the Golden Lizard said. 'The Tokyo police have been circulating our descriptions for months.'

'Use the women, and kill them. Then return to your haven. Do not leave there until I send for you.' His pockmarked face creased in an exultant smile. 'Soon you will have the power to walk the streets freely. Peasants will fall on their faces before you. The mighty will seek your favour.'

It was almost two a.m. when Udo entered his apartment. 'Are you still awake?'

'Hold me,' Gin-ko said.

He felt her trembling in his arms. 'I almost ate that fugu,' she sobbed. 'I have been sitting here too frightened to move. I used to think I wanted to die. Now I fear death because it would take me from you and the children.' She buried her face in his chest and breathed his comforting smell.

'Shhh. Shhhhhh,' he crooned. 'It will be all right. Everything will be fine.'

'I worry you will die and leave me. Hold me tight,' she pleaded.

There was a tapping on the door. Udo brushed Gin-ko's tears dry. 'Enter,' he called.

An imperial guardsman stalked into the room and examined every corner.

'That will be all.' Princess Atsu dismissed the samurai. 'I was awakened by the extra guards placed in and around my apartment,' the plump young woman said. 'When I heard Lord Koin was dead, I feared it was Iyeasu.'

'No, your highness,' Udo said. 'His older brother, Danjuro, was poisoned.'

'Yes, I have heard the story.' She looked down at Gin ko. 'May I help you?'

Tears brimmed in Gin-ko's eyes. 'You are a princess.'

'I am your friend.'

'My wife and I would be grateful for your presence,' Udo said. 'I am late for a meeting and would not like to leave her alone.'

'We ladies shall have a talk and some tea,' Princess Atsu said. 'You may go about your business.'

Udo entered Jiroo's apartment, and stopped short. His eyes went from Jiroo to Iyeasu, and back again.

'Do not fear,' Jiroo said. 'Iyeasu Koin wants his brother dead.'

'It was not Hideyoshi who killed Danjuro,' Udo said.

'He planned it,' Iyeasu replied. 'Wada Zenshichi's Yakuza confirm that the Golden Lizard and his henchman purchased the fugu and delivered it to the restaurant. Both met with Hideyoshi before and after the poisoning.'

'Your brother is preparing to destroy Mung.' Udo told of the newspaper article.

'The exposure of Mung's conversion will finish him,' Jiroo said. 'We have just returned from a strategy meeting with him. Because of his vow not to kill Hideyoshi, we did not tell him of our plans.'

'Before we do away with Hideyoshi,' Udo said, 'we must find those in the imperial army who remain loyal to him. He is planning to take over the army. He must have men in key positions, just as Saga did in the Satsuma army. We must kill them and make an example of them.'

444

'No killings should take place until the Sakhalin agreement is ratified,' Iyeasu said. 'In that way we gain Hideyoshi's votes on our side in the National Assembly. Then we can kill him and his traitors.'

'To protect the Black Dragon, that newspaper article must also be destroyed,' Jiroo said.

'That is not enough.' Iyeasu leaned forward over his big stomach. 'Mung will always have political enemies. Someone else might come across the article at another time. Mung must be protected for all time, and I think I know how it can be done.'

'The sooner the better,' Udo said.

'How will you fulfil your promise to the Russian woman without bankrupting Japan?' Jiroo asked Udo. 'The assassination of a senior foreign diplomat would invite severe retaliation.'

'I am counting on the ambassador knowing his wife has a lesbian lover, and the Eurasian keeping us informed. Remember that I placed her in that household.'

'All Tokyo knows about Tala Derzhavin and her lover,' Jiroo said. 'The Russian ambassador is a frequent guest at the House of a Thousand Delights. Sandanj's girls report he attributes his posting to Japan, which he looks down upon, to his wife's sexual excesses.'

'Hearing that, I can assure you there will be no repercussions,' Udo said.

Sandanj entered the room. His clothes were dishevelled and he smelled of smoke. 'The devils raided the newspaper,' he said. 'They tried to burn it down.'

'Who?' Udo demanded.

'The Golden Lizard and his men. Thank the gods the printing press is safe. Most of the building too. The paper and ink powder were ruined by the water. It will be at least a week before we can print again, but it could have been worse.'

'Let your people deal with that,' Udo said. 'From now on, stay close to us. I suggest we all rest, then meet again to plan for the killing night. We must finish Hideyoshi and his followers in a way which will give a clear message they are traitors.'

At midday, Udo still slept. Gin-ko and Princess Atsu were playing with the children when an imperial guard entered. 'Your highness, there is a girl asking to speak with Mistress Gin-ko.'

'Send her in.'

'Your highness, this is a waif from the Yoshiwara. She refuses to state her business.'

'Allow her entrance.'

The frightened girl prostrated herself before the princess.

'Rise up, young one,' Princess Atsu said. 'We no longer bow in that fashion.'

Gin-ko helped the girl to her knees, recognizing her former apprentice in the Yoshiwara. 'What is it? Why have you come?'

'I was afraid to tell the police,' the girl said. 'My new workplace is not yet licensed. I came directly to you, Mistress Gin-ko. I fear they will kill my employers.'

'Who will?'

'The Golden Lizard and his henchman.'

Gin-ko went pale. Memories of Kagoshima and Ukiko came flooding back. She could hear the hissing sound of his voice, see the scaly head and hooded eyes. She rushed to wake Udo.

Half-dressed, Udo hurried out to question the girl, and saw Princess Atsu. He bowed. 'My apologies, your highness. I did not realize you were present.' He motioned the girl into the other room. Gin-ko helped him dress as he questioned her.

446

Udo tucked his weapons away and went to the door. 'I must alert Mung and Iyeasu.'

The princess perked up. 'I will inform Iyeasu,' she said. 'You notify the inspector general. It will save time.'

'But, princess,' Udo protested, 'it is below your dignity to carry a message to a minister.'

The young woman flashed a coy smile. 'Not to this minister.'

Udo, Sandanj, Mung and Rhee met Iyeasu, Jiroo and ten Black Dragons at the palace gate. They set off at a run for the Yoshiwara.

'Let us hope we are in time to catch the lizard-man,' Mung said.

Iyeasu puffed as they ran. 'Did you send Princess Atsu to inform me?' he asked Udo.

'Me send the princess? Never. She insisted on bringing you the message.'

'Why would she do that?' Iyeasu panted.

'Gin-ko says the princess is considering you as a husband.'

Iyeasu stopped, putting his hands on his knees, trying to catch his breath. The others hurried on. Iyeasu stood alone. 'Me,' he gasped. 'A woman would consider me for a husband? The charming princess? This is most disturbing.' He smiled and stood straight. 'She thinks of me as a man, not a fat joke.' A rickshaw passed by and Iyeasu hailed it. He scrambled in. 'To the Yoshiwara!'

For an entire night and part of the next day, Muso and the Golden Lizard had used and abused the two Yoshiwara courtesans. It was when the tattooed men decided to entertain themselves with the apprentice that they realized she was gone.

The lizard-man spoke in the secret language of the Yakuza. 'That brat will inform on us.'

Muso grabbed his clothes and dressed. The Golden Lizard knelt naked between the two young women stretched out on the tatami mats. Although frightened, they were mesmerized by the black-edged golden scales that covered the muscular body. They watched him place his palms on their soft, defenceless bellies. He ran his hands slowly up their smooth bodies, between their breasts, and up to their necks. He clamped the scaly fingers of each hand around a throat. The women choked. Saliva gurgled from their sweet lips. Their slender backs arched as he closed his grip tighter and tighter. Their legs thrashed, then fell limp.

'People outside,' Muso warned.

The Golden Lizard ignored his clothing. Taking only his steel hook and dagger, he moved to the wall. 'This side is closest to the foreign compound,' he said. 'We will be safe there. Apply the tactic they used on us at the villa by Tamieka pond. Just before they break in, we charge out through this wall.'

Muso crouched next to the lizard-man and cocked his double-barrelled pistol.

Outside, Mung whispered, 'We must not lose them. Separate into four groups of four, one team on each side of the building. At my signal, we enter through the walls.' He waited until all were in position. 'Now!' he shouted.

The four groups charged through the sides of the building. The two tattooed men broke out opposite four Black Dragons coming in. Muso shot and killed the first. The Golden Lizard left his hook in another's throat, and they raced away. The other two Black Dragons took up the chase, sounding an alarm as they went.

At the far end of the street ahead of the fleeing Yakuza, Iyeasu's rickshaw turned the corner. The Golden Lizard skirted the rickshaw but Muso, coming behind, was caught by Iyeasu's thick arm in his face. Muso was knocked off his feet and flat on his back. Four Black Dragons followed the lizard-man.

'Keep that Yakuza alive!' Mung shouted. 'Jiroo, I want information from him, and quickly.'

Following in the direction the Golden Lizard had gone, Mung was met by a Black Dragon coming towards him. 'Sire, we have the lizard-man surrounded in a house in the foreign compound. We cannot explain the situation to the foreigners.'

'I will explain and that reptilian bastard will be mine.'

Iyeasu cleared his throat. 'There may be complications.' But Mung did not hear. He was running towards the compound.

A Black Dragon pointed out the building next door to the French ambassador's residence. The plaque near the entrance read, SOCIÉTÉ DES MISSIONS ETRANGÈRES DE PARIS.

'Missionaries,' Mung mumbled. He marched up to the French ambassador's residence. His way was blocked by a marine lieutenant. 'I am the inspector general of Hokkaido. My men have followed a criminal to that building.'

Iyeasu rode up in his rickshaw and stepped out. 'Lieutenant, I am senior advisor to the Emperor. We should like to speak with Ambassador Montigny.' He addressed Mung. 'This is why your men could not find the Golden Lizard. It is now the fashion for our worst criminals to become Christians in order to escape Japanese justice.'

'We shall drag the lizard-man out from under his religious rock.'

'Ahh,' Iyeasu sighed, 'you have forgotten about extraterritoriality. Its effect is even larger than the word. These

449

priests promise foreign citizenship with each conversion. It exempts the Japanese from our laws.'

'Ambassador Montigny will see you,' the lieutenant said, escorting them into the house.

The French ambassador sat behind a large ornate desk. At his right stood a Catholic priest. The lieutenant took a place at his left. 'The ambassador will hear you,' the officer said.

'Ambassador Montigny, a professional killer is hiding in your church,' Iyeasu said. 'He belongs to a brotherhood of criminals who can be identified by the tattoos on their bodies. The Golden Lizard is a leader of these outlaws.' He indicated Mung. 'This is the inspector general of Hokkaido. He was a victim, and witness to this murderer's work in Kagoshima.'

Mung's burning eyes and rage-filled face dominated the room. Although Iyeasu had spoken, Ambassador Montigny addressed Mung. 'Monsieur, I have heard about you. You must understand the man you speak of has taken God as his feudal lord.' The ambassador turned to the priest, and nodded.

'Joseph is the baptized name of the man you seek,' the priest said. 'He traded his local loyalties for a universal one when he received Christ to his bosom.'

Mung's eyes turned a fiery black, his shoulder muscles bunched. In street-level French, he growled, 'That painted son of a bitch killed my wife.'

'Sir,' the lieutenant snapped, 'you are in the presence of the ambassador of France and a Catholic priest.'

'I would not give a damn if it were Bonaparte and the goddamned pope. I want the lizard-man.'

'You will have no such thing,' the priest said. 'According to international law, you are on French soil. The man you speak of received French citizenship when he converted.' The priest softened his harsh tone. 'My son, this man may

450

not be able to change the colour of his painted skin, but when he received Christ into his heart, he changed his way of life. His everlasting soul has become part of the kingdom of God. Can you understand that?'

'Are you mad or stupid? That scum murdered two young women today. He killed two of my men. The blood is fresh on the ground. It was the serpent who tempted Adam into sin,' Mung raged, 'and you are protecting this snake.'

'The Old Testament was replaced by the New,' the priest said. 'Just as the laws of Japan have been changed to incorporate Christian law.'

'Enough,' Montigny said. 'Father, please see to your charge. I am certain he will benefit from your moral guidance.' The ambassador looked up at Mung. 'The man you want is protected by international law. Japanese *corpus juris* has no power here.'

'He is protected by you,' Mung growled, pulling his pistol. He shoved the muzzle in the ambassador's face. The lieutenant reached out but Mung cocked the hammer and the officer withdrew his hand.

Looking over the gun barrel into Mung's angry eyes, Ambassador Montigny said, 'Mr Mung, you will do your country far more harm if you pull that trigger than that painted savage could achieve in two lifetimes. I admit the clergy in France has an unhealthy amount of political power. I am not naïve. In China, Burma and India, missionaries are in competition for souls. Some of them abuse their privileges. I sympathize, but cannot contravene international law to help you.'

Mung pressed the muzzle against the Frenchman's forehead. 'Will you surrender the Golden Lizard?'

'No, I will not.'

The four men remained frozen in time. Mung's finger quivered on the trigger. Iyeasu reached out and gently raised Mung's arm. 'Please,' the round man said, 'do not do it.'

Slowly Mung let the hammer down. He tucked the pistol into his obi. Then the lieutenant drew his weapon.

'Put that away,' Montigny ordered. 'All of you, listen to what I say. Nothing, I repeat, nothing of this incident will ever be mentioned or in any way communicated to another person outside this room.' He addressed Mung. 'You lost your wife and I am sorry. Public figures are often the object of undeserved hatred and violence. The tattooed man you seek truly appears to have accepted Christ into his heart. It is possible he will reform.'

'He is a traitor and a killer. He murdered after he supposedly accepted Christ.'

'Our French missionaries teach their converts the two J's – Jesus and Japan,' the ambassador said. 'We hope they will be loyal to both.'

'Teach the Golden Lizard this,' Mung said. 'If he leaves here, he will die. Furthermore, your priests and missionaries of all faiths are restricted to this compound until he is turned over to me.'

'I doubt if the inspector general of Hokkaido has the power to do that,' Montigny said.

'I have,' Iyeasu said. 'I hereby order the restrictions for the safety of your missionaries. If they leave this compound, they will come to harm. We seek to protect them.' He waddled closer to the desk. 'You see, Mr Ambassador, the man you protect is guilty of poisoning my brother, Lord Danjuro of Mito.' Iyeasu's large round face swelled with anger. 'You and other foreign dignitaries are scheduled to attend the funeral tomorrow. Know, when you stand at the grave side, you have given sanctuary to my brother's killer.'

'We will have a confession from the Golden Lizard's accomplice very soon,' Mung said.

'You will use torture to loosen his tongue,' Montigny said in disgust.

'Yes,' Mung replied. 'We Japanese learned from the best torturers ever. The Catholic missionaries who arrived here in the sixteenth century were part of the Inquisition.'

Muso, bound and gagged, strained to get free. His eyes flashed, his brain raced, seeking a means to escape.

'I want him spread-eagled face up on that low rectangular table,' Jiroo said. 'Sandanj, you look in the kitchen for a sharp knife, a mallet and a pitcher of water. Udo, find a long rope and a square patch of silk.'

Jiroo pointed at the bodies of the two young women. 'Take them out of the room.' He looked down at Muso. 'Even in death they should not have to be witness to what is about to happen to you.'

Muso squirmed but made no sound.

'I have everything you asked for,' Sandanj said.

'Cut his clothes off.'

Udo returned with a thick rope. The naked tattooed body was tied to the table. A bundle of torn clothes and a folded piece of rice paper lay on the floor. He picked up the paper.

'This is a list of names.' Udo glared down at the Yakuza. 'Who are these men?' he demanded.

'No questions just yet,' Jiroo said. He probed the tattooed body as a doctor would a patient. He looked down into Muso's eyes. 'You are a miserable excuse for a human being. I have no reservations about hurting you. You are gagged only because I do not wish to hear you until I am certain you will speak the truth. I can cause you an infinite amount of pain. If you are honest with me, I promise to release you from it by death. You are going to die. Have no doubt about that. The question is how long will it take.' Jiroo held out his hand to Sandanj. 'Knife.'

Sandanj handed over a keen-edged kitchen knife. Jiroo cut two parallel slits in the tattooed skin of Muso's quivering belly. He closed both ends with two quick cuts that formed a bloody square. He worked the tip of the blade under one corner and peeled off the patch of coloured skin. Muso bucked and squirmed. He moaned, but the gag muffled the sound.

Jiroo flipped the tattooed skin to the floor. He inserted the flat part of the blade under the Yakuza's penis. 'Mallet,' he said, holding the penis back out of the way.

Muso scrunched his chin on his chest. He watched Jiroo raise the hammer and smash down on his right testicle. The Yakuza's body jumped, kicked, convulsed, then fell limp in puddles of his own sweat and urine.

'Remove the gag,' Jiroo said. 'Udo, hold his head. Sandanj, keep his jaw open.' Jiroo snatched a tuft of hair on each side of Muso's temples and jerked them out. The Yakuza's eyes snapped open with the shock to his brain. Jiroo took the silk and shoved it into Muso's open mouth. Pouring water from the pitcher into the silk pocket dropped it deeper and deeper into Muso's throat, gradually cutting off his air. The big man coughed. He choked. He tried to twist his head away but it was held firmly by Udo and Sandanj. His starved lungs expanded, sucking the silk further down into the oesophagus. Muso's body arched from head to toe, his rib cage expanded until the bones were about to burst through the skin. Jiroo watched the man's eyes widen until they were popping from his head. The moment he saw them begin to cloud over, he pulled the water filled silk patch from Muso's throat. The Yakuza sucked great gulps of air. 'I will tell everything,' he wheezed.

Following Jiroo's instructions, Sandanj cut Muso's bonds. Udo threw the long rope over the centre ceiling beam. 'Now tie his hands behind his back and haul up the rope until he stands on tiptoe,' Jiroo said.

'I will tell you,' Muso sobbed. 'Enough! The list you found is of the officers loyal to Hideyoshi. They will revolt . . .'

Jiroo slapped his hand over the Yakuza's mouth. 'We shall do this my way. I am certain you can enlighten us on many things. In a moment I will allow it. First we will lift you off the floor by the rope tied to your hands. From the pressure on your hands behind your back, the muscles in your shoulders will begin to tear. You are a strong man. I estimate it will take two hours for your hands to come over your head and dislocate your shoulders. Two painful, piercing, hideous hours. If you speak quickly and answer all my questions, your pain will end in minutes.' He turned to Udo and Sandanj. 'Haul this turd up in the air.'

Later that evening, Jiroo reported to Mung. 'Muso spoke freely with us. He spent his last breath confirming everything Udo reported about the Russian ambassador, the poisoned fish, and the assassination attempts on you. It was the work of the Golden Lizard in conjunction with Hideyoshi. We have a list of fifty-six officers in the imperial army loyal to Hideyoshi, who are prepared to lead a revolt. There are thirty Yakuza in Tokyo working with the lizard-man to depose Wada Zenshichi. Some we know by name, others by tattoos, a few by addresses.'

'The chief Yakuza will deal with them,' Mung said. 'We will attend to the fifty-six traitors. They will be disgraced and forced to commit seppuku.'

'What about the Golden Lizard?' Iyeasu asked.

'Tomorrow is your brother's funeral. The day after, I stand before the National Assembly. With Hideyoshi's backing, passage of the Sakhalin agreement and cancellation of the Korean venture are assured. Immediately after my appearance at the assembly, I want fifty Black Dragons armed and ready to accompany me to the foreign compound. I will take the lizard-man out of that mission, law or no law.'

Udo, Sandanj, and Jiroo bowed to Mung's decision. Iyeasu looked at the Black Dragon's grim face and knew there would be no reasoning with him. He nodded his approval, but reflected silently on a way to stop Mung from ending his career for the sake of revenge.

Jiroo, Sandanj and Udo sat in Iyeasu's apartment. 'If Mung attacks that church, he is finished,' Iyeasu said. 'The foreigners would demand his head.'

'We three have sworn to obey the Black Dragon,' Jiroo said. 'Although in this case, for his own sake, we must seek a way to have the Golden Lizard ejected from that church.'

'We could kill him there,' Sandanj said. 'It might as well be two international incidents as one. When Udo kills the Russian ambassador, there will be hell to pay. The death of a converted criminal will hardly matter.'

'I promised you before,' Udo said, 'that there will be no repercussions. I plan to use the services of the Chinese chef.'

'If you are thinking of poisoning the ambassador so soon after Danjuro's death, it will be suspect,' Sandanj said.

'Not the way I intend doing it,' Udo replied.

'Protecting the Black Dragon from destroying himself must be our first concern,' Jiroo said.

The four men talked late into the night, but could determine no acceptable method of diverting Mung from his revenge. They adjourned their meeting until the next day.

Iyeasu asked Udo to remain after the others had gone. As soon as the door closed behind them, Iyeasu said,

'Please repeat what you said yesterday regarding Princess Atsu's consideration of me for marriage.'

'It is true. My wife told me. I apologize for blurting it out that way.'

'Do not apologize. You did well to tell me. But I do not know how these things work. If I ask for Princess Atsu's hand and she refuses, I am disgraced and must commit seppuku. On the other hand, she cannot lower herself to ask me.'

'We must find a nakoda,' Udo said. 'May I suggest Gin-ko?'

'Oh yes. Most certainly, if she is acceptable to the princess.'

'It was the princess who suggested Gin-ko. The Emperor already knows.'

Iyeasu rocked back onto his heels. 'By the gods, the young princess has been quite active.' He leaned forward. 'What did the Emperor say?'

'His imperial majesty indicated that in this matter tradition must prevail.'

'What does that mean?'

'The nakoda speaks to both parties, then to the Emperor. If he agrees, there will be a mi-ai. The yuino follows with an exchange of gifts, then the san-san kudo and you will be married.'

'Is it a long process?'

'For royalty, yes. The princess says it will take six months.'

'Oh. She has calculated everything. How remarkable!'

Ambassador Montigny stood next to American Ambassador Townsend Harris. 'This is my first state funeral,' Montigny said. 'The cortege is more than a mile long. It must have cost a fortune.'

'A million yen,' Harris said. 'There have been many

innovations in the traditional ceremony. Tuxedos and top hats are the most obvious concession to western tastes. The Japanese used to cremate the bodies weeks after the death. Now they use coffins and inter the deceased within twenty-four to forty-eight hours. They believe it is more European.'

'But the coffin is sitting on end, and there are Buddhist priests in attendance. The little I know of Danjuro, he leaned towards the older religion of Shintoism.'

'The body is seated upright in the coffin in the Buddhist position of meditation because there is a government organized division of religious labour in this country. The Shinto priests attend all births and the Buddhists officiate at deaths, even of Shinto priests. In that way each group is guaranteed a fair share of the religious market.'

'Danjuro's brother, Iyeasu, asked to see me later,' Montigny said. 'He appeared more concerned with our appointment than his brother's funeral.'

'I am certain he is,' Harris said, pointing to the large ox-drawn wagon carrying the coffin. 'Danjuro was murdered. There is only one thing Iyeasu can do for him now. That is to seek revenge. You harbour the man who killed his brother.'

'How can you know for certain the lizard-man did it?' Montigny asked.

The procession began to move. The foreign dignitaries followed the lords of the realm. The ox-cart's solid wooden wheels creaked and groaned behind them. Then came thousands of warriors, retainers, and priests holding paper lotus petals, the Buddhist symbol of peace and tranquillity.

'I know the Golden Lizard is guilty because I have more spies than you in Tokyo.' Harris smiled.

'Will the other brother, Hideyoshi, also seek revenge?' Montigny asked.

'Hideyoshi paid the Golden Lizard to kill Danjuro. I

suggest you listen carefully to Iyeasu at your meeting. It could prevent a blood bath.'

Ambassador Montigny sat alone with Baron Iyeasu Koin. 'Sir,' Montigny said, 'you have my sincere condolences.'

Iyeasu bowed. 'Thank you, but it pains me to inform the ambassador that if he does not give up the lizard-man, there will soon be many more funerals to attend and condolences to be given.'

'You would attack a foreign embassy?'

'That tattooed beast must die. If you continue to protect him, your priests will never be safe in Japan. And many of your converts will suffer because of him.'

'You are referring to war between Japan and France?'

'That could happen later,' Iyeasu said. 'I speak now of your converts being slaughtered. How many Christians are there in Tokyo?'

'Including the Protestants, three thousand.'

'Our Japanese lords may copy western dress and technology, but they fear that Japanese criminals and even honest citizens who owe large legitimate debts will prefer to convert rather than stand before Japanese law. Our people are quite ambivalent about religion. No one takes it seriously until it affects his economic, political or social status. We are a country obsessed with status and the privileges which accompany it. Your priests are breaking the legal status quo in Japan. For that alone, the Golden Lizard will die. He deserves to die on moral grounds. Your priest made a bad conversion. If you do not rectify the situation, there will be catastrophe.'

'I ask again,' Montigny said. 'Would you attack the embassy?'

'To capture the Golden Lizard, yes. And, if there is a battle at the foreign compound, others in Tokyo may use it as an excuse to kill Christian converts.'

Montigny felt his legs weaken. He gazed at the pudgy man in front of him. 'Mr Minister, I will try my utmost to avoid bloodshed.'

Iyeasu bowed. 'Please do it quickly. Time is short.'

Chapter 47

Mung held a meeting in his apartment. 'Tomorrow noon I present myself to the National Assembly. Jiroo, those fifty armed Black Dragons are to be ready when I come out of there. Udo, you will accompany me to take the Golden Lizard.'

'And where is my position in this scheme?' Iyeasu asked.

'With Sandanj, far from the foreign compound. Choose a public place where people will notice you.'

'With a shape like mine, that is not difficult.'

'When this is over,' Mung said, 'I want you and Sandanj free from suspicion. The Emperor will need your advice and his expertise with influencing people through the newspaper. Udo will leave for China the following morning.'

'How will you protect yourself?' Jiroo asked.

'I will either be disgraced or exiled again.' Mung had expected opposition at this meeting and was pleased they were accepting his decisions. He did not suspect the four men were formulating plans of their own, to use the fifty-six traitors to draw attention away from his attack on the Catholic mission.

'Prior to coming here I spoke with the Emperor,' Iyeasu said. 'He reminds you to mention the forty million yen to the assembly only as an agricultural loan. Nothing is to be said about purchasing weapons or the secret agreements.'

'I understand. If Hideyoshi does support my proposals, there should be no problem.' Mung turned to Jiroo. 'After we deal with the Golden Lizard, I do not wish to receive any messages until Hideyoshi and his traitorous officers have been taken prisoner. For that, use an additional two hundred Black Dragons.' Mung was applying Saga's tactic of isolating himself until the action was complete. Neither the National Assembly nor even the Emperor would be able to stop him. 'Udo,' he asked, 'did you speak with Wada Zenshichi?'

'He was most pleased to receive the list of outlaw Yakuza. They will be disposed of tomorrow night when we move against the others. The chief Yakuza also expressed his satisfaction with the fur trading arrangements and the profits he has already made trading gold with the Shansi banks in China. I believe you have repaid any debts the Black Dragon Society may have owed Wada Zenshichi.'

'In the event I should die in the attack,' Mung said, 'Jiroo will become the Black Dragon.' He noticed the four men avoiding his eyes, and assumed they were embarrassed by his words. They bowed and Mung was pleased. The Black Dragon Society would continue to serve the Emperor and Japan, as he had carried it forward after the death of Gompachi.

In his apartment, Iyeasu Koin sat propped up by several cushions. He stared at Udo and his voice rumbled from his massive chest. 'How can you justify killing fifty-six officers of the imperial army when it is possible to disgrace them into committing seppuku?'

'It is not a question of cruelty,' Udo said. 'It is one of strategy. Since the Emperor moved to Tokyo there have been five serious uprisings to restore the power of the shogunate and limit the Emperor's ability to govern. Unless we make an extraordinary example of these traitors, we will face the same problem sometime in the future. Every one of them must be found dead with a rope around his neck, even if he was killed by the sword or a bullet. Your brother, Hideyoshi, too.'

'I agree,' Sandanj said. 'Such a method will put an end to further revolts. The property of those traitors should revert to the Emperor, including the three houses of Mito.'

'There is no heir to Mito,' Iyeasu said glumly. 'It means the end of the paternal line in my family.'

'The immediate addition of Mito's property and income to the imperial treasury will be a major step towards centralized government,' Udo said.

Iyeasu found he was annoyed at the others for pushing him, and angry at himself for knowing they were right although not wishing to admit it.

'I also agree,' Jiroo said. 'An example must be made of the fifty-six. But Hideyoshi is a lord of the realm. You are a government minister, and his brother. You alone should decide if he lives or dies.'

'I will kill him,' Iyeasu said.

'Agreed,' Jiroo said. 'And all with ropes around their necks. A point has been reached in the reformation of Japan where a public stand must be taken. The raising of an army for the invasion of Korea is a threat to centralized government. Only the state should have the right to put men under arms. A democracy will be achieved once a stable power base has been established. Not before.'

'Mung is influenced by the American concept of justice,' Iyeasu said. 'He will consider our actions a violation of his orders. My rank protects me from his wrath. I believe, in time, he will forgive the three of you, unless Udo causes an international incident by killing the Russian ambassador. The deaths of the fifty-six, Hideyoshi, and even the Golden Lizard are all between Japanese. The Russian's death will have repercussions beyond the borders of Japan. The Europeans will exploit it. Udo, you may be Mung's son, but I doubt he would ever forgive you if Japan suffered further humiliation because of your action.'

'I swear on my son's life,' Udo said, 'there will be no

repercussions.' He turned to Sandanj. 'When will I see the Chinese chef?'

'He waits outside.'

'I suggest we adjourn this meeting,' Udo said. 'Tomorrow when we reach the foreign compound, Jiroo and I will isolate Mung and send our Black Dragons into the church after the lizard-man. Keep in mind that Mung must come out of this confrontation unscathed.'

Outside Iyeasu's apartment, Udo led Sandanj and the chef to a courtyard where they could not be overheard. 'Kang Shu told me you are an expert in poisons,' he said to the chef in Mandarin.

'I am.'

'Is it possible to place poison in a sealed bottle of wine without affecting the taste?'

'Depending on the poison and the wine, but it is done with a hot needle punched through the base of the bottle.'

'Is it possible for me to drink the same wine and not die?'

'Yes,' the chef said. 'The others who drink will die within minutes, without even tasting the poison. You will be safe if I administer an antidote. But it will not be pleasant.'

'Prepare two bottles for tomorrow night,' Udo said. 'Bring enough antidote for two. You will drink at the same time I do. If we both survive and the others die, I will take you with me back to China. You will be set free with enough money to open your own restaurant.'

The chef bowed. 'It will be a pleasure to serve you, and to see China again. I will need several bottles of the wine to be certain the concentration of poison is correct.'

'Sandanj,' Udo said, 'find out from the Eurasian which wine Tala Derzhavin prefers. See that the chef has ten bottles of that wine, and make an appointment with Tala for two a.m. tomorrow. We are to meet in the kitchen. Tell her I am coming to kill her husband.' He turned to the chef. 'Bring a quilt with you.'

'I believe Mung has reservations about me,' Udo said. 'I know Jiroo recommended me to the post of Black Dragon if anything happens to Mung. Yet Mung chose Jiroo.'

Gin-ko massaged the tense muscles in her husband's back. She snuggled her belly up to his buttocks. 'You are too sensitive. Mung will be here long after Jiroo is gone, but whoever inherits the Black Dragon Society will be hemmed in by established traditions. You will have the opportunity of building Genoysha, the Black Ocean Society, as you wish it. You will be able to put your personal imprint on the overseas organization.'

'Building Genoysha means constant travelling.'

Gin-ko rested her chin over the back of Udo's shoulder and nibbled on his ear. 'As long as we are together.'

Udo rolled back. He slipped his arm and leg under her and lifted her naked body onto his. 'I am glad you do not mind travelling. In little more than twenty-four hours we are off to China.'

Gin-ko tried to rise but was trapped by Udo's arms in a bear-hug. He rolled over on top of her, working his legs between hers. He probed with his erection into her softness, and pushed himself in.

'Why did you not tell me this before?' she asked.

He worked his hips slowly for she was dry inside. 'I've just found out. Can you and the children be ready?'

'Of course.' Her hips began to move in time to his. Her juices lubricated his throbbing penis. 'How long will we be gone?'

'A year or more.' Udo worked his body up higher between her thighs to plunge straight down into her.

Gin-ko locked her arms behind his head and hugged him

with her legs. 'Who will replace me as nakoda for the princess and Iyeasu?'

'At this moment I do not care.' Udo's body worked harder, pumping, pumping, up and down, in and out. 'I-do-not-care,' going deeper into her with each word.

'I-care, I-care, I-care,' Gin-ko responded, her body moving to his rhythm, faster and faster, until they stiffened and climaxed, then slumped in each other's arms.

Gin-ko kept her legs around Udo to hold his golden rod inside of her. 'Where in China are we going?'

When he did not reply she opened her eyes. He had fallen asleep. She smiled and kissed his forehead. 'Pleasant dreams, my beloved.'

But Udo was trapped in his dream vision of the killing night.

Chapter 48

By appointment, Mung and Iyeasu met the French lieutenant near the Hall of a Hundred Mats. 'Mr Minister.
Inspector General.' The officer bowed. 'I have a most
confidential message from the ambassador of France.' He
looked around, and seeing no one, continued, 'Ambassador
Montigny wishes to inform you of a technical oversight in
the religious conversion of the lizard-man, which makes
his baptism to Christianity invalid. This was brought to
our attention by the priest of the Catholic missionary
service.'

'No matter to me if he dies baptized or not,' Mung said.

'Monsieur, you do not understand. Without conversion,
the tattooed one does not enjoy French citizenship. He is
now simply a Japanese criminal on our property. Ahhh,
there are certain conditions.' The Frenchman raised one
finger as he mentioned each point. 'Take him soon. Do not
invade embassy grounds. Remove restrictions on all
missionaries.'

'You pose an interesting problem,' Iyeasu said. 'The
inspector general can take the Golden Lizard, but cannot
enter the building where he is hiding.'

'That is correct,' the lieutenant said.

'Inform the ambassador that all restrictions on missionaries are rescinded,' Mung said. 'Notify your priests and
soldiers to leave the compound by dark. I will personally
pay for all damages incurred. Also, there is to be no
interference from other Europeans in the compound. Can
those conditions be met?'

'It shall be as you wish.' The officer bowed, and departed.

'I worry when things go this right,' Mung said.

'How can you force the Golden Lizard from the mission?'

'Burn him out. With Ukiko's money and mine, there is more than enough to rebuild a dozen churches. Tell Udo to arm half the men with torches, the other half with repeating rifles.'

'Another obstacle overcome,' Iyeasu said. 'Perhaps after the National Assembly vindicates you for your policy in the north, you can help me.' He waddled up the wooden steps to the great hall at Mung's side. 'I need someone to act as nakoda between Princess Atsu and me.'

'I thought Udo's wife agreed to that.'

'Gin-ko will travel to China with Udo.'

'The children too?' Mung asked.

'Yes, Udo told me this morning.'

'Where are they now?'

'Udo is preparing the fifty men who will accompany you to the foreign compound.'

'I mean the children, Shimatzu and Yaka.' It was the first time Mung had pronounced his son's and grandson's names.

'Gin-ko and the children are still in the palace.'

The two men removed their clogs. They waited in the rear of the hall for the master of protocol to complete the formal opening of the National Assembly. Mung was pleased to see the lords in their kimonos. No western dress was allowed in the assembly.

'My lords,' the master of protocol called out, 'the inspector general of Hokkaido, Moryiama Ishikawa, will present himself for examination before this assembly. The subject to be discussed and voted upon is the Sakhalin and

469

Kurile islands agreement with imperial Russia. Will Moryiama Ishikawa come forward.'

Mung walked alone down the long, narrow aisle. Every one of the 250 lords and their retainers was armed. As Mung passed they sat back on their heels, resting hands on sword hilts, waiting for him to mount the dais at the head of the hall and be seated.

Iyeasu remained at the rear, listening to Mung give his honorific greetings and opening statement of intent. Mung launched into a concise political and geographical history of the Sakhalin and Kurile islands. Abiding by the restricted guidelines set by the Emperor, he outlined the process of negotiations, and benefits derived thereof.

Udo came up behind Iyeasu and whispered, 'There is trouble. The Golden Lizard's Yakuza have reported his situation to Hideyoshi.'

'Does my brother know about Muso's capture?'

'Probably. Several of our Black Dragons are certain Hideyoshi's allies will now vote against the treaty, and renew their efforts to obtain official approval for the invasion of Korea.'

Iyeasu looked down the long aisle. Mung seemed relaxed and confident as he reached the conclusion of his presentation. Iyeasu looked at Udo and shook his big head. 'Mung was forbidden to reveal half of what he has accomplished. If what you say is true, he will surely be defeated when they vote. Hideyoshi will destroy Mung and leave here the most powerful man in Japan.'

'Can we alert Mung before he finishes?'

'Only a lord or his heir may speak from the floor of the assembly.'

'What if I were to run in there and shout a warning?' Udo said.

Iyeasu pointed to the husky six-foot imperial guards posted every twenty feet on both sides of the centre aisle, and all around the four walls of the great hall. 'You would be cut down before you said two words. Mung has revealed all that is permissible. I must think.' He rolled his eyes up into his head and inhaled, long and deep. He concentrated his thoughts, willing his mind to search out a solution, trembling with the exertion. His face reddened, then purpled. For two minutes he did not breathe. Udo reached out to hold the swaying block-like figure upright.

With a mighty sigh that drew the attention of the guards near the door, Iyeasu Koin opened his eyes and looked up at Udo. 'Summon the Black Dragons. If it appears Mung will lose the vote, we shall invade the great hall and stop the ballot.'

Udo was frozen by the master of protocol's summons of Hideyoshi Koin to the dais. He watched the Lord of Mito mount the stage and sit beside Mung. Both men bowed. Udo sensed Hideyoshi's supporters waiting like sharks for the attack on Mung to begin.

'If I lead the Black Dragons into the assembly, Mung will be held responsible,' Udo said to Iyeasu. 'I have a better plan.' He rushed from the hall and ran towards the imperial palace.

On the dais, Hideyoshi stood up and began to speak. 'Honoured lords. My brother's tragic death has dominated my mind and heart these last hours. If I stray from the point or wander off the subject, bear with me, please.' He found the role of humble petitioner humorously unfamiliar. He had practised his opening statement many times. He had memorized facts in the best possible order to defeat the treaty, gain acceptance for the invasion of Korea, and finish Mung. Upon hearing of the Golden Lizard's entrapment and Muso's capture, Hideyoshi had realized he must abandon the Russians and revert to his original plan. He looked at Mung, then turned to the lords before him. 'We have listened patiently to the inspector general's explanation that Russia's loan to us was meant to establish a few thousand Japanese on Hokkaido. He told us there will be an increase of trade with the czar's maritime provinces. But, he neglected to mention the 30,000 square miles of Sakhalin island he traded for 1,500 square miles of the Kurile islands. Even that might be acceptable, if Russia could be trusted.' Hideyoshi pointed his fan at Mung. 'What Mr Ishikawa did not tell you is that Russia has violated the treaty of Nirtchinsk with China, and is preparing to violate the agreement with us.'

Mung was stunned by the unexpected, well-informed attack.

Hideyoshi went on. 'The Russians pushed beyond the agreed boundaries with China, past the Amur river. They now use that river as a water highway to the Pacific. Count Reznov, the new governor general of that area, is expanding the seventy colonies along the Amur river all the way to the Tatar strait. He is strengthening the maritime colonies along the east coast of the Japan Sea to Vladivostok.' Hideyoshi held the rapt attention of everyone in the hall. He congratulated himself for underplaying his role. He struck a classic pose with his fists dug into his sides, and challenged the lords, 'Does anyone know the meaning of the name Vladivostok?' He waited, then leaned forward and said, 'Someone please tell me the name of the country bordering Vladivostok.' Again he waited. Tension built. This time Hideyoshi pointed to Mung. 'He knows. The inspector general of Hokkaido knows that Vladivostok in Russian means Ruler of the East. He also knows the name of the country bordering Vladivostok. It is Korea. More than that, he must know Russian surveyors are measuring a path parallel to the river settlements for a trans-Siberian railroad.'

There was much whispering and murmuring among the

lords and their retainers. Mung was certain the information must have come from one of Hideyoshi's spies in the foreign compound. He watched the new Lord of Mito sit straighter, staring defiantly at the lords in the hall as if to hold them responsible.

When they quieted, Hideyoshi continued, 'The Japan Sea will soon become a Russian lake if Mr Ishikawa has his way. The inspector general should have asked himself why a man as capable as Count Muriev would want such a forsaken, freezing, windswept island as Sakhalin. The answer, of course, is coal. The Russian engineers know there are vast deposits of coal on that island. We have been told by the inspector general that iron-hulled ships with improved steam engines can increase the fishing season up north. Undoubtedly the best fuel for a steam engine is coal. If we can build propeller-driven fishing ships, the Russians can build warships and have the coal to fuel them.'

Mung was shocked by the revelation of coal deposits, but knew it must be true. Muriev was too clever to have given up so much for what Mung had considered so little. Yet even so, Mung felt he could defend his position if allowed a rebuttal. However that did not seem to be a possibility. The warrior lords hung on Hideyoshi's every word.

'The Russians will violate their treaty with us,' Hideyoshi said. 'Vladivostok was named Ruler of the East because it is to be used as a base to conquer the Orient. The Russians' first move was to cross the Amur river into China. The next move is from Vladivostok into North Korea. Everyone is familiar with the saying, "The Korean peninsula points like a dagger at Japan's heart." It is only one hundred miles from Pusan to Japan. After the Russians invade Korea, we are next. The insult to our trade delegation was cause enough to go to war with Korea. Now we have a strategic reason that warrants our military intervention.'

The lords of the realm whispered among themselves. Their voices raised, their arguments raged like a summer storm. Anger, resentment and national pride surged through the Hall of a Hundred Mats like a tidal wave. Mung stared straight ahead, knowing that if a vote was taken no one in the world could prevent his denouncement and the invasion of Korea. He looked across at Hideyoshi's exultant pockmarked face and read the cold black eyes. The new Lord of Mito was not done.

'Japan is not prepared for war,' Mung said.

Only Hideyoshi heard him over the roar, and cocked his head at the inspector general. 'It may not be ready, but I am.'

The master of protocol finally succeeded in restoring order to the hall. Hideyoshi wet his thin cruel lips, savouring his triumph a moment longer. He had rehearsed his concluding remarks more often than the opening. He flicked his fan in Mung's direction. 'Moryiama Ishikawa was recalled from Hokkaido where he was exiled, because another man took responsibility for using foreign warships to shell Japanese troops. The man who committed seppuku to protect Moryiama Ishikawa was Lord Hotta of the Fujiwara.'

Mung felt as if he had been whipped across the face. He flinched, and the lords saw his reaction. An ugly murmur swept the hall, but Hideyoshi cut it short with a wave of his fan. 'Why did you not tell the honourable lords that Russian sailors man half the ships in the Korean navy?' he asked Mung. 'And that there are Russian military advisors on the other half?'

The hall rumbled to an uproar. Fists were raised at Mung, swords partially drawn. Mung felt as if he had been bludgeoned with his own weapon. He tried to maintain a proud exterior but his shoulders sagged and he had not the strength to square them. He knew Muriev had not intended to invade Korea or Japan, but doubted there would be a chance to say that. The information Hideyoshi had was so accurate and up-to-date, Mung knew it must have come from the Russian ambassador himself. He heard calls for a vote. Many took up the cry.

Hideyoshi turned to Mung. 'Fisherman, you are finished. In another minute you will be in the cesspool of disgrace.' He withdrew the newspaper from his sleeve, opened it and showed Mung the article circled in red. FIRST JAPANESE CHRISTIAN CONVERT IN HAWAII, was printed in bold letters. 'When they quieten down I will accuse you of being a Christian spy,' Hideyoshi said. 'A traitor who has betrayed Japan for the European god.'

'My death is unimportant,' Mung said. 'Japan will be defeated in a war with Korea.'

'Why worry, you will not be here to see it.'

The two men on the dais suddenly realized theirs were the only voices in the hall. Everyone, including the guards, was bowed down. Mung and Hideyoshi could not believe their eyes. Udo and Iyeasu were leading fifty imperial guards down the aisle, followed by the Emperor of Japan carried in an open sedan chair. The two on the dais bowed down.

Seated on a raised platform behind the dais, the Emperor signalled to the master of protocol.

'Raise up your heads and gaze upon the descendant of the Sun Goddess, Amaterasu-o-mi-Kami,' the master of protocol intoned. 'The Meiji Emperor, divine ruler of Japan!'

'Lords of the realm,' the Emperor began, 'hearken well to my words. The issues debated here go beyond an agreement between Japan and Russia, or an invasion of Korea. The issue facing us is whether we continue with a

475

government whose members are responsible for their own welfare and no other. Or do we become responsible for our people's welfare. I advocate the latter, as did Lord Hotta. It was for this reason he sacrificed himself. For the establishment of a constitutional monarchy. Moryiama Ishikawa was prepared to take the consequences of his actions. I sent him to Hokkaido to protect him from your unjust anger. I muted him by imperial decree. I have muted him until now. He was forbidden to tell you of the entire agreement with Russia for fear some in this hall would relay sensitive information to the Europeans.'

There was an embarrassed hush. The Emperor tapped Mung's shoulder with his fan. 'I now order you to explain the treaty in full.'

Mung felt the veins pulsating in his forehead. His nostrils quivered, and he flexed his muscles. I am to have a fair chance to refute Hideyoshi's argument, he thought. The Emperor supports me, not Hideyoshi's policies. The lords are free to vote with their consciences. Mung faced the lords and began to speak with passion. 'It is true that Vladivostok means Ruler of the East. It is true Russians man Korean ships. It is probable Sakhalin has coal in large amounts, the best fuel for a steamship. But, you see, the Russians had only one steamship north of the thirty-eighth parallel, and we captured it.'

There was a brief but encouraging tapping of fans. 'My lords,' Mung said, 'if there is coal on Sakhalin, there must be coal on Hokkaido. Earlier, when I described the geographical makeup of our northern islands, I explained that Muriev proved Hokkaido was not a natural part of Honshu, but belonged to Sakhalin. If there is coal on one island, there must be coal on the other. It is true the Russians are strengthening their posts along the Amur river and surveying a pathway for a trans-Siberian railroad. And it is one of the biggest mistakes in history. Those plans were made long before the sale of Alaska to the Americans. The Amur settlements were originally established to funnel back furs brought from the Alaskan colonies to central Russia. The decision to build a railroad was made when the sea otter was plentiful, and whaling profitable. The sea otter is almost extinct now. Paraffin oil, or kerosene as it is called, has replaced whale oil for lighting. And America now owns Alaska. The Russian expansion across Siberia will take many years, involve tens of thousands of men, and require investments of billions of roubles. If Count Muriev was alive, he would have stopped it. In fact, the loan to Japan was meant to save Russia money by attending to the needs of their maritime provinces. The czar sold Alaska to pay his debts for the Crimean War. Now he has placed his country in debt again, which means he does not have funds to invade Korea. One third of the forty million yen loan to Japan is to be used to settle Hokkaido, and one third to purchase weapons for the imperial army and navy.'

There was a sigh of approval throughout the hall. Mung glanced at Hideyoshi. His face was sallow, cheeks sucked in. His eyes flicked rapidly from side to side.

Mung continued speaking. 'The final third of the loan will be used to bribe Chinese officials to support our claims to the Ryukyu islands, and for the Chinese to encourage the Korean government to give us favoured nation status in trade. Furthermore, there is an unwritten agreement confirmed by Russia after Muriev's death, of their support for international recognition of our rights in Ryukyu and the Kuriles.' He heard the lords suck wind through their teeth. He pressed on. 'It is true the total land mass of Sakhalin is four times greater than the Kuriles and Ryukyu combined. However the smaller islands extend north and south of Japan, covering fifty times the area of Sakhalin. These islands form a protective chain that can be fortified. They lock Russia in from Kamchatka to Vladivostok. They block off Korea and China, from their northernmost provinces to Shanghai.' Mung flung out his left arm. 'For a thousand miles north of Japan,' he flung out his right arm, 'and a thousand miles south, we will have control of the fishing grounds. I have traded 30,000 square miles of frozen land for 300,000 square miles of ocean.'

Mung levelled his eyes at the warrior lords before him. Many had fought, bled and lost kin in battles to keep the foreigners out. All felt a sense of shame for the unequal treaties forced on them by the western powers. He came to his most convincing point. 'As part of the unsigned agreement with Russia, they will support our demand to end the unfair treaties forced on us by western countries. I also have an official letter from the American State Department supporting us in ending the unequal treaties.'

Profound silence and proud faces showed the respect the lords felt for Moryiama Ishikawa.

'Lords of the realm,' the Emperor said. 'You have been schooled in Confucian philosophy, Shinto religion and Buddhist ritual. Yet we have a history older than any of those. Among the stories from our ancient past is the one told of the Shishi. It is related as a fairy tale for children. The story tells of the Emperor's personal champion who secretly carries out imperial orders without recognition or reward. And that story is true. From the time Amaterasu-o-mi-Kami sent Jimmu Tenno, the first in the imperial line to rule the Dragon Islands, each Emperor has had one personal champion. The valiant deeds you recall to your children by the warmth of a winter fire or on the evening of a full moon, are not make-believe. My father told them to me, and his father to him, as now I reveal to you. Lords of the realm, look upon the Shishi.' The Emperor pointed to Mung. 'Here is a man of high purpose. The Shishi!'

The warrior lords of Japan bowed. Hideyoshi looked across at Mung with savage, undisguised hate, then lowered his head. Mung fought back tears. How much this would have meant to Saiyo and Ukiko, to Yoshida, Hotta, and all the others who were gone.

'The Shishi has neglected to inform you of a most important order he has issued regarding the resettlement of Hokkaido,' the Emperor said. 'The first group sent north will all be Christian converts from Tokyo. The Shishi has come to this decision in order to influence western missionaries not to harbour criminals.'

Mung was surprised by the Emperor's statement, but Hideyoshi was devastated. The colour drained from his face. His body shook uncontrollably. Mung saw him touch the newspaper and realized it was now useless. The deportation order declared by the Emperor in Mung's name meant no one would ever again hold his conversion over him as a threat.

'Master of protocol, take the vote on the Sakhalin agreement,' the Emperor ordered.

Hideyoshi, seeing that not one fan opened against the proposal, kept his shut in his lap.

'Those in favour,' the master of protocol intoned.

Throughout the hall, fans snapped open like the cracking and splintering of a tree broken by the wind. Hideyoshi's shoulders slumped and his chin dropped on to his chest.

Again the Emperor spoke. 'You brothers of Mito – Iyeasu, Hideyoshi. Accompany me to the chamber of meditation.' He tapped Mung on the shoulder with his fan. 'Shishi, your last assignment awaits you in the foreign compound. Destroy the Golden Lizard.'

Chapter 49

The Meiji Emperor addressed Hideyoshi Koin in the chamber of meditation. 'I will install you as Lord of Mito in a formal palace ceremony only if you agree to leave for Hokkaido on the next mail-boat, there to take charge of the Christian convert deportees.'

'Your imperial majesty,' Hideyoshi said, 'the lordship is my right by birth.'

'The tenets of Bushido require your brother and the inspector general to avenge Danjuro's death. If you do not comply, I shall allow them to do so.'

Hideyoshi was in shock. He dreaded Iyeasu's wrath. He feared Mung's Black Dragons. He bowed to the Emperor. 'I hear and obey.'

'Officially you will be responsible for the resettlement plan in the north,' the Emperor said. 'Actually it will be organized and directed by an appointee of the Black Dragon. Let me warn you. If it is reported to me that you have spoken against my policies, the government, or Moryiama Ishikawa, I will declare you disgraced. Get out of my sight.'

Hideyoshi backed quickly from the room.

The Emperor turned to Iyeasu. 'If you desire to continue serving me, if you wish to marry my sister, Princess Atsu, you will forswear vengeance against your brother.'

'He deserves to die, your highness.'

'That is true, but Japan cannot afford it. He has no heir. There are those lords who would believe I ordered him killed to confiscate his property. It might cause them to

480

rebel against my constitutional reforms. When all hereditary titles and privileges are abolished, Hideyoshi's rank of lord will make little difference. I will leave him to freeze up north.'

'Sire,' Iyeasu said, 'I am your humble servant. If it is your wish, I hereby forswear vengeance against Hideyoshi.'

'There is still Mung,' the Emperor said.

'Mung will obey you as I have. He feels obligated to his oath to my father. If you would extend an urgent invitation to Mung and me, then keep us waiting until tomorrow noon, it would prevent the Black Dragon and me from being involved in a nasty piece of work planned for tonight.'

'You are both invited to wait in the anteroom for as long as you like. Now, about my sister.'

Iyeasu swallowed hard. 'I would like very much to marry her, your majesty.'

Mung, Udo and Rhee, leading fifty Black Dragons, set out from the Hall of a Hundred Mats. Half the men carried Henry repeating rifles, the other half oil-soaked torches. They moved quickly through the Yoshiwara, then cut across the Ginza towards the foreign compound. Lights showed through shuttered windows in the embassy residences, but doors were locked and the long, wide street deserted.

'The French ambassador has kept his word,' Mung said. 'I hope the Golden Lizard will fight. I have never killed a defenceless man.'

Several Black Dragons appeared from the shadows around the church. Their leader came forward and bowed. 'Sire, my men are in position. The lizard-man is alone inside. All French nationals have been evacuated.'

'Deploy the men with torches on three sides of the building,' Mung ordered. 'Form the riflemen facing the

481

fifty-foot lane between the church and the ambassador's house. No one is to cross the picket fence around the church. If the Golden Lizard tries to escape to the ambassador's house, the riflemen are to shoot to kill. At thirty feet they cannot miss. If he surrenders, he is to be taken alive.'

The order was relayed and Mung watched the riflemen form up. The first row assumed the prone position, their weapons pushed through the picket fence. The second row knelt, resting their rifle barrels on top of the fence. The third row stood, weapons at the ready. Suddenly the church bell rang.

'There is a figure in the doorway,' Udo said.

'Lizard-man,' Mung called across the neat green lawn, 'for the attacks on my family, I will kill you! For the death of my wife and Danjuro, you will die! For the sake of Japan, give yourself up. I promise your life will end without pain.'

'Fishmonger,' the Golden Lizard's voice rasped from the shadows, 'you have been in pursuit of me for a long time. I was not easy to catch, and will be more difficult to kill.' He rambled on, hoping to engage Mung in a verbal argument long enough to pick him out of the crowd and kill him. 'Did you bring along your son and his whore wife to watch?'

Mung ignored the lizard-man's words. 'Light up,' he ordered the Black Dragons, feeling grim satisfaction the Yakuza had chosen this way to die.

Udo struck the first match and Mung saw the hate in his eyes reflected in the burst of flame. The fire was passed from torch to torch around three sides of the building. Udo's face was disfigured by the fury he directed towards the dark doorway of the mission church.

The lizard-man stepped from the shadows into the eerie, smoky light, wearing the black vestment of a Roman

Catholic priest. The white collar under his face and shimmering skull had a chilling effect. The tilted head appeared to float above the black suit. The voice was a rasping hiss, forewarning of primeval danger. 'Fisherman, I may die, but not before I kill some of you.' He raised his right hand, light reflected off a pistol barrel, and he fired. The bullet clipped the torch behind Mung's head, sending a shower of sparks bursting into the night air. Mung grabbed the torch from the man behind him and flung it onto the wood-shingled roof. Twice more the lizard-man fired, and missed. Twenty-four flaming brands arched through the air, crashing through the tall windows and framed glass doors. Flames leapt up the draperies, setting the wood building ablaze. The Golden Lizard was perfectly framed in the doorway.

Suddenly Mung was pushed aside. Udo took careful aim with his pistol, firing three quick shots. The door splintered around the lizard-man's head, and he ducked back into the mass of flames in the church. He tried again to come out through the burning door. Udo fired once more, driving the Yakuza back into the sea of fire.

'Why did you not kill him?' Mung asked.

Udo ran to the leader of the riflemen, keeping his eyes on the inside of the building. He could see the lizard-man running between burning pews. 'Stand by,' he ordered. 'This side is his only choice. Do not kill him when he comes out. Drive him back into the flames.'

There was a crash of splintering glass. A chair came through one of the floor to ceiling windows that faced the ambassador's house. 'He is coming out!' Udo cried.

The black-clad figure leapt through the window, landing on all fours. Repeating rifles cracked and bullets sprayed dirt in the Golden Lizard's face. He jumped up and more bullets tore the ground at his feet, knocking him against the burning building. His clothes caught fire and he ripped them off. Naked, he was driven back inside by the marksmen.

With a loud crash, the front wall of the church collapsed. The nude man was seen running back and forth, hemmed in by flames. The golden scales of his sweat-sleek body reflected the fire. The floor was burning under his bare feet and he jumped for the bell rope. He swung back and forth slowly, ringing the bell. The gongs came to a halt when he began to climb up, away from the fire. Then a spray of burning shingles fell from the roof around his head. He looked up. The flames had burned through the ceiling. He looked down into an inferno.

Mung pulled his pistol and rested the barrel on the stump of his left arm. He aimed at the slick, scaly figure clinging to the bell rope, and fired. The tattooed head snapped back. The Golden Lizard dropped into the raging fire.

Udo ran to Mung and grabbed his arm, spinning him around. 'Why did you shoot the slimy devil?'

Mung eyed Udo's hand on his arm until it was removed. 'I am the Black Dragon,' Mung said. 'I am your father. No explanation is necessary.'

Udo stepped back and bowed. 'It would have been better had you let him burn alive.'

'You cannot kill every man who remembers your wife's past.'

'This one deserved worse,' Udo said.

Jiroo had waited outside the foreign compound on instructions from Iyeasu. Now he approached the Black Dragon. 'The Emperor summons you.'

'I gave orders no messages were to reach me until the fifty-six traitors were taken into custody.'

'This is a direct order from the Emperor,' Jiroo said. 'I could not refuse to carry it, nor can you disobey.'

'Rhee,' Mung snapped, 'come with me. Jiroo, Udo, move against the traitors. I will join you as soon as possible.'

When Mung was out of sight, Jiroo spoke to Udo. 'Sandanj is waiting with two hundred Black Dragons. We have fifty-six nooses. Every traitor will die with a rope around his neck. Wada Zenshichi has already moved against the rogue Yakuza. Hideyoshi has been exiled. The Chinese chef waits for you outside the Russian ambassador's house.'

'Good,' Udo said, 'all goes as planned.'

'Yes, although I find it hard to accept your promise of no repercussions after the ambassador's death,' Jiroo said. 'I saw you overtaken by brain sickness upon hearing the Golden Lizard's words. You cannot afford another mistake.'

'There will be no repercussions,' Udo said. 'Of that I am certain.' He turned away and walked down the long street of the foreign compound, towards Ambassador Derzhavin's house at the end of the row. As he walked, he willed a coldness into his heart, a method he had learned from Kang Shu in China. The tong chief had taught him to treat his enemies without mercy. Tonight he intended doing just that.

'Sire, I am here,' the Chinese chef called from the shadows opposite the ambassador's house.

Udo went to him. 'Do you have everything we need?'

'Yes, sire.' He held up a sack. 'All I must do now is whistle and the Eurasian will bring the lady to the kitchen.'

'Show me the poisoned wine.'

The chef produced two long-necked bottles. Udo tapped one. 'Open it and drink.'

'I must first prepare myself.'

'You take the antidote before the poison?'

'Olive oil coats the stomach. Afterwards we clean the poison out of the stomach with the antidote.' He uncorked a small flask, drank, and handed it to Udo. 'You had better finish this.'

Udo drank the oil, shuddering at the taste. He pointed to the wine. 'Drink some of that.'

The chef uncorked the bottle. He took a deep breath, put the tilted bottle to his lips and swallowed.

'Good,' Udo said, 'now signal. You will come inside with me.'

The chef whistled, and they waited. Then a light moved through the house to the kitchen. They hurried across the dark street to the servants' entrance. The Eurasian stepped back from the door to let them pass.

'Who did you bring with you?' Tala demanded.

'My servant,' Udo said. 'He understands no French and is here to help me.' He motioned the chef forward. 'Give me the wine.' Udo took the bottle and showed the label to Tala.

'A good wine and a better year,' she murmured.

'I brought this to seal our friendship, no matter what you decide. Do you actually wish me to kill your husband?'

'What are you talking about?' Her face turned vicious.

I should not have given her this opportunity, Udo thought.

Tala Derzhavin moved towards him. 'We made a bargain,' she said through gritted teeth. 'You had better keep it.'

'I hoped you would change your mind.'

'I have not!'

'Then let us drink to your husband's death.' Udo uncorked the bottle. 'In a few minutes you will hear no more of him.' He turned to the Eurasian. 'Glasses! We drink to the ambassador's death.'

The Eurasian brought the glasses and Udo poured a bit of wine into one. He sniffed its aroma. 'Where is your husband now?' he asked, taking a sip. He swished the wine in his mouth, and swallowed. 'Ahhh, a clean robust flavour.'

'You may be able to ape the ritual of wine drinking, but I doubt an Oriental can tell wine from water,' Tala said. 'You will find my husband in the study on the other side of the house. He works until ten, has a nightcap and goes to bed, alone. Thank God I shall never have to put up with him again!'

Udo filled three glasses. He raised his and toasted, 'To a successful killing.' The women raised their glasses and sipped.

'Isn't it bad luck to leave half the toast in the glass?' Udo said.

The women emptied their glasses and set them on the table. 'The wine has a smoky flavour,' Tala said. 'Not robust at all.' She began to sway. 'Possibly it is stronger than it tastes.'

Udo placed a chair for her and she fell into it. He saw the Eurasian's legs tremble, her body begin to shake. She reached out and fell against the wall, slipping slowly to the floor.

'What have you done?' Tala's tongue was large and furry in her mouth. She reached out for her lover. The room reeled about her. She fell off the chair onto the other woman.

'How long do we have before the poison takes effect on us?' Udo asked.

There was no response. The chef was gripping the back of a chair, his mouth open, his eyes starting from his head. Udo jumped up and slapped him. The man's expression did not change. Udo hit him again, panic welling up in his chest. He did not know the second part of the antidote. He clamped his hand over the chef's mouth and pinched the man's nose shut. The Chinese struggled for air but Udo maintained his grip until the chef fought desperately to free himself. Udo took his hands away. 'How much time do we have?' he demanded.

'Twenty minutes,' the chef gasped. 'I had no idea you were going to kill two women.'

'Nobody did,' Udo snapped. 'Spread that quilt on the floor. Help me undress them and lay them on it.'

The silk nightgowns slipped easily from the two nude bodies. They placed the lovers side by side on the quilt in an embrace. Udo took the wine bottle and two glasses from the table and put them near the lifeless heads. 'A lesbian lovers' suicide pact,' he said. 'The ambassador will never ask for an investigation of this.' He cleaned the third glass and returned it to the cupboard. 'Where is the antidote?'

'We cannot take it here. It will cause us to vomit.'

'Damn it!' Udo grabbed the man and threw him out of the back door. 'We have less than ten minutes.'

They ran to a deserted place on the dock. The chef pulled two vials of foul-smelling liquid from his sack. He gave one to Udo and they gulped down the antidote. Soon they were kneeling over the edge of the dock, retching into Tokyo bay. The nausea came in gut-wrenching waves for half an hour. Both men leaned weakly against the edge of the dock.

'In my sack,' the chef whispered.

'In your sack what?'

'There is a skin of goat's milk. It will soothe our stomachs and absorb any poison left in our bodies.'

Udo reached into the sack. He touched a cool hairy skin and brought it out to drink, feeling immediate relief from the milk. He sucked more.

'Please,' the chef said, holding out his hand, 'save some for me.'

Udo dragged himself to the man's side. 'Is this the entire antidote?'

'Yes.' The chef took the skin and raised it to his lips.

Udo slipped the Arkansas toothpick from his sleeve. He grasped the handle and drove the point into the chef's heart. He took the skin from the dying man's hands and drank it dry. 'I swore there would be no possibility of repercussions.' He withdrew the blade, cleaned it on the skin, then dumped it and the chef into the bay.

Mung and Iyeasu passed the night in the outer chamber of the Emperor's reception room, waiting to be summoned. Mung fumed but could do nothing. They were totally isolated, except for the silent servant who brought them breakfast.

When the sun touched the peak of Mount Fuji, twenty-seven Yakuza were dead. Fifty-six officers of the imperial army were laid in front of the army barracks, each with a noose around his neck.

At noon, Iyeasu was called from the chamber. In the Emperor's reception room, Udo, Jiroo and Sandanj reported the events of the night.

'You have done well,' Iyeasu said. 'The Black Dragon is protected, although he will resent our actions. Certainly he will be angry about the bloodletting, and Udo's solution.' He addressed Sandanj. 'Udo, Jiroo and I will take responsibility for last night's events. You must never admit to having been part of the killing night. The Emperor needs your newspaper and cultural societies to press forward his reforms. Jiroo, you will leave for Hokkaido immediately. Keep watch on Hideyoshi. Udo, your belongings are already aboard the ship for Canton. Take your family and go. The Black Dragon's wrath will mellow in a year or two.'

'What about you?' Udo asked.

'I am protected from Mung's anger by my proximity to the Emperor and my impending marriage to his sister. Mung is also my friend. In time he will forgive me this deception.' Iyeasu pointed to the door. 'You may all leave.

Mung will be kept waiting another two hours before the Emperor sees him. Good luck.'

Udo stood in the doorway and bowed. 'Enter,' Princess Atsu said. 'Your wife and children are waiting. I have come to say goodbye.'

'Thank you, your highness. My family and I have been ordered to depart immediately.' He looked at Gin-ko. 'Is everything ready?'

'Yes, but I must speak to Mung before we leave. It is most important.'

'I am forced to avoid my father before our departure,' Udo said.

Princess Atsu knew what Gin-ko planned. 'I will accompany your wife and tend the children,' the princess said. 'We will meet you at the main palace gate. You may leave from there.'

Mung was meditating in the lotus position when Gin-ko entered the chamber. Holding three scrolls in her hand, she bowed in the old way, touching her head to the floor. 'Honourable father-in-law, I promised Ukiko you would have these.' She placed the scrolls at his feet. He did not move.

Gin-ko knelt in front of Mung. 'Ukiko often spoke of you and your exploits. She told me that when you agreed to marry her, you swore to treat her children as you did Yoshida.'

Mung's voice was flat and emotionless. 'I said her children would also be my children.'

'Ukiko told me how you braved the death penalty to return home to sire a son who would honour your grave and those of your ancestors.'

'It is so,' Mung replied, 'but Yoshida is dead.'

'Your son, Shimatzu, will fulfil that dream if you will

490

only accept him.' Gin-ko watched the man people called Stone-Heart. He showed no intention of answering. 'We are overdue for the sailing ship to Canton,' she said. 'In a few minutes it will be too late. Your son and grandson are on the other side of that door. Please, I beg you for their sake and yours, allow me to bring them to you.'

Mung's eyes looked through her, his lips remained sealed. Slowly Gin-ko backed away. She opened the door and still he did not move. She held out her hands. Princess Atsu placed the two little boys in her arms.

Gin-ko approached Mung on her knees. She held the older child forward. 'This is your son, Shimatzu.'

The child looked wide-eyed at his father. Mung did not move.

Gin-ko leaned forward and placed the boy in Mung's lap. The child's head rested in the crook of his arm. Gin-ko watched the distant look in Mung's eyes fade. They became misty. They pleaded with her.

'Look at your son,' she whispered.

Mung lowered his head. Shimatzu's bright dark eyes rolled up at him. The child raised his pudgy hands to Mung's mouth. The small fingers prised his lips open. Little fingernails clicked on his teeth.

A long, piteous sigh was torn from Mung's heart, frightening the boy. Mung kissed the little hands and embraced his son. 'I see Ukiko,' he sobbed. 'She is in his face, and Saiyo looks at me from his eyes.' Mung rocked back and forth, cradling Shimatzu, murmuring. 'It is too much. Oh, it is too much for me.'

There was the booming sound of the port signal cannon indicating the turn of the tide. 'We must leave,' Gin-ko said.

Mung nodded at Yaka. 'Please let me hold my grandson.' He took the smaller child in his right arm and nuzzled both of them, his tears wetting their round, red cheeks. 'How can I care for Shimatzu?' Mung whispered.

'I wish to continue as his mother,' Gin-ko said. 'Udo and I love him.'

Mung nodded. 'Please write to me,' he said. 'Write often and tell me about both boys.'

'As often as possible.' Gin-ko held out her arms.

Reluctantly Mung parted with the children. He bowed to her. 'Thank you.'

At the door, Gin-ko bowed. 'I will return from China with another grandchild for you.' She watched Mung pick up the first portrait scroll of Ukiko, and open it.